NOTHING VENTURED

RODERICK PRICE

Published by R Price
ISBN: 978-0-9907466-5-2

Copyright © 2020, R Price

Cover Design by Lieu Pham, Covertopia.com
Book Design by Guido Henkel

CHAPTER 1

HE HAD STARTED COLLECTING AND CARING FOR THESE
Hudson automobiles in the late fifties. Frankly, Melvin
Baker could never have afforded a new one, but when an
old Finn up in Oulu had put his Commodore up for sale in
1958, Melvin had scraped together all the money he could
and bought her for two hundred and eighty-five dollars.
Hudson Automotive Company called it Pacifica Blue Green,
so he called her the Green Hornet. Later he bought a couple of others under similar circumstances—even drove over
to Lake Minocqua back in 1969 and bought a Commander
off some smart-ass savings-and-loan guy from Chicago who
had been keeping it at his summer house and wanted to get
rid of it. Hudsons really were the best cars ever made—sad-
dest day in his life when he heard they were going to stop
making them. Even got one of his sons interested in collecting, but now the son had had an aneurysm and was laid up
in the big Veteran's Hospital down in Indianapolis. Melvin
was alone. Every day, every night, every meal, Melvin was
alone. Biggest event was walking out to get the mail; maybe

drive the Green Hornet down to the convenience store to get an ice cream bar.

Larry Walker drove up the drive especially slowly that day. There were big old boxelder trees on either side of the road. Larry rounded the big overgrown patch of lilacs and parked behind the woodpile. It seemed to Larry like every house up there had a five-year supply of rat-infested wood that had been stacked up for the winter. For northern Wisconsin, Melvin's house was a big one; old and unkempt. Inside it reeked of old newspapers, wet carpet and stale pipe tobacco. It needed paint. The rusted screens on the back porch were torn, waving quietly in the gentle breeze. Some of the outbuildings were in disrepair. While the barn was structurally sound, the Quonset-style tin roof was rusting and giving way to age. The windmill still pumped the water into an above ground concrete cistern that was oddly placed not ten steps from the front door. The old cistern was long ago covered with dark grapevines that would bear some beady little grapes in the odd year when late summer brought extra rain. Larry entered through the screen door onto the back porch. The back door was unlocked, ajar, but Larry knocked with growing impatience, waiting for Melvin to come to the door. What a rat hole. There were four feet of old newspapers stacked right by the door. The cold December drizzle was coming down more unequivocally now. The first time, Larry had just stopped by cordial-like and politely asked Melvin to sign up. Then he had tried to reason with the toothless old fool. Then last time he brought a bottle of Dewar's and tried to drink him into submission. Larry had gotten belligerent; Melvin was going to sign the lease or else. Melvin was old, but he knew something was going on and he didn't like it. Didn't need the money anyway—could live just fine off social security, especially since Ma died from female problems. He was sitting on the biggest chunk of private land in the middle of Chequamegon State Forest and he knew it. Didn't know what he was going to do with it, but it was his.

He was probably napping, was Larry's guess. Larry could feel the steel on his handgun turning cold in the damp, December air. Larry leaned in over the threshold and called out for Melvin, but there was no answer. Melvin still had relatives—a son down in Indiana. Nobody around here even looking in on him. A dreary, darkening, late afternoon and Larry could smell death. It didn't have to be this way. Melvin had had a choice. Larry tapped open the door a bit farther and called for him again, but no one answered.

As he turned back toward his car, Larry spotted a long, sliding door on one of the sheds that was cracked open, yellow light shining faintly through the opening. Larry moved quickly across the backyard and edged up alongside the doorway. AM radio was playing Jim Reeves, "Put Your Sweet Lips A Little Closer to The Phone." The hood was up on one of the Hudsons; a long, brown model hunkered stoically at its station. A light was on under the car. Melvin was out in his shop. Larry could smell the Prince Albert. Larry's grandfather had smoked it. The roughnecks down around Bastrop had smoked it too, back in the early-70s oil boom. They were living in those six-foot-high, metal culverts with the ends boarded up, making twenty dollars an hour, drinking Shiner beer, driving new pickup trucks and smoking Prince Albert. The car was up on blocks and Melvin was under it putting a new gasket around the fuel pump, the shadows jumping across the room from Melvin's movements. Peering out from under the car, Melvin saw the stranger enter through the doorway and quietly shut the door behind him. He saw the sharp crease in the smooth slacks and knew immediately it was the guy from Texas back to put the squeeze on him. The guy just didn't get it. Melvin didn't need the money that would come from harvesting the jack pine and poplar trees by some big pulp mill company and he wasn't interested in signing a lease to have somebody come in and clear off the timber. Larry could talk all day long if he wanted, but there was no way Melvin was signing a contract to do it. By now, Melvin knew that many of his neighbors had signed up and got a pretty nice chunk of change upfront from Larry as well. Melvin wasn't driving a hard bargain. He simply was not going to sign. He pushed himself out from under the car. Larry was smiling.

"Melvin, how are you doing?"

"Doing okay, Larry, how are you?" Said Melvin. He actually kind of liked Larry—kind of a southern gentleman. Melvin felt a little uncomfortable in his oldest set of coveralls. Even by Melvin's standards, they utterly filthy from top to bottom in grease and grime.

Larry spoke first. "Melvin, I'm getting in trouble with my boss and I need your help. I really need you to sign the timber lease, Melvin. You're the only one around here who hasn't signed up and I'm afraid I am running out of time."

"Don't plan to sign it," said Melvin, pulling his pipe from the top left pocket of his coveralls. "I like you a lot Larry, but I don't want anybody tearing around on my land and I wouldn't know what to do with the money if I had it."

"Mr. Baker," said Larry, quietly pulling the lease from his pocket. "You are putting me in a very precarious position. You're the only landowner who's surrounded by the state forest that hasn't signed up. I really need your signature in order to get the company bonus that is coming to me under this program."

Melvin glanced toward Larry and then looked down at his own shoes. "Nothing against you, Larry, but I'm really getting tired of you coming around my place, and I think you need to go."

"Look, Melvin I like you really a lot, too. I am going to make you an offer, but I really don't want you telling any of your neighbors about this deal. I am authorized to pay you twice the signing bonus we paid your neighbors if you will sign up today. Now if you tell them about this, they aren't going to like me very much and they aren't going to like you very much either, but I'm not leaving here until I get you signed up."

They were now standing in front of the car less than six feet apart. Larry seemed different. Melvin could see how much pressure he was under. Larry threw the contract down on the hood of the car and handed Melvin a pen.

"Well, I would like to help you out Larry, but it's my land and I just don't want to sign," said Melvin.

Melvin caught just a glint of silver from Larry's oncoming hand and then heard the sickening sound of his own jaw cracking inside his head. Clumsily, as if in slow motion, he felt himself backpedal and crash into the heavy oak tool bench. His head slammed against the ancient steel anvil that was bolted firmly onto the top of the large tool bench. He went down flat on his back, staring strangely into the yellow light washing over him from beneath the car. Larry was standing over him, holding the gun he had used to strike him across the face.

"I've been patient with you up until now, old man, but now it's time for you to do your part and sign the lease." Larry gripped the gun tightly.

Melvin just lay there in disbelief. He had never been in a fight in his life.

Larry lifted his foot and stomped down hard on the old man, grinding his heel deep into the old man's belly.

"I'm sorry I have to hurt you like this, Melvin, but you get up here now and sign this thing and I'll get out of here."

Melvin remained frozen with fear as Larry reached down and dragged him with surprising ease up onto the fender of the car. Melvin could feel the warm blood running off his lip, torn from the butt of the pistol. Looking down dumbly he saw his own blood dripping over the car hood as he lay over it, wheezing and feeling lightheaded. He was no match for Larry. Larry shoved the pen back into his hand and brought the cold barrel of the handgun up against Melvin's temple.

"Now sign it, you old bastard or I'll kill you where you stand."

Everything was a blur. Melvin was hurt; he could feel the tears rolling warmly down his cheeks. He could barely make out the thick black signature line on the bottom right side of the contract, but he took the pen and signed. The rasp of the paper sounded deafening as Larry grabbed back the pen and paper and with his left hand folded it into the breast pocket of his overcoat. Melvin was now a liability. He could report Larry to the county sheriff. It would be clear that Melvin had taken a few blows. Melvin could go back on the deal, go to a lawyer or call a cop and say he was forced to sign. Larry moved the gun from his left hand to his right hand. There was only one thing left for Larry to take care of.

Halfway back to Deep Lake Lodge, Larry pulled off Forest Road 411, shut off his lights and drove the car slowly through the woods on an old, abandoned railroad grade that was now used only by hunters and fishermen. The moon that night wasn't particularly bright, but once his eyes had become accustomed to the darkness, he could move the car confidently, if slowly, over the hill and down the primitive forest road. Perhaps a quarter mile off the road, he put the car in park, left the engine running and pulled the heavy black duffel bag up into the front seat next to him. Easing out into the freezing night air, he carefully pulled the floor mats out of the car and laid them neatly side by side in the orange, leafy dirt of the old trail. He stripped off his blood-stained overcoat first, the blood-splattered shoes he had bought in Superior next, and then the rest of his clothes. He shivered uncontrollably in the night air as he rummaged through the black bag pulling out a complete change of clothes. He pulled on his favorite slacks, a sweater, and his lace-up shoes, then tucked his gun into his belt. Then he pulled on the topcoat he'd worn every day since arriving in northern Wisconsin. In a minute, he had everything else back in the bag, and with just four quick strides over to the old stump he had spotted the previous day, he dumped the bag, contents and all, and covered it with leaves. By eight in the evening, he had returned the rental car to the airport in Superior. By ten, he had made it back to the bar at the lodge in his original rental car. Along with several regulars, he took in the late news with a cold beer, some batter-fried cod and french fries.

Every day, Larry wondered how they would find the old man. Initially, he just assumed some passerby would see the fire and within hours everyone in the county would hear. On the fifth day, it was Willie Olson, the propane gas delivery-man, that didn't get the answer he always had when visiting Melvin. Walking back around the outbuildings, he found the remains of the burned-out old shed, the car, and a half-empty bottle of booze just feet from the charred remains. Later they found Melvin—what was left of him—burned to death, probably in a drunken stupor trapped under one of those old cars he had been working on. Looked like he had been smoking a pipe while changing a gasoline fuel filter. Bad idea. With the fire, the autopsy was difficult. Melvin had been ill. He was ancient. Didn't take very good care of himself. Always working on those cars. There wasn't much to autopsy but the old coroner did find a bullet in the body. It was damaged, but it had survived the fire. The bullet appeared to be lodged in the abdomen. Hard to tell. Melvin had seen plenty of action when he was in the Army. That bullet could've been there for years. Murders didn't really happen in this part of the state. The death was ruled accidental. It seemed nobody would ever discover the truth about the final fleeting seconds of Melvin Baker's life.

CHAPTER 2

"WHY DON'T YOU BE REALISTIC—JUST FOR FIVE MINUTES."
It was Sheldon Mack, chief environmental negotiator for
Arbor Resources. Arbor was seeking to do a major expansion
at a medium-sized refinery in Superior, Wisconsin. All of
that shale oil coming out of North Dakota was creating a
real opportunity for refining oil in the northern U.S. and
they were in Superior at a hearing for the Department of
Natural Resources.

"And in whose world should we be realistic," asked Taylor, "*your* world or the world everyone else lives in?" Taylor
glowered over her horn-rimmed glasses and looked down
the full length of the conference room table to Sheldon.

"My world is the real world," shot back Sheldon. "I live
in the world where people have to put bread on the table
and a roof over their head."

"...and an environmental nightmare in their backyard,"
continued Taylor.

"No, not an environmental nightmare," bellowed Sheldon, "a comprehensive and responsible plan for managing environmental impact."

"The people of the state of Wisconsin don't want environmental impact, much less a plan for dealing with it," Taylor interrupted. "Your proposal is neither comprehensive or responsible and the people of Wisconsin just won't accept it. I can't believe I made the trip up here to Superior to listen to the same old crap."

Jansen, the Empire Oil representative, could not stay out of the fray any longer.

"To which people of Wisconsin are you referring, Ms. Thompson? Certainly, you are not including the more than eleven thousand people in the Superior area who signed the petition to ask the DNR to grant the waivers required to expand the refinery?"

"I am sensitive to the economic importance of your facility to the people of northern Wisconsin. But I'm not about to mortgage the health and well-being of future generations of our people, our water, or our forests while big oil companies pillage our state," said Taylor matter-of-factly.

"We are not pillaging your state," said Sheldon angrily. "We have proposed more than eleven million dollars in environmental investments specifically designed to meet your concerns."

Taylor was hot. "You know as well as I do that eleven million is the absolute minimum amount you think you can get away with to do business here and you are wrong. If you don't get serious about making a commitment, I'm recommending to the governor that we shut this expansion down."

"Shut us down? You can't just shut us down! This would create three thousand jobs. And frankly, the area could really use it." Said Sheldon.

"Not only can we shut this down, gentlemen—we *will*," said Taylor. "Now, you boys better do some serious talking with your management before we get back together on the tenth. I don't want to keep wasting my time. Thank you all for coming today. Unless there is something else, I believe we are adjourned."

Both sides of the table had been lined with representatives from Big Oil, Big Labor and state government. With Taylor's concluding remarks, a thunderous squeaking, groaning and grinding ensued as the more than two dozen big old leather chairs slid back across the old oak floors and people rose up from around the table. It was a show of the power—and the respect—commanded by Taylor Thompson, the Director of the Wisconsin Department of Natural Resources. The entourage rolled out of the Douglas County Courthouse, a beautiful, brick-and-limestone building, constructed in 1919. As she exited the Belknap Street side of the Courthouse, the camera crews were ready. This afternoon, like so many others, Taylor was likely to be a good lead-in to the six o'clock news. She was not only flamboyant, but was also able to put environmental issues in a light that made them seemingly relevant to some of the most pro-capitalist, conservative businessmen in the state. Taylor Nicole Thompson, often called "TNT" by friends and foes alike, was always ready for a good fight—and a good show.

The cameras were rolling, and the sun was low in the wintry, afternoon sky as they poured out through the impossibly tall, double oak doors of the Courthouse. Taylor paused judiciously at the top of the steps. Her crowd of adversaries from the meeting were packed closely behind her, awaiting her next move.

"Ms. Thompson," asked the first reporter, "what is the timetable toward ending this dispute?"

The microphones were all clustered around her now.

"We are doing everything we can to assist these large corporations in the development of a sound and coherent plan to meet the environmental needs of the people of Wisconsin. We're doing everything we can to help them develop a solution as soon as possible. We would love to bring more jobs to this area."

"Taylor, Mr. Mack, the Senior Vice President from Empire Oil, has publicly referred to your Agency, the DNR, as *Damn Near Russian* in the enforcement of government regulations. What is the DNR's response to this?"

"The Department has not and does not intend to engage in frivolous name-calling or innuendo. Frankly, our hope is that Mr. Mack and his associates can channel such creativity and resourcefulness in a positive direction. We need these big oil companies to craft a constructive program that enhances the health, safety, and environment for the workers of northern Wisconsin and Minnesota. Surely, they can simultaneously expand their refinery *and* protect the environment."

Behind her, Taylor could hear the grumbling of the company executives. They sensed the scene unfolding before them and surged forward, enveloping Taylor, the cameras, lights and reporters, creating the kind of carnival-like atmosphere that television news stations—even networks—look for in every story.

"So, Taylor," beckoned the next reporter, "you're rumored to be the leading candidate for lieutenant governor in the April election. What are your plans?"

Just for a moment she smiled ever so slightly. Only last week she had arranged for a couple staff members to float that rumor at the monthly meeting of the Mifflin Co-op. It had been no big deal. They had just mentioned it, ever so discreetly, over decaf latte after the main meeting. Now it was coming around very nicely.

"I can't think of anything right now other than safe-guarding the people and incredible resources of the state of Wisconsin. You'll have to ask the governor whom he wants for lieutenant governor next spring. Now, I'm very sorry, you'll have to excuse me. No further comments for today."

It was eighteen steps down to the nondescript black sedan waiting at the curb. Jason, her top litigator and advisor, was right by her side. She stood silently on the wide sidewalk for just a moment and took a deep breath of the cold, fresh air. Only the afterglow of the setting sun was left now, falling over the shoulders of Superior's lakeshore. Here it was, just before Thanksgiving, and her only plans were to spend three days with her parents in Iron River, and then make the drive back to Madison on Monday morning before Thanksgiving. She hadn't even thought about the actual Thanksgiving holiday. Starting tomorrow, the state offices were shut down for the next ten days, but she sure wasn't spending a week with her parents. Madison was going to be quiet. Even the students in Madison would be gone for the holiday. It would be a good time to get some work done.

"All right Taylor, let's do it." It was Jason as he opened the door of the Department's car and guided her easily into the backseat. With her settled—oversized briefcase and all —Jason abruptly slammed the door and rapped on the roof for the driver to get moving. It was an easy, half-hour drive down Highway 2 from Superior to Iron River, and another fifteen minutes to the old house where she was raised, on the shore of Spider Lake, south of town. By 5:30 p.m. she was with her parents, watching her courthouse press conference on Channel 11. It had been a long Thursday, and she needed to get some rest. She was taking Friday off and planned to sleep in her old bed until noon.

CHAPTER 3

THE FLIGHT FROM MINNEAPOLIS SHOWED A 9:20 P.M. scheduled departure time but it was 11:35 p.m. before the announcement came. The feedback from the microphone jarred Martin from his nap. "Flight 4655 from Minneapolis to Lacrosse will now begin boarding. All passengers with tickets should report to Gate D-11 on the green concourse for immediate boarding."

Martin Cantrell rose carefully from his seat and approached the counter.

"Well rested, Mr. Cantrell?" asked the young woman smiling from behind the counter. "You know there's terrible weather on the way to Lacrosse."

"Sounds like show time," Martin replied evenly as she handed over his ticket.

"I would normally say have a good flight," she smiled. "Have a *safe* flight."

"Thanks for that," said Martin.

In her mid-thirties, she had appraised him hours earlier when he had first gotten in from Houston. He was athletic, obviously a seasoned business traveler, flying first class alone on pleasure. While the weather cleared, and the crowd of travelers thinned, she had watched him as he napped innocently in the departure area. The small plane to Lacrosse was going to be one of the last ones out. Lacrosse did not have the most sophisticated airport equipment, and farther south, the weather was severe.

As a group, they headed out to the waiting plane. All eleven of them—those who had waited it out—were led down the ramp by a balding man dressed in a burnt-orange, polyester blazer over which he had pulled a cotton-lined navy windbreaker. Martin silently admired the fiber of the man; his sense of duty. The man was sallow from countless nights under these dirty fluorescent lights. His eyes shone the gray of the knowing, the pursued, and the beaten. His mother would have never let anyone take him for granted as this airline had. His cheap, chalky black shoes were worn smooth on the soles. But tonight, he drove on as the leader of this tiny platoon because he took pride in his job. It was just his job.

Down the steps they went, clutching carefully both their belongings and the polished, aluminum rail. They emerged from the grimy, nicotine-scarred boarding room and heaved forward in a dark huddle, arrested by the bitter, spitting darkness of late November. Leaning into the wind and rain, their guide pulled them forward to the plane and wished them well as they vanished into the lean, taut belly of the Twin Otter quivering on the tarmac.

A half-dozen, middle-aged salesmen had already fallen into seats ahead of Martin. To his left, an older woman with a Russian accent was cursing as she tried to stow her tired bag under the seat. There was a young, college-looking kid

behind him, followed by an average-looking man in a business suit accompanied by a good-looking woman.

Martin eased into the left window seat of row 7, as the
rear cabin door slammed shut. The de-icers pulled away
from the plane. Hunched over in the rose hue of the passenger cabin, the co-pilot gave brief, uninspiring flight in-
structions. Along with every other passenger in the cabin
this night, Martin looked coldly and cleanly through the boy
co-pilot and felt a knot twist in his gut. He glanced again
out the window. It was only 150 miles from Minneapolis to
Lacrosse. In fair weather, he had himself flown the route at
night a dozen times, as a young private pilot in an old
Cherokee 140. But it was icy, windy, and black out there
tonight, and the plane shuddered knowingly with each Arctic blast from the north. As they started the engines, the familiar whirring sound of the gyroscopes pulled Martin's attention back to the cabin. From his unique vantage point,
he looked toward the pilot's seat and saw the old man request clearance as the big props roared to life. Suddenly relieved with the sight of the veteran pilot, Martin pushed
back in his chair and extended his 6'2" frame. He pulled the
collar of his leather jacket up and around him and wandered
off toward dreamland. He was going home. Lacrosse.

CHAPTER 4

IF ELIZABETH CANTRELL WAS A TOUGH ONE, SHE JUST couldn't help it. She blamed her father. From the day she was born, she was his. Powerfully built, with an intensity foreign to most men, her dad had meant what he said, did what was needed, and helped to write the rules. Liz had two older brothers, but she was the one to whom he tried to teach everything. She almost died with him, at his funeral, her senior year in college. He had taught her every single thing he knew about living, yet not a single, damned thing about dying.

She had worked as a financial analyst for Prudential for three years after they got married. When her second child came around, she retired from her full-time job, but she kept busy. After a couple of kids, everyone told her they couldn't believe how great she looked. Most of them knew she made it to the gym six mornings a week after dropping off the kids. Had to work off that edge, almost every day. She'd also spend a lot of time running out in the Memorial area, in the deep humidity of Houston's summer mornings.

After they had been married for four years, she and Martin bought their little bungalow in Bunker Hill. She had joined the Houstonian Club and started the women's tennis club. The past five years she had worked part-time as a professional fund raiser. It had started when she was running the annual benefit for the kids' school. When that event became incredibly successful, she was offered part-time work on other fundraisers. The expansion at the zoo. The Children's Museum. One thing Houston had was a lot of money, and they didn't mind spending money at a charitable event. With the family, the house, and her occasional job, Liz kept busy. She met many of Houston's rich and famous, too. Her life was fine, but it wasn't like it used to be with Martin. Back when they were first married, they would make love all the time. Candles. Laughing. They had gone to Yellowstone, of all places, for their honeymoon, and in six days they had left the Lodge just twice to walk out and see Old Faithful. She knew things always changed, but she was only forty-one years old—not exactly ready to hang it up.

"Earth to Mom, earth to Mom, come in Mom."

She bolted upright, cutting away from her sea of thoughts. It was her fourteen-year-old daughter who had been watching her from the kitchen table. Liz was working over the sink, slowly, meticulously, cradling her fine wine glasses after a rough night.

"What's up honey?" said Liz.

"Oh nothing," said her daughter, "it's just that when someone in the house uses half the water in Ethiopia to wash two wine glasses, I want to make sure they are held accountable."

"I thought you had homework to do," Liz suggested in a flanking maneuver.

"All finished. Guess I better get out of here before somebody asks me to start building an ark or something."

"Guess so," said Liz as she carefully set the crystal upside down on a towel on the blue-tiled countertop and turned off the water.

It was quiet in the kitchen. The kids didn't know yet. Hell, Liz didn't know for sure, but rather than tell the girls anything now, she had asked Martin to wait until he got back from his deer hunting trip to Wisconsin.

She had told him last Sunday night that they "needed to talk." Maybe go out for dinner on Wednesday. It wasn't like they hadn't had this conversation before. She said she was unhappy. Martin said she was impatient, or bored, certainly "hard to make happy." If there was one thing they were not suffering from, it was open communication. She thought he was too relaxed, too easy-going. She told him maybe he needed to get more of a "killer instinct," even though she didn't really know what she meant by that. When Wednesday night had come, they were both tired. She had been running errands all day and he got held up at work and didn't get home until 7:30. She was finishing her second glass of wine and as soon as he got changed, they were through the door and headed out for dinner.

Bunker Hill was a beautiful little village in the heart of the Memorial area in Houston. Many of today's residents built their dream home there fifty years ago when a lack of good roads, central air conditioning and industrial infrastructure stifled Houston, and made Memorial, at best, a frontier bedroom community with a long drive to downtown. Times had changed. Now it was easily one of the most sought-after areas.

Liz knew when she first drove through Memorial that someday she was going to have a house there. That was when she had been apartment hunting years earlier. With the villages having their own police it would be safe enough for a small-town girl from Wichita Falls, Texas. Its winding, tree-lined streets spoke tacitly of comfort and discretion.

She liked the retired man in the royal blue jump suit carefully mulching around his newly planted fruit trees in the front yard. She had longed for the day when her children could swing on the huge, gray jungle gym at Bunker Hill Elementary. It made her a little sad, but she liked it when an older four-bedroom ranch on an estate-sized lot would occasionally get scrapped to make room for one of those large, two-story brick houses with pillars that lawyers, doctors and oil men were building all over Memorial.

Last night it had started amazingly easy, and yet it was exceedingly difficult. As Martin eased out of the driveway, Liz finished her lipstick in the mirror.

"Cody's?" Martin half asked, half stated, as he surveyed the road ahead.

"Sounds good," said Liz. "You know we really haven't been there since Stephanie's birthday party."

"Don't remind me," said Martin, thinking back to the night. Cody's was *their* place—*had* been their place. When they first got to Houston, they'd go there two or three times a month for late dinner and then close the place down listening to jazz by Angel McGill or Film At Eleven. They would talk and dance for hours, sharing their dreams and often just holding each other in warm silence during the drive home.

Stephanie's birthday party had been different. Coarse. It was all of Stephanie's friends from the Houstonian. Liz knew every single woman and every single man. It wasn't that Liz had done anything wrong; she just had had too many laughs and too many looks. Martin finished the evening retreating into himself, analyzing the Houston skyline and suddenly feeling exceedingly small in a big city. When they got home, he berated Liz, her friends, her behavior and her lack of respect for him. He said she had ignored him all night. She told him that he was no fun. He sulked stoically about the house for several days afterward. He told himself he was going to do the things he wanted to do, and he found himself vindictively waiting for the small-est infraction from his wife. At first Liz didn't recognize her feelings toward Martin as he sulked about. She tried to cat-egorize them. She tried to analyze them. Her feelings were different, awkward. Then one evening Martin went to bed early. As she caught his reflection in the large mirror over the double sink vanity, she thought deeply of him and came face to face with this newfound feeling. It was sympathy for him. Sympathy for her husband. For the first time in fifteen years she was scared.

"Their" maître de had died long before from AIDS, but his replacement took one look at Liz and led them directly to a table perfectly suited for dining and dancing. Martin followed Liz confidently across the dining room floor. He eased into his chair and unfolded the crisp, neatly-creased napkin across his lap. The view from the twelfth floor was beautiful; looking back across the city skyline as the sun closed with those golden rays framing the towers against the far-off ship channel. Shell Towers. Pennzoil Place. The Pe-troleum Club on top of the Exxon building. Then Martin looked across the room to see if there was anyone he knew. For the first real time today, maybe the first time this week, he looked unwaveringly into his wife's eyes. Liz set her el-bows wide apart on the table, leaned ahead with her chin set evenly on her firmly-clasped hands, and matter-of-factly said, "Martin, I want a divorce."

"A divorce?" Martin repeated. "You want a divorce?" He knew she had been moody, not her normal self, but *divorce*?

"I don't like saying it. Never thought I would have to say it. But yeah, divorce." Liz was looking straight at him with an unblinking stare.

"Where is this coming from? I mean, I know things have been a little rocky lately, but lots of people go through rough patches," he submitted.

"Yeah, well, the last three years hasn't been what I would call a rough patch. It's been going on for a while; at least for me."

"Three years?" said Martin.

The waiter showed up. Liz looked at him. "Vodka and cranberry juice on the rocks for me, and a double vodka rocks for him."

The waiter turned on his heel.

"Well, I remember when the girls went to camp in the Ozarks. I was basically alone for six weeks that summer and that was three years ago in July. So yeah, three years," said Liz. Not angry, not smiling, just very matter-of-fact.

"So… you've been unhappy for *three years?*"

"Unhappy. Frustrated. Tired of it. Wanting something more. I could go on," she shrugged.

"Jesus, that's pretty harsh. Better get you on suicide watch. I didn't know it was that bad," Martin responded, trying to make light of it.

"Bad time for a joke, Martin," Liz said.

"Sorry," said Martin, hesitating and looking out over that skyline. "Just from the outside looking in, it doesn't seem that bad to me. I like our house. The girls are doing great—as far as I know. My job's going pretty well…"

"Wow, now I know you're joking."

"Well, I get frustrated with management, as you know, but we aren't exactly starving to death."

Liz looked him over. He was a good man. Still good looking, too, even if he had got a little thicker around the middle. "As weird as this sounds, we can talk about other things. I just wanted to put it out there. I want a divorce. A separation for sure... you know, just to see."

"Just to see what?" said Martin.

"Well, I guess, just to see how it feels... For both of us, really," said Liz.

"What's going on?" said Martin. "You've met someone."

"No, no I'm not saying I'm having an affair. I'm just saying we need a break," said Liz.

"Come on what's going on? Really. What's going on?" said Martin, looking her directly in her eyes.

"Well, this isn't a newsflash Martin, but I just think you've lost your edge. You're not the same guy I married. You don't want to do things or go out with friends. It doesn't seem like you're going anywhere with your job. I just want more, Martin. I want to live, really live my life, even if you're content on just getting by." Liz stopped and waited.

"I'm working my ass off!" said Martin. "I don't like your "cool" friends from the Houstonian. I'm fine hanging around the house with my family."

"I wasn't going to get into this; I was just putting the separation idea out there," said Liz. "But the truth... is we're not going anywhere. We've lived in the same crappy house for fifteen years. You go to bed at nine o'clock and you won't even *think* about interviewing for another job."

"We've got bills to pay! I can't just randomly look for a new job. We'd lose our unvested stock if I left!" Martin was angry. "I go to bed because I'm fucking tired from working all day."

"You are better than this, Martin. Tell your boss to screw himself if they won't make you a VP. You're the best damn geologist at the company and you know it. Fight for it—they're not going to just hand it to you." Now Liz was angry, too. She'd had enough. They had been over this.

Martin changed course. "Look, I don't think our life is that bad. I like our house. I know it needs some updates, but we can do that. I like our neighborhood. The kids are doing great in—"

Liz wasn't taking it again. "Look Martin, all of this might be good enough for you. But for me, getting by isn't good enough any longer. Period."

Martin looked at her carefully. It was clearly his move. He knew it didn't work to push Liz—she just pushed back. "I guess I would say, you have an interesting way of introducing the idea of divorce." He looked across the room and picked up his menu. "I guess this conversation is to be continued."

CHAPTER 5

THE FOUNDATION FOR THE GLORY YEARS OF CRUDE OIL trading began being laid in the summer of 1973. In August, Petroleum Intelligence Weekly reported that "near-panic buying by US, European independents as well as the Japanese" was resulting in "oil prices sky-rocketing." In the U.S. alone, oil imports stood at nearly 6.2 million barrels per day compared to only 3 million barrels per day just three years earlier. For twenty years, the Arabs had threatened to use oil as a weapon to stem the influence of Zionism around the world and fight back against American Imperialism. Now was their chance. With the 1973 Arab-Israeli war, the disruption in production, the embargo and the panic in gas lines in the United States, the world was set for one of the strongest economic shocks of the century. Oil prices went from an astoundingly low $2.80 per barrel to nearly $20 per barrel in the open market. The official price was finally set at $11.65 per barrel. At the end of the day, the major oil companies banded together to form a managed market with

Arab suppliers, and a nervous path of seemingly stable operations was preserved.

In 1979 fortunes were to be made. With the Shah sent into exile in Iran, five million barrels of oil a day disappeared from world markets. This time, a total disruption in world supply lines was scattered unevenly across companies and countries. Then with the Three Mile Island incident, the threat of freezing homes, fuel rationing and anarchy sent prices this time from $13 per barrel in early 1979 to nearly $40 dollars per barrel in early 1981. By trying to restore order and balance, and with the politically-correct intention of harnessing Big Oil's obscene profits, legislation was enacted to limit the margin that a company could make in the purchase and subsequent sale of a barrel of oil. In addition, in order to balance now short supplies on an equitable basis, an artificial allocation system called "entitlement" was put in place, which allocated oil on a pro rata basis using prior years' demand profile. Predictably, the governments around the world—most notably in the U.S.—failed miserably in their attempts to legislate fairness and equity in the world oil market. In some cases, the consequences were almost laughable. Small- and medium-sized refineries, which for years had been at best marginal operations, now had a "grandfathered" right to buy an allotment of tens or even hundreds of thousands of barrels of oil a day at official prices substantially below open market. They could then sell these barrels on the open market and turn large profits—much larger profits than they could make running an outdated, inefficient refinery.

Out of the chaos was born a new breed of oil trader. For years, U.S.-based oil trading operations had acted as mere third-party service companies to clear market imbalances for oil producers and consumers. Many of these traders were given a government entitlement to buy or sell hundreds of thousands of barrels each day based on their prior years' business activities. They often owned no refining capacity, and they never did have the desire or the capability to take physical possession of the product, but this entitlement made them rich and powerful. Offshore independent trading houses, and a few dozen offshore corporations, soon began to represent countries from the Middle East, Africa, and Latin America. These trading companies were set up as shadow operations providing legal entities that acted as clearinghouses for establishing, transferring, and cleansing the title on cargoes of oil from sources wishing to remain anonymous. Some crudes, such as those from Iran, were officially under embargo by the U.S., but a good trading company could take possession of that crude and get a seemingly clear title to it.

Oil price controls were established in many countries in an attempt to control speculation. In the regulated market, areas such as the United States set a profit limit of perhaps thirty cents per barrel on the spread for each transaction. This meant that if a company purchased a million-barrel cargo at, say, $17 per barrel, they could, in turn, sell it for no more than $17.30 per barrel, limiting their trading profit before expenses to only $300,000. However, a savvy oil trader might arrange to pass these cargoes through a series of buy-and-sell transactions within the crude oil trading "fraternity," and a given cargo could ultimately be returned to your company with a legal chain of title after it appeared to have changed hands four or six or eight times. This process would enable you to buy it back now for $19.70 per barrel and subsequently sell it for $20 per barrel. This gave the original owner of the cargo a beginning-to-end, trading profit of $3 million on the cargo instead of $300,000. Such a string of transactions could be made quickly and easily, with just a telephone and a telex machine. Hundreds of such chains could be in progress on any single day between the traders, most of whom were on a global, first-name basis.

Meanwhile, the huge oil tanker moved steadily and quietly over the water on its thirty-five-day journeys from the Middle East to Baytown or Baton Rouge, or St. Croix or New York.

The traders who directed such activity shared uncommon tenacity and ruthlessness. With this ruthlessness came money and power. Self-assuredness. They always lived on the edge of the law, often, clearly above the law. Among themselves was a world of cold-blooded integrity, where a phone call, or a nod of the head, was enough to settle on the purchase of twenty or thirty million dollars' worth of oil. Paperwork to follow.

Eventually, the government came to understand the dark ways of the traders. They knew that their system of controls and price limits and regulation was not working. They launched inquiries. Senators formed Committees. Representatives held hearings. Prosecutors filed injunctions. But finally, after years of fruitless effort, the agency officials, special prosecutors, legislative panels, and judicial subcommittees packed up their charges, and their unraveled research, and gave up. By then, the traders, like jackals—those willing, and in many cases needing to live on the edge— simply moved on. Such a man was Hilton Sinclair. Houston- and global-oil trader.

CHAPTER 6

MARTIN WAS DEEP IN HIS DREAMS, DEER HUNTING AS A kid in northern Wisconsin, when he suddenly jolted back rigidly in his seat at the crack of the rifle. But it wasn't a rifle at all. The plane was taking on ice, and thankfully the deicers had come to life. As the wings heated, the ice had begun falling away in sheets. An occasional sheet of ice would catch the propeller, and it would be hurled violently against the fuselage of the plane with a deafening crack. It sounded like the whole damn plane was breaking apart as it lunged forward through the wintry black of night. A prayerful silence filled the cabin and Martin realized he had been the only one tired enough—or foolish enough—to sleep.

Now the captain, the old man, was sitting straight-backed in his seat, cradling the yolk of the craft in a tender embrace. About every thirty seconds, the boy at his side would reach across the glass in front of him and, using a navy-blue blanket, he would wipe away the condensation and fog that was gathering on the inside of the cockpit window. It took a moment for Martin to see that the wipers were, in fact, on. They were bundled in ice, laboring piteously in a battle to keep the glass clear. Now Martin was worried.

"Lacrosse Tower, Otter one three five seven Tango, two four miles north at 11000 heading one seven zero. Over." Even from his seat, Martin could see the knuckles whiten on the co-pilot's hand as he clenched the radio mike.

"Roger five seven Tango, we're open for business." The response was so cheerful that Martin could almost smell the hot coffee brewing inside the warm, snug traffic control tower two miles below.

"We've got a problem with our cockpit defog and de-ice. We're losing visual, and navs are erratic. Request clearance to 3000 now, over."

"I copy you, Tango, authorized now for 3000." The voice on the other end had gone dead serious. "Be careful. We are IFR only with light rain and ground fog. No sleet, repeat, no ice. No known local traffic in area, over. You boys are the only ones crazy enough to be up there."

"Roger that, Tower, on our way to 3000 now. Will report at the three-mile marker. Out."

Without looking, the young pilot returned the mike to its Velcro holder and vainly wiped the old navy-blue blanket across the glass again.

"Five seven Tango," replied the tower. "Good luck."

Luck. So now it was coming down to luck, thought Martin. Lately, he had not enjoyed much luck. He had seen it coming a mile away, yet when Liz said the word "divorce," he just sat helplessly as she went over all of the soul searching, all of her concerns, all of her struggles with what was the right thing to do. Now he sat helplessly again staring emptily as the amber lights reflected off the intense faces in the cockpit. He had not really spent much time thinking about how he might die, or even how he might live. Suddenly, another rifle shot echoed as the plane lurched without warning, prompting shrieks from the passengers.

His first thought was that they were going down, and they were. They weren't necessarily going to crash; but the immediate and abrupt way in which the old man took her down to a lower altitude convinced Martin of the immediate danger. Martin understood the problem and he understood the plan. The deicers on the cockpit windows were not working, and the ice was building up across the top front of the plane. This was fogging up the cockpit windows and beginning to ice over the navigational sensors required to measure basic functions like airspeed, altitude, and direction. Very soon, the pilots would not be able to see, and they would lose their sense of direction. The pilot had bet that he could get to a lower, warmer altitude before he lost navigational instrumentation. Even Martin calculated that it ought to be nearly twenty degrees warmer at 3000 feet. It had always amazed Martin on international flights when temperatures routinely got to sixty or seventy degrees below zero at thirty or thirty-six thousand feet elevation.

As the seconds ticked by, they continued to descend. At last, the plane leveled off at three thousand feet. Then they waited. Thankfully, the sleet turned to rain. Through the patchy fog they found themselves gliding over the mercury vapor lights scattered across the fields and hills of the houses and farms of Minnesota and Wisconsin. Far to his left, Martin could discern the outlines of what he believed to be Winona, Minnesota. Ahead of him, he could see the glass in the cockpit starting to clear.

"Lacrosse tower, one three five seven Tango now three miles north at 3000, bearing one six zero. Request clearance to land," the young co-pilot stated dutifully.

"Roger, Tango," cracked the tower. "Welcome back, guys. Kind of a rough ride tonight."

"Roger, Tower," said the veteran pilot, "rock and roll for a while, but now we're out of the freezer."

"You're cleared straight in on runway one eight zero. I'm bringing on the ILA for you at 2500 to bring you through the ground fog. We've got a few ice patches on roll out. Tower over."

"Copy, Tower, ILA at 2500. We've got visual now. Ice patches on roll out, over."

The flashing ILA strobe lights on approach gave a queer brilliance to the dense fog that seemed to overwhelm the tiny craft. Soon they fluttered over the threshold of the runway. The plane seemed to hesitate as the pilot cut back power, and then, like a tired warrior, the plane dropped to the runway and pulled up to the official terminal building of the Western Wisconsin Tri-State Regional Airport in Lacrosse.

CHAPTER 7

HILTON HAD BEEN AT PROLEA ALMOST TWO AND A HALF years now and he still couldn't stand the damned French. They didn't come down from New York very often, and never stayed more than two nights. But each time they came, it took Hilton a little more time and a little more scotch to recover from his latest round of interrogation. He'd never met a trader worth a damn anyway who couldn't drink his weight in scotch.

"So, Mr. Sinclair," said Gerard, peering over his pewter-rimmed glasses. "what do you believe is the basis for the buildup of our East Coast fuel oil position over the last six weeks?"

Alain had been the one to hire Hilton, and both had agreed that Hilton was the perfect man for the job. Now Alain had moved to a new job, and Hilton was stuck dealing with Gerard. Shortly after coming to terms with Hilton, Alain had been offered an opportunity to run the French operations for Latin America-West Africa, Prolea's largest operating unit. Gerard showed up three weeks later.

For the first eight months, Gerard had been respectful—almost reverential—toward "Mr. Sinclair." He didn't know anything about the business at first, but he asked a lot of questions, and soaked up information. At first, Hilton found some of the questions almost comical, but Gerard had stayed out of the way. He never offered advice, and as long as Hilton's people sent him plenty of reports to look at, Gerard seemed content.

During the first year with Gerard, the market had been quiet, but that was soon to change. Over the next eight months of the Gulf War, Hilton's unit had made $360,000,000 net income. During this time, Gerard had become increasingly involved in the business, and frankly, Hilton had appreciated his help. Together, they had gone before the board of the parent company in Paris to lay out their strategies, beef up their financing, and successfully secure higher trading limits to support their positions during the Gulf War. As the war wound down, Gerard had gotten credit from Paris for his astute oversight of the trading unit; and, in turn, Gerard had become downright friendly, almost jocular, with his new American colleague, "Heelton."

Financially, Hilton's first year at Prolea had been break-even. He got a nice salary, but no bonuses. During his second year, that all changed. His employment contract with Prolea had paid him over a million dollars in bonuses. He needed the money, too. He was on his third wife and he had a huge house in River Oaks. Among other things, he had just bought a new sailboat that he kept down in Clear Lake. Now, that seemed like ages ago. Things had changed very quickly. Business had gotten rough again. It was beyond belief to Hilton that Gerard was now treating him like a second-class citizen. It wasn't just Gerard, either, it was this conference room full of chain-smoking, second-guessing lieutenants that seemed to accompany Gerard on every visit now.

"Mr. Sinclair," chirped Gerard. "I was asking about your east coast fuel oil stocks." Hilton jolted back to reality.

"Wel,l Gerard, as you know, we've been watching European product inventory levels as they've neared historic lows. We see continued escalation in U.S. east coast manufacturing activity." Hilton spoke carefully. "All of our models are showing latent demand for products moving into strength as we approach winter."

"But Mr. Sinclair, your laid-in costs on diesel fuel alone are now more than four cents above the New York Harbor market price," said Gerard, apparently no longer on a first name basis with Hilton. Gerard was glaring from side to side at his fellow Frenchmen who lined both sides of the huge mahogany table. Gerard, too, was clearly under pressure now that things had been rather inauspicious over the past six months. "Who is going to be pleasant enough to pay Prolea four cents a gallon more for our fuel oil than they can buy it on the spot market?"

"For Christ's sake, Gerard, you know that four cents can be made up in a week when the market is short. Everyone knows that the market is short on product. When things get tight, they just aren't going to be able to get physical product in fast enough to cover the holiday season, and we are going to clean up. Prices are already starting to climb," he implored.

Unmoved, Gerard looked down the table and barked to one of his lieutenants. "Mr. Guideau, what was the price on New York Harbor number six fuel oil at opening this morning?"

"Fifty-two and one tenth cents," snapped the impeccably-dressed young man. He quickly placed his cigarette down to peer at the stack of paper in front of him.

"And yesterday?" Asked Gerard.

"52.45 at close, sir."

"And last Friday?" Demand Gerard.

"53.11 sir," the response came curtly.

"And one month ago, and two months ago today, what were the prices then?" continued Gerard.

After a hurried shuffle of paper came the answers, "53.51 and 53.85."

"So, Mr. Sinclair," Gerard continued, again peering over his pewter rims and glaring down at Hilton at the end of the table, "it would appear that, in fact, prices are not coming up now, are they?"

"Prices are coming up," shot back Hilton. "We're building our positions in number two and number six fuel oil and I think it's clear you have my ass if prices do not come up."

"To be clear," Gerard replied coolly, "we have no interest whatsoever in your ass. You are an employee of this company and you are charged with preserving and enhancing the value of our hydrocarbon production from around the world. For several months now, it seems that under your direction, we have been neither preserving nor enhancing anything other than your continued good fortune with this company. On this book alone, we stand nearly twenty million barrels and almost $33 million dollars out of the market. We will take no further positions toward this strategy, Mr. Sinclair. At your request, we will hold the portfolio we have; and we will be back in exactly thirty days to take appropriate action based upon our standing at that time. Am I making myself clear?"

"Come down anytime you wish," said Hilton. "It's always a pleasure."

"Am I making myself clear?" Said Gerard again. Hilton was getting to him; Gerard was flushed with anger. At the last moment, Gerard restrained himself and waited for an answer.

"Yes Gerard," replied Hilton. "You are making yourself perfectly clear."

CHAPTER 8

LACROSSE WAS AN OLD RIVER TOWN ON THE BANKS OF THE Mississippi River. The French explorer Lafayette named Lacrosse when he passed through the area on a fur-trading expedition in 1720. Indians playing a racquet-like sport on the river plain reminded Lafayette of the sport he knew from his native France as lacrosse. Western Wisconsin was beautiful country, with dramatic limestone cliffs, tree-covered hills and meandering valleys known by the locals as "coulees." This area of Wisconsin had been mysteriously left untouched by glaciers millions of years ago.

Lacrosse was really settled in the 1820s and 1830s when Scandinavian and German farm families came seeking new opportunities and religious freedom in America. They found this land to look stunningly similar to their Motherland. Beginning in 1870, powerful lumber barons built huge sawmills along the rivers: Mississippi, Wisconsin, Black, Chippewa, Bad Ax, Zumbro and Saint Croix. Like a storm, they mercilessly clear-cut virgin timbers for burgeoning Chicago, Cleveland, Philadelphia, populations East and

New York. Twenty years later, the barons, the mills and the huge, old trees were gone. For decades, only the sweat of the Norwegian dirt farmers enabled the land and the towns to further develop, masking over the scarred face of the land.

Martin always liked the drive from Lacrosse "Up North" to northern Wisconsin. From the Minneapolis airport, Martin called his parents several times the previous night to keep them informed of his delayed departure. Even though it was almost one in the morning before he landed, both of his parents were there to meet him at the terminal. Each time now, they seemed smaller than he remembered them. He found himself watching their steps, holding their arms as they walked together, and hugging them longer at the close of each visit. After a short drive and an hour or so around the kitchen table discussing how Houston and the family were doing, Martin collapsed into bed at a little after two.

Before sunrise, he and his dad were heading north up State Highway 53 to meet his brother and the rest of their gang for breakfast in Whitehall. Five minutes into the darkness, with Martin at the wheel, his dad rustled through the back seat and came out with his trusty old forest green stainless Thermos bottle and poured two steaming cups of black coffee. Over the background of the Milwaukee Stockyard livestock quotations, Martin tried to relax back in his seat. He knew it was time to talk.

"Liz and I have a problem" Martin began. He could not believe his voice cracking even now as he said it.

A deep harbor, his father took his time responding. "What kind of problem is that?"

"She says that we've drifted apart. She says we're going nowhere. She says she needs more…" his voice trailed off. Again, there was a measured silence. Martin had the sensation of being underwater. He recalled those days of diving headlong into the greenish-brown waters of the Mississippi. He winced at the thought of stepping barefoot into the muck on the bottom. The pressure on his ears was piercing. Martin peered forward into the darkness as his ears filled with the dull thud of pounding pavement.

"What did you say?" his father said.

"I'm not sure it makes a difference what I say, " said Martin. "She says she wants a divorce."

Actually, Martin thought, she had a helluva lot more to say than that. After dinner the other night, she began with a recounting of their plans, their hopes, and their dreams. Their early days of lovemaking and the way they used to do crazy, spontaneous things like the Thanksgiving they rented a car and drove to Santa Fe and back, just because they'd never been there. When they had the girls, they were in Houston with no extended family around them. At the time it didn't seem like anybody else really cared. At the restaurant, Martin had sat listening to her in total, unblinking silence. He sat numbly watching her lips as the words flowed. He shouldn't have gotten angry, but he did.

He was a "good man," she had said; a hard-working, dedicated father. But she was tired of "going nowhere" as she described it. She recounted one by one, at each point over the last three years, when she had slowly given up. Other people, it seemed, had become more interesting, doing more things, building bigger houses, making more money and going more places.

She had loved it in the early days when Martin had done so well as a geologist, when he was so excited by his work. Almost twenty years later he was still a good geologist, but he was just an employee. He wasn't really in a management position. He couldn't stand his boss. These days it was great to be so secure in his job, she had said. They were "getting by" fine on his hundred thousand a year, but she she wanted more. Unfortunately, Martin was not making a difference anymore.

Martin was still angry. Most women would love having a nice house and a hard-working husband. He wasn't really surprised, though. Increasingly, Liz had been hanging with a pretty fast crowd, people with nice cars. Maybe he *was* just getting by. Maybe he did need to acquire that "killer instinct," as Liz called it.

The drive home that night had been beyond sobering. With the end drawing near—the end of *everything* drawing near—Martin's thoughts were singular and unresolved. What does a man do when he learns from his wife that "getting by" just isn't good enough any longer?

CHAPTER 9

IT WAS ONLY 8:15 A.M. AND THE PHONE WAS ALREADY ringing off the hook.

"Basin Energy, Mr. Cantrell's office. How may I help you?" She said mechanically.

"So, can you come out and play today?" He asked.

"My, aren't we frisky for so early in the morning," she said as the switchboard lit up. "I need to get the other line, baby. I'll be back in just a second."

Anita would be a catch for any man. She was a handful, that was for sure. Young, attractive, divorced, she had first met Hilton almost two years ago at the NPRA Conference in San Antonio. They had both fallen into too many margaritas that night. When she saw the big, gold Rolex and the wedding band, she liked the smell of this kind of trouble. A woman had to be a hell of a lot more careful these days.

She didn't just get out-of-town opportunities, either. Her Mom was back in Houston watching Anita's daughter for the weekend. Besides, Hilton looked like he had a lot to offer, so they had spent the night together. It had been good. When they got back to Houston, Hilton just kept calling; first just to visit, then for a drink or lunch, and one thing just led to another. Now, whether they liked it or not, they had a relationship that could lead to just about anything.

"Sorry, you still there?" Anita came back on the line.

"Didn't Marty take off to chase Bambi? I was thinking we could take a long lunch," said Hilton.

Anita hated it when he called Martin, "Marty."

"Yeah, Martin left for Wisconsin yesterday, deer hunting for almost a week."

"So how about I pick you up at 11 a.m.?"

"I don't know, maybe not today. Martin left me a stack of stuff, and the guys just gave me a bunch of slides they need for a big project they are presenting tomorrow on the Kazakhstan deal." She understood that Basin Oil, like most other big oil companies, was doing whatever they could to gain a strategic foothold in the former Soviet Union. All it meant to her was a doubling of workload, in what used to be a pretty easy job in the exploration and production department of a major oil company. Good benefits. Nice office.

"Come on, two hours won't hurt. It'll clear your head," said Hilton enthusiastically.

She loved it when men acted this way—women's ultimate power in the universe.

"Oh, okay, see you at eleven on the Ashford side of the building," said Anita.

"See you, baby."

Without looking, she hung up the phone and went back to her computer. It had been confusing when they had first gotten off the word processor. There were all kinds of passwords, commands, file, diskettes, and things. But after a few classes, she found she had a knack for it. Now she was publishing spreadsheets, word processing and even creating slide presentations for the guys, and they loved it. Before, she had always called in sick at least once every month or so, but now she really made a difference. Her group—Martin included—would give her grief for hours when she'd still try and play hooky for a day.

Martin had been a hard one for Anita to figure out. He was smart. She found him at once attractive and intimidating. He showed her the ropes and helped her with the computer at first. There was a time when she had mistaken his engaging style and the way those clear eyes hung on her every word, as another easy mark. Later, when she got to know him better, she'd met Liz and then came to realize that Martin was the same with everyone. Even the plant lady had asked about "that very attractive man in the corner office." She knew there was just something about Martin. Often, in bed with Hilton, she just couldn't help thinking of Martin. But Martin was a forest too dark. There was an animal within him, and nobody had brought it out.

Hilton had an hour before he had to pick up Anita. He scanned through on-line news, looked over his Argus oil price faxes and reviewed Prolea closing positions from the previous day. New York gasoline was down another eight basis points, but American Petroleum Institute product inventory levels were still drawing down. He had one more very important call to make.

"New York Brokerage, Gannon speaking."

"Jerry, this is Hilton. What's going on?"

"Nothing special, Hilton. Volume is heavy. Light oils still looking for support. See Platt's this morning?"

"I saw it. Where do we stand?"

"It's not a pretty picture, Hilton, I'll tell you that," Jerry replied.

"I'm a trader, not a mind reader—where do we stand?" Hilton wasn't known for his patience.

q"Well Hilton, "Jerry proceeded cautiously, "On paper, Prolea is out of the market $37.23 million the way it stands right now."

There was a long, uninterrupted silence as Hilton considered his next move. "Roll it another month," he finally stammered.

"Yours, Hilton? — or Prolea's?" Asked Jerry.

"Just Prolea's. We can worry about what to do with mine later."

"Hilton, this is getting pretty big. It's going to take me some time."

"Just do it," said Hilton, and he hung up.

The striking thing was that Hilton thought there was nothing unusual with having his own "private" trading book, along with the position he managed at Prolea—illegal, maybe, but not unusual. Traders playing their hunches or working off their company's data would open accounts, willing to bet a hundred or two hundred thousand dollars of their own money. They were always hoping to make an extra hundred thousand here or there when they were the first to get news of a sudden Middle East skirmish or a refinery fire that would drive prices suddenly and unexpectedly down—or up, for that matter. He always said a good trader could make just as much money when the market was going down, as he could when it was going up.

Hilton had started his own trading account almost six months earlier. He had called one morning to buy a near month futures contract for 100,000 barrels. He had chatted amicably with Jerry. At the time, Hilton's lead futures trader was in Naples, Florida for a week at a convention and Hilton placed the order himself. Hilton and Jerry had shared perceptions on overall market conditions. It turned out they had some old mutual friends. Hilton had complained loudly about the increasing foreign influence on his decision making and how it was keeping him from making the decisions he wanted to make on every deal. They had talked openly about Hilton opening his own personal account with Jerry where he could always do exactly what he wanted, even if it differed a bit from the French influence at Prolea. It had been a good conversation. Hilton wired Jerry some money, and Jerry placed the first order. By eleven the next morning, West Texas Intermediate was up $1.30 a barrel in Cushing, and Hilton's purchase from the day before had made $130,000 on paper.

Jerry also made a lot of corporate transactions under Hilton's Prolea business. Keeping the two accounts separate had been easy for Jerry—for a couple of months. Shortly before the Iraq war, Hilton was filling in for a trader again, and called Jerry to purchase 500,000 barrels of Brent oil. When all hell broke loose with the U.S. bombing of the Iraqi forces, Jerry was inundated with calls and couldn't confirm the trade right away. When he talked to Hilton only two hours later, the 500,000 barrels of Brent oil was worth 1.3 million dollars more than he had paid for it. Jerry had booked the original order for Prolea because Hilton had indicated it was a Prolea purchase, but now Hilton said it had been for him. There had been a heated debate. Jerry had told Hilton to get somebody else for a broker; Hilton had threatened to take his business—and Prolea's—elsewhere, if he "couldn't trust" Jerry. When Hilton finally said he'd only ask this favor one time, Jerry thought about it for a day and then changed the paperwork, placing it all under Hilton's personal account. Hilton put over a million dollars in his own pocket, and about a week later, Jerry got a wire from Hilton for a hundred grand. Big, sudden market moves like that don't come along that often, but a man like Hilton was more than willing to use his power to put a million bucks in his pocket.

That was months ago. Now Hilton was doing it often. If Hilton made a good trade, he'd take the margin and keep it in his account. If things went wrong, Prolea ate it. Lately, things had been going wrong for Hilton and Prolea. Hilton had lost two million dollars from his account in the last four months, but he was still carrying almost six hundred thousand of profits in his personal account. On fundamentals, Jerry and Hilton were both convinced that the product-fuels market just had to improve. If it did, everyone, including Prolea, would be fine. But if prices didn't rise, even Hilton wouldn't survive much longer at Prolea, and whoever came in would take a long and careful look at the trading records of Prolea Energy- and Jerry Gannon would be finished at the New York Mercantile Exchange.

Hilton said, "roll it ahead a month," so Jerry took a long draw off his Diet Coke, huddled over his computer screen in the center of the trading floor and began to enter the first order, rolling over Prolea's problem to the next month.

CHAPTER 10

MARTIN SLOWLY PULLED THE EXPLORER OVER TO THE CURB directly across from Elmo's Diner. Except for the uneven crunching of yesterday's melted snow under his feet, the town was quiet. The air was crisp and fresh. Even though the red sky of morning was beginning to stake its claim, the stars hung expectedly over Main Street, waiting to see what the day would hold. Martin listened for the telling slam of the door on his father's side of the truck and then stood patiently waiting for him to come around the car and join him. The stark lights of the Farmer's Co-op gas station shone silently through his breath. A passing pick-up, loaded with corn for the mill, labored by in the morning silence. With its passing, they walked stiff-legged across the street into the simple, earthy warmth of Elmo's.

Inside the diner, large unshaven men in wool, plaid shirts were congregated together in small circles around the beat-up tables. The high, worried walls and hand-crafted, dark oak counters vouched for the ancestors of those in the room. As the interior door slammed shut behind them, Martin and his dad drew calculating stares from all around. Martin saw several large Formica-topped tables clearly unclaimed near the back and he strode forward with assurance while his father headed for the restroom. Martin quickly pulled two tables together for their crew. He asked for two pots of coffee, black. By the time his father had returned, his brother and the rest of the deer hunting gang had arrived in two more vehicles. For twenty-two years this had been their rally point on the Friday before deer season opened.

They quickly grew loud, and an occasional glance from the front of the place reminded them that they were not necessarily welcome. Two of the men in their group had been participating for years, and immediately went back to recounting the infamous missed shots at a trophy buck, or when he dragged out a deer in deep snow late at night, and various other stories covering the last three decades of hunting. Martin, his dad, and Martin's brother, made up the core of the group; the other three had joined up along the way and brought their own collection of nicknames and mischief to the foray. Martin knew he could rely on any one of them, including his dad, to get him out of the deepest woods in the deepest snows, if he ever found himself in trouble. Martin sat quietly in his thoughts, and, with no conversation directed specifically toward him, the chatter faded into the background. He thought of Liz. She would be getting up about now. The girls still had school today. He wondered if she had told anyone about their discussion just three nights ago. As he warmed up by the big wood stove in the corner, he wondered again if he should have come hunting or stayed back in Houston to patch things up with Liz. He had wanted to stay, but Liz had insisted he go. Said she needed some "breathing room." In the end, he'd only gone because staying would have meant an awkward time around the house. Liz had suggested she'd go stay with a girlfriend for a few nights, giving Martin time to look for an apartment. Finally, she'd agreed to think it over and do nothing until he got back from his hunting trip. Reluctantly, he had packed up his stuff and headed out the next day. Now he realized he was a million miles away from his wife and her thoughts.

After wallowing through an assortment of eggs, sausage, pancakes, bacon, French toast and tall, cold glasses of fresh, chalky whole milk and then more coffee, each of the group picked up his bill and headed to the front cash register to pay.

Finally, they were ready to depart Elmo's. It was daylight. Martin's dad slid behind the wheel. Martin's brother also sat in the front, and Martin took the back seat, piled high with blaze-orange hunting clothes and supplies for the week. Martin had not seen his brother for more than eight months. When the subject of family came up, Martin's father had shot him a warning glance in the rearview mirror. Now was not the time or the place to open this up to a three-way discussion. They drove north toward Osseo to get on the Interstate. The conversation quickly turned to local sports and then moved to a fight brewing in Lacrosse over a proposed freeway that the damn environmentalists were fighting. Martin was tired from the night before. His back ached from sitting on the curved- back plastic chairs in the Minneapolis airport, and the five hours on the plane from Houston and Minneapolis. It was cooler in the back seat and he was getting toasty in his down vest. He leaned his head against the frosty glass of the back window. The voices in the front seat drifted farther and farther away. Soon he was breathing deeply in a well-deserved sleep.

Deer hunting season each year in Wisconsin is from the Saturday before Thanksgiving until the Sunday after. During these nine days, over four hundred thousand men, women and children put on warm clothes and head for the Wisconsin woods. Some find comfort simply in spending time outdoors with friends, interested in game only if it presents itself. There is a broader band of young and middle-aged men, set on getting a kill during these nine days to fill a license they have purchased and to finish something they have decided to do. There are other slices of hunters too, from women who like the thrill, to boys going with their dad on an annual journey toward manhood. Some drive all night from Chicago to enter the woods in the predawn hours Saturday to wait in the foreign darkness for the onslaught to begin. Martin had first gone with his dad when he was only twelve years old. He remembered the drive "Up North." He remembered the seemingly large, old men with oversized knives strapped to their belts, talking loudly as they played cards late into the night. The cabin would smell of beans, bacon and cigar smoke. The frost on the windows would grow heavier and heavier as the temperature dropped ever lower and the heat from the ten men and boys in the cabin made itself known on the windows.

In his dreams, Martin could remember the alarm clock go off in the darkness at around 4:30 a.m. After some shuffling about, Don Larsen would usually be the first one up. He would start by throwing several short, stout logs into the woodstove. Next could be heard the hissing sound of gas as it raced out of the stovetop before a quick match caught it and held it captive. Taking a huge old frontier-day black iron kettle, Don would stand over the sink and fill it to the brim. Then he would clang the huge pot down mightily on the stovetop to boil coffee for the day. As the door of the refrigerator was swung open, cartons of jumbo eggs, thick sliced smoked Canadian bacon, orange juice and homemade bread were ceremoniously unloaded and stacked roughly on the counter beside the blazing stove top. Don was standing in his insulated underwear with a heavy, plaid wool shirt hanging almost to his knees. Finally, when all was set, Don picked up an oversized roasting pan and began vengefully beating it with an old, bent-up stainless soup ladle. The sound was deafening, the image memorable, but the glimmer in Don's eyes let everyone know that it was a special time of the year again. A time to begin the hunt.

Martin awoke from his nap. They rolled up Highway 53 in caravan now. As they neared Hayward, the roughness of the land continued to build. Abandoned homesteads and unused cabins, each with its own furtive legacy, stood off in the woods along the road. The soil was poor, and many that had come later had finally just given up the idea of farming the land or raising their family on poor soil so begrudging. An old log home with a tarpaper roof now served as a wintering stable for some steers, worriedly watching for winter's onset. The wind, now clearly blowing in from the north, swept across the dull gray skies of late November.

"And yes, I remember Graybeard," said Martin's brother excitedly from the front seat. "Remember him, Marty? Remember? I'll never forget that we were walking down North Country Trail off Ruth Lake Road. It was just Marty and me and it was near dusk. It was a Tuesday. We hadn't seen a hair all day."

Martin could feel the excitement building in his brother's voice, even though he'd relived this story a hundred times.

"Well, the doe came first. She was a big doe, stood right in the center of the trail. Big doe eyes. No kidding—big doe eyes. We froze in our tracks; she was looking right at us, no more than sixty yards away. She was big, but she didn't move. She looked and she smelled, looked and she smelled. But we were downwind. Then she looked back. When she did, I knew he was back there." Martin's brother loved hunting.

"Wasn't Rich over on your old stand?" asked Martin's father.

"Just left. I think Richie kicked them through because he had just gotten back to the road when he heard us shoot. Anyway, after about a minute, and I mean a really long minute, you know, I see a flash of gray. There's a huge buck standing directly behind the doe. Nobody's moving. They're just looking and smelling, looking and smelling."

Now even Martin was getting caught up in reliving it.

"Yes, I was actually just behind your right shoulder, right? So, I whisper, 'I'm bringing up my iron' and slowly, slowly, slowly I raise my rifle over your right shoulder. I look in the scope and all I see is horns. I can't see a leg. I can't see a body or head. All I see is horns sticking up from behind Mrs. Doe."

Now Martin's brother is very excited. "All of a sudden, they are off like a rocket. I mean they are crashing through the woods. His rack was so huge he had to hold his head back when he was crashing through the brush. Even without scoping him you can see he's big and he's old. He's so old he's got a gray beard. You could see it with the naked eye couldn't you Marty? He had a gray beard."

"I couldn't open up because I was behind you," confessed Martin. "But when he got out there in the opening, I just unloaded on him. Never touched a hair."

"Don saw him two years ago," said Martin's father. "Don's sitting on his stand. Windier than hell, and he looks at a tree and sees a nose and some horns—that's it. When the damn thing starts running, it looks back at him and he can see the gray beard."

"There were shadows everywhere, Marty," offered Martin's brother. "He was gone like a ghost. We'll get him this year. I'll get him. This is my year."

"How long ago was that?" wondered Martin.

"It was your senior year in college," said Martin's dad. "I remember you took the train up to Lacrosse from Madison. That was fifteen years ago."

Fifteen years, thought Martin. Where had he gotten in fifteen years? He had felt his jaw tighten minutes earlier when his brother announced that this was his year, and now, thinking back, Martin wondered how he'd gotten where he was. Twenty years ago, he had been cruising through life looking for all it had to offer him, and now... his thoughts drifted away. He thought of his diligence at work, the dedication, and now with this divorce looming, it all seemed meaningless.

Things were good. Martin, by most standards, had a good, stable job. That was what Liz had called it—stable. She said she didn't need stable. She needed more, but she just could not seem to articulate exactly what she needed more of. He knew it was money, for sure, but money was not enough. Martin had to admit that it had not been great these last few years. Basically, she just was not interested in maintaining the status quo for twenty more years. He loved her more than he ever could say, or ever would say. But even love, simple love, was not good enough. Love meant willing to make a difference, start a venture, take a risk. He was angry, and he was getting ready to do something about it. Management at work had taken him for granted. Hadn't promoted him. Fuck them, he would show them. Good old Martin.

Rich was driving the lead vehicle in the caravan. When they got to old Highway H, he pulled his Jeep over onto the far-left side of the scarred pavement and waved the other two vehicles up alongside. From the back-seat, Martin could view the scene unfold as a spectator. Three abreast, they sat idling steadily on an all-but-abandoned road in the wilderness of northern Wisconsin. They were a hundred miles from any city that most people had ever heard of. Martin could feel the gray cold creep into the cabin of their vehicle as the exhaust-laced air rolled in through the open windows.

"Okay Don," Rick started in, looking across the front seats of two vehicles to address the elder statesman of the group. "I'm thinking it's getting a little late in the day and we got a light dusting of snow. Rather than go by the cabins first and stow our goods, we need to settle on who's standing where in the morning."

Don's worn, wool-checkered cap rested easily as he nodded his head in agreement. "We're with you," he replied. Steve and Patrick and I will follow you down as far as the old game farm and come in from Silver Lake."

"We'll go down to the new clear-cut north of you and walk south," said Rich. "How about you, Bob?"

At a very young sixty-four years of age, Martin's father replied without hesitation. He had hunted various parts of this forest since he was seventeen years old. Before there were roads, or resorts or stores, they used to ride the train in as far as Delta and get dropped off with enough supplies to last for ten days. "We need to check out the Triangle. We got cold and snow coming in tonight. I'm thinking they will be in the big pines before sunup. We'll walk in a couple of miles and if we don't see any fresh signs, we'll meet you on the east side of 411 around four o'clock."

"Sounds good, General," Rich said, smiling at Martin's dad broadly. "Let's get 'em!"

With that, he dropped into full-time four-wheel drive and floored it. Snow, ice, rocks, and mud flew up from all four wheels as he churned wildly off the shoulder, gained control, and led the charge on down Old County Trunk Highway H. Rich wasn't the best pure hunter in the group. But his love of the sport, and his understanding of the importance of fellowship, easily made him the most welcome member. At any second, he could drop his truck into a frozen rut, run over an old log or skid across a boulder and rip the bottom off his vehicle. Nonetheless, the truck rocked and churned through the muck and he fishtailed on down the road.

"Crazy bastard," said Martin's brother admiringly, "look at him go."

Martin's father slowly shook his head and smiled as he eased in behind Rich and headed down the old road. By four o'clock that afternoon they had seen thirteen deer between the eight of them. Each of them had settled on a special place to start the season in the critical early morning hours of opening day. By six that night they had unpacked clothes and supplies back at the Ruth Lake Lodge.

Martin wasn't a good card player, but he liked to sit around, play cards and drink beer. He had never been much for hard liquor. He had worked two summers at a brewery in Lacrosse when he was going to college. During that time, he had found that he not only enjoyed drinking beer—he was good at it. College down in Madison had been a party. This night had started off extremely well. Martin had been a partner with his dad playing pinochle, and they were cleaning up. The more they won, the louder they got. For the Cantrell's, pinochle wasn't a game, it was a religion. When Martin was a kid, and the weather was bad on summer weekends, they would sit around the kitchen table for hours and play game after game. One year on a deer hunting trip, the weather had turned to a cold slushy rain around 11 a.m. on Monday morning. After two hours, the whole hunting gang had been chased back to the camp, soaked to the bone in freezing rain. Somebody got the cards going and Martin and his brother had won seventeen games of pinochle in a row. They still occasionally reminded everyone of that fateful day. Tonight, there wasn't enough time for seventeen games. In fact, after three devastating wins in a row, Martin and his dad declared victory. Then they all headed for the

Log Cabin restaurant for dinner. Martin pulled on a coat and followed everyone out the door and down the rock steps to their vehicle below. In five minutes, they were walking into the bar/store/restaurant/lodge for dinner.

Somebody had Hank Williams Jr. on the jukebox, and the pre-hunt crowd was the biggest Martin had ever seen "Up North." Rough looking locals with torn hands and wind-worn faces were eating fish baskets at the bar. Nice-looking families from Madison were sitting at orderly tables across the dining room. The Ripon Bunch and the Delta Gang were there. Martin didn't really know any of the members of those hunting groups, but they would occasionally see each other out in the middle of the wilderness during the hunting season. After a while, each group had come to mutually respect the toughness of the others. For starters, they had all learned the lay of the land in the three hundred thousand-acre boundaries of the Chequamegon State Forest. In fact, three years earlier, the Delta Gang had gotten those new blaze-orange hunting caps with their green delta insignia sewed on. From then on you could look through your rifle scope a quarter mile away and pick them out with their fancy damn caps.

"All right," said Rich, "I got the first round." He had to holler over the music. The older guys slid onto the bar stools around one of the standup cocktail tables while the younger ones checked the crowd and pulled popcorn out of the machine and cradled it in nasty looking red plastic baskets. The popcorn was delicious.

"Hi fellas. What can I get you tonight?" asked the woman hustling drinks. She just looked too good to be doing this during hunting season. She was wearing jeans and a tight black t-shirt. She looked perfectly at home, oblivious to the crowd around her.

"Well given Richie's shaky financial standing I'll just have another light beer," said Don. He had that big round face and sparkling eyes, even in his sixties he could get away with just about anything.

Martin's dad went next. "Old-fashioned for me."

After they ordered drinks, they got back to the serious business of talking up the hunt. Martin's brother had been bow-hunting with Rich in early fall. Over a long weekend they had hunted most of the regular territory. They had also gotten two really nice bucks from their vantage point in the tree stands. The conversation was pretty animated walking back through the fall hunt. Martin had lost track of which forest trail intersected with which logging road. He was having trouble picturing in his mind the contours that lay north of Canthook Lake. Soon his dad and Don were talking about their Florida winter homes and his brother was caught up in conversation with his buddies. Martin very much belonged, but he found himself to be somewhat of an outsider. He drank two beers in almost no time, matching the two he had had back at the cabin. He realized the jukebox had run out of money. He went to the bar to get change. Then, standing over the jukebox he surveyed the list of available songs, turning the quarters slowly in the palm of one hand while sipping a beer in the other. He tossed in his first three selections.

A woman came up beside him.

"What are you doing in here buddy?" She said. "Are you going to pick out some Texas music for us Northerners?"

He turned and saw Taylor Thompson. She was giving him that big smile and then looking with him down toward the bright lights of the music box.

"Taylor. Taylor, what are you doing here?" A nearly speechless Martin stumbled.

"Umm, you forgot I live here, right?" Said Taylor. "Well, actually my parents live up here."

"Oh, that's right. I'm just so used to thinking of you being from Madison, I did forget," said Martin.

Taylor smiled, "Well, after twenty years I guess it's time you meet my parents." A nice-looking old couple was standing behind her. "Mom and Dad, this is Martin Cantrell; guess you could say we used to date back in college. Martin, these are my folks." They shook hands all around and then stood awkwardly looking at each other.

"Wow, I can't believe bumping into you like this," said Martin.

"Up for the hunt, I assume," said her dad.

"Yeah, there's a crew of us, including my dad," he responded, nodding toward their table.

"So, we're going to get our name on the list and see if we can get a table," said Taylor.

"I'm guessing you're in for a wait tonight," said Martin, looking around at the overflow crowd.

"We're pretty good friends with the owners. You know, we live about five minutes from here," said Taylor's mom. "There's a chance we won't have a long wait." She smiled.

"Well, very nice to meet you," said Martin. "Don't want my buddies to start missing me and send out a search party."

"They seem to be doing just fine without you," said Taylor smiling. "Unreal to see you."

Martin slowly turned and weaved his way back through the crowd to his buddies. Another twenty minutes went by. Martin had his fifth beer. It was pushing 9:00 p.m. and they hadn't eaten. Somebody tapped him on the shoulder. It was Taylor. All conversation stopped and all eyes turned to Taylor.

"I think you're going to like this next song," said Taylor. "How about a little dance?"

Before Martin could speak, Richie nearly hollered, "Sure babe, I'd love a dance with you!" Laughter from the group.

"Guys, guys, let me introduce Taylor Thompson. She and I were good friends down in Madison. She's up here visiting her parents," said Martin.

"Let me just say," Richie said, looking at Taylor; "if that means you guys dated in college, you have very poor taste in men." Again, laughs all around.

"You gonna dance, or do I have to downgrade to one of these guys?" she said, smiling at all of them.

Like just about every other bar "Up North" there was a hardwood dance floor out in front of the jukebox. This one was about average size, no more than fifteen by fifteen feet. There were four couples who had been doing the two-step. The next song came on—a slow one—one of their favorites from twenty years ago. They danced slowly, her leaning in, so she could talk in his ear over the noise.

For just an instant, Martin felt a little bit light-headed. She grabbed his shoulder and gave it a good squeeze, brushing against him, ever so slightly. Martin looked across to the other side of the bar. His buddies were back to their lively conversation. His hand now held her head against his shoulder; her collar was damp against her hair. Ever so softly, she was sighing as they moved slowly in a tight circle around the floor. For some reason, Martin felt relaxed. He found himself leaning into her. Closing his eyes, he listened to the music. The thought of Liz swept by him, a thousand miles away.

"You still in the oil business?" asked Taylor.

"Yep, part of the evil empire, trying to kill the planet. And you."

"Head of the DNR, trying my best to put guys like you out of business," she laughed.

"Still married?" asked Martin.

"Wow, still Martin. You get right to the point, don't you?" she said. "Divorced, three years ago. You?"

"Married, trying to stay that way," said Martin. They went on to ask about old friends. She was only in Iron River for a couple of days. He was going to be busy hunting. The dance was coming to an end.

"Listen," said Taylor, "I'd love to see you sometime. Maybe at one of the oil conferences we could have dinner, if you are okay with it."

"Yeah, yeah, that would be great," said Martin. He paused, contemplating his next words. "You know I still think about you."

She was taken aback. "Really?"

"Well, I'm not a stalker, obviously, but we had something special."

Taylor took moment, "I thought so too. Well, I gotta get back to my parents. Good to see you." And with that, she walked off.

Martin quickly went over by the deer gang's table and tried to work himself nonchalantly into the conversation. Of course, there was a lot of good-natured ribbing for Martin. Richie was first, "Jeez, season's not even open and Martin has a doe already." Big laughs again. Everybody was having a nice time. Martin was feeling the alcohol now. Finally, their table was ready. As their group headed toward the table, Martin peeled off to use the men's room, running directly into Taylor on the way. Slowly, he steered her over against the wall to give her a hug. Unexpectedly for both of them, he kissed her on the lips. She arched her back and grabbed him by the hair on the back of his head, returning a long, deep kiss. His brother had waited back to pay the bill and saw everything.

Across the dining room, Martin caught passing glimpses of Taylor as she enjoyed spending time with her parents. She gazed across the room. When their eyes met, she gave him a big smile, shook her hair back over her shoulders, and then looked very businesslike back at her table as she and her parents placed their orders.

It was near the end of the meal when Martin headed for the restroom again. Too many beers. The knotty pine walls reminded him that he was really "Up North." The painted concrete floors showed this to be a place of practicality and prudence. Martin liked it. He was standing at the urinal when his brother walked in.

"What in the hell do you think you're doing out there?" said his brother.

"What do you mean?"

"What were you trying to prove with that tramp?" He continued. "Showing us all what a big man you are?"

He was talking very loudly, almost angry. Martin had seen him get this way before on a number of occasions—usually at parties where he drank too much and would pick a fight. Martin wasn't in the mood to humor him this time.

"Frankly, it's none of your damn business," said Martin, barely masking his anger.

"It sure as hell is my business. We all come up here together and you make an ass out of yourself with some tramp."

"She isn't a tramp and all I was doing was having a little dance with her. You are really starting to piss me off," said Martin, raising his voice in return.

"You were practically screwing her right in front of us. You are a married man for Christ's sake! Grow up!" And with that he rammed his pointed finger into Martin's chest.

Things had been building up in Martin. His work. Liz and the divorce. He was tired and in no mood.

"Just get out of my face, brother—you're drunk."

His brother was red-faced, "No *you're* drunk," he retorted, giving Martin a push.

"Now you're going to get it," said Martin. He pulled back his fist and then struck out fiercely in the close confines of the bathroom. The blow landed evenly across the chin of his brother who fell back against the wall. He didn't go down, but his head snapped back decidedly as he came to a stop. Momentarily stunned, he was then back on Martin with fists flying. Martin rammed his shoulder into him and slammed him a second time into the wall. Just as they were hitting the floor, two other guys came into the restroom and found them groveling about on the cold concrete floor. After twenty seconds of scuffling and cursing, the strangers pulled them apart. Martin's brother was still enraged and was getting the short end of this fight. He had a set of deep red dots where Martin's knuckles had made their mark. Martin was regaining composure.

"Leave me alone. You're my brother, but you're not my big brother anymore," said Martin.

"Jesus, Martin, cool off. I was just telling you to watch your manners in this place," said Martin's brother.

Martin said, "Just stay out of my business."

"You're still a tough little son of a bitch. You get pissed off enough, you're liable to do anything. Turns out you're still kind of a tough bastard." Said Martin's brother.

They walked out of the restroom, and shortly they were back in their cabins, all asleep, with visions of trees and lakes and trophy bucks dancing in their heads.

CHAPTER 11

MORNING, THE RUFFIAN, RUSTLED THEM FROM THEIR beds at 4:30 a.m. Martin was never the first one up. He looked hazily from beneath the heavy covers as the others slowly rolled out. As he rose to his feet, the sick smell of greasy bacon almost brought Martin down. In one move, he ran his long stockinged legs through old jeans and into his old leather-topped sorrel boots, waiting patiently at the foot of the bed. A down vest over a flannel shirt and he was in the bathroom splashing cold water in his face. Soon they were rocking back down Forest Road 411 toward the huge, empty dark forest. Martin had the farthest to walk to get back to his deer stand. He liked it that way.

It was fifteen degrees. A gentle breeze was coming down from the Lake to the north, just as his father had predicted. The stars were out, joined by a quarter moon now low on the horizon. Martin was walking, rifle in hand. He was headed west on the North Country Trail. Without breaking stride, he levered a cartridge into the chamber. In the darkness he checked the safety. Reaching in his left pocket, he pulled out a clip of four more shells and listened as the clip clicked reassuringly into place. The cold was quickly eating into his hands. Quickly he completed his maneuvers and pulled on his wool gloves. His hands were feeling thicker with each passing second. Without breaking stride, he unzipped a game pocket in the back of his coat. Cradling the rifle in one arm, he reached back with the other and produced a small, halogen flashlight from the pocket, then continued down the snow-covered path. He could clearly make out the path in the lingering moonlight. Intermittently he flipped the flashlight on and off, showing the path ahead. No fresh footprints were in sight. He would be the first of anyone into these backwoods today.

For forty-five minutes he pressed on. It was almost three miles back to his stand. His only companion now was the snow speaking softly to him as it squeaked under his broad boots. He paused briefly to unzip the top and bottom of his heavy jacket. He also unzipped the side seams of his pants. The wear of carrying himself over this distance now had his body overheating. His glasses steamed over in the morning air. The sweat was beginning to roll off him. He had to get cooled down before he soaked through everything he had on. He pulled open his jacket and unbuttoned both his goose down vest and heavy, red wool shirt. The white wisps of steam silently dissipated out into the starlight. He sensed motion in the black fringes beyond him. He held his breath. He moved his trigger finger over the safety. He listened. An animal of some type moved from left to right behind him, across his trail. His heart beat rapidly in his throat. His glasses were still fogging over. For two minutes he stood motionless. Now the cold was creeping over him again as he remained motionless. He moved carefully to silently survey a full circle of territory around him, then he dutifully launched off again down the trail. In twenty minutes, he came upon a deep drop of the trail angling decidedly south as it fell over the hill. Again, he stopped and looked to his right. The forest floor rose steadily over a distance of perhaps a quarter mile. In a long, even line across the dark horizon he could make out the ridge. This was his jump-off from the trail. He moved toward the ridgeline. Moving in the darkness and using his flashlight sparingly, he picked his way along, avoiding downed trees and the thickest brush. After six hundred yards he came across the run. He could see it first in the powdered snow ahead. The beam from his flashlight fell across tracks that had been left by more than a dozen deer during the night. The snow flurries had begun to softly fall. He paused briefly over the trail. At least three or four of the sets of tracks were fresh. Gazing about, Martin picked a group of three aspens standing together in easy reach of the deer trail. The spot was downwind from the deer run. This was to be his deer stand, his point of vantage for the day. Each of the trees was about a foot in diameter. Martin stood in the center of the three trees and looked carefully for a few minutes in each direction. There was heavy brush behind him downwind, running parallel to the trail. Facing into the wind he could look to his right for the final distance up to the top of the ridge. To his left and ahead he could look clearly across the falling landscape. He checked his watch—5:50 a.m. The legal time to begin shooting was six thirty. Another forty minutes. Martin scraped away the snow to enable himself to change his stance quietly without the crunching of snow. He unshouldered his pack and leaned it gently against the outside edge of one of the trees. With his knife he sliced off a half dozen sprigs that protruded from the trees across his newly claimed space, enabling him to freely swing his rifle if needed. Any one of those branches could rasp loudly across his clothes or block the swing of his rifle or vision if they were not cut back. He was a bit over three miles from any road. The moon was long lost over the horizon, and the cold, light breeze still wafted through the trees. In total silence he clicked the safety off, and then on. The simple click seemed deafening. He rolled the rifle back into the cradle of his arm. Then he again scraped the snow in a tight circle in front of the largest tree. He zipped up his legs and outer jacket and leaned back squarely against the tree. Alone, in the predawn wilderness, Martin was ready for anything.

Time passed slowly. The predawn emptiness now gone, Martin took a break and poured a cup of steaming black coffee. He unconsciously calculated the length of the walk back to the trailhead. Already, his eyes were raw from the cold, dry breeze. Five hours of standing motionless had taken their toll. With each graying swirl in the brush he had stared intently and fully in search of the all-too-elusive prey. With the day had come the rumbling of distant gunfire across this wilderness. For the most part, the sound of gunfire was distant. But along the way there was also an occasional sharp, close crack of a rifle, perhaps only a mile or so distant. Some shots were in sequence. Three or four shots close together was probably a hunter firing as his target followed a weaving, slicing path through thick woods. A lonesome shot followed methodically with a second telling shot was an experienced hunter. He had awaited his trophy and brought justice to it. Next, Martin heard, off in the distance, four shots. Each shot was spaced seconds apart. It was a hunter, most likely in a tree stand with a large caliber rifle, taking careful aim at his quarry as it ran breakneck across an open field. The seconds between shots followed the deer as it raced across a field likely to be littered with the stumps, treetops, and new pine fingerlings of a summer's past pulp harvest.

For Martin there had been nothing. He had not seen a deer. He had not seen another hunter. He stood quietly in the middle of the three trees. His three friendly sentinels rocked aimlessly and silently in the breeze. Martin had plenty of time to think. What had brought him here? What had gotten him to this point? What does a man do when he begins to understand that getting by isn't good enough any longer? It was a Saturday morning. By now Liz was on her third cup of hazelnut and was readying the kids to be out for the day. The initial excitement of the morning was gone. Martin could feel the cold air and snow slowly numbing his feet. He hadn't moved more than a step for almost five hours. He remained standing. Rigid. The first day, the slightest movement of a hunter could scare off that one trophy buck of a lifetime.

From his deer stand, Martin looked down through the forest toward a stand of pines about three hundred yards away. It looked a bit swampy just on the other side of the pines. Sometimes, Martin would find a trail where the deer would tend to run toward the thick cover of pines, skirting an adjoining marsh. Standing silently, he slowly rotated his head to the right, and then back again left. Nothing in sight. Breathing shallow, he paused a bit longer, listening intently for any tell-tale crunching of snow or snapping of twigs. He heard nothing. Looking back toward the pines again, he shuddered from the cold creeping down his back. Finally, he snapped the safety on his rifle off and then on again. It was time to stretch his legs. He strode off cautiously through the open woods. It was easy walking, but at first, he found his steps deafening in the quiet, gray woods of winter. He thought he would walk down to the swampy area.

As he neared the pines, he began to make out open shallow pools of water near the marshy area. The pools weren't frozen, even though the air was still a good ten degrees below freezing. Pausing every fifteen steps or so to look around, Martin knew there had to be natural warm springs under the forest floor, keeping the water from freezing here in the early winter. At last he found himself under the broad boughs of the pines. He had heated up again and he stopped momentarily to unzip his jacket and slip off his gloves. He looked north now up the little tree-covered valley. Old hummocks of earth and peat, scattered along the bottom of the valley were strewn with marsh grass, berry bushes and prickly ash. Beside one of the swampy pools, he turned to check the path on which he'd just come. As he turned, he carelessly grazed his hand across one of the one-inch spurs of a prickly ash, slashing the back of his hand from the wrist to his middle knuckle. Martin let out a low, painful grunt as the limb snapped away. Grimacing, he shifted his rifle from his left arm to cradle it in his right and then lifted his left hand to inspect the damage. It wasn't dangerous at all, but it was deep enough to bleed like crazy. Martin stood there senselessly watching as the blood ran down the heel of his hand and splattered brilliantly in the stark, white snow. Kneeling now in the snow, he leaned his rifle carefully against a small sapling and reached with his good hand into the zippered back pocket of his blaze orange coat. In a second, he retrieved a large, weathered roll of toilet paper. After rubbing freezing snow across the wound to clean it out and wipe away some of the blood, he quickly wrapped the toilet paper around his hand a number of times to stop the bleeding.

Martin was on his knees. Suddenly, from the rise to his right, came a crashing sound so loud that Martin's first instinct was to duck down; perhaps it was a rifle shot. Instantly, three deer careened through the brush and trees, running with heads down, obviously spooked. Still kneeling, undetected and sheltered, Martin reached for his gun. In a second, it was on his shoulder. He picked an opening and held on it. Deer Number One went blazing through his scope, no horns. A second later and Number Two followed. Martin held his position; no horns. And then immediately, Number Three came into view—all horns; a huge, beautiful buck deer. Martin stuck his sights on the big buck, waited for a clear opening and ripped off two deafening rounds. As quickly as it had begun, it was over. Martin heard the dull thud of the stag's body drop to the forest floor, less than seventy feet away. Jumping to his feet, Martin raced forward through the trees, gun in hand, fearing that perhaps a graze or a flesh wound had only momentarily stunned the magnificent animal. Then he was upon the big deer lying on the ground, and saw that he had shot it through the heart. It was lying in a contorted position in the snow. Its dance with life and death was now complete. Martin's heart was racing. He sat down on one of the snow- and ice-covered hummocks and stared at his trophy. For several minutes, he stared alternately at the big buck and gun. An indescribable feeling of power came over him, turning quickly to feelings of guilt and sadness. Even when he was hunting as a kid, killing never bothered him. He still offered a silent tribute to this beautiful animal. In the last three days, Martin knew he had become a different man. He would do whatever had to be done. Maybe he still had the killer instinct; it had just been buried for a while. He looked silently up the quiet little valley as more flurries of afternoon snow began to drift through the trees. Martin steeled himself against the wind. The death here, and the thought of his aging parents, and the thought of his family back in Houston melded together. Staring at the small pools of water in front of him, he followed the snowflakes as they dropped into the oily, iridescent glimmer of each small pool in the swamp.

During his childhood, when he'd first seen these iridescent pools, he had dreamed of deep oil fields; of oil seeping to the top of his father's farm down by Lacrosse, making them all very rich. But what if there was oil here? What if no one had ever looked for it, here in the woods of northern Wisconsin? As a geologist, he knew that the oily, iridescent film was from algae and decaying vegetation. Now in the silence of the snow, he smiled blankly as the flakes melted innocently in the warm spring's shiny pools.

After a while, he got out his big knife and went to dress out the deer. In an hour, he had neatly cleaned the innards from the huge buck and then dragged it a few hundred yards back up to the trail he had come in on that morning. There was no way for him to drag it out to the road on his own. He strung it up in a big pine tree which camouflaged it in the dense undergrowth. Only the most veteran hunter passing by would be able to spot an irregularity in the long shadows of the late, gray afternoon, and spot the deer. About an hour before dark, Martin's brother came striding down the trail, dressed light and moving fast. Martin eased off his stand and moved briskly across the forest floor to meet him.

"You get one?" His brother asked bluntly. "I figured when you weren't at the car, you needed some help."

"Yeah," said Martin dryly. "Had some luck today."

"What in the hell did you do to your hand?" Steve asked.

Now dried and frozen, as stiff as cardboard, Martin had forgotten about the ugly, dark stains of blood on his glove from the prickly ash tear.

"Wasn't watching what I was doing," answered Martin. "Ripped it on some thorns."

"That's going to be a great scar there, slick. Where's the deer?" Martin motioned silently toward the big tree where the deer was hanging. "Can you use your good hand to help me pull the deer out to the road?"

"Yeah, I'm all right," said Martin. "Let me show you the deer."

Martin led his brother back up the trail and over to the hanging deer. The sun was losing its vitality, and twilight would come in only thirty minutes on this cloudy, winter day. Martin could see his brother look admiringly at the deer.

"You know Martin, I've been hunting up here every year since high school and I've never seen one bigger than this."

"Well," said Martin, "I appreciate that. He is a beauty, isn't he."

"Hey kid, good shooting! Richie's gonna go ape shit when he sees this."

"Bro, thanks for inviting me up this year. I'm sorry about last night," said Martin.

"That's okay. You were right, it was none of my business. Anyway, I'm glad to see you still got it in you, kid. Now let's drag this monster back to the truck. It's going to take us awhile."

CHAPTER 12

LEANING OVER THE MARBLE-TOPPED VANITY, ANITA PUT on fresh lipstick and eyeliner. In two minutes, she had her hair brushed out, and the rest of her makeup touched up. From her bag, she grabbed a pair of black heels, slipped off her flats and put on her heels. It was only by chance, but at the last minute this morning she had put on a black-knit dress and she smiled silently to herself knowing Hilton would like the look. Glancing at her watch, she saw that it was already 11:05 a.m., and Hilton was always on time. After he had left her waiting in the doorway a couple of times at lunchtime, she let him know the importance of being on time for her and he had gotten the message. She needed to be on time, too.

Quickly she snapped her compact shut, picked up her bag and headed for the elevator. It was only two floors down, but she never walked it. Looking out over the atrium she could see Hilton's black Mercedes waiting outside. She walked directly to the car, Hilton watching her every move. In a moment, she was settling in on the big leather seat, and letting Hilton see some good leg as she leaned back for the seat belt and shut the door.

"Damn, you look good today," said Hilton. "I've been thinking about you all morning."

"Oh, you have not," said Anita. "You've been thinking about your oil company." Anita knew Hilton. Often out for a drink, over the phone or even after making love, Hilton would go into a long, rambling discussion. He would talk about who was saying what and where in the world. And he'd explain why oil prices were therefore going to go up or down or stay flat the rest of the day. Hilton lacked a lot of things a woman looks for in a man, including fidelity, but he loved to trade oil. He also knew how to make money. She had dated her share of deadbeats over the years, and at this point in her life, she'd take money over a lot of things.

Hilton swung the car out onto Ashford Lane and headed north toward I-10. Just before reaching the freeway, he turned left at Threadneedle and took the back entrance into the hotel. She went to the lounge and ordered their drinks while he made arrangements at the front desk. This was a pretty well-rehearsed routine. In five minutes, he was by her side at a corner table, running his big hands teasingly over the inside of her thighs as they talked.

"So, are you doing all right?" Hilton asked. Nobody but Hilton ever asked her that question. And whenever he asked, he listened until he had a real answer.

"Well, Amanda's got a cold. I finally took her to the doctor yesterday after work because she's just not getting over it. That cost me sixty dollars and a prescription for Amoxicillin that'll cost me another sixty. My annual deductible's a thousand. But, as long as they continue letting her go to school, I guess it'll be all right."

"So, you've been working a lot, huh?" Asked Hilton.

"Yeah, quite a bit. I haven't been working any overtime unless Martin personally approves it, but the guys are really busy. I think they're thinking of selling some West Texas stuff to help fund this Russian deal. Several of the guys were out in Odessa all last week again and now I've got slides for three "show-and-tells" and they just keep changing and changing and changing the slides."

"Damn you look so damn good. I want you bad, baby. Let's head up to the room," said Hilton.

"Hilton, I'm not even finished with my drink."

"I'm just going to bring mine with us."

Hilton looked damned good himself today, Anita thought. Always tan and trim, it looked to her like he had lost a few pounds. He didn't smile much, but when he did, it was that big smile, white teeth and tan, with lots of wavy black hair brushed just right over the collar. Anita squeezed his hand under the table and moved it closer to her. She could feel overwhelming heat.

"You know Hilton, I'm really glad you called me today," Anita said slowly.

They picked up their half-finished drinks, eased out of the table and headed for the room.

CHAPTER 13

IT HAD BEEN A GREAT OPENING DAY OFF THE NORTH COUNTRY TRAIL. Early in the day, his brother had laid down a really nice three-year-old forked buck, not more than two hundred feet from the Jeep. Don had gotten a six-pointer in heavy brush at dawn. They had all seen plenty of deer. Martin's dad had seen thirteen, not a horn to be found. After forty years of deer hunting, he was not about to settle for a doe. It was legal to shoot does in this area on opening weekend. The last two winters had seen light snow and there were plenty of deer, given the mild winter. Three years ago, with a heavy snow, the deer had yarded up early and had starved by the thousands. Even though he was down in Houston, Martin remembered seeing news clips of some groups trying to feed the deer by air, dropping giant bales of hay and corn from huge, odd looking helicopters from the National Guard over in Superior. In the end, it was hopeless. There were too many deer and it was too expensive to do much about it. Winterkill, as they called it, was just one method of herd management. The gun season was another.

Dragging the huge buck, Martin and his brother had their hands full and needed to stop and rest. It was pitch black. The woods had long ago cleared from that day's hunt. After standing around for thirty minutes after closing time, a couple of the guys had trailed after Martin's brother. The two of them met Martin and his brother only a mile from the road, and they were exhausted from dragging the giant deer through the snow. This buck was, in fact, a big one. Martin's dad said it was one of the biggest he had ever seen north of the Chippewa River.

By the time this State Forest was formed back in the thirties, some of the oldest families had already lived on their homestead more than fifty years. Many of the original settlers had left almost immediately in the 1880s and 1890s when the promise of gold and silver riches in South Dakota and Colorado lured them away. Another wave left in the early 1900s when western Minnesota was taking shape. The deep rich loam of Rochester and Albert Lea, and even western Iowa was attractive to the homesteaders. That soil compared favorably with the coarse, rancid soil of northern Wisconsin that had been found when their fathers or their grandfathers had cleared this land for the original homestead. By the time that Roosevelt's Civilian Conservation Corps laid down the markers for the state forest lines, there were only twenty-six families left living on land within the boundaries of the state forest. The government offered very nice relocation packages to each of the twenty-six families, and a few families happily accepted and moved on. Later, the government offered very attractive buyout options to the twenty or so families who still kept their struggling farms within the Forest. The state threatened to condemn their land for public use. The government even got tough and said if the families didn't take the buyout offer, they'd be paid only a pitifully small amount for their land. Most of the families didn't want a legal battle and they took the buyout and left their homes.

But there were still eighteen farms left. The remaining families, either too proud or too foolish to move, vowed to fight it out. In the end, only eighteen families stayed. Together they controlled nearly four thousand acres of poor farmland and marginal forest. Still, they stood out curiously, in the middle of the huge Chequamegon State Forest, which was otherwise uninhabited. After years of idle threats and legal saber rattling, the government finally gave up. The state, terming it "socially symbiotic" for the farmers to stay, finally got the settlers to sign an agreement that they could never subdivide their land. This would keep the parcels barren and prevent the landowners from selling off their land in small pieces to other families or vacationers who might want to build a lake house or hunting cabin back off one of the secluded forest roads.

As the Deer Gang drove back to camp in the darkness, Martin noticed the occasional, lonely, rusted mailbox along the road. Through the trees he could see the houses or outbuildings, still perfectly square from the Old-World craftsmen who had put them there. They needed paint, many were in disrepair, but most still housed family members. Most of them were barely hanging on by their teeth. The livestock were gone from the land that once used to grow hay in the government's Soil Bank program. One of the yards had a two-year-old Oldsmobile sedan in the yard. No doubt somebody in the family, maybe an older son, had caught on with the pulp plant over in Ashland where they could make upwards of eight dollars an hour.

At last they pulled into their cabins and strung up the deer. In no time they were all showered and hunkered down around the big plank table at the Green Top. It was the Saturday night before Thanksgiving, and time for the annual Deer Hunter's Ball. The group recalled again their most memorable hunts, their finest moments in sports, and of course, their greatest exploits in the art of womanizing. As the evening waned, Martin sat back and watched, he listened, he laughed, and among friends he found himself more alone than he had ever been in his entire life.

By seven Wednesday morning they had eaten breakfast, loaded up, and gotten on the road. By 8:30 a.m. they were in Hayward, home of the annual Lumberjack Championship and the Sportsman's Bar featuring the world's largest Muskie fish ever caught. The tone was subdued. Martin woke from his nap as they exited off Interstate 94 and came to a complete stop in Osseo. The windows were covered in salt and slush. You couldn't begin to see out any window except the windshield. Eyes barely open, Martin heard the whir of the power window as his dad cracked open a window to see the intersection. Outside, in the grays and whites and blacks of town, Martin saw neat little houses lying peacefully in the late morning mist.

"So, we stopping here or Whitehall?" It was Steve. Six days' beard. Eyes bloodshot. The appetite for deer hunting satisfied for another year.

"Let's stop here in Osseo," said Martin's father. "I haven't seen Lee for at least three years, and they get all their lefse from Whitehall anyway."

Martin smiled an easy smile. This was a tradition. Nobody had to remind them; no one ever said a thing. There would be a big Thanksgiving dinner; a true feast. And every year, on the way back from deer hunting, they would stop here in one of these small Scandinavian towns and buy lefse. It was a sort of tortilla-like flat bread made of potatoes and flour in round sheets and then folded into triangles and placed in packages of three. A lot of wives and mothers still made it the old-fashioned way in farmhouses up and down the hills and valleys. It was tricky to make properly, and it was expensive in the store. Lefse remained somewhat of a holiday delicacy for most.

They pulled into the IGA and all three of them got out —jeans, wool shirts, Redwings, and Steve with his huge Buck knife still strapped in his belt. They pushed through the front door, the smells of warm produce and wooden floors enticing Martin's memories from narrow clefts and deep caverns of years long passed.

"There's Lee back behind the meat counter," said Martin's dad. "I'm going to go back see if he recognizes me."

"Guess I'll join you," said Martin's brother, peering toward the back of the store. "Man, old Lee's gained some weight."

"Always been kind of heavy," said Martin's dad.

"Look, I'll get the lefse," offered Martin, "and meet you guys in the back."

They nodded and parted ways. Martin could see loaves of bread stacked neatly in the left corner of the store. The aisles narrow, the wooden floors smooth from a hundred years' wear. Martin turned right at the bread and headed down the far aisle, looking, looking, and looking. There was a cart half full and a woman with her back to him, staring at the lefse. It used to be that lefse was lefse. These days some of the packages were wheat flour, some were multigrain. She seemed to be checking her options.

He was waiting for a second behind her; waiting for her to make her selection. She saw they were both after lefse and took half a step to one side. Black hair, a ski vest with last year's lift pass from Telluride dangling off the back of the vest.

Martin looked back at the lefse. "I better take my time here; this might be the biggest decision I make all week."

She turned. It was Taylor. "Oh, this is too weird," she laughed. "You really are stalking me!" She laughed again.

Less than a foot between them,Martin said, "I really am with the guys! I'm not stalking you. My dad knows Lee, the owner of the store."

"Sure, sure, stick with that story." Taylor had the most beautiful smile.

She stood for just a moment, keys dangling from her left hand, then stepped into him with both hands around his waist and said, "God I've missed you, too."

They kissed again. Together, back in college at Madison, he had entered Wisconsin's geology program and she was a history major, hellbent on going on to law school. In August of his senior year, he had been sitting out on the patio at Memorial Union. Camden, Steve, Doc, Paula, and Stark had all been with him. It was Friday afternoon—happy hour; dollar pitchers; sitting out overlooking Lake Mendota. It was still hot and humid, but in the shade of late afternoon, ending the first week of classes; they were in fine form. Martin had watched her out on the patio for a while. First, she had been alone, reading the Capitol Times, drinking a Shiner, and carrying the biggest backpack he had ever seen. After about twenty minutes, a couple joined her, and they engaged in deep conversation. She was tan from the summer. There was just something about her. He could see she had a big smile and yet an uncommon intensity. It would be weeks later in the library before he could get up the nerve to talk to her.

Now, here in the store in Osseo, they talked. She was now actually Head of the Department of Natural Resources in Madison. She had finally gotten what she wanted. He was with Basin Oil, of course, as a geologist. She had heard of Basin but didn't know much about them. She had gotten to know many of the oil companies over the last few years; it hadn't all been pleasant. They exchanged business cards, laughing at the titles on each other's cards. After her divorce, she just hadn't gotten around to getting remarried. "Too busy," she said. He lived in Houston, of course. Texas was a lot different—and a lot warmer—than Madison had ever been. She was driving back to Madison, had stopped here to buy some snacks for the rest of the drive, and ended up grabbing some lefse.

"So, are we buying lefse or are we getting the Osseo weather forecast, or what?" It was his brother, with his dad, of course, in tow.

"What the Hell," said his brother, "how did you arrange this, Martin?" His brother and his dad laughed. Everyone stood around nervously stomping their feet for a few minutes trying to make normal conversation.

Finally, Taylor spoke up. "Martin, it was really good to see you and I hope you have a good time over Thanksgiving." Always the diplomat, thought Martin, she could be sending off the Ambassador to Japan with that salutation. Taking his cue, he reached out oddly to shake her hand and wish her the best.

A smiling Taylor looked over at Martin's dad and said, "And can you tell your son to stop stalking me?" They all laughed. On cue, the three large men and Taylor turned back down the aisle toward checkout. In a few minutes, everybody was out of the store and back on the road. The questions about this woman—and Martin—no one asked.

It was late afternoon when Martin pulled into his parents' drive. On Thanksgiving Day, he couldn't sleep so he had gotten up at five and gone for a long walk up behind their house. He had spent the last day around the house, visiting with the relatives, playing ball with his nephews, eating leftover food and inventing new reasons to get outside and get some fresh air. Finally, Sunday had arrived. It was time to head back to Houston. After lunch he had said goodbye, and his brother came by with his kids to take him to the Lacrosse airport. The weather conditions were a little different this time, with crisp, clear blue skies. His brother's youngest boy had cried when Martin had hugged him goodbye. They hardly knew each other, but Martin could feel the love between them.

Martin arrived in Minneapolis all right, but there was a long delay again and his plane didn't take off until after seven. He tried to sleep on the plane but couldn't. He was going home... or was he? The pilot announced their approach to Houston. Martin had always dreaded Sunday nights. In the heavy, humid air of evening, he could see the long, neat lines of houses over Houston. He thought of their house. They had painted over the brick two years ago, in a fashionable light gray that Liz had liked. The dark shutters had looked good too. Even he had grudgingly admitted it. The azaleas had been neatly trimmed around the front entryway. Perhaps the time away had been good for them both. Maybe things would be different. Clearer. At the same time, he felt powerless to deal with Liz and her complaints, mostly because many were valid. Liz wanted more. Hell, Martin wanted more. He just hadn't taken the time or made a plan or maybe he had lacked the guts to go after it—whatever "it" was. What exactly was he going to do?

CHAPTER 14

WHEN THE LIGHT TURNED RED ON MEMORIAL, MARTIN swung his Acura out onto the road and headed west. Thankfully, he was going against the traffic as it wove its web into downtown Houston, each of the drivers peering intently over the steering wheel, meeting the morning sun. It was 6:45 a.m. and Martin would probably be first into the office again that morning. Sometimes his colleague, Krenovich, would come in extra early so that he could run his high-end geological simulation programs with dedicated computer power. Martin and Liz had talked to the kids. They said they were having some problems and they needed a break. Liz had done most of the talking while Martin sat idly by, trying to be calm, reassuring. She had said that sometimes "friends" need time apart to plan and think about what they want to do, and that things had changed between Mom and Dad. His oldest daughter asked all the hard questions: "Are you getting divorced? What are you fighting about? Why does Dad have to move out?" It wasn't so much that she was on his side; she was just giving Liz maximum grief. Liz didn't tell Martin she wanted a divorce; she just kept saying she needed time to think about things. He had talked to his attorney and he knew it was bad for him to agree to move out, but at this point he really didn't have much leverage. Liz said she would probably just file for divorce if he didn't move out.

It hadn't been that hard. In fact, the whole family had pitched in as he pulled together his stuff and made a few trips back and forth from the house to his apartment at the Memorial Creole. Liz and Martin had actually rented there, when they had first moved to Houston, and the place was still safe, clean and well kept. He was free to do whatever he wanted. He had time of his own.

He hated it.

He was alone. He was angry. He was starting to feel desperate. What does a man do when it's just not good enough? Where does he go? Why are we even here? These questions haunted him. For the first time in his life he lay awake, sleepless, desperately chasing his dreams over the last twenty years, always ending up back where he was with no way ahead. In many ways, Liz had been right. He had just been getting by, but in lots of ways they were doing great—much better than most people—but it just wasn't good enough any longer. Liz had said she was tired of waiting and waiting for something, even if she wasn't sure just what. It wasn't only to work out at the Houstonian with her friends. It wasn't to pick the kids up from soccer to take them to piano. She wanted more, and Martin concluded that one way or the other she was going to get it, either with him or without him. She was hungry, and she was bringing out things in him that he hadn't felt in a long time: anger, determination, and unyielding focus. He had always known that he could do almost anything; he just never had had to do it before. He would be the ruler of his own world; that's what he wanted; or at least that's what Liz wanted for him.

As he walked up to the door at Basin Oil, his thoughts came back to the business at hand. For some reason, he genuinely liked the smell of his office. His desk—or more accurately, a huge, old viewing table—was teak wood, worn smooth from the miles of maps and drawings that he had dragged across it over the years. The lock turned tightly in the steel frame of the glass door in the lobby, and then clacked open in the morning stillness. He was the first one in today, after all. He always left all the lights off, navigating his way nicely to his office in the northwest corner on the second floor. Again, the lock to his office, and then some sense of being home, he silently smiled as he found himself exploring the irony of thinking this was home. He didn't have a comfortable, high back chair in the office—never had —but he settled down on his gray, Steelcase drafting stool, and put his feet up on the table. Quietly looking about the room, he took time to view each item carefully, individually. As the minutes passed, he could hear the early traffic out on the Katy Freeway, muffled through the tinted glass. It had been two weeks since he had gotten back from Wisconsin and moved out, and he had been thinking. He had thought of their friends, many of whom had made it big; mostly friends through Liz. Last week, he had been up to Oklahoma to review some stuff on their deep gas wells and he had been thinking. He had thought about how men had chased their dreams, taken risks, done what they had to do. He had been looking at the whole geophysical process and he had been more than thinking. He had been formulating a plan. It had started "Up North" in Wisconsin. He was ready to begin. He didn't have much time.

Conceptually, the entire oil exploration business is not that difficult to comprehend. In its earliest days in Pennsylvania and even some parts of the South like Louisiana, prospectors would literally walk back hollows, valleys and lowlands, looking for oil oozing from the ground. Before the wide acceptance of the combustion engine and electric lighting, much of the early oil was refined as lamp oil to light the homes of early Americans in the mid- and late-19th century. Finding these places where the oil pockets were close to the surface was really quite straightforward, and the sinking of a simple pipe driven to a hundred or eventually several hundred feet into the ground was a well-defined set of tasks. They called them "oil wells" because they weren't that much different from water wells. At that time, much of the effort in the fledgling oil business centered on handling the oil once it was out of the ground, and sending it via wagon, barge, and eventually railroad, from the early fields around Titusville, and Oil City Pennsylvania, and over the hills to the industrial cities of New York, Boston and Philadelphia. Battles were fought, and fortunes were won in those days; none of course bigger than that of John D. Rockefeller, effectively the father of the modern integrated oil company. Rockefeller made money on oil all right, but he made a fortune as well on the transportation networks he built to move oil and other goods around the northeastern U.S. After a time, giant oil fields were discovered, like the Permian Basin in Texas that held thirty billion barrels of oil —not even to mention natural gas.

By the 1960s and even the mid-1970s it had become a different world. In the United States oil and gas were abundant but harder to find. The prospective fields of hydrocarbons, or "prospects," as they are called, were deeper, resulting in greater need for investment, higher demands for engineering execution and, as a result, much higher risk than the early oil barons had ever known. Companies would even band together as working interest owners to share the cost and the risk of failure and pool their intellectual capital to successfully reach even deeper down for some of the largest of fields called "elephants," those with reserves of more than five hundred million barrels of oil. These days it was exceedingly rare for big oil companies, or even an especially gifted independent geologist or geophysicist, to find a colossal new field. In some smaller, independent oil companies, a big oil find could make fortunes for all of the executives in the company. Famous Texans like Clint Murchison, Sid Richardson, Roy Cullen and H.L. Hunt (who had fifteen children), headed some of the world's richest families, sometimes on the discovery of just one good oil field on which they held the mineral rights.

While the majority of the well-known major fields were under full development; advanced methods, computers and horizontal drilling continued to unearth a rare mammoth find here and there. Later, as oil prices fell in the 1980s and 1990s, the investment and exploration efforts increasingly focused on essentially untapped resources in underdeveloped areas of the world, where the proliferation of commerce, greed and technology had not yet come to pass. Exploration efforts shifted from the U.S. to places like Malaysia, Indonesia, Brazil, Sakhalin Island, across Africa; these were the "ladies-in-waiting," now subject to the onslaught, offering the spoils of man's unquenchable thirst for oil.

Essentially, much of the work is based on measuring gravity, density, porosity, and amplitudes; familiar to any first-year college engineering student. On land, huge trucks with sophisticated listening devices lay cabled devices across the land surface of broad expanses suspected of holding potential hydrocarbon reserves. Once such cabling devices are laid, highly explosive charges are set off to send shock waves down into the bedrock below. Echoes from these shock waves would be received by "listening" devices spread across the surface. In some cases, explosives would be replaced with a mobile, three-ton "weight-drop" which would trigger similar shock waves. Differences in density in the underlying earth impact the speed and manner in which these waves echo back to cabled receptors. Sophisticated modeling programs and scientific analytical techniques blend together all of these reflected waves into a seismo-graphic picture of the types of materials that lie beneath the surface. Oil reserves are often thought of as deep, unmiti-gated lakes of oil, hidden far below the surface. These are actually prevalent in some basins of the Middle East. In Saudi Arabia oil can be discovered and brought to the sur-face for less than three dollars a barrel. But in most of the rest of the world, oil is most typically ensconced in tiny pores of sedimentary rock, in varying layers, depths, widths and concentrations. Mixed in with these reservoirs are pools of saline solutions and massive caverns of varying grades of wet sand and rock that make reading exploration data a skill that very have ever mastered. Then, even the best geolo-gists and geophysicists have their own share of big, dry holes.

CHAPTER 15

LIZ WAVED AT THE GUARD AS SHE DROVE UP THE ENTRANCE to the Houstonian Club. When she got closer, the guard who saw her coming raised the gate as she came down the lane. The club had nearly two thousand members, but at least a thousand only used the club for an occasional business lunch. Perhaps two hundred used the fitness center and tennis courts. Liz was one of the warriors who actually took advantage of her membership. She was more than a regular, showing up day in, day out to get a serious workout. She zipped past the guard house and into the parking garage under the huge two-story fitness center. Cruising down the ramp, she turned left against traffic and parked by the west wall next to the stairs. When they saw her on the monitor, they buzzed her in through the door and she came up the steps right next to the women's locker room. It was a huge facility: three restaurants, two pools, an outdoor spa, tennis and squash courts, aerobics studio and a salon. Down on the south end of the property there was a nice-sized hotel and conference center. Martin would have a meeting at the conference center every once in a while, when his company would have a group in for a show-and-tell or a deal-making session.

This morning it was pretty busy for 8:15 a.m. but it was getting close to Christmas and all of the holiday parties were coming up. By the treadmills, there were a handful of people watching the morning news and working out. Liz dressed in no time and found her spot in the 8:30 a.m. aerobics class. Looking in the mirror at the front of the room, she checked herself over. It wasn't like she really missed Martin, but she did feel as if something was missing. The kids knew that she had been unhappy for a long time, but now she knew they blamed her for the separation. She had tried to tell him over and over again what she was feeling. She wanted to be gentle, but in the end, she had been brutally direct. It was the only way he would listen. Maybe they could work things out. Maybe things were okay. Her life was slipping away from her and Martin wouldn't do a damn thing about it. She wasn't getting any younger, either. It wasn't a single event that had occurred. It had been a process. Martin had gotten increasingly frustrated with his work. He had gotten good reviews and worked on Basin's biggest projects, but when it came to a promotion to a management position, they told him he was not quite ready. He was not "dynamic enough" or he needed "more seasoning." He would come home sullen, angry, and quiet. She would listen, but the story remained the same, and her empathy had waned.

"Hey Liz, pumping some iron today?" It was Hilton Sinclair. He was always at the club. She knew he was working at the French Company, Prolea—one of the executives. It seemed to Liz that these days he worked only when he wanted. She had finished aerobics and had made it upstairs for some weightlifting.

"Nothing special, Hilton," said Liz, "just trying to work some flab off the old lady here. You're early today."

"Yeah, well nothing going on today. The market was flat in London this morning. There's a big OPEC meeting tomorrow so everyone's sitting tight. I thought I would come over and get in a little extra work out before tomorrow."

He was older than Liz, probably in his late forties or early fifties. Jet black hair, showing some balding, he had grown a mustache about six months ago and actually looked a lot better. Rugged. But basically, he was a body builder type guy masquerading as a businessman, and he spent too much time working on his tan. Liz had known a dozen guys like him at the club. Most of them worked out as avidly as she did and spent the balance of their time talking about making it big. She had heard Hilton had already made it big back in the late seventies. He was an oil trader. They made a lot of money, but it seems they spent a lot of money, too. One of Liz's friends had told her that Hilton was on marriage number three. He was always direct, matter of fact, but low pressure.

"So, what are you doing today?" asked Liz.

"Legs and abs today. A bunch of us are meeting at the pool for lunch so I've got some time to get in a good workout." Hilton was big at poolside. Frequently out there on really nice days. "Why don't you come by for a while today and visit? I'll buy you lunch."

Liz was just slightly taken back. "Well, I don't know," she hesitated. "I've got a ton of stuff I need to get done today. We'll see."

"Great, maybe see you later. Lunch at 11:30." He was off in the opposite direction, walking all the way down to the end of the giant weight room where the ab boards were tilted up looking out the windows over the tennis courts.

At 11:00, Liz was still in the club. Usually, she was long gone by now. She had showered and done her makeup and hair. She hadn't been out to the pool for three months, but it was an unusually warm day out there for this late in the year. She checked her watch—11:25. She looked in her locker and saw her suit hanging there for her. The kids were in school, a perfect day, Martin certainly wasn't around, she did have errands to run...

The iron gate creaked as she slowly swung it open and then slammed it shut with a clang as the big spring pushed it back to latch. She moved slowly, careful not to look too long at any one thing, or in any one direction. She stepped off the pebbly surface up onto the wood cedar deck that bounded the north end of the pool, out of the slight breeze and into the direct sunshine. A flock of chairs languished on the deck, some older, retired men dozing in the midday sun or reading the Financial Times; others with dark sunglasses chatting amicably on an extended lunch hour. In the corner, back against the building, six or seven people were gathered. Hilton Sinclair turned as she walked over, the group following his gaze. He greeted her with a big smile and the wave of his arm.

"Liz. Come on over, let me get you a chair." In one movement, he was out of his chair, dragging a chaise lounge into the circle for Liz.

"Glad you could make it, Liz, let me grab you a towel." Hilton took about ten short steps to the towel rack while she stood there waiting. He returned with two oversized towels and tossed them down on her chair. The rest of the group never left their conversation but followed Hilton's movements all the way. They were talking about some guy who had opened a new restaurant down in the village. Liz had seen two of the three women many times before but had never introduced herself. The rest of the group seemed vaguely familiar, but she really didn't know any of them.

95

Finally, Hilton settled down in his chair and leaned back. "So, everybody, I think if you've been around the club you may already know her, but if you don't, this is Liz Cantrell. Liz, this is Sheri, Michelle, Peggy, Ron and Rick. Everybody, say hi to Liz."

It was nice. Everybody smiled at her. She fit right into the group. Hilton bought her lunch. She was home in plenty of time to welcome the girls back from school.

CHAPTER 16

TAYLOR HAD RETURNED FROM NORTHERN WISCONSIN A few days earlier and had spent the time painting her master bathroom. She had lived in the old house now for a little over eight years. When the realtor first showed it to Taylor, it had been beat up, and divided into two student apartments. Still, the dovetailed wood siding and the hardwood floors and the turrets that towered over West Washington Avenue had won her over. From the east turret she could look right up the avenue to the Capitol dome. No matter how many times she found herself looking at it, she found it inspiring. Sometimes at night she would sit for hours, alternately gazing at the Dome and reading the seven newspapers she subscribed to from around the State. It wasn't the best neighborhood in town, especially after dark. If she wanted, she would still walk the eight blocks to work in the morning. Even though she was somewhat of a celebrity in the city, everybody in the neighborhood left her alone.

She was upstairs just getting out of the shower when she heard the deadbolt click in the front door. Jason had let himself in. Taylor could hear him walk to the kitchen in the back of the house and rustle the ice cubes in the icemaker. He always showed up twenty minutes early when they were going out. Taylor knew she'd find his coat lying across one of the chairs in the living room. He'd be drinking a vodka tonic and watching CNN on the small television on the bar in the kitchen. She had bought that little TV at Arnie's when she was in college. She had gotten a free ten-speed bike to go with it. Now the cheap old bike was long gone, but the TV was still serving her pretty well.

She picked the beige suit tonight; the one with the dark brown, suede collar and lapels. It was formal enough to fit right in, but it was casual enough, if she ended up somewhere else for a drink later on. She spent an extra few minutes on her hair and let it fall free. In reality she would be working tonight, but this look was not for the office. In her public work she pulled her hair back and wore glasses with tortoise shell frames. But tonight, Governor Conlan wouldn't let the photographers within a mile of the governor's mansion. The mansion was over on the east side of Lake Mendota and Taylor knew there'd be a big crowd. Conlan was up for re-election in the primary and he had invited anybody with big money in as his guest tonight. In November, there had been a lot of legislative action, particularly in the Wisconsin Assembly. Conlan was milking it for all it was worth.

Taylor could hear an outcry from Jason over some bit of news from CNN. There was a burst of laughter. Undoubtedly, Jason's ruthless sense of humor was at work. She could hear him in the ice machine again. Apparently, not all had gone well with the staff in the late afternoon. Jason had probably lost his patience. He was getting a good start on the evening's festivities. Taylor found herself hurrying with her make-up. It was best if Jason didn't get too far ahead of her. The outcomes were not always so positive when Jason started giving people his honest assessment of political matters.

Taylor had actually gone to modeling school one summer in Milwaukee and had gotten borderline expert at putting on makeup. Now just a little Pimento Spice lipstick as she moved down the big open staircase. Jason didn't even look as she entered the kitchen. He was trying to get the market wrap before they left for the party. A few minutes later and they were moving briskly toward the mansion in Jason's 1988 Saab 900 Turbo.

"I swear," Jason said, "if Conlan has the house full of pulp heads tonight, I'm hiding all of the toilet paper when I go to the john."

Taylor laughed right out loud at the thought. "Don't call them pulp heads. They're paper companies. You know they are the largest single employer in Wisconsin?"

"I swear to God, they'd be better off if they just dumped all their stuff in the river without even trying to treat it. Last week, Brownie was going over the toxin reports with me on the upper Wisconsin River and I almost got sick to my stomach. Oil companies and paper companies. I love my job."

The pulp and paper industry had been tough ones, even for Taylor. She had met with their best chemists and environmental people. They all agreed that none of their remediation options were very attractive. Even Taylor didn't have the heart to put somebody out of business. Most of them were doing the best they could. Unfortunately, together, the paper and pulp industry had put more than 300,000 tons of particulates into the air and water in the last two years and it wasn't going to get a lot better than that.

"You know," said Jason, continuing, "last year at this event, one of those idiots suggested to me that if we could be even half as cooperative as the people they were working with in Indonesia, that they would be willing to make a much more substantial investment in Wisconsin. Like we want the state blanketed with paper mills!"

"Jason, you need to be more understanding of your capitalist brethren," Taylor taunted him. "Those are, after all, the people who are paying your salary."

"You are so right, Master," said Jason. "If only I was as politically astute as you, I would have a future in front of me."

It was classic Jason. He was stitched close enough to the lining to risk an unraveling. "Well, I am sure you will be in fondest company this evening with your capitalist supporters."

Taylor smirked. "You do know that it's the capitalists that have the money for campaigns, right?"

Jason had been with her for a little over four years. When they had first started working together, he had been mad at everyone, including her. He was vehement in his dedication to the environment. Typically, in internal staff meetings—even meetings with outside companies seeking a variance—Jason would turn out to be the only one in the room that had actually analyzed all of the documents. On more than one occasion, it had been downright embarrassing when Jason would take apart an entire corporate team of lawyers and executives. They would have a license request or an environmental impact statement that had huge holes or inconsistencies in it. After letting them talk for an hour, Jason would nod in Taylor's direction and take charge. He would propose a dozen or more solid recommendations that would typically make the proposed venture more palatable to both the business and the state.

On big public reviews, like the one going on with the oil companies' Superior project, Taylor would debate with Jason for hours. Each of them would take alternate positions of the state of Wisconsin DNR versus the Oil Company's point of view, and then really go after each other. Then they'd switch sides and debate again until they were so exhausted, they couldn't think of another new thing to say. Like Taylor, Jason's job was his life; at least for now. They had a rare combination of both love and respect for each other. Not love, love. Just love and respect.

There were valets swarming all over the front entrance at the governor's mansion. The valets were from some fraternity house where one of the fathers had a connection to Governor Conlan. Jason and Taylor were running a little late. The crowd was large, even by Conlan's standards. The mansion was huge, right on the shore of Lake Mendota, sixteen thousand square feet. Fifty years ago, a banker had sold it to the state for $47,500. It was one of the few governor's mansions in the country located on a lake, not on the grounds of the capitol.

"Looks like Conlan has a good hatch," Jason commented dryly as they walked up the steps to the grand foyer. Taylor thought for a moment for an appropriate comeback and then let the remark drop softly in the cold dead air of early winter. She stepped through the oversized doors and felt the rush of stale warm air fleeing past her, out and up to the stars. Taylor cut a narrow path through the clusters of business suits and dinner jackets toward the old hand-hewn bar in the back of the grand dining room. The room overlooked the length of Lake Mendota. The shimmering images of the attendees were reflecting on the large single-paned windows. She could see the lights on the north shore. Directly west she saw the sprinkling of security lights on the new running path that wound itself all the way out to Picnic Point. Back in law school, she would pack up her books and ride her bike out there on fall afternoons. The lights reposed patiently in the satiny black darkness.

Governor Conlan, as always, was tucked securely into the alcove just to the right of the bar. Taylor knew she would find him there. He used this alcove as a kind of harbor where he could reach out and shake hands with anyone he wished. If needed, he could also step back into the privacy of his adjacent office and discuss more private matters with a special friend or wealthy donor.

Taylor leaned against the bar with a drink. Jason knew that others would begin to gather around her. She was in her element. He needed to get out of the way. After a few minutes, he nodded to her and then disappeared into the crowd. Jason could work a room, too. He would carefully share a snippet or two of rumor and fact. He'd also take time to cross-check his stories with colleagues in other departments. Along the way, he would take time to commiserate with friends on the evils and shortcomings of the political process.

After an hour Taylor was warming to the evening. The huge fire was burning mightily under the ancient, oversized stone hearth. Unfortunately, Sheldon Mack had stopped by and tried to make small talk. Taylor knew right away the old gizzard was out of character, drunk and bitter. Addressing her as Ms. Thompson, he added an extra sampling of Z's to the Ms. Finding he had humored himself; he had abruptly shared the thought that Taylor certainly did look like "a cute little thing this evening." Taylor did her best to ignore him. She turned back to visit with a friend, but Mack just continued on talking, saying he guessed that Taylor "just plain enjoyed getting her picture on television." He was obviously baiting her, hoping to get her to her boiling point. She looked away again and her eyes met Conlan's. He had been watching the interchange and he nodded for a conference toward the side stair. When the governor was well out of the room, Taylor told Mack she needed the ladies' room and graciously excused herself. Returning from the re-

stroom, she took a turn up the stairs. The library was directly over the dining room, where they always met. The library
had a second-story balcony that looked wonderfully out over
the lake. She and Conlan had met there often when they
were working through natural gas deregulation plans last
summer. The two of them would step out on the balcony
together and make sure they were in agreement on key
points of the regulations. Conlan was a chain smoker, so it
was a natural spot for him. Even in the wintertime, she and
Conlan would still meet up in the library, although usually
with a couple of politicians or businessmen who were trying
to work a deal. Before she entered, she heard voices; fairly
loud voices. She grabbed the worn, scarred, brass doorknob,
turned it and walked into the room.

She had always taken pride in her ability to see things
coming. This time, Conlan blind-sided her. It was Sheldon
Mack from Arbor Energy and Dick Jansen from Empire Oil.
They were both smoking cigars, perched on the arms of the
big, overstuffed leather chairs by the fireplace. Governor
Conlan was with Ricky Amery, the head of the Finance
Committee for Conlan's reelection campaign. This conversation was going to be about money. Taylor had come up
here alone, thinking she and the governor were going to
have one of their pow-wows. Jason was downstairs, debating
the issues of the day with his buddies. Nobody else even
knew where she was, unless they were looking for her in the
lady's room. Just for a second, she thought about turning
right around and going back out the door, but Sheldon Mack
had already taken a shot at her earlier in the evening, and
she relished a go at him in private quarters.

Conlan talked first. "Thanks for breaking away, Taylor. I
thought you would want to be in on our discussion."

"Nothing like mixing business with pleasure," said Taylor smoothly. "What have you got on the agenda?"

"Taylor," said Mack, his speech slurring ever so slightly. "Despite our efforts to work cooperatively with you and your people, we don't think you are listening to us on the Superior deal."

"We're listening," said Taylor flatly. "It just so happens that so far you haven't had anything to say." Taylor was rather pleased with herself for jumping right out ahead of him.

"Now Taylor," said Mack, "before you start getting your panties in a wad, I want you to know that this project is very important to Arbor Energy. It's even more important to me personally. I have raised certain expectations at Arbor that I'm going to deliver on this one and now everybody is asking me when. If we keep going where you're leading us, we aren't going to end up where we need to be. I assure you; such an outcome will make us all very, very unhappy."

The room grew suddenly still. Taylor could see the deep blue smoke roll slowly off the men's cigars. It floated aimlessly toward the high ceiling. Taylor glanced over at the fireplace. On the mantle was a vintage Carmody horse clock, mounted on a varnished mahogany block of wood. On one end of the base was the clock, on the other end was a bronze statue of a saddled horse, standing upright on all fours. The bridle of the horse was a stainless key chain that looped through the horse's mouth and hung loosely over the saddle horn. It was Taylor's turn to speak.

"Look Sheldon, if you want to send some people over Monday to work with Jason on some modifications, we can do that. But I am not going to stand here and tell you that the fundamentals of the deal are changing, because they are not. Gazing over at Jansen, she continued. "We know you guys are already making a fortune off that plant because we've run all of our own models to prove it. The development tax credit the governor gave you three years ago will let you make all of your capital improvements without spending a dime of your own money. When do we get something back, Sheldon? When?"

It was Jansen's turn. He was a quiet one, but he had been in the business a long time. Taylor knew he was dangerous. He eased off the arm of the chair and walked slowly to fireplace and stared at the Carmody. He angled himself toward the group, being careful not to face anyone directly and then he slowly exhaled smoke out his mouth and nose at the same time.

"Look Taylor, we think you're damn good at what you do. Honestly, I wish we had you on our side. We'd like to see the governor get re-elected. In fact, we think Governor Conlan and you would make a great team as governor and lieutenant governor of the state. When Empire Oil feels good about something, we go out of our way to show our support, if you know what I mean."

In an instant, Taylor got it. Money and power. Money, that's why Amery the campaign finance guy was here. She shot him a quick glance, but he was looking at Conlan. When she looked back at Jansen, he had followed Taylor's look over to Amery too. When she looked back at him, his eyes met hers in a heartless, expressionless stare.

"Taylor, all they're asking for is that we be flexible," said the governor. The governor wanted her to back off on the Superior refinery expansion. "We could be a great team if you have an interest in being my next lieutenant governor."

"What does your current lieutenant governor think about that?" Asked Taylor. "Does he think I'd be great in his job as well?"

Conlan shifted uneasily back in his chair. "Look, I know you're close to the lieutenant governor, but I'd appreciate you not telling him this quite yet."

"So officially, you want me as your running mate?" asked Taylor. "Do I have to cave on this refinery deal to run with you?"

Amery spoke up, "The truth is, he's a loser, you're a winner. All the polls tell us that. Even if he ran for governor next time, he wouldn't make it through our own party primary."

Conlan rested his elbow on the arm of the sofa. He was tense. His head dropped sideways resignedly, and he rested his chin onto the back of his knuckles. The long hours at government meetings and long evenings had taken their toll. He knew it was not easy to get Taylor to do something she did not want to do.

"'Loser' is probably a fair description," said Jansen. "We've been running a few polls ourselves, and Governor Conlan himself is looking at a pretty tough battle just to win this election. We're not sure he can win it without you, Taylor."

"So, I say "yes" to Superior," said Taylor, "and you throw your financial backing to our ticket."

"We're not asking for the moon here, Taylor, but you got to ease up," said Jansen. "You know we're talking to the "Kensington for Governor" team, right? Representative Kensington, your buddy from Milwaukee, has been talking to us consistently about his ideas for a 'Commitment to Commerce' program. He doesn't have any problem with the refinery expansion. Compared to some of the treatment we've been getting from your DNR, we find some of Kensington's ideas very intriguing."

Kensington was one of the few politicians in the state to successfully attack Taylor in public. She had taken a lot of hits from him on the Kickapoo Valley Dam Project. She had finally gotten the Corp of Engineers to shut down the project. But several hundred farmers had been thrown off their land. Now most of Vernon and Sauk and Dell counties were mad as hell at her. First, the feds and the state had condemned all of the farmland behind the proposed dam. Then the farmers had been thrown off their land and Taylor got the project stopped. Now the land was just sitting there idle, while the DNR and federal government were trying to figure out what to do with it. They'd been working on it for more than three years. Kensington had gotten time on Nightline, not six months ago, and he had roasted Taylor as the villain. He was leading a "grassroots" effort for reopening public hearings on the project and giving the land back to the farmers. If Kensington beat Conlan, the first thing he'd do is put Taylor out on the street. The governor appoints the head of the DNR.

"At any rate, "Jensen continued, "when we don't know where you stand on key issues like this, Taylor, it puts us in a very difficult situation. That's why we wanted to get the attention of you and the governor this evening."

They were threatening her. They were offering to buy her. She either needed to let them off easy on the permitting process for their stinking refinery in Superior or they'd do everything they could to get rid of her. Not only did they want to scare her, now they had Conlan offering her the lieutenant governor position in the next election as part of the package. She had calmed down as Jensen had eased her back through it, but now when she took a step back, it made her mad as hell.

"Oh boys," she started in, "I think I'm starting to get it. You want to buy me off so you can make a fortune up in Superior. We should have shut that stinking, inefficient, old refinery down twenty years ago and you know it. Now I get to keep playing politics with you fellas. If I let you buy me off on this deal, you've got me over a barrel for the rest of my career. No pun intended."

"Taylor," said Amery, "nobody is buying you off. This is a great opportunity for you, and it would be good for The Party." He was a snake if there ever was one, thought Taylor. The money guy wants the money. They were all ganging up on her.

"If you lie down with the dogs you get fleas, Amery. Did anybody ever tell you that?" said Taylor looking at the oil company guys.

Things were clearly not going as the four of them had planned. The harder they pushed, the deeper they sunk.

Taylor wasn't finished.

"Nobody is going to bring me in here and threaten me like this and not suffer the consequences!" Taylor thought she could keep her cool. She always kept her cool. But this wasn't the steps of the Douglas County Courthouse; this was a private setting and she was going to let them have it. Looking about the room, she was sure at least one of them had shared the thought that this might go very badly and now she was waiting for the next move.

"Look honey," said Sheldon, "we didn't really want to get into this tonight, but you are forcing the issue. So, we want to let you know we understand if you have other concerns about your so-called political viability." Sheldon's sudden smugness took her by surprise.

"I'm not thinking about my political viability," said Taylor, "I'm thinking about what's right and wrong. You guys just don't get that, do you?" Taylor caught the four of them exchanging glances.

"Well, on the scale of right and wrong, Ms. Thompson, where does banging the lieutenant governor fall? Would you say it falls on the "right" side because you had fun doing it, or on the "wrong" side, because it just so happens the dumb shit has been married twenty-two years and has three kids.

What do you have to say for yourself now, you self-righteous little bitch?"

Taylor felt ill. Why hadn't they just come out and told her they knew right away. She was speechless. She stood looking from Mack to the governor, back to Mack. Mack continued; "Now we need to know right now whether you are going to work with us on this or not. Because if not, we think the good people of Wisconsin need to know that they are using their hard-earned tax dollars to have the Head of the Department of Natural Resources screw the lieutenant governor, on government time no less. Personally, based on the pictures I've seen, I think you could do better, but we'd best not get into the details right now, should we, Ms. Thompson?"

Taylor shuddered. Jesus, they had pictures? Somehow, they had gotten pictures. Clearly, they had already shared them with the governor. She could tell that by looking at him. The room was closing in around her.

"Now one more time Taylor, let me say it slowly. We need to know if we've got your attention on this matter or not, and Taylor, we need to know right now what it's going to be. Don't start telling us you need to consult with that faggot litigator of yours, Jason, and that you'll get back to us. And please don't start telling those little stories about dogs and fleas because they'll just come back to haunt you now, won't they, Ms. Thompson?"

She was done unless she said yes. In six months, she'd be lieutenant governor and positioned to inherit the governorship when Conlan completed his next term. If she said no, they'd pour all their money into beating Conlan and getting rid of her—even if it took a scandal to do it. Taylor walked easily over to the set of decanters on the table and poured herself a nice, big scotch with no ice. She defiantly looked around the room at each of them as she sipped the scotch. Just five minutes later, the men were back downstairs enjoying the evening. Taylor left word for Jason that she wasn't feeling well, and then asked for one of the governor's cars to take her home.

CHAPTER 17

THE NATIONAL PETROLEUM REFINERY ASSOCIATION wasn't really a refinery association at all. Oh, it had been one a long time ago. Now the NPRA had functions for all kinds of people throughout the year and anyone even close to any part of the industry was welcome to attend. A lot of the meetings were still held by short-sleeved-shirt engineers to discuss the latest cat cracker technology or read the latest heat transfer papers they had written. Some would center on the latest trends in computer technology or information technology issues. Occasionally there would be an executive lunch out at Turtle Creek in Dallas or the Westin Galleria in Houston, where one of the industry's veterans would rail away at the lack of a national energy policy or the error of the latest addition to government regulations. Easily the most interesting group, and also the ones who usually started their two-day conferences with a brief informational presentation out behind the first tee, was the NPRA Crude Oil and Products Supply and Distribution Group—the oil traders. They were made up principally of a group of not more than two hundred and fifty men from twenty or so companies around the U.S. Most knew each other by name and company, many dealing with each other daily in the sale and purchase of dizzying volumes of oil and petroleum products. Some had worked together at one company or another along the way before, perhaps, falling on particularly rough times at one company or moving on to another with greater promises of responsibility, benefits, and bonuses.

Martin's secretary had been to a bunch of nice NPRA dinners over the years. Anita knew firsthand what a good time the guys had at these things. She was single, with a child, so some of the guys thought she made for a good date. And when she got dressed up, she looked damn good. Anita had been looking forward to the Houston NPRA dinner coming up. She assumed that Hilton would find a way to invite her. But then Hilton had let her know that he would have to take his wife to the annual dinner again this year because to be seen in such a setting with Anita would just be, in Hilton's words, "bad for business." Anita knew that Hilton and his wife had themselves "taken some time away" from each other. She was surprised that he couldn't figure out a way for them to go to the dinner together. Most of the traders usually brought their wives, or if single, then their best girlfriend to this event. It hadn't helped Anita's chances that this year it was at Café Annie in Houston. It was right in Hilton's backyard and Anita surmised that Hilton's wife might find out about it if Hilton attended with somebody else. Often, these events were in Boca Raton, or New York, or Laguna Nigel, and then, lots of girlfriends showed up. When Hilton first told her about it a couple of months ago, she tried to shrug it off. She was sure he would try to make it up to her by asking her to the next West Coast or Phoenix getaway. But in the last two weeks leading up to tonight, it had just eaten at her, and she had made up her mind to do something about it. Lately, she found herself thinking more and more about what it would be like to be Mrs. Hilton Sinclair. If she was ever going to get anywhere, she was going to have to start taking some steps to move in a direction that held some promise for her and her young daughter.

"You know Martin," Anita began, "you just aren't any fun to be around anymore."

Back in March she had used some petty cash to buy an expensive coffee maker for the office, along with a dozen exotic blends of beans. Now part of her morning ritual was to select a specialty coffee for the day, grind the beans and keep the pot full. Martin had started letting her know which ones were his favorites, and over time she made sure she only stocked the ones that he really liked.

"What makes you say that?" said Martin.

As he often did, Martin never looked up when she came into the room. He was staring intensely at the oversized display monitor of his computer workstation; a seismic map, not unlike a giant thumbprint, was absorbing all his attention. Anita put the cup down on his hot pad next to the computer, and Martin, still without looking up, reached over and grabbed the steaming cup and sipped it carefully.

"You just used to always be doing stuff ,and now, as far as I know, you don't do anything but work." Martin continued looking carefully at the screen, but Anita could tell she had his attention.

"Just because I don't keep you updated on my calendar doesn't mean I don't do anything."

It sounded a little hollow, even to him, and of course the truth was he hadn't done anything but work since he moved out. There wasn't much to do, so he had found himself working. There had been more nights than he wished to remember getting home at eight or nine in the evening, eating a microwaved dinner, watching television and going to bed. Doing anything else just didn't seem to make sense right now.

"I'm not saying you're getting boring in your old age," said Anita good naturedly, "I'm just saying you're taking all of this stuff, including work, much too seriously. You've got to live, too, you know."

He was still looking at the computer screen quietly, thinking about what she had said. It had taken him four or five days to tell her they were separated. He really didn't have anyone else he could talk to about it. As they talked, she said she had felt some of the same things he had been feeling when her husband moved out, leaving her alone with her daughter. If I just had the kids, I could make it through just fine, thought Martin.

"I'm not saying you're not living," continued Anita; "I'm just saying you need to give yourself a break once in a while. Have some fun."

Martin slowly pushed back in his chair and grasped the coffee cup opposite the handle. Anita was half sitting on the edge of his desk, leaning toward the workstation. The cup was hotter than Martin had thought, and he switched it quickly to his other hand, glancing casually toward Anita. Martin had always found her attractive but was careful to never show her much attention. She was looking especially nice today. Martin knew she had a thing going on with some oil trader named "Hilton" and Martin wondered if this was another day when Anita and Hilton had "lunch plans," as Anita usually referred to it. Suddenly, he realized he couldn't remember how they had gotten into this conversation and he had no idea where it was heading.

"Hey, by the way, where are the Athabasca slides? Are you done with those yet?" He was trying to steer things back toward business. Easier that way. Definitely simpler.

"Finished them Friday, "said Anita, "Karl's got them, said he wanted to make a few changes. Big surprise." She laughed, seeing Martin nod and glance back at the geological image on the screen. Anita took a breath and continued. "Look Martin, I was wondering if you would do me a favor."

Martin hoped she would keep talking, but she stopped, awaiting his reply before she went on. "Sure, what do you need?"

"Well, almost every year I go to this fancy dinner for the NPRA. I really have a blast seeing everybody I know and getting all dressed up and I really want to go again this year."

"Then you should go." Martin felt like it was his turn to say something more, but he was careful to not say anything more before looking back at Anita.

"Well, this year I can't go with the guy I usually go with, and I was wondering if I could go with you."

Martin could feel his face flush. Flattered, he tried to stay cool but then floundered around for the right thing to say next. "So, you want me to take you to this dinner?"

"It wouldn't be like you were taking me as a date or anything. I just really want to go to this thing and I'm certainly not going to go alone. That would look desperate. It'd be like, you know, you were my escort."

"I would be your escort," Martin repeated haltingly. He knew Anita well enough to know what this was really about. She wanted to see and be seen. In a way he felt sorry for her. Probably wanted to see if she could find some husband material. He didn't blame her.

"Well, maybe not my escort. More like my friend. We would sit together at dinner, but there are a lot of people who just bring a friend along because it's just a really good time; and it's free! Basin's a corporate sponsor."

Martin was dumbfounded, yet comfortable with the idea. He really hadn't been out for some time and he wasn't going to get a better, safer opportunity than this to get out and see some people. There would be a lot of his old Houston geologist buddies there from Empire Oil. Carefully he ceded his last chance to retreat.

"Just for the record, when is this dinner going to be held?"

"Tonight," said Anita with a big smile. "It's at Café Annie. Drinks are at seven, black tie optional, but everybody wears a tux. Jessie loaned me a great dress. You're going to help me out, aren't you?"

He wanted time to think about it. He really needed a week to get mentally prepared to go out like this. He had the tux, but he needed to get a new tuxedo shirt. He needed more time. "How about if I pick you up at about seven at your place?" said Martin.

Anita gave him a big smile. "Yes! You gotta deal, Martin. I'll go draw you a map so you can find my place."

Martin sat stunned. He stared blankly back at the computer screen. His watch said it was only 10:45, but suddenly it seemed as though a lot had gone on that day. Today, tonight, thought Martin, I'm going out tonight. Just the sound of it seemed foreign, distant, calling to him as if it were not him. But it was. He left at 11:00 and found himself picking through the stacks of tuxedo shirts and bow ties at Jack's Formal Wear. For some reason, it seemed to him like these places were always named after a Jack or a Harold or a Walter. He took his time letting the salesman finally convince him that he needed to go with a more updated look, and in a little over half an hour he was out of the store and driving down Westheimer. Instinctively, as he came up on Chimney Rock, he put on his left-hand turn signal and waited for the green arrow. It was still one of the longest lights in town. The day had remained humid, but was unseasonably cool. Looking toward downtown he could see only the west end of the Galleria. The Williams Tower, still billed as the tallest building west of the Mississippi, loomed above him. Looking south he saw Rodeo, or whatever remained of Rodeo. It had been out of business now for almost a year. It was one of the last, nice country-and-western dance bars to close. Weeds were six feet high in the parking lot. There was a "For Lease" sign right out front, but for some reason, the building sat empty.

Chimney Rock was finally open now after they had widened it to four lanes. Martin hadn't actually been down it since he had moved out. Houses that had once sat back proudly on their haunches, masterfully overlooking their surroundings, now seemed teetering precariously on the edge of the curb. His thoughts wandered as he slowly drove through the old neighborhood. He wanted to drive by his house, but he was uncomfortable that the neighbors, or even Liz, would see him here in the neighborhood. They had met a lot of people in the neighborhood, mostly through school, but for some reason they had never made the real friends they were looking to find. The husband was always way too intense, or the wife wasn't any fun, or the kids weren't the kind of kids you wanted yours to hang with, or they had too much money or they didn't have enough. It just had not happened. They slowly gravitated to friends that Liz had made, mostly from her fund-raising business, and the Houstonian, of course. There was a nice cul-de-sac at the end of the street where he could easily make the turn in one pass, but if Liz was in the kitchen, she would spot his car immediately. If she were standing at the sink, she would not miss it. He would seem desperate, vulnerable, and lonely. He slowed to a crawl as he passed the intersection and scanned the block for all he was worth. No action. No cars in the driveway. No kids in the yard, nothing going on. Continuing up the street, he made a big, slow turn onto Memorial and less than ten minutes later stopped by his apartment.

No messages on the answering machine. No mail of any consequence in the box. He thought about leaving immediately and stopping somewhere for a sandwich, maybe Allegro. Then he thought better of it and found himself drinking an extra-large glass of milk from a plastic cup and downing a huge slice of Swiss cheese, buried in butter between two dark slices of heavy, rough rye bread. Back at work, the afternoon dragged on without mercy. He told Anita she could leave at four. He found himself slinking out the door at four thirty, hoping that no one would really notice or think anything of it. Finally realizing that no one would care, and even if they did, they would probably just assume he was off to a late afternoon meeting at some other oil company to do the geologist thing.

Anita looked almost too good when he picked her up. He had never thought about it much before, but she generally did not wear much makeup at work, and tonight, with a bit more makeup, and a great dress, she looked awesome. She talked nonstop all the way to the party, leaving Martin little time to sort out his thinking or put on a frame of mind for the evening. Together they had decided to refer to each other throughout the evening simply as "friends from work." Somehow this helped Martin feel okay. At the same time, he realized he had been separated now for just over six weeks, and he was escorting a woman who would undoubtedly be one of the better-looking women at the dinner. Martin pulled up to valet and together they entered the restaurant. It was a beautifully done place, heavy in dark oak, pale wheat-colored walls and gentle, even lighting. It was large, and they had closed the whole place for the evening. Only in the oil business, thought Martin wryly as they walked up to the reception desk. Anita found her nametag immediately, and then, much to his surprise, found one made out for him, learning that she had given them a quick call to finalize Basin's reservation. There were people in the bar area to the left. People standing out in the dining area with drinks. Platters of hors d'oeuvres. Even in the Wild Game Room upstairs, Martin could see couples visiting out on the small balcony that overlooked the main dining room. All of the men were in tuxedos, just like Anita had said. Many were in cowboy boots, some smoking cigars, almost comical in appearance. A few even had on cowboy hats, which eight or nine years ago would have been de rigueur for a party such as this. The ice sculpture was an old pumping rig and there was some sort of black liquid—Martin guessed coffee—that was supposed to look like oil flowing out of the rig and washing back down around the base of the sculpture.

After some drinks and socializing, it was time to be seated, and they found their table to be in the wine-tasting cellar. It was not a cellar really, but a large private dining area off the main salon. Martin mused that there was no doubt Anita's last-minute RSVP was to blame for not getting preferred seating for the evening. What he didn't know is that she was friends with one of the women who had organized the event, and Anita had told the woman exactly where she wanted to sit. Most of the best tables would be taken by the group's officers for the year, the officer's friends in the business, and likely a group of older guys from the major oil companies or "majors."

Martin had been back in this very room a couple of years ago when there had been some promotions to vice-president at Basin Oil. He had been bitter as hell that night, watching a co-worker get a promotion that he felt he was due, but he had been too proud not to attend the dinner party. It had turned out to be a tolerable evening. Martin had actually met the owner/chef of Café Annie when he had been dove hunting down in Mexico a year earlier. They had spent time entertaining the group telling bird hunting stories, mostly the kind that are half true. But when you are listening to these stories you are never sure where the truth stops, and the embellishment begins.

Martin moved easily through the shuffling crowd as others moved to be seated, too. They were at a large table with seats for a dozen. He found their nameplates and was standing patiently by the table, waiting for Anita who was talking to a girlfriend. A couple walked up to be seated next to Martin and introduced themselves and Martin had a nice chat with them. Finally, Anita joined him and the four of them took their seats. Ten minutes later, the final couple showed up. Martin's draw dropped. It was Liz with a tall dark-haired good-looking gentleman in a striking Armani tux. Liz locked eyes on Martin.

Finally, the man with Liz said, "Hey everybody, sorry we're late. I know most of you, but my name's Hilton Sinclair and this is Liz. Hilton locked his eyes on Anita. Martin and Liz were still staring at each other. Anita hadn't seen Liz in a couple of years, but in a few seconds, Anita figured out that Hilton was with Martin's wife. About the same time, Martin recalled that this Hilton had to be Anita's "lunch pal." Martin wondered silently how Anita possibly could have known that Liz was going to be Hilton's dinner date. Liz thought that Anita was Martin's secretary, but she wasn't certain. Liz had no idea that Anita was Hilton's "lunch date." Hilton had never met Martin before and certainly didn't know that Liz was Martin's wife.

At this moment, the head waiter walked up. Hilton spoke quietly to the waiter, and then Hilton turned to the table and said, "I just bought us six bottles of Cristal. I hope everybody's thirsty."

One of the guys next to Hilton gave him a high-five and Hilton and Liz took their seats. Anita leaned over and whispered in Martin's ear, "Martin, I had no idea. No idea."

The champagne arrived, and in no time the table was off to a rollicking time. Anita quipped to one of the guys at the table that she didn't drink champagne without strawberries, making a passing reference to some movie she had once seen. Immediately, the guy ordered the largest tray of big juicy strawberries that Martin had ever seen. After appetizers, Hilton ordered several bottles of Opus One. Martin knew it was four hundred dollars a bottle. Hilton suggested that while other attendees could drink the house wine, he and his "new" friends would be drinking Opus the rest of the night. It wasn't apparent to Martin that Liz had told Hilton who her husband was. By now, it was clear Anita was having a great time, alternately joking with the guests, and then hanging on Martin's shoulder. She would laugh at the crudest jokes and then shake her head in disbelief as one of the traders told of this escapade or that. A mini food fight with sautéed crawfish ensued. Hilton remained cool, but periodically he would cast a cautious glance toward Anita. Around ten, it was announced there would be desserts and drinks out in the main dining room, along with a brief recognition ceremony for new officers. Anita dragged Martin by the hand around the far edge of the crowd, and up to the center of the bar. They were actually behind the stage for the presentation ceremony, but the minute it was over, the bar would be packed. The bar was already two or three people deep. Anita and Martin stood in close quarters pushing in for a drink. The crowd parted for just a second to let a couple through and Martin found himself standing face to face with Liz and Hilton.

"Oh Martin, wow," Liz was the first to speak. "We didn't really get a chance to talk earlier." She looked over at Anita.

Martin had seen her do this before. In the face of adversity, Liz could put on a perfectly happy face. He was suddenly angry that she was out with some sleaze ball.

"What are you even doing here?" said Martin. He hadn't meant it to come out so judgmental. He immediately realized how petty that sounded.

"What do you think she's doing here? Having a good time." It was the sleaze ball, Hilton, nearly in his face—totally uncalled for.

"I wasn't talking to you," Martin shot back. "I was talking to my wife."

"It's all right Martin, I knew what you meant," Liz said quickly, trying to smooth things over.

"Well, since you knew what I meant, when you get some time, maybe you can explain it to your friend here." Martin could have let it go. He was jealous, and besides, Hilton had jumped in for no reason. Everybody had had far too much alcohol.

Liz tried again. "I guess I should introduce you two. Martin, this is Hilton Sinclair. Hilton this is Martin, my husband."

Anita had been off to Martin's side watching this, and now she moved up quickly to face Liz.

"Hi Liz, good to see you again," said Anita evenly. "Hello Hilton, good to see you too." Martin saw Liz carefully look Anita over from head to toe and back again.

"Man, how many good-looking women were you planning on coming to the party with anyway, man?" said Hilton, his remark gracious under the circumstances.

"She's my wife, okay?"

"Ex-wife. Get used to it."

"We're separated."

"Let's not get technical, Martin." Hilton smiled.

"It'd satisfy me just fine if you'd just not refer to her as my ex-wife, when she's not my ex-wife." Martin was about to boil over.

"Well, I'm glad that would satisfy you. At least then, maybe one of you would be satisfied for a change," said Hilton smiling over at Liz. Liz knew this was headed for trouble and she didn't like it.

"What's that supposed to mean? Martin retorted.

"If I've got to explain it to you, no wonder she booted you out," said Hilton.

Martin was at once enraged and speechless. He charged headlong into Hilton. Drinks flew in every direction as Hilton hit the bar with a dull thud. Martin could feel the thick, meaty muscles of Hilton's back as he arched upward trying to escape the bear hug Martin had on him. Although momentarily stunned, in an instant Hilton was pummeling Martin around the head and shoulders. Desperately, Martin grabbed Hilton by the left leg and dragged him awkwardly forward causing him to fall hard onto the floor on his back. Immediately, Martin dove on top of him like a crazed animal and the two flailed about on the floor, their tuxedos flapping oddly about as they flailed at one another. Quickly, the men in the crowd closed around them, pulled them up off the floor, and managed to separate the two. Anita was at once both efficient and elegant. While Martin was brushing himself off and trying to get his bearings, Anita gently reached into his coat pocket and grabbed the valet slip to the car, handing it off to one of the employees to fetch the car. From a distance, Martin found himself still glaring at Hilton, then he looked at Liz, then Hilton, then Liz again. Anita pulled Martin toward the front door. The car was waiting. Anita jumped in the driver's seat, and off they sped. Martin slowly settled down and began to feel relaxed.

"You know Martin, you might have a future in boxing," said Anita, smiling.

"I know, I know," said Martin. "Might do with a little more training, though."

"You really went off on my boyfriend, Martin." Anita was still smiling. "Who says you're no fun at a party!"

"You know what Anita; I've been thinking about this a lot. From now on I'm just not going to take shit from anybody." said Martin. "Nobody, no shit, no more."

"Well," said Anita. "I think you're off to a good start on that tonight."

CHAPTER 18

AS USUAL, THE NEXT MORNING MARTIN WAS IN THE OFFICE before 7:00. Anita brought him his third coffee an hour later when she got in.

"Hey slugger," she smiled. "Sleep well?"

"As a matter of fact, I did," he smiled back.

"Well, you know how I called you "boring" the other day?" She continued. "Um, let's just say, I take it back." She smiled and left his office.

The next few days found Martin in his office hovering laboriously over his computer long before Anita got in, until long after she left. She could count the used coffee cups and the sandwich wrappers in his trash and know how long he had been working. She had continued to try and smooth over things from the dinner incident, assuring him that it was no big deal, but he had shrugged politely. He had looked more than a little hurt, but then he would dive back into the details of his work. He had always informed Anita when he had an especially important call or when he needed to leave the office for an appointment. On Thursday, at 4:15, he abruptly walked out of the office with his coat and car keys, telling Anita he'd be back the next day. No explanation. Driving as fast as he legally permissible, he got to the Westside Public Library in just over ten minutes and then waited patiently in the private phone booth to dial the number. He had been to the library a number of times with his kids. And he had called from there a number of times, always finding it odd that they had built a couple of little wooden, private phone booths inside the library. Now they seemed the perfectly anonymous, untraceable place to make a call. Finally, at exactly 4:30 he dialed and felt his heart race when someone picked up the phone. He drew in his breath when he heard the familiar voice of Taylor Thompson.

They had started off haltingly, appreciatively professional. He had called earlier in the week at dinnertime, hoping to catch her late at work. The phone was answered by a man, who called himself Jason. Once Martin had convinced Jason that he really was an old friend of Taylor, Jason took a simple message with Martin's name and an agreement to schedule this time for a callback later in the week.

Taylor could tell from his tone that Martin was up to something, but he started out telling her about his job, the challenges he had faced in the last few years and the recent struggles he had been having with Liz. All of this seemed to be fairly normal stuff. Taylor had done well for herself; he always knew that she would. But increasingly she was frustrated with her job and the realities of how big money had such an influence over everything that she said and did. She even let him know that she had had it with the oil industry, and gave him a summary of the Superior project, though not sharing the shady details.

When she mentioned Jansen by name, Martin told her how he had worked with Dick Jansen eighteen years earlier in the management development program at Empire Oil. Together, they spent a few fun minutes comparing the guy's mannerisms to those of a snake. It was clear Taylor had taken enough from big business and was ready for a break. Taylor asked how Martin's dad and brother were doing, joking about their lefse encounter. Taylor said she had been working like crazy. Again, Martin mentioned that he and Liz were having some "rocky times" and taking a break for a while. Martin mentioned that he had noticed she was speaking at an API sponsored industry forum the following week in Chicago. Martin was planning on attending the forum for the first two days and Martin wondered if she would have time for that dinner they talked about. She was leery of seeing anyone on a rebound from divorce, or even separation, but she wanted to see him. Taylor realized that this was the same Martin she had known twenty years earlier, even if he was working through some issues now. They set up their dinner plans in Chicago.

When Martin got back to the office it was pushing five o'clock. Anita was finishing up for the day and Martin plunked himself down oddly in the chair next to her workstation. Soon they were talking a mile a minute and taking parting shots at co-workers as they streamed past Anita's desk, leaving for the day. While she was having a lot of fun fooling around with him, she apologized for having to leave to pick up her daughter from after-school day care. Not a problem, Martin said, wondering if they shouldn't just continue the conversation at lunch tomorrow, being Friday and everything. Before she knew it, she had a lunch planned with Martin for the next day. Carefully, he helped her out through the front door with her purse, a backpack, and a shopping bag. Ordinarily, she would have changed into her flats before leaving the office, but she suddenly felt a certain self-consciousness in front of him and decided to stay in her heels. He seemed genuinely sad to see her go, reassuring her that he would take responsibility to lock up before he left, asking her only to think about someplace nice for lunch tomorrow. Maybe someplace not frequented by Hilton or Liz, suggested Martin. More than anything else, she felt relief as she walked to her car in the brisk evening air. All week she had felt guilty about getting Martin into his little altercation, last Thursday night, exactly one week ago. Now, just seeing him back in a good mood did her a world of good. It would make life a little more bearable around the office, too.

After Anita left, Martin strolled leisurely and confidently back to his office, only stopping by the lunchroom to pull a Diet Coke out of the fridge. He smiled to himself as he thought sarcastically that one of his biggest fringe benefits at Basin was free soda. Most of the vice-presidents now had gotten club memberships and cars; here he was enjoying his free soda. Back in his familiar chair, he looked admiringly over the mass of maps, plots, computer disks and geological analysis littering his drafting table. The sun was already kissing the horizon and the cars were lined up on the Katy Freeway for their long trek back to Houston's western suburbs. Momentarily, Martin found it ironic that everyone had to put so much effort into going back and forth from their home to their office. He could sit right here in his office and transport himself from the deep waters of the Gulf of Mexico, to the top of the Wind River Basin in Wyoming and over to the northern reaches of Kazakhstan. He had spent the last couple of weeks carefully poring over the seismic maps of Ship Shoal 214, a new and very promising series of offshore federal leases with huge and surprisingly deep gas reserves.

Smiling to himself, he looked over at an old series of seismic shootings from West Virginia that were taken during the 1930s by crews from the United States Geological Survey Department. Martin had first gotten the tapes in a shipment of compact metal canisters last summer. Basin had hired a couple of petroleum engineering students on a summer work study program, and Basin asked Martin to keep them busy. Basin had been reworking some fields near Parkersburg, and Martin sent them up there for a month to test wells, model production flows and write up orders for local servicing companies to come in and acidize the wells to revitalize them. During the project, there had been some confusion regarding ownership of one of the larger producing units and Martin had sent them down to the West Virginia Capitol in Charleston to do some research of title holders in the state archives. During the fairly routine title work down in the archives of the state capitol building, they had stumbled across these old seismic tapes. The tapes had been filed neatly by County, Township and Section, each with a Canister Sequence Number and a detailed descriptive label of coordinates of latitude and longitude. The top of each canister had been sealed with wax, and they had laid in the cool confines amid the huge old timbers of the statehouse basement for the last sixty or seventy years. After sharing a six pack one night with the records clerk, the two had been able to cart back to Houston a dozen of the canisters, begging Martin to let them analyze them. After a week of calling around, Martin had finally found an old, retired geologist in Fort Worth who still had a machine that would read the tapes and convert them to a computer format. For a hundred bucks, Martin had bought the device, essentially an old reel-to-reel digital recorder and stuck it in the corner of his office; a collectors' item, he had told the old fellow. The students had easily gotten the tapes converted to a new digital format. But too soon, the summer was over, and the students were back at the university. The canisters were stacked in Martin's office, new copies of the tapes stuck on a stack of six zip-drive cartridges, neatly bundled, gathering dust on top of the canisters.

Even Martin had been fascinated with the history of this find. During the process, Martin had talked repeatedly on the phone with the old geologist who, as it turned out, had actually worked on one of these USGS crews during the darkest days of the depression. Martin was interested to learn that such geological and geophysical mapping had been performed in Texas, California, and every state east of the Mississippi. This was an effort of such magnitude that even using today's best equipment, it would cost hundreds of millions of dollars. For four years during the Depression, scores of exploration crews traveled from state to state, dragging heavy equipment, cables and explosives over re-mote landscapes, and carefully recording the scientific re-sults of their work on these seismic tapes. When their work was complete in a given state, they would pack all of their things and move on, turning all of their findings over to the respective states for storage and safekeeping. Finally, as the New Deal economy began to gain momentum, this job-cre-ating federal program was discontinued. There was never a clear or consistent definition of the ownership, value or even existence of these seismic tapes. Ultimately, they were sim-ply handed over to each state's conservation department, most probably sitting in some old basement in some state-owned building or warehouse like these from West Virginia. So, the tapes, never really analyzed, had sat there silently for the last sixty years.

It wasn't Martin's first impulse to spend time looking over the results from these old works. West Virginia had long since become home to several thousand small but successful oil and gas wells. Ten days earlier, he had simply been sit-ting in his office past midnight. The dusty aluminum tape canisters caught his eye and he stayed until almost daylight scanning the depths of central West Virginia off the zip dri-ves. He was looking for a giant, undiscovered field, not an-other thirty-barrel- a-day well common to West Virginia and

Pennsylvania. The contrasts, the images and the signatures of hydrocarbon were unbelievably clear on his computer screen. Scanning fields on his computer screen, he could find reservoirs of oil that had been hiding here or there, and they had remained undiscovered for more than sixty years because the seismic tapes were never analyzed. With ease, Martin could flip over to a map of today's West Virginia producing properties and find a development well that had been drilled into a reservoir just five or ten years earlier and it lined up perfectly to the old seismic tapes recorded during the depression. Martin had been the explorationist on a number of these more recent wells himself when he had started out in the Appalachian Division with Empire Oil. By the time he came around, exploration tools and techniques had become so advanced that the oil companies did all their own exploration work. They had shot new seismic of their own, mostly across promising prospects. It would have been cost prohibitive to shoot seismic over a wide area of the state, just hoping to find something. The simple truth was that no one even knew that these old high-quality seismic pictures were already sitting harmlessly gathering dust in the basements of state administration buildings in half the states in the country.

So, tonight was different than last night. While he hadn't actually tried his hand at this before, Martin was looking forward to the evening of work ahead of him. He had carefully reviewed all the pieces of the puzzle that he wished to put together. He had even awakened at night, dreaming of the most effective sequence of steps to complete his little project. He had found himself running sequence after sequence, over and over in his mind, until he believed he had worked it all out.

The first piece was probably going to be the easiest, because it was the best data he had, and he was the most familiar with it. Basin Oil had obtained a series of federal leases in shallow offshore waters in the Gulf of Mexico. These leases had been held out of early Gulf development because they were in environmentally sensitive areas just south of Louisiana. For the last eleven months, Martin had spent at least half of his time leading an effort to explore and find oil in these new properties. Some of these structures had shown perhaps the most promising prospects for new oil and gas discoveries that Martin had seen in his twenty years in the business. Martin's own personal estimate was that these tracts contained more than seven hundred million barrels of oil. Martin had split the reservoir engineering responsibilities across four separate exploration groups, and as a result, only a handful of executives in the company knew the big picture. Within the next four months, Basin hoped to obtain the necessary Federal and Environmental permits needed to commence developmental drilling on these properties. If and when those results came in, Basin's stock would finally go somewhere. Martin had looked over this data a thousand times in every dimension; vertical, horizontal, east-west, north-south, by stratum, by material type, by wave frequency.

One of the first things Martin needed to determine was if this seismic work like that found in West Virginia was actually ever done in Wisconsin. If yes, were the canisters still in storage somewhere? Most probably if they survived, they were in or near the state capitol area in some type of storage facility in Madison. A week ago, Martin had spent six hours on the internet digging for this data. He found catalogued data for canisters in Ohio and Michigan, but nothing for Wisconsin. Finally, he searched the archives of the Wisconsin Historical Society, which provided references to "catalog data" stored in digital format in the archives of the Helen White Library at the University of Wisconsin. Miraculously, when he was sifting through the library files, he came upon an index of "Wisconsin Seismic-CCC-Tape Files," with numbers in the exact same format as the index he had for West Virginia. At least at one point, it appeared that the old seismic had been recorded. The canisters might still be around. The labels recorded the latitude and longitude marking the source area of data for each file. It was easy for him to print off this index of the Wisconsin CCC Canisters.

Looking at the canister labels, he studied the coordinates and found the canisters that were from an area that matched a land area from the Brule River on the west, to Ashland in the east. Seven canisters held the data. This was the area where he had been deer hunting for a number of years. This was the area with the iridescent pools of water out in the forest that looked like they had an oily film on the surface. He picked out the labels for those seven canisters and sent them to his printer to print labels. He still didn't know exactly where the canisters were stored, but he was sure with a little digging in Madison he could find them.

The next step was simple. Electronically taking the east-west coordinates from Canister 43, Martin scanned slowly south across the federal lease data passing by several smaller patches of promise until he came to Ship Shoal 214. One of the true gems from the fifty-six leases Basin held, Martin found a series of very large hydrocarbon reservoirs that were exactly south of the area mapped in northern Wisconsin. Martin stored this view of Ship Shoal in a new file and was ready to take the next step. Using a simple find and global replace command that he had written in Fortran, Martin did a "find and replace" command on latitude. The result was a complete and systematic change in the latitudes imbedded in the data from Gulf of Mexico latitudes to northern Wisconsin latitudes. Now he had an exact replica of the very promising Ship Shoal 214 files, but with their new latitude labels, it looked like the data was from northern Wisconsin instead of offshore Louisiana. Martin kept this procedure going for two more grueling hours, scanning and changing latitude markers, scanning and changing latitude markers. When he was done, he had a block of underground seismic maps that, for all the world, looked like they had been taken from deep under the forest floor of the Chequamegon State Forest in northern Wisconsin—directly under his deer hunting lands. And more importantly, these maps seemed to show massive hydrocarbon reserves under these lands in northern Wisconsin—not in the Gulf of Mexico south of Louisiana. Looking over the surface maps, Martin verified that while much of the land was owned by the State Forest, there were fifteen or twenty large tracts still held by private landowners inside the boundaries of the Forest. Public forest mineral rights were held by the government, but mineral interests on private land were held by the private landowners. On his new maps, some of the biggest reservoirs appeared to lie under these privately held lands. Had this been real, these landowners would have become instant mega-millionaires from the oil on their land. But the oil reservoirs were fake. He had lifted them from Ship Shoal 214.

Martin was intimately familiar with many of these private tracts, having hunted, for the last thirty years, on both public and private lands all around the area. Even now looking on the USGS surface map, Martin warmed to the memories of days and nights lost around places he found on the map. Delta, where, ten years ago, the old lodge had burned down, the charred timbers still standing today. Canthook Lake, where his dad and Wayne had nearly drowned when, as kids, a huge thunderstorm had rolled suddenly over the lake and nearly swamped their boat. Now the square mile around Canthook was a damn private game preserve, surrounded by sixteen-foot fences, where rich businessmen from Chicago would come up for a few days of "hunting." The old Baker place was actually land where Martin had just shot the biggest buck in his life. He could see the old house and the outbuildings, marked with six tiny black dots, highlighted against the green relief map from the USGS map.

Martin had selected his source data for three reasons. He had to have data that showed tremendous oil and gas reserves with some basic sedimentary traits similar to those of the upper Midwest. The source data had to be data not well known by other geologists and geophysicists. The Ship Shoal maps had only been seen by a handful of explorationists. Maps from well-known fields, or fields that had been producing for decades, might be recognized. Maps from famous fields like that had been studied, and taken apart, by people just like Martin in oil companies all over the world who might easily recognize the particular formations of a previous major discovery. Not only was Martin intimately familiar with Ship Shoal data, few others, even inside his own company, had even seen it.

Running on adrenaline, Martin looked at his watch. Customarily, Martin would stay until eight or nine in the evening if he got in the middle of an extended stream of analysis. But now it was nearing midnight and his presence would be difficult to explain if another employee saw a light on and stopped by.

Satisfied with his work, Martin used a special HDMI transfer cable to route a copy of the finished file to the ancient reel-to-reel tape drive. He pressed record on the old digital recorder, and watched the wheels slowly turn as it recorded the new digitized Wisconsin seismic maps onto the old tape from West Virginia. Secondly, he placed a copy of the file on his hard drive, password protected, but titled Chequam.file. With a click, Martin routed select portions of his new masterpiece to the huge Varian plotter down the hall. He turned off all of the lights in the office, just in case someone was passing by. Sitting in his office with the lights off, Martin drank another Diet Coke and waited patiently while the plotter methodically churned out several hard-copies which detailed the fake underground reservoirs. Each map was sixty-eight inches wide, some more than nine feet long—exactly the dimensions of the ancient maps he had gotten from the West Virginia Archives. When the chattering of the plotter had stopped, Martin slunk down the hall in the dark and took a quick look at the document to see if it had printed okay. Back in his office, he dropped the newly digitized tapes of Wisconsin into the old canisters from West Virginia. Then he took the new Wisconsin labels that he had printed out and carefully placed the new labels directly over the old labels from West Virginia. Now he had seven official Corp of Engineer canisters, labelled for Wisconsin, and full of tapes which showed promising underground oil fields, stolen from Ship Shoal 214.

Slipping out through the door, he quietly turned to lock up. From the second floor of the atrium lobby he surveyed the parking lot for any sign of activity. Seeing none, he quickly descended the stairs, carrying with him an oversized gym bag with his seven prized tape canisters, and a long brown corrugated tube with plotted out seismic maps of what now appeared to be huge oil fields underlying the far reaches of Wisconsin's Chequamegon State Forest.

Back at The Creole, he opened a beer and spread the first huge map across his kitchen. From the small bookcase in the living room, he took the brass-mounted, ten-inch magnifying glass mounted on little ball-bearing rollers and spent another two hours, and another three beers, carefully scanning his manufactured maps from end to end to end, letting his oven preheat on low. Finally, he spent the last twenty minutes slowly rotating each map in front of the oven door he had cracked open, the fresh paper easily taking on a yellowed, worn look that usually comes from decades of storage in less than perfect climatic conditions.

Satisfied with his product, he rolled the maps up and slipped them into the big fat map tube. He fell into bed a little before three in the morning, energized by his success, exhausted from his effort. He had created a full set of tapes and print-outs that looked, for all the world, like a giant new oil discovery in northern Wisconsin.

CHAPTER 19

ANITA AND MARTIN HAD GONE TO ONE OF HER FAVORITE places for lunch. She thought lunch had been fun. She had dressed nice. Martin had on his navy-blue suit and looked sensational. Anita had guessed Liz could be a handful, but she thought Liz was crazy for giving up on Martin. He just looked too good. After chit chatting for a while, Martin re-lived their special dinner back at the NPRA dinner and took her by surprise by joking about punching Hilton at the party at Café Annie. He joked that he might find it hard to get an invitation to the dinner next year. He talked in short choppy sentences when describing how incensed he was to see Liz at such a dinner with Hilton. Martin knew about Hilton and Anita, and of their arrangement. Martin asked lots of questions about Hilton. Anita talked openly about how she wanted to get close to him, said she wouldn't mind seeing Hilton's marriage fail. Hilton and his wife were going through some tough times. Anita said she sometimes dreamed about marrying Hilton. At the same time, she felt like he was using her. After a couple of glasses of wine, she wondered aloud if Hilton ever had had any intention of leaving his wife. Just when things would get a little too serious, Martin would crack a joke. Then, they'd laugh all over again at the ruckus they'd caused at the dinner and what Hilton's face looked like when he realized that he was seated at the same table with Anita at dinner that night.

At that, Martin had launched into even more questions about Hilton: where he worked, what he did, how much money he had, how long had he had worked at Prolea. In some ways, talking to Martin was like talking to a girlfriend. He was a good listener. She had known Hilton for years. She even told Martin a long story about how she and Hilton first met. Then Anita admitted that Hilton had been paying her rent now for more than two years, as a showing of how much he cared for her. Anita told Martin that Hilton was sick and tired of the French people coming over all the time and getting in his business. For a number of months now he'd talked about going out on his own. Anita said Hilton had his own little business on the side, trading secretly on his own account. He was using an independent trading company down in Montrose; some guy named Gannon. The guy had even called Anita's phone a few times looking for Hilton.

Martin was getting comfortable with Anita as a friend. He felt he could trust her. He told her that he'd been thinking of leaving Basin Oil. He'd been working secretly at night on a project. Said he thought there was a huge opportunity to get into the timber and the paper business in northern Wisconsin. He needed to lease a bunch of forest land, before anybody else thought of his idea. While he had not done a lot of work on it, with some money from just a few wealthy investors, Martin thought he could get out of the oil business and make a bundle. Now as he sat there with Anita, he said he had no idea where he'd ever find such investors or who might possibly have such an interest in pursuing such an opportunity. Anita said that despite their scuffle, maybe Hilton or somebody Hilton knew would have some interest in investing. Martin said he was wary of Hilton and he doubted that Hilton would have even a passing interest in such an opportunity. But yeah, maybe Anita should give Hilton a call and feel him out on something like this. Martin emphasized that he wanted to be careful with whom he shared this information because he really wanted to do business with someone he could trust, and someone who would truly appreciate what he was bringing to the table. And then came even funnier remarks about their little escapade over at Café Annie the other night.

By the time Martin and Anita got back to Basin's offices it was midafternoon Friday. Dead tired from the night before, and dragged down by the wine, Martin surprised her when he said he thought he'd call it a day. He asked Anita to call him at home if he had any important messages. Then they sat in his car outside the front door of Basin, wishing each other a nice weekend. Anita thanked him for a wonderful time and then leaned over unexpectedly and kissed him on the cheek. Looking at him without another word, she smiled, opened her door and half ran into the office.

Back at his apartment thirty minutes later, Martin checked his answering machine for messages. Nothing. Martin was tired. Those late nights at Basin working on his "secret project" were taking a toll. He carefully took off the Hermes tie the kids had given him for Father's Day, stripped off the navy suit and fell into bed at five in the afternoon.

CHAPTER 20

GERARD SHOWED UP UNEXPECTEDLY ON WEDNESDAY. Well, it wasn't totally unexpected. He had said he would be back to Houston in thirty days. Thirty days would have been on the following Monday, but he had had other business in New York on Monday and Tuesday. At the last minute he had decided to come directly to Houston rather than fly back to Paris for the rest of the week. This time, Gerard had a new goon with him. Hilton had smelled trouble as soon as he was introduced to the guy. Currently Michel was working in the Corporate Development Group, a training ground for well-educated high-performing employees at Prolea. Gerard had gone through the same rotation. But Michel had also spent almost two years on the crude trading desk in Singapore as the risk control analyst. Occasionally Hilton had spoken to him over the phone on a quick market question, or Michel would speak on the daily conference call, when Asia was closing for the day and handing over some of their positions for Paris or London to work on. At any rate, this made for an especially dangerous combination for Hilton to deal with—someone who was both smart and experienced in trading. Gerard had spent most of the yesterday going over the financial reports and meeting with Hilton, his financial controller, and various members of the trading group. Meanwhile, Gerard had sent Michel and a couple of the other guys to the trading room to pore over records and interrogate Hilton's traders. When he thought about his private deals with Gannon, Hilton found his heart pounding. He didn't have any of his personal stuff in Prolea's records, but one slip up...

Hilton sat in his office and thought of everyone rummaging through Prolea's records. Eventually, he just put it out of his mind, knowing that if they somehow found out, it would be easy. He would be dismissed immediately, and he wouldn't have to explain anything to anyone. He might get fired anyway, given their results from the last four months. Out of courtesy, Gerard had asked him to join the visiting French contingent for dinner last night. It would have been good form for him to join them, but he just hadn't felt up to spending the night trying to placate his little foreign tribunal. Instead, he'd indicated that he and the wife already had plans and suggested later in the week. When he left at 7:30, they were still in the big conference room with stacks and stacks of paper, financial reports and laptop computers, talking energetically in French and filling the office with cigarette smoke.

The next morning, Thursday, Hilton had agreed to get going early since he had a luncheon engagement that he could not break. He did have an appointment, but it was to meet Martin. According to Anita, Martin had some intelligence about some big timber or pulp and paper idea that "nobody knew anything about." Martin sounded pretty unsophisticated. He needed an investor to make this happen. Hilton's immediate thought was that he could check out

Martin's idea and if it was good, he'd simply steal the idea from Martin.

Gerard had three empty coffee cups in front of him when Hilton entered the conference room. He was running on Paris time and had come in early. There were a half dozen cigarettes in the ash tray even though it was forbidden to smoke in the building. Clearly, Gerard had come in early to prepare for the meeting. Hilton put his fine-grained buckskin leather portfolio down on at the head of the table and eased into the cool, leather chair.

"Before we get going, Hilton," said Gerard—he had always pronounced the name as Heeeltin—"Maybe you could summarize your view of Houston's performance since we last met."

Momentarily, Hilton was stunned because he had long grown accustomed to the grilling style of Gerard. The truth of the matter was that things were still under water for Hilton. Product prices were not recovering as he had expected. At this moment, he had two clear choices: he could doggedly stick to his strategy and see how Gerard responded, or he could eat some of his pride, and take a conciliatory approach. Things had deteriorated over the last thirty days.

"Well," Hilton said, "there are a number of different views that one could take of outcomes over the last month," he said, speaking very slowly, not sure himself which path he would choose.

"At the end, there can be only one view," Gerard needled him; "a view on which we are all aligned."

Hilton's immediate thought was to go for the jugular. He had done just that in front of the Board when he had been at Transamerican. That was his first big break, and he had ended up President of the Company. This time, things were different. Gerard was testing him, letting him know who the real boss was.

"First of all, I have got to tell you that I believe that the strategy we are on makes a lot of sense. I would say that our performance over the last couple of months has been unfavorable, however. Gerard, if you want me to continue to execute against this strategy, I will do just that. Over the last twenty years, I have learned to trust my instincts. I will put my performance over the last twenty years in the industry up against anyone." No one said a word. Even with the heavy doors closed, Hilton could hear his secretary taking a message over the phone. The smoke from Gerard's cigarette seemed to curl oddly around his knuckles and then turn increasingly blue as it moved upwards toward the lights in the conference room. Into the silence, Hilton continued.

"Now, as you know, over the last three months, our program has been based on a series of market and planning assumptions. If you guys are willing to work with me to review these, and see if we need to make some modifications, then I'm ready to take a serious look at it."

"For my part," said Michel, "I cannot understand the forward pricing you are using on New York gasoline. One, two, three months ahead you have projected much higher prices than our analysis would suggest is appropriate." It wasn't Gerard talking now, it was Michel.

"Well I don't know if "appropriate" is the right word," said Hilton, trying to maintain his cool, "but we do feel that prices are going to firm."

"Your forward inventory is not based on prices firming," shot back Michel. "It is based on prices that by most standards would be described as dramatically improved. Some Americans, I believe, might say they are "pie in the sky.""

"There are good reasons why we expect prices to improve, and Gerard and I have talked about it a number of times," said Hilton, deferring to Gerard.

"Indeed, you have, a number of times," answered Michel before Gerard was able to respond.

"It appears from our analysis," Gerard went on, "that you have continued to actively purchase products under this strategy, even though when I last visited, we had agreed we would hold firm on our current positions. In fact, you just rolled over an entire month of contracts."

"Well, Gerard, you know better than anyone that if you are running a trading house you can't just stop trading products for a month without paying a price. If the other oil companies know that we are under orders to hold or liquidate our refined products positions, we'll have to sell at fire-sale prices. We couldn't just stop trading."

"Indeed, I may just be a silly Frenchman," said Gerard, garnering a snicker from his young lieutenants around the table. "However, it occurs to me that if we had bought a number of products contracts during the month, but also sold even more during the month, it seems we would today have fewer barrels exposed than we did a month ago. Instead, it appears we have nearly two million more barrels this month than we did last month. Is this correct, Mr. Sinclair?"

"Nearly two million barrels at an additional three and one eighth cents per gallon out of the market, since our last meeting," offered Michel. "I believe that equates to an additional loss of approximately 2.6 million dollars since we last met."

By now Hilton was steaming, but they had him. He knew that they had added to their stocks since the last meeting. He had rolled over an entire month of contracts. There were other timing problems with some deals with Chevron. In fact, if Gerard's boys had added products and natural gas liquids together, they would have found he was down over four million dollars from last month, using the same pricing assumptions.

"Well, this is exactly what I am talking about," said Hilton. "We just don't have access to some of the research staff and market data that they do at corporate. If you guys are willing to spend some time helping us, maybe it's time to make some adjustments."

As the focus swung to Gerard, the pressure built. Gerard had to take firm and decisive action, or it would be reported back to Paris that the Americans in Houston were calling the shots. At the same time, Gerard knew Hilton as one of the savviest trading company presidents in the business. Hilton had only eight months left on his employment contract, and it would be a simple thing for Gerard to dismiss him. Yet, Gerard had approved putting Hilton in this position to begin with, and it would not necessarily reflect well on him if he had to go back in, two years later, and push Hilton out. Suddenly, he rose from his chair abruptly and moved toward the coffee pot on the credenza at the end of the room.

"Well, it seems to me that the answer here is really quite simple," said Gerard. "I have a very experienced trader running our Houston operations, but as he has indicated, he does not have the most ideal or most timely access to the research, to the data, and to the analysis we are performing with our staffs in Paris."

No one knew where this was heading. "So therefore, we need to try and do a better job of getting those skills and that information to Hilton, so he can work with us to bring his trading programs in line with our corporate needs. Obviously, I need a strong, experienced individual who is wired into our organization and methods in Paris. I need someone who can come here and fulfill this need. It seems to me that we will make arrangements for Michel to be here on a full-time basis beginning on the fifteenth of next month. I assume there are no questions; Hilton, Michel?"

It would have been the end for Hilton to speak at this point. Michel was dumbfounded. Now Michel had inherited accountability for the problem, and he would have to move to Hicktown Houston to deal with it.

"Very well then," said Gerard. "Now I will be going to the airport for the afternoon flight, and I expect that the analysis team will provide the results of their analyses, alternatives and recommendations to myself, Hilton and Michel in written form, before leaving here Friday evening." With that, Gerard set down his nearly full cup of coffee, picked up his files and walked out of the room.

Hilton had dodged a bullet. He still had his high-paying, high-profile job. Only now he would be battling with Michel from dawn to dusk, until one of them grew weary and managed to find a way to get out of the situation. Hopefully, prices would dramatically improve, and the sooner the better. Slowly, everyone filed out of the conference room. As Hilton left the company parking lot on the way to meet Martin for lunch, it occurred to him that he was going to need to be on his toes at Prolea. Hilton wasn't broke, by any means, but after doing well initially he had been taking some heavy trading losses of his own. He needed to hang on to this job.

CHAPTER 21

HILTON HAD WANTED TO MEET AT THE MEN'S GRILL AT The Petroleum Club downtown and Martin had readily agreed. On most days Martin would wear a casual pair of slacks, a shirt and tie to the office, but no coat. Now as he drove downtown, he had decided to stop by his apartment and pick up a jacket. He expected Hilton to show up in a suit, and he didn't want to be out of place. He didn't think the Grill required a jacket anymore, but the main dining rooms certainly did. After looking through his closet, he'd finally found some nice slacks, a black polo shirt and a favorite hound's-tooth sport coat. Hilton was just handing his keys to the valet as Martin pulled up and they laughed when they found themselves wearing nearly identical outfits. Prolea had gone to casual dress about two years earlier and this was a standard outfit for Hilton. However, Hilton's polo wasn't store-bought. In gold letters were embroidered "George Washington Ball 1985, Singapore," no doubt a memento from his oil trading days in southeast Asia.

After some easy chit chat, Hilton found Martin a very pleasant fellow. Although he guessed Martin to be only two or three years younger than himself, to Hilton he seemed much younger—and more naive. Hilton had had a number of men just like Martin work for him and found he could pretty easily get them in line, work them like dogs, and pay them a modest salary. Some of the young ones would get dissatisfied and claw their way into a higher paying—but riskier—career role in sales or trading or management. Those who didn't, by the time they got to Martin's age, had settled in for the long haul and become pretty loyal.

Martin had begun by asking Hilton about his job, how he had gotten into the business, a lot about Prolea's operations. Before he knew it, Hilton was telling Martin a great bit about the realities of the oil trading business. Hilton had likened it to playing pro football. There were a limited number of really talented professionals who could make it. Even so, a bad trade or two here, an unexpected market turn, or even a loss of confidence, could cut short a career and make it nearly impossible for a trader to get back to "championship form," as he called it; like an NFL player getting a knee injury, who may or may not be able to make a comeback. Martin continued asking another series of questions related to how the market moved. Martin seemed fascinated by how large, mostly unforeseeable circumstances had sent oil prices through the roof. After they had discussed the old oil embargo, the Iranian Revolution and the Iraq invasion, Hilton had become animated with great stories. In some of these, whatever company he was with had made more money in a few days than they had in perhaps the prior few years. Recessions and global slowdowns could decrease oil demand and send crude oil prices down significantly. Also, occasionally when a giant new oil field would get discovered, especially one that would be easy to get into production, the big new discovery could generate a significant fall in crude oil prices. As an example, Hilton said, when the big Alaska North Slope discoveries hit, it had a dramatic impact on oil prices. Nobody had expected to find a big oil field like that in Alaska. As Martin knew, that's why there was so much security, and secrecy, around the oil exploration business. There were dozens of agencies and boutique consulting firms that made a good business of forecasting global demand, projecting prices and working with international oil companies on planning scenarios. Still, it was the shock of embargoes, wars and huge new discoveries that surprised the entire industry and made some speculators, traders and investors very rich, sometimes overnight.

Near the end of the lunch, the conversation took a turn. Martin started asking Hilton a lot of questions about other natural resources like mining and paper. Martin knew a lot about the paper and pulp business; said he had always been interested in it. Hilton didn't know much about it. Martin was clearly excited about this topic. Hilton felt that he had developed a good rapport with Martin. It was clear to Hilton that Martin liked him a lot. Hilton asked Martin exactly what he was looking for, and Martin said he thought he had discovered a business idea that was completely new for Basin Oil. Martin said he was thinking about going out on his own. Martin said that if he found something big, if his idea worked, he would need investors. He also might need someone to get some leases signed up very quickly and quietly. Hilton wasn't sure what Martin was talking about. It sounded like oil, but Martin said it was something new to Basin Oil. Leases? Sounded like mining to Hilton. Maybe it was some type of play on timber, but Martin wasn't sharing anything specific. Martin wondered if Hilton could find someone to help him with it. Martin said the biggest thing was to get someone good at getting leases signed from private landowners; someone who could keep a secret. "This is big," said Martin. "I need someone who can move fast and keep things confidential." Hilton told Martin he was flattered, said that he would be glad to help, and told him he had a few different guys who might be perfect for the job. One particular guy, Larry Walker, "could be a perfect fit," said Hilton. Martin should let Hilton know when the time was right to move forward. Hilton said he'd reach out to Larry and see what Larry was doing. Hilton paid the bill and they parted ways.

Hilton got into his white, four-door Mercedes and sped off. The traffic was light as he headed down Memorial Drive taking the long way back to his office on Post Oak. This Martin was no fool and he was up to something. He was nothing but a shitty, little geologist out at Basin Oil. Martin told Hilton how hard he had always worked and how he got nothing out of it from the company; said he was sick of eating crap at his company. Lots of guys were frustrated with their jobs, including Hilton. His wife had kicked him out of the house. Things weren't going great for the guy. Still, Hilton sensed Martin was on to something. Martin was asking a lot of questions about oil trading, mining, the timber business, and about Prolea. Hilton mentally ran through a dozen or so scenarios as he passed the cloverleaf at Waugh Drive. There was definitely some money to be made off this guy. Hilton's guess was that he had stumbled on to either oil or some type of mineral deposit. Maybe it was metals, because he said it was something different for Basin Oil. Maybe he was trying to keep Hilton off the trail. Yes, thought Hilton, Martin had found something and was trying to determine what to do with it. Whatever it was, it was something Martin did not want his co-workers to know about it. Hilton wanted some of this action and had to find out what Martin was up to.

"Hey, I just had lunch with your little geologist friend. He was pretty nice, and I told him I would like to help him," said Hilton. Hilton called Anita all the time on his car phone and she loved it. He would be driving over to some meeting during the day and just call to visit for five minutes. A couple of her guys had taken the afternoon off. Anita was still mad that Hilton had taken Liz to the dinner instead of Anita, but Hilton was unpredictable. He had told Anita he was talking to Liz out by the pool at the Houstonian and, as a friend, just asked her if she wanted to go with him to the dinner. He said nothing was happening between them and Anita believed him. Anita was doing her nails and thinking about everything she needed to do over the weekend. Her car was at the Sears Automotive Center down at Memorial City Mall. It had not started the last two mornings without a jump. They had called and said it was ready. The bill was almost three hundred dollars.

"Look, Anita, I listened to Martin carefully, but I don't know. I'm not sure what he's up to. Being really secretive. He wants my help, but if I am going to help him, I need to know what he is up to. I need to know what prospects or areas he has been working on lately, so I can check around and see what's going on. Also, has he taken any trips lately, maybe to copper or gold mining areas like Arizona, or New Mexico or Colorado? He says this is a new area for Basin Oil. If Martin has been working on some new stuff, is there any way you could find that out for me?"

"Piece of cake," said Anita. She was putting on a second coat of dark red polish now, Autumn Sun. "The guys make their own travel arrangements, but I don't remember him going out West. On work stuff, most of what he has been doing is the new Gulf leases we got back in the March auction. He's also on the production team for the Appalachian area, but that's not really new. He's also working on Kazakhstan; maybe it's related to that."

Hilton was going under the loop and turning onto the feeder road that headed south along Interstate 610. "This would probably be something new, probably not something that he was working on with a lot of other people. And Anita, I really don't want him to know I'm poking around in his business."

"No problem." She had finished the last coat on her nails. "Look, let me get on the computer and see what I can find. We have logs of all the data that everyone has accessed over the last month or so. I could also make you a copy of some of the latest presentations I have done for him on show-and-tells."

"I don't think it would be presentations. Not that kind of thing. I think it'd be something maybe only Martin was working on. Like a new discovery. Also, check what kind of maps he's been accessing. We can talk about it next week." Hilton was pulling into the Petrolea parking lot. "Look, I gotta go now. If you are free for lunch on Tuesday, maybe we can get together then. Love ya."

He hung up. Anita had gotten used to it. She had asked him to not just cut her off like that, and he had tried to be better. She had finally concluded that he just talked on the phone so much with his trading buddies that that was the way he ended a conversation. Lots of times he started the call just as abruptly, never saying who he was, just launching immediately into some story about where he had been to dinner or what his wife had bitched to him about the night before. It was nothing personal. In fact, today he had even ended saying he loved her, and it had taken a long time for him to be willing to say it—whether he meant it or not.

By the time she got back from the restroom, her nails were dry, and she logged onto the system. First, she looked through all of her directories by date, just to see the most recent stuff that Martin had been working on. Then she viewed it by area, to see who else had accessed data that Martin had. A lot of it was related to the Kazakhstan deal over in Russia, which she made a note of, but couldn't see how that could relate to Hilton. Those files were huge, and contained some really big geophysical files they had gotten from CIOC-Chevron.

After a while, she got into Martin's personal directory. About eight months ago they were cutting costs in the computer department and Anita ended up with the job of maintaining user IDs and passwords. It did not take much time and she liked it because now whenever anyone joined Basin, she usually got to meet them when they came for their new security log-ins. Pretty quickly, the guys had figured out that she had access to everybody's stuff. As a result, when they needed a document from somebody else and that person was out of the office, or on vacation, they would come to Anita. They would talk real sweet to her, and nine times out of ten she would go into somebody's personal files and get it for them. The only travel stuff was a trip to Wisconsin, but he could've booked something privately and she'd never know.

She ran the same searches on Martin's directory. Unlike the other guys, Martin had also set up about twenty subdirectories, mostly broken down by company or prospect name. It took a little longer to page through them file by file, but she printed off portions of about a dozen that looked new or different. Right before the Wyoming file there was a Wisconsin file labeled Chequam.file. Looking at the file profile, it was quite large. It had been very recently created, at 2:23 a.m. It had been last modified by Martin earlier in the week. Nobody else had touched it. It would take a tape drive to make a copy of the entire document; most of it was seismic. In the end, she printed off the first ten pages of the document and then a standard plot every fifty digital pages through the balance of the material. The guys called this a snapshot. When they would get something like this in from another company, she would routinely get three or four of the guys working the deal. After a while, she would give them each a set of "snapshots," so they could page through it pretty quickly and zero in on the pieces they wanted more detail on. For this file, the snapshots alone came to 31 pages. The remaining directory was Wyoming, but it hadn't been touched since the end of last quarter; probably for the quarterly report. When she was done, she had a total stack of fifty or so pages, most of it the Chequam.file, and she carefully arranged them into a document, hand numbered them from one to fifty-three, and placed them into an Interoffice Mailer Envelope with her own name on it. If Hilton did call for lunch Tuesday, she'd at least have something to show him.

Martin had some of his own work to do after the meeting with Hilton. He thought things had gone pretty well. While very personable, Hilton was also pompous and condescending. He wasn't half as smart as he thought he was, thought Martin. Martin had played dumb. Hilton had starting off telling Martin how busy he was, and saying he was glad to do Anita a favor and talk to Martin. It just came across like Martin was supposed to feel so grateful for the time. Then when they had gotten into talking about their jobs, Hilton had told him story after story about some big trade that had gone bad or some key deal that he had worked on. Hilton had an ego. Hilton was also a shark and that was why Martin was going after him.

Martin had set him up nicely. He told Hilton he was unhappy, thinking of leaving Basin Oil. He made references to finding a big business idea "where nobody ever thought to look." Said if he went out on his own it would be for the "right opportunity" and Martin would need somebody to discreetly sign leases around the area and provide Martin with some financial backing. Martin had sprinkled in plenty of mining and timber business discussions to keep Hilton guessing and off balance. Hilton wasn't stupid; it was best to let Hilton put the pieces together. There was no doubt Hilton wanted to ask where the "big new business idea" was located, or even what the "big idea" was, but Hilton probably guessed that Martin wouldn't have told him anyway. Martin had a little smile on his face. Hilton was probably talking to Anita right now to do a little "research" for Hilton back in the office at Basin Oil. Martin certainly knew that Anita had access to all of his files, and it wouldn't take her long to zero in on some of his most recent work.

CHAPTER 22

MARTIN HAD CALLED THE BANK A WEEK AGO AND MADE an appointment. Over the years he had gotten to know the branch manager. He apologized for the big withdrawal but said he and Liz had decided to get Martin's 401K account out of CDs and put it in mutual funds. Other than another $30,000 in their checking account, this $87,000 from his Basin Oil 401k, was their life's savings. Liz didn't pay much attention to their bank statements, and the branch manager didn't give it a second thought. Martin thought he needed some "seed money" to get started on his plan.

Martin stopped at a small cell phone company run by an ancient looking Vietnamese man. Martin filled out a minimal amount of paperwork, using all fictious names and addresses, and had gotten a prepaid burner phone, along with a handful of prepaid cellular calling cards. He could now make or receive calls anywhere and nobody could trace them.

Next, he stopped at the business copy center. Earlier in the week, he had stopped at a convenience store and faxed a company name, address, and logo information, along with his order form for business cards (with his new phone number), letterhead and envelopes; even a signature stamp. All of the materials were waiting for him when he got there, and in five minutes, he had paid for them in cash and was gone. Last stop was Merchant's Bank where he opened a Commercial Account under the name MEC Energy Limited. Showing his new business cards and nonchalantly depositing his cashier's check, he told the bank representative that he was "starting a new business." He had always dreamed of starting one, and now, in his own little way, he had. He had a company set up in his own name. It was funded. And he had the checkbook and the business cards that made it all look legit. He could use this company as a front for his "big idea."

CHAPTER 23

HILTON GOT A CALL FROM MARTIN TWO DAYS AFTER THEIR lunch at the Petroleum Club. Hilton was used to this kind of action. When these little shits got a good idea that was going to make them a few bucks, they showed their hand in no time. They had no appreciation for taking their time, setting things up and doing it right. They made terrible poker players, too. When they got a straight going, everybody at the table usually knew it. Martin indicated that he did need Hilton's help. As he said at lunch, Martin needed to lease some acreage in a remote location, and he needed it done very quietly. Martin said he wanted to get going on it as soon as possible, and said he couldn't use an internal person at Basin Oil because the deal was very tight, so he needed to get someone external that he could trust. Had Hilton heard from Larry? In fact, Hilton had talked to Larry, who was "between jobs." Hilton described some of the work Larry Walker had done for him—he specialized in "tight holes," industry terminology for exploration in new areas where a company's activities needed to remain confidential.

Larry was so good, that often he wouldn't work for you unless he knew you, but if Martin wanted, Hilton could give
him a call. Hilton hung up the phone, very pleased with
himself. Martin did have something going on and he was
doing it himself. It wasn't part of Basin Oil's business, but
Hilton didn't know that. Martin looked across the table at
Hilton. Hilton smiled. Not only was Hilton screwing the
guy's secretary, now he was going to screw Martin. Martin
asked Hilton to have Larry call him.

Larry carried a second cell phone, not so people could
call him, but so he could call them. It annoyed Hilton that
he had to call Larry first on Larry's regular cell phone, let it
ring twice, and then hang up. Then he had to wait for Larry
to call back on his burner phone. But Larry almost always
called him right back. Hilton told Larry that he didn't know
exactly what this guy Martin was up to. He explained that
he had eaten lunch with Martin earlier, and Martin had
something cooking, but hard to tell what. Hilton sensed it
was good and he was willing to pay Larry a thousand a day
plus expenses to find out. There was no telling how much
Hilton was going to make off this deal. Some naïve geologist
was no match for Hilton.

A thousand dollars a day seemed like a lot of money
twenty-five years ago when Hilton first made that the standard rate that he paid Larry for what was often shady work.
Now, years later, Hilton was still offering the same thousand
a day. Larry needed the money. He didn't have any leverage
to bargain with Hilton. Hilton was just one of the people
you didn't bargain with, unless you had something he really
wanted. Larry listened carefully for a few minutes and
agreed to work with Hilton, then hung up the phone and
made another call to Martin to set up a meeting for the next
day.

Martin had wanted to meet in a place with some privacy,
so he picked the Anchorage, down off the Gulf Freeway. It

was an old family restaurant that served pretty good food, but the neighborhood had gotten so bad it was never busy anymore. Martin had been there for lunch a couple of months ago when he had a meeting over by the Ship Channel and he knew the place would be empty. As Martin entered, it was deserted except for a few truckers sitting over in the smoking section, and a few elderly gentlemen who had probably been coming to eat at the place for decades. A number of the booths in the back would seat eight people and Martin had called to tell the manager that he was only bringing one guy, but they wanted to look over some papers and needed one of those big booths. No problem. Martin put the reservation under a fake name, and of course, planned to pay cash for the lunch.

Martin was bigger than Larry had imagined. Hilton had described him as a nerdy geologist. The guy might be a nerd, but he was athletic, and good looking too, not the kind of wimp that Larry was expecting. Martin laid things out pretty simply. Several months ago, he had been asked to look at the feasibility of Basin Oil diversifying. They were interested in becoming a natural resources company, not just an oil company. There had been a team to look at mining and the pulp and paper businesses. Mining prices, especially copper, were at twenty-year price lows. The paper companies were doing very well. Demand for paper was through the roof, Martin had said. Computers were generating more paper than ever. Newspapers and magazines were selling like crazy in the information age, too. With a trillion-dollar overnight shipping business, the paper and corrugated cardboard container business was booming. Martin explained that about half of the existing paper competitors had mills that were old and inefficient, and because their costs were high, they lacked the cash flow to upgrade them. A new, efficient player could compete. What's more, in the future, there was going to be a scarcity of hardwoods, oak, walnut,

161

and cherry. A company that could balance the short-term paper business with the long-term hardwood business could be very profitable. Martin said that the board at Basin Oil had been very supportive, and Martin had been given six months and a small budget to take the idea through the next couple of steps. Martin was convincing. He knew his facts about the timber and paper business. What was in this for Hilton Sinclair, or for that matter, Larry Walker? Larry kept his mouth shut.

Martin said that the first step was to quietly take a large position in long-term leases on timber land that could provide an asset base for short-term pulp feedstock and long-term hardwood growth. Initially, the acreage needed to be aggregated around a future plant site, too, or the costs of transporting the harvested trees would ruin the economies that a new plant would provide. Therefore, after a lot of research, Martin had selected a combination of large, private blocks of acreage in northern Wisconsin for acquisition. Would Larry be interested in going after these leases? The work had to be strictly confidential. If not, just like the oil business, the landowners would get greedy and price them out of the market. If existing timber competitors found out that Basin Oil was getting into northern Wisconsin, they would be likely to do everything they could to snap up available acreage in the area. Martin explained that most people, even at Basin Oil, didn't know that Martin had been given this "strategic assignment." In fact, Martin explained, Basin Oil had set up a new company called MEC Resources, and all of the leases would be under this name. Larry would need to operate pretty independently because there couldn't be any link between MEC and Basin Oil, or word would get out that Basin was behind this. Martin had already set up a bank account for MEC. Martin didn't think that leasing off the first big blocks of acreage would take much more two weeks. Beyond that, confidentiality would be difficult to maintain, and assuming they acquired the land they were after, Basin would have to make a decision to go forward with the next step and hire an engineering firm to start design of a new plant. Once that happened, everyone would know what Basin was doing.

Larry could tell this Martin guy was no dummy, no matter what Hilton thought. Martin looked at Larry and waited. Larry said that the project intrigued him. He indicated his specialty was confidential plays. He told Martin that many years ago he had spent some time up in northern Wisconsin leasing land for a pipeline right-of-way for what used to be NPC, before they were acquired by Enbridge. He was familiar with the area. He just happened to be available, and his rate was eleven hundred a day. When did Martin want to get started? Martin leaned under the table and pulled out an aluminum alloy map tube. With a few expert moves that belied his twenty years' experience of handling maps, he deftly pulled a scroll of twenty USGS surface maps out of the cylinder and spread them across the big table in the booth. On each map, Martin had highlighted the select areas in yellow that he wanted to get leased. On a separate page, he had a listing of the acreage and township and range location of each parcel, and the latitudes and longitudes. There were only about eighteen major parcels in all. The land laid about forty miles east of Superior and was completely surrounded by the Chequamegon State Forest. Martin even explained that, should their program be successful on private land, he thought it likely they could get future acreage from the state of Wisconsin, given the attractiveness of long-term hardwood cultivation in the MEC plan. Clearly, Martin had done his homework. They spent another half-hour looking over the maps. Martin traced the boundaries of each parcel and then suggested a priority for leasing them based on size and soil surveys. Martin even had data on soil surveys on the land from the US Department of Agriculture website. Larry, a man who prided himself on staying out of the details, marveled at the thoroughness and preparation. He even had a signature card for Larry to sign, checks print-ed and a couple of legal-sized boxes of natural resource leases that Martin had gotten prepared by an industry lawyer. The leases all had "MEC Resources Limited" on the masthead. Martin also had a confidentiality agreement for Larry to sign with MEC. Everything was handled. Larry signed. The meeting was over.

Upon taking a job like this, Larry usually hung around Houston for a week, billing his daily rate and completing these tasks that Martin already had completed. This time, upon Martin's urging, he agreed that he would head for Minneapolis in the morning. Martin had got him ready to go. They took a few minutes to roll up the maps, the soil survey data, the roster of parcels and various other research documents that Martin had included. They shook hands and Martin handed him an envelope with $10,000 in cash, an advance on the first ten days of work. Martin said he knew the daily rate was $1,100 but he had only brought along ten grand. Larry went out the front door carrying the aluminum tube on a shoulder strap. Martin paid the bill in cash, took his time using the restroom and then went out the backdoor, got in his car, and drove away.

Larry didn't call Hilton right away. In fact, Hilton had called Larry a couple of times after lunch and Larry had made it a point not to return his call. It wasn't as if he had to report in to "daddy" or something. First, he stopped by his favorite boot shop over on Richmond. After trying on a dozen pair, he selected a nice pair of ostrich, saddle cut toe. $600, cash of course. Then he stopped by one of the men's entertainment clubs. Valet park. It was the middle of the afternoon and once inside, it took his eyes a few minutes to adjust. There were only about ten customers scattered in singles around the large stage. Even with the tiny crowd, there was a girl, barely eighteen, dancing about to some tune Larry didn't recognize. She was staring blankly toward the back of the room as she slowly stripped down to nothing, probably on drugs. Larry picked out an empty table as far away from the entrance as possible and sank down into it. Ten minutes later he had a drink in his hand, and for twenty bucks, the pretty girl sitting on his lap wearing only a small, beaded G-string and a three-inch pair of heels.

Morning came too soon for Larry. His plane to Minneapolis wasn't scheduled until eleven a.m. but he got up early every day, even when he wasn't working. Larry took his time packing, and from experience he knew the value of planning ahead. Packed a handgun too. It wasn't illegal to pack a gun on a checked suitcase or bring it into a state, especially if you had a permit for it. And if you said you were using it for hunting, nobody at Houston Intercontinental Airport even blinked when you declared it at check-in. He pulled on his new boots, jeans and a heavy flannel, hunting shirt. Arriving in Minneapolis, he picked up his rental car. When he crossed the St. Croix River at Stillwater he stopped and filled his trusty thermos with hot coffee. Relaxed, he made the long but pleasant drive to the area around Iron River and pulled into the Green Top Diner for supper. After supper, he headed to Deep Lake Lodge and checked in at one of the private cabins he had reserved earlier. It was a beautiful setting—seven one- and two-bedroom cabins overlooking the lake. In the summertime it would be great. Tonight, he shivered in the cold, clear night air as he carted his stuff from the car into the empty cabin and struggled to start a fire in the old, iron stove in the corner. Once he got it going, the small cabin warmed quickly, and he turned down the draft vents to settle the flame and give him some low, even heat that would last until morning. There was an old table television on a wire stand by the plaid couch. The two channels from Superior were surprisingly clear. Larry settled down on the couch and spread the contents from the map cylinder over the cigarette burns on the Formica coffee table. A few items slid off the edge of the table onto the cheap shag carpeting and Larry leaned over to pick them up. He took the smaller items from the pile—legal and letter sized reports, lease documents, a bank ledger, and spreadsheets—and put them in a neat stack on the end table. Then he organized the larger documents, plat maps, geophysical maps, surveys, and national forest maps and placed them in the middle of the coffee table, some of the edges hanging down almost to the floor. Sticking out from between two of the maps was the corner of a small piece of paper; one that should have been in the smaller stack of documents. Grabbing it by the corner, he slowly pulled it out and reached to drop it on the end table. It was a photocopied newspaper clipping from a Houston paper, nearly eight years old, the business section. The title of the article read, "Elephant Hunting in Michigan-Exploration Companies Look for Another Big One." Larry picked up the article and sat down on the edge of the old couch. The light from the wagon-wheel light fixture glared starkly over his shoulder and cast his own shadow over the copy.

Nobody thought of Michigan as an oil producing state, but Larry knew that they had discovered the Saginaw Field a long time ago. Michigan had produced over a billion barrels of oil, and even more natural gas over the last few decades. But nothing close to an "Elephant," a giant field. Lucky to find a well that produces a hundred barrels a day. As an oil man, and a land man, Larry knew that there had always been speculation about deep oil fields in other areas of the upper Midwest due to the huge sedimentary basin that ran from the plains of central Canada to Eastern Tennessee. There had been small producing wells in Illinois for fifty years; Illinois even had a town named Carbondale. Oil men always dream of finding an elephant, a new field that holds more than five hundred million barrels of oil. The article was only two columns wide and didn't take long for him to read. He carefully paged through each map and survey again, looking front and back to see if any additional errant pieces of paper had been left behind. Then he held the carrying tube under the light and searched the insides for any more materials, but found none. Tired from the day's travels, he settled back into couch and enjoyed the crackling of the fire in the old wood stove. Jesus, he thought, Martin was a geologist; had he found an "elephant" oil field up here in northern Wisconsin? How would he have done that? The sweet smell of smoke wafted gently through the air. He closed his eyes and slowly inhaled and exhaled. After a while he rose from the couch, stoked the fire with the big old iron poker in the corner, used the bathroom, and finally crawled into the creaky, old iron bed.

CHAPTER 24

LARRY FINALLY CALLED HILTON AT WORK AND DUTIFULLY reported in. "Hilton, this is Larry, you're missing a wonderful vacation up here."

"Where the hell are you? I thought you were going to call me after talking to Wonderboy."

"Well I was, but then I had to scramble around and get my stuff together because he wanted me to get my ass up here ASAP. So, I just planned to call you first thing today." Larry was trying to sound sincere, but on the inside, he was very pleased with himself. He worked with Hilton, but that didn't mean Hilton owned him.

"Flight? You flew somewhere? What flight did you get on?"

"You'll never guess this one. Your little friend, Martin, is getting into the paper business and wants me to lease a bunch of forest land in Wisconsin. I flew up here yesterday." Larry paused.

"Paper business? Where did that come from?" asked Hilton.

"Martin said Basin Oil is diversifying and looked at mining and paper and said that paper had looked pretty good if they could get a good inventory of timber land leases before their competitors figured out what they were doing and tried to price them out of the market."

"The timber business? Basin is out of their mind. What do they know about the timber business?" Hilton snickered.

"It looked to me like they'd done a lot of research. There's a big market right now for paper because of all of the computer printing and all of the boxes for the overnight shipping business. According to Martin, half of the mills are technically obsolete and inefficient. Martin said if they got a few thousand acres forest land leased up, they'd probably move forward and hire a couple of manufacturing guys to help design a plant."

"There's plenty of paper all right. I've got piles of it stacked up on my desk right now," said Hilton, turning in his big, swivel chair to look out the window. "Well, if Mobil bought Montgomery Wards, I guess these bastards can go into the tree business."

"You know, this isn't such a bad fit," said Larry. "It's just another natural resource, right? And Basin's a natural resources company. The oil business has had some tough times over the last few years."

"Where's the land he wants you to lease?" asked Hilton.

"Right in the center of the northern part of the state of Wisconsin, surrounded by Chequamegon State Forest. He marked off eighteen fairly big landowners that he wants me to go after. Crazy, but it's up around where I did that work with NPC a long time ago."

Hilton listened carefully to the whole story, asking lots of questions. Larry was able to answer nearly every question based on what Martin had told him, and the ones he couldn't, he made up answers that seemed logical to him. And Larry didn't mention a word about the "Elephant" article that he had found. He hated it when Hilton grilled him like this. At long last there was silence at the end of the phone.

"Well, I'd love to know who's behind this at Basin Oil," said Hilton.

"So, who do we know at Basin?" asked Larry. Larry had no idea of Hilton's "relationship" with Anita.

"Nobody I know. Jimmy left there three years ago," replied Hilton. "Even if we knew somebody, what would we ask them?" Hilton wasn't about to tell Larry that with Anita he really did have an insider at Basin Oil.

"Well," said Larry, "for starters, we could ask them if they're getting into the timber business. Martin says it's a top-secret project and not a lot of people inside Basin even know about it."

"I don't see how they keep that a secret inside Basin," said Hilton. "Let me dig around and see if I can come up with anything."

"So, do you want me to stay on this or not?" asked Larry. Larry was half hoping that Hilton would tell him to pull out, especially since they now thought it was timber and paper.

"Yeah, I guess stick it out for a bit. I didn't plan for you to go to Cheeseland to be a forest ranger. But I was the one who asked you to check this out, so I guess if I've hired you for ten days, you should see where it leads."

"Well, just so you know, I got Martin to pay me eleven hundred a day so I'm officially off your payroll."

"Well that's nice. Now I know for sure that I want you to stay. But I'll still pay you the thousand a day. Let's see how this goes. Keep me in the loop. And call me in a few days to give me an update. I might nose around Basin and see what they're up to."

"Okay, I'm going to go get some leases signed up," said Larry. "But be careful when you're poking around. Martin made it clear that if word got out on this deal, it could easily kill it. If you start asking questions, it won't take a rocket scientist to figure out that you and I and Martin are all talking."

"Yeah, yeah. I'm not an idiot. Like I say, I might just nose around a little bit if I get the chance. Not sure I know anybody over there anymore anyway since they chopped all those heads last year." Hilton was lying again.

"Just be careful. I haven't been real busy over the last two months and I can use the eleven grand. And neither of us wants this in the business section of the Chronicle tomorrow."

"Yeah, yeah, I know," said Hilton. "I gotta go."

From Larry's perspective, the conversation had gone extremely well with Hilton. As long as Hilton didn't poke around with the wrong guy at Basin, this would stay quiet. Larry shaved and got dressed in his favorite land man outfit: a nice pair of gray slacks, well pressed, and a long-sleeved shirt with the Sears Arnold Palmer logo over the pocket. Most of these farmers weren't that much different from the ones in Texas or Oklahoma. They expected people to wear nice clean clothes, and if they owned a dress shirt, odds are they bought it from either Sears or Penney's or Wal-Mart. He took his "leasing briefcase" out of his suitcase and set it up on the table. Larry smiled at the worn "AAA" and the "Go Army" stickers he had put on the side of it twenty years ago. Nice touch.

Larry reached down into his briefcase and took out the stack of legal lease forms that Martin had given him, the box of business cards, the MEC checkbook and threw them into the fire in the big pot-bellied stove. Next, he took from his suitcase his own standard lease forms in the name of one of his companies that he had set up for prior work, Walker Resources LLC. He hadn't used this company for a while, but he still had his own Walker Resources LLC check book and business cards. He looked them over carefully and then placed them into the weathered leather briefcase.

This time Larry didn't care who was paying him or how much. From the old newspaper clipping, Larry figured that somehow Martin must have discovered oil up here in northern Wisconsin. This time, Larry wasn't about to let either Hilton or Martin get rich while he stood by and watched. These leases were going to be in Larry's name. Picking up the briefcase, he stepped into the bathroom one last time to check his appearance, pushed his shoulders back and smiled his famous smile. Still had the "southern gentlemen" smile. This was the start of something very good for Larry Walker.

CHAPTER 25

TAYLOR HAD GOTTEN UP AT 5:45 AND SAT IN THE CUPOLA overlooking the capitol to the east. She didn't always get up this early, but she always set her coffee pot to come on at 5:30 as an extra incentive. She didn't merely *sip* coffee; she *drank* it down. She had an oversized mug at the office, too. Still, in one of the big, oversized flannel shirts she slept in, this one from her dad, she skirted down the stairs and headed for the kitchen. Her message machine was blinking emptily at her on the counter. She hit the messages button and began pouring coffee. The first two messages were hang-ups; she got a lot of those. A call from the movie rental place. Then the fourth call was odd, even by her standards—a long pause, a man breathing, and finally a simple phrase: "We've done our job, now you do yours." Another long pause, and a loud clank of the receiver as the caller hung up. Even with her first taste of steaming coffee, a shiver rocked down through her body to the soles of her bare feet. She had unlisted her number a couple of years ago, but she still got her share of crank calls. This was not, however, a crank call. It could be an accident that she had gotten this unnerving call. She wasn't sure what it meant, but she wondered about a number of things, including the Superior deal. Lots of people had threatened to politically destroy her along the way, but she felt physically threatened by the blunt message from this unknown caller. Slowly, she walked to the bay windows around the back breakfast room and peered carefully around the yard. Nothing. Carefully, she walked to the front of the house, checked the street through the side windows on the porch, then quickly opened the door, grabbed the stack of morning papers, and slammed and dead-bolted the front door.

Retreating to her sanctuary upstairs, it was still a few minutes before six. Like many mornings, relaxing a bit up in the third story of the big old house, she settled into looking over all of the documents on her PC that Jason and her staff had put together for the day. And at the same time, she would alternately find herself drinking her coffee, watching the city get going, and scanning the morning papers: The Cardinal, The New York Times, The Capitol Times and others. Nothing in the Cardinal, but her stomach knotted on page one of the Cap Times. It was buried in a larger article about the upcoming gubernatorial election—an unconfirmed source saying that Clark Everson, the lieutenant governor, might not seek re-election. She thought of the message on her answering machine. Her heart skipped a beat and she wanted to call Jason. She knew from her experience that state capitols all over the country had rumors like these floating around all of the time. This one was a bit unusual because she was reading it here in the paper instead of hearing it at work. Someone must have directly called the paper last night for the express purpose of getting it on the front page before it could be denied. They had done their job, now she was supposed to do hers.

It was perfectly clear and crisp out. The sun was shining on the statue of Lady Liberty at the top of the capitol dome. It was time for Taylor to eat some cinnamon toast, get dressed and get to the office. She had a big day ahead. Any big press day was navy blue. She was dressed in ten minutes. Jason would pick her up at 7:15 a.m., but it was just after 6:30 a.m. She brushed back her earlier fears and took off for the three-block walk up to the Capitol.

Three hours later, the hearing chambers at the capitol building were more crowded than she had ever seen. Last time, the press was composed mostly of campus communication majors, middle-aged reporters from the local papers and television, and a handful from northern Wisconsin; two from the Superior newspapers—now that it was clear that the hearing had statewide impact, and represented a battle between the big oil companies, liberals and the Greens. Both the Chicago Tribune and the Houston Chronicle had sent people; so had the St. Paul Pioneer Press. One of Jason's guys had said the local stations were doing a segment for the national evening news. Not many knew it, but two weeks ago, The Wall Street Journal had actually assigned a staffer to develop a story around this. Taylor couldn't believe it hadn't hit the press yet.

For the last two hours Taylor and Jason had closely pored over the oil companies' "best and final offer." Even Jason had to admit that they had come along way. They had made some very nice concessions to conservation initiatives underway in other areas of Wisconsin, but then they had actually slightly expanded the refinery addition from what they had originally proposed. Their entire message was built around one of what they called "balanced growth," and it would play extremely well in every place outside of Madison. Most of Madison residents wanted nothing to do with harming the environment, regardless of the economics. Taylor hadn't made any promises to Jason. In fact, she had indi-

175

cated that if things were going the right way, she would look for a deal. Finally, they headed off to the hearing.

There was such a crowd that Taylor had to physically push herself behind Jason to get into the chambers. Suddenly inside, it seemed unnaturally quiet as her team unpacked their briefcases and supporting materials for the hearing. The gallery was packed with reporters. All of her old buddies were here—Dick Jansen from Empire Oil and Sheldon Mack from Arbor Energy. At 9:30, the administrative judge brought the gavel firmly down on the old oak conference table and called the meeting to order. Taylor found herself in a tough position, if she didn't work out something agreeable to the oil companies, they'd expose her and ruin her. If she went off too quickly in a conciliatory manner, her staff and most of Madison would sense betrayal. The environmentalists would be picketing her before she got back to her office. Of course, many would be unhappy no matter what she did. The gallery was packed full as the judge called for opening comments from big oil.

"Your honor," the oil company lead counsel began, "I want the court to know that under the leadership of Ms. Thompson and the DNR, the oil companies have arrived at a compromise solution. We believe this solution will provide new jobs and growth for the people of Wisconsin, and we believe it rightly reflects an investment we are ready to make in six major conservation initiatives already underway in Wisconsin. Not only have we made tremendous strides in reducing the environmental impact of our facilities, with some adjustments we have added a greater number of jobs to the entity with an addition of a high tech, state-of-the-art lubricants-blending and packaging facility."

The judge was shaking his head sternly back and forth. He had seen it too many times. This case had been dragging on for more than eight months, and now the oil companies were changing their design plans. His guess was that "Ms.

Thompson" was going to live up to her TNT nickname and just explode. God, he hated running a circus for the press. Grimacing slightly, he looked down the DNR side of the table as Taylor sat calmly staring at the oil company counsel as he droned on. At one juncture, counsel handed out a two-page summary of the oil company final proposal that was actually slightly better than the draft she and Jason had been reviewing less than an hour ago. In the next minute, maybe five, it was going to be show time for Taylor. Even though the deal wasn't so bad, she felt dirty giving in to them, especially under the circumstances. Momentarily, she had a flashback to the library back in the governor's mansion less than a month ago. If these guys decided to crush her, they would probably be successful unless she somehow could outmaneuver them.

"Ms. Thompson, you or your designee now have the floor," the judge said, his somber tone jarring her back to reality. He looked at her over the top of his glasses, motioning toward the State's lectern. He had been the faculty advisor to Law Review her second year. If some lawyers from New York or Houston thought they were going to come into Madison and pull one over on the locals, they were sadly mistaken. If she ever needed a recess, a motion, a multi-day stay of proceedings, with her old law school professor, all she had to do was ask. If it was even close to the realm of appropriateness, she had it. Today was a little different, even though she had Jason beckoning for a morning break to review the latest proposal, she slowly gathered various compilations of documents, and after some length, moved to the lectern. The entire courtroom focused on her every move, awaiting the state's response.

She spoke with no benefit of prepared remarks for she had just been handed the latest oil company proposal minutes earlier. Still, she seemed completely at ease, to the point of taking her coffee cup with her to the podium.

"Your honor, esteemed colleagues, all of us have worked long and hard to craft an approach which balances our over-riding concern for the environment with the real needs for jobs, growth and economic prosperity for the people of Wisconsin. We will need additional time in committee with state and industry representatives to review and finalize the details of the proposal as outlined this morning. However, I would like to say that the state of Wisconsin believes that the proposal by these oil companies represents a break-through in providing balanced growth to the people and in-dustry of Wisconsin. I applaud the efforts of the senior ex-ecutives of these companies, and your Honor, I believe we have the basis for granting approval to the oil companies the right to move forward on this facility. At this time, the State will seek no injunctions that would impair the progress of Superior Oil Refining and Lubricants Company as outlined in defendants' draft proposal, and we look forward to finaliz-ing the terms over the coming days."

The stunned Judge looked from Taylor, to the oil com-pany table, back to Taylor and then up to the huge old Waltham clock on the wall. Finally, no more than fifteen minutes into the proceeding, he slammed down the gavel firmly on his desk and announced to all that no injunction would be granted against the oil companies in the State vs. Superior Refining matter. Court was adjourned. As the fat, balding, graying oil men in suits warmly congratulated each other, jeers from the gallery overwhelmed Taylor with "trai-tor," "wimp" and "sucker," and worse. Jason, not looking or speaking to her, quickly packed his things and deftly darted out through the clerk's alcove. She was left alone to slowly pack the huge stack of documents in front of her chair into her worn briefcase. There would be no big press conference today. She had let the day belong to the oil companies.

CHAPTER 26

TAYLOR HAD CALLED THE FAIRMONT HERSELF TO REQUEST a lake view room. There was a commuter flight down from Madison, but she had taken off right after lunch and took her time driving down. When she got to Elgin, she stopped for a rest. She spent over an hour drinking coffee at the over-the-freeway McDonald's, just watching the cars and trucks streaming below her. Most of the cars had one passenger, possibly a businessman on a client call, a worker returning from her day, a student, a trucker, or a nurse. An occasional car had a nice family in it, with Dad sitting very upright driving and Mom looking across the seat toward him, engaged in conversation to pass the time, probably catching up in their busy lives, kids dozing in the back seat. She poured the sugar packet out onto the serving tray and made tiny designs in it with her stirring stick. Then she would stare at the cars for a while—even found herself counting them—and then turned back to her little sugar pile, first piling it all closely together, and then spreading it broadly and evenly out over the thin paper cover on the tray. A couple of men had waited to catch her eye, and smiled at her, but she returned a cold, lifeless stare that immediately made them glance quickly off in another direction.

It had now been two weeks since Martin had called her. He had seen that she was a speaker at the Chicago API Conference, talking about environmental regulations and issues. He really wanted to have dinner with Taylor and catch up with her. She thought back to their steamy encounters in northern Wisconsin. Martin also said he needed to talk to her about some business. When she started joking with him about what kind of "business" he had in mind, he had immediately gotten very serious and asked that she not mention to anyone that they were meeting. Strange.

CHAPTER 27

"GOOD MORNING, MA'AM, I AM LARRY WALKER WITH Walker Resources, and I am wondering if I could speak with you or the man of the house about some timber-related business."

Jesus, this was easy. Not only was he good at this, these people were just so trusting. He had been in Houston too long. Maybe he could come up here in a few years and buy a small piece of land on a lake. Great fishing. Long bow season for deer. A man could just live off the land. Get a double-wide like this guy had done. Good people up here, too. Kept to their own business.

"Why Mr. Walker, Roy went down to the co-op about an hour ago to pick up some drill bits. He should be back any minute. You can either sit and have a cup while I put away these dishes or stop back later."

"Oh Ma'am, I couldn't trouble you for some coffee, I'll just wait out in the car for your husband to get back," he said, turning convincingly back out the door.

By the time Roy returned, Larry and Helen had become pretty good friends. Roy was sixty-two, on disability from the phone company for the past ten years. A lineman, he had taken a bad fall and hurt his back. No brothers or sisters so they owned the land themselves. That was the worst, when one of the kids was living on the family farm. They were both on their second marriage. Helen's dad had actually bought them the land when they got married. The factory had towed the double-wide all the way from Wausau to the site back here in the woods. One daughter was divorced, working in Superior as a nurse's aide.

"Is that the new Oldsmobile?" asked Roy as he came through the front door.

"Yeah," said Larry, never missing a beat. "They call her the Aurora. It's a rental of course, but I really like it. This one's got the V6 in it, so it's got pretty good get-up-and-go for one of the newer cars." Roy was smoking a pipe, looking a lot younger than sixty-two. Didn't look like his back was hurting him much, either. He still looked lean enough to strap on those spikes and walk a pole.

"Ain't that the truth," said Roy. "Seems like you can't even buy a car with a V8 anymore. Name's Roy, what can I do for ya?"

A helluva handshake. Larry would need to be pretty direct with this one.

"I'm with a small timber company called Walker Resources. We're in the pulp and paper business, supplying pulp feedstock to the mills down in Georgia."

Roy leaned back in his chair and folded his arms across his chest. "We ain't really interested in pulping off the land, Larry."

"I couldn't agree with you more," said Larry. "If all this was about was pulping off the land, I don't think I'd have the stomach to do it. For years, all the company would do is clean off the pulp trees and replant them with the cheapest, fastest growing trees they could find. Then in another five or six years, they'd be back in, cleaning off the land again and replanting the same old cheap trees. They made a fortune. But a couple of years ago, the company founder came down with lung cancer. He started thinking about, you know, giving something back. It turns out that when he died, he left his estate and company in a trust dedicated to conservation. That's when I decided to come to work for the company. So now, rather than just pulp off land and replant it with cheap stock for the next round of milling, we replace it with top quality, hybrid hardwoods."

"What kind of hardwoods," asked Roy. He was leaning forward over the table now, puffing slowly on the pipe.

"We analyze lands all over the country to find prime spots to do this and we think this area around the State Forest is best for a mix of oak and walnut. I am told oak was one of the primary hardwoods here more than a hundred years ago." Larry had perfected this story. All of his leases contained language that gave him all of the underground mineral rights to the land, as well as the right to clear-cut. But he wasn't telling anybody about the oil reserves, right under their noses.

"Yep, was mostly oak, and of course, white pine. Not jack pine like the junk that is out there today, but big white pine. Grandpa said that some of those trees were so big that sometimes one forty-foot section of a tree would fill up a whole flatbed rail car."

"Actually," said Larry, "my grandfather was one of the boys that did some of the original cutting up here. His dad was a no-good drunk who finally just up and left them when Gramp was just a little boy down in Shreveport. When he was twelve, he hitched a riverboat ride up here on the Mississippi from New Orleans to Prescott. Came right up the St. Croix with some loggers. Got a job carting sawdust in a wheelbarrow at one of the big mills down by Spooner. He got paid fifty cents a day and all he could eat."

Larry took a long drink of coffee and a breath. Best to slow down with people. "So, he never talked about himself, but one time when my brother and I were squabbling over some candy, he said he worked the entire first year and sent back every single penny he made to his Mom and two sisters. Joined the Army as one of the first machine gunners back in the First Big War and made it through all right. Settled back in Shreveport after the war and never made it back up here."

"You got family?" asked Helen.

"Well, not really," said Larry. "Divorced, no kids."

Larry looked over at Roy and Helen. Helen had stopped working on the dishes and just stood quietly leaning against the Frigidaire; one of those short, rounded ones you see on My Three Sons reruns. She was holding a dish rag and a pan, as if drying it, but she just stood there motionless, listening to Larry's story.

"Ma and I are against pulping, that's for sure. But this one's a little different ain't it Ma?"

Helen nodded her head slowly.

"I don't expect to barge in here and hit you guys with this cold. I understand you want some time to think it over, so I really just stopped by today to meet you and tell you what we're trying to do. I'll also leave off a copy of this standard lease here in case you want your lawyer to have a look at it. The only thing that's different is the length of it is pretty long, given the time it takes to grow out those big trees, and there are very restrictive conditions on the selective cutting that can begin no earlier than five years from the date the lease is signed."

Roy gushed with laughter.

"Five years from now, let's see, I'll be pushing seventy. Probably won't care what you cut."

"Well to tell you the truth, if a landowner is only thinking about money, he maybe shouldn't sign up for this, because at this point the company is more like a Conservation Agency than a big money-making corporation. You'll also see in the fine print that we are paying the same going rate as what you could get from any of the other pulp companies, it's just that we aren't coming in and stripping off the land like they are. The other favor I need you to do for me is to keep this quiet for the next three weeks or so when I am going around talking to your neighbors about it. For this to be successful, I need to work real hard and privately to get all of the fifteen or so acreage owners around you to sign up. The old man who left all the money made it clear he didn't want somebody putting up a Dairy Queen in the middle of his forest. If I don't get all of the landowners in an area, Walker Resources will make me just walk away and not proceed with the venture. To tell you the truth, we can't afford to have one hold out asking for more money than what everybody else is getting. It just isn't fair to you or economical for the long term. But you guys take your time and talk it over. I've taken too much of your time already."

"Well, it wasn't like we had a big day planned," said Helen, smiling at Roy carefully as she turned to put the old aluminum pot in a big drawer underneath the oven.

"Yeah," said Roy straightening up in the chair, "my motto these days is if you don't get it done today, you can just get it done tomorrow." Then all three of them laughed together.

"Roy, if you want, you can ask Mr. Walker to stay for some lunch. It's almost eleven thirty."

"Oh," said Larry, "I wouldn't feel right putting you out like that."

"Not putting us out one bit," said Roy. "Would you like to stay and eat with us?"

"I wouldn't want you to go to any trouble. I usually just have a sandwich back at my cabin over at Deep Lake."

"No trouble at all," said Helen. "We'd be glad to have you stay."

"Well maybe just for a bite, but then I need to let you get on with your day."

"I'll put on an extra plate."

Larry never went in to one of these initial meetings expecting to get a signed lease. Mentally, he always planned for three visits and then, if it happened on the second, it would be a nice surprise, and if it took a fourth, that would be okay, too. But an hour and a half later, when he backed his Aurora away from the house, they were standing on the porch waving good-bye, and he had a signed lease for fifty years of oil and timber rights on three hundred acres in the heart of Chequamegon State Forest.

The truth was, he already had fifteen leases, and those leases were sitting safely back in the cabin in a big, red accordion file. Well, that included Mel Baker's "signature," if that's what you want to call it. He just told every single one of these landowners to swear to secrecy, and how he needed to get everybody to sign up, or they wouldn't get big money. And of course, he lied about the timber and pulping too. He was after the mineral rights—the oil—but nobody had come close to suspecting that. After that big lunch, Larry was ready for a nap back at Deep Lake Lodge.

CHAPTER 28

LARRY HAD LAID LOW FOR A FEW DAYS AFTER THEY HAD found Melvin Baker. Now he had only to sign up the two remaining landholders inside the bounds of the state forest. Late in the morning he had walked out of the rustic, wooden cabin overlooking the lake and trudged steadily across the old cinder drive to his car, his cordovan penny loafers grinding unaccustomedly on the path. Throwing his leather case into the back seat, he grabbed the ice scraper from the floor behind the driver's seat. He began scraping away the thin layer of crusty ice that had gathered on the windshield. Very light snow flurries were whirling about in the leftover fall leaves. The snow was coming in off Lake Superior, bringing with it silent little promise after promise of the winter to come. Occasionally, an errant flake would catch Larry by surprise on the open skin behind his collar and spread an icy chill over him as he leaned over the windshield.

It wasn't as if Larry had to explain his actions to anybody. Larry knew that going about his business in a consistent and predictable manner could only serve to continue to build his legitimacy with the small number of people at the lodge or in the community that knew enough about him to strike up a conversation. Larry was no stranger to this area. He had been up here in his early days as a lease hunter. Northern Pipeline Company, NPC, as they were called in Minneapolis, had been intending to build a new natural gas pipeline across northern Wisconsin and Michigan since 1978. At the time, Larry had been doing pretty standard work in the West Texas oil fields, working leases for NPC, and they had asked him to take a six-month assignment in northern Wisconsin to lease the right-of-way for the pipeline. He was single at the time, and though he moaned and groaned about it, he had actually relished the idea of being up in "Sportsman's Paradise," living high on the company expense account. At that time, he had stayed, for the most part, in hotels in Superior and Ashland. They were two of the only towns up around there that had more than five thousand inhabitants—something to keep a young man occupied. But even though his hotels were miles away from Iron River, he became familiar with the entire area. The NPC pipeline was to run north of Federal Highway 2, through the aptly named "Barrens" country north of Chequamegon. On many days, Larry had eaten lunch in Iron River.

When Larry first arrived on the scene at that time nearly twenty years ago, he first thought his task hopeless. The first three landowners that Larry had called on that year, had actually ordered Larry off their land. One of them had threatened him with a deer rifle. NPC had the right, through legal court proceedings, to take "non-participating" farmers and landowners such as these to court and sue for eminent domain. This would legally require those in the path of the pipeline to finally give up and lease their right of way to NPC for a settlement price. But such court proceedings would take the company much longer to gain approval for the pipeline and were likely to cost the company four times more than a landowner would, who'd be willing to lease his land in a friendly business transaction. At the end of the week, when Larry had reported his lack of progress back to his manager in Houston, the man had become belligerent. His boss told Larry to essentially get off his ass and get some leases signed, or else. His manager closed the conversation by suggesting to Larry that perhaps he would not need a return trip back to Houston, if he did not start showing some progress on his assignment. Today, Larry would consider killing a man who would dare to talk to him like that. At first, the then young Larry had become worried that his job could be at risk, and then he became angry at the lack of respect and support he was getting from his home office. Depressed, Larry had found himself sitting among the beat-up Formica tables and Naugahyde barstools of the Green Top in Iron River. Behind the bar hung a weathered picture of Eisenhower, grinning into the camera and clutching a rainbow trout from a visit there after the Big War. Eisenhower had come to fish the Brule River—some of the best trout fishing in the world. It was on that night that Larry had met a man named Vern Patterson. Vern was a long-time local guy. Vern and his father had gone to the same high school in Iron River. His grandfather had gone there to school through the sixth grade. They were third generation in this god-forsaken town. After seeing action in Saipan during World War II, Vern had worked for the county for thirty-five years; first as a mechanic, and then on the road crew. On the side, he had dabbled in selling insurance and real estate. After six children, he and his wife enjoyed a meager existence in a double-wide trailer home overlooking Bluebird Lake down by Delta.

Vern had come into the bar that night on crutches, his leg in a cast. He had "twisted his knee funny" falling over a log out in the woods, and torn cartilage. Having had surgery earlier in the week, this was he and Pat's first outing since he had gotten out of the hospital. Vern was depressed because he was going to be laid up, out of work for eight weeks while his knee healed up. He was going to get almost ninety dollars a week in worker's compensation, but after just two days, Vern was getting cabin fever laying around the house, drinking beer and listening to Guy Lombardo music. Vern had struck up a conversation with the young Larry, and before Larry knew it, he had made a deal with Vern, where Vern would accompany him on his leasing activities. It turned out that Vern knew every single one of the landowners in the whole area—how many kids they had, where they worked, how much land they owned. Vern had either maintained phone lines on their property, installed or fixed their phone, or tried to sell them some insurance along the way. In planning for the new pipeline, NPC financial and planning experts had figured that it would take Larry at least four months to secure leases from the two-thirds majority of landowners they needed to push the deal through. As it turned out, Larry and Vern had gotten every single landowner to sign up in just over four weeks. Larry had gotten a big enough bonus out of the deal to buy a used red Mercedes 450SL. For years, NPC used Larry and this experience, as an example of how to make things happen in the oil business. Vern was rewarded with a more than acceptable hourly wage for his "consulting services." He was happy most of the time to be exploring the countryside with Larry, hobbling into a local café, restaurant or bar for a steak and fries or fish and chips lunch. He would routinely chastise young Larry, the "southern gentleman," as Vern called him, for remaining unerringly cordial and polite, and leaving a hefty tip, no matter how bad the food or service.

This morning, after clearing the car windows of ice, Larry tossed the ice scraper in through the still open back car door and slid onto the cold seat of the rental car. A lot had changed for Larry over the last twenty years. Then, he had been a young buck, innocent, above-board, looking to be recognized for his efforts, and seeking to work his way to the top. These days, he found himself a hardened man. Long ago, he had realized that since nobody was going to look out for him, he was going to have to look out for himself. Settling into his mid-forties, twice divorced, he had made some money along the way, and for the most part had spent it. Working on a contract basis, he still had one club membership, but he was renting an apartment in west Houston and driving an old car. His parents were gone. No family. While most people thought Larry was still doing pretty well, in reality he had his life savings, consisting of eighteen thousand dollars in a checking account. His Walker Resources business account still had a revolving line of credit, but all of these checks he was writing would have to be repaid one way or another. Once in a while, Hilton, or one of his other old buddies, would throw a job his way. Larry was scraping by. Larry was alone. Maybe this was going to be the big one for him.

CHAPTER 29

IT WAS A BIG DAY FOR LIZ. HER YOUNGER DAUGHTER HAD gotten serious about swimming, and Liz needed to get her to early morning practice and get back by the time her older daughter finished breakfast. Liz lumbered out of the driveway and made the trip to drop her off. One third of all the Chevrolet Suburbans sold in the United States are sold in Texas. Generally, they are not being driven around by tall, lanky, dusty cowboys out by Big Spring. And they are not being driven around by big, husky, refinery workers down along the Ship Channel in Pasadena. They are family vehicles often driven by women just like Liz who are living in Houston and Dallas and San Antonio and Austin. Off Liz went with her trusty cell phone by her side. Thankfully, they were only ten minutes from school, but that was still twenty minutes round trip before most people in the neighborhood were even up. A quick stop by Starbucks on the way back to the house. Then she'd drop the older one off at the start of school. She always tried to do maajor grocery shopping on Wednesdays, and she was playing racquetball after lunch. The younger daughter had lost a little screw on a pair of glasses, so Liz also had to stop by an eyewear place and get that fixed. Every day it was something that took twice as long as it was supposed to.

Finally, tonight she was "going out," as she told the kids, which meant she either had a date or was meeting one of her girlfriends from the club for dinner and maybe going to a movie or something. Tonight, it was a date—her fourth with a guy named Kerry. It was a little bit weird, but she continued to insist on driving to a neutral location to meet, usually the Houstonian, and then go out from there. She didn't need Kerry coming by the house to pick her up. Not only was it easier on the kids, she told herself, but it gave the neighbors a lot less to talk about.

It had been different with Martin gone. She felt it the most right after she got the kids to bed. Most of the days he had left early in the morning and so he wasn't around much at breakfast. He'd usually be home in time for dinner, but it was such a busy time with the kids coming and going, that they really didn't have much time to talk. It was really only at the end of the day, when they got everybody settled down for the night, that the two of them would sit around the kitchen table and talk, and it was those times that she missed now. He had called several times since the split, mostly just to ask how she was doing. It had all stayed strictly business. She would give him a complete rundown on the girls, tell him a number of things she had spent money on, and then they would cordially end the call.

She was exhausted by the time she got done playing racquetball. Stephanie had been divorced for two years and practically lived at the club. She was in great shape and probably played racquetball five days a week. Liz was lucky to play five days a month. Both drenched, and now starving, they retreated to the juice bar to talk and get something to eat.

"So, how are things going with Kerry?" Stephanie was always either asking who Liz was going out with or telling Liz about her own latest boyfriend.

"He's fine, it's going fine."

"So how many times have you been out now?" She was putting a huge handful of alfalfa sprouts on her salad.

"Actually, we met for coffee twice. Dinner once. Dinner again tonight."

"Oh, four times. Just for the record, have you been out with anyone else yet four times?"

"Sure, lots of them, but that was twenty years ago," and then they both laughed like schoolgirls. In some ways, Liz didn't like Stephanie—or anyone else—talking about her private life, but at times it was really fun. A few times they had spent hours talking over all the men they knew, mostly talking about all of the stupid stuff the guys had said or done. They also spent a fair amount of time talking about how much money they thought some of them had. A couple of the guys Liz had met had also dated Stephanie. At first, it seemed weird that they both had dated the same guy, but by now Liz had gotten used to it. Most of the time Stephanie had gathered a lot more intelligence on the guy than she had, and they would cross check their stories. When one of the guys got talking about his ranch out in Brenham, Stephanie had learned it was his uncle's ranch. One of the other guys took a pretty nice trip every month or so, but he worked for a wealthy guy who liked to have sales meetings in resort locations and charge it all off to company expense. One of the only nice guys Liz had been out with, was real quiet and lived in a nice, but pretty meager bottom-half apartment in a big house in Montrose. Stephanie had showed her an old newspaper article one time with a story about this guy inventing and founding a computer disk drive company and being bought out for a couple hundred million. She had even gotten on the net to see how many shares of stock he still had in the company. He was modest and living way below the radar. Yes, he was loaded, but Stephanie had found him so boring, she sure wasn't going to marry into that. In fact, on one of their "dates," he had taken her to dinner and then to Astrohall Convention Center and walked through a computer exposition. Liz had laughed until tears ran down her cheeks when Stephanie had told that story—definitely not what Stephanie was looking for. Besides, with that much money, the guy's lawyer would demand a pre-nup anyway, so a divorce later wouldn't do anybody very much good.

"How's the sex been?" asked Stephanie.

Momentarily, Liz was taken aback. "Actually, I haven't had that much of it, but it has been good."

"Yeah, most of these guys are older and they know they've got to work for it. Or they act like they've got something to prove." Stephanie was smiling.

"It's a welcome change, I'll say that. Martin always said he was too tired," said Liz.

"That's such bullshit. I wouldn't have guessed that with Martin." Stephanie paused. "So, what do you think of Kerry, could he be the right guy?" continued Stephanie.

"I don't think anybody could be the guy right now," said Liz.

"Why not?"

"Well, for one thing, I've got the girls to think about. It's not like Martin is out of my life. it's only been a month since I asked him to move out."

"Jeez, when you say that, I still can't believe you had the guts to tell him to move out."

"It wasn't guts. I didn't want to do it. We *had* to do it. We were hardly even talking anymore; we didn't agree on anything."

"What were you fighting about?"

"We weren't fighting; we just didn't agree on anything. He hardly talked at all."

"Like what? What didn't you agree on?" Stephanie and Liz had been over parts of this a number of times. Stephanie should have been a marriage counselor or a therapist. Her own personal life was screwed up, like most marriage counselors, but somehow that just made her more of an expert on how not to screw up somebody else's life.

"Well, we didn't agree on the house," said Liz flatly.

"What about the house?"

"I thought we needed a big addition and some remodeling, and he liked it just the way it was. He said it was homey, and if we started ripping it up, it was never going to be the same house again."

"So, did he tell you that you couldn't remodel the house?"

"No, he just said he didn't want to."

"What kind of addition do you want?"

"Big master bedroom and bath, and closets—*lots* of closets. We also talked about putting a big family room out behind the garage."

"So why didn't you do it?"

"Martin didn't want to. He just said he was okay with the house the way it was."

"Gee, I can see that's grounds for divorce," said Stephanie, now grinning again. "He didn't support you in your desire to add on a master bedroom and bath."

"Actually, when I think about it, that's not the main reason we are separated. It's not the addition; that's just one thing. It's the thing about just being okay with the way things are. He was like that on everything. If the kids were doing okay in school, if the neighbors didn't invite us to a party, he didn't seem to care. It was like he had just lost heart. He wanted more with his job, but he seemed resigned to accept the way it was. I'm still young. I want more for our family and our kids—and myself, okay—and Martin was just giving up and saying, "Okay, this is it." Goodness knows he's a hard worker. He just lost his sense of adventure."

"He's still pretty cute. I saw him grocery shopping at Randall's over on Woodway on Tuesday, and he had on jeans and a flannel shirt. Looked like the Marlboro Man to me. It looked like he was eating real healthy too, lots of fresh fruit and veggies in his cart. Maybe when your divorce goes through, you'll let me have a crack at him."

"You are the worst! Can't believe you checked out his grocery cart!" Liz laughed. "You stay away from him. He's always liked brunettes, especially brunettes with nice butts."

Liz was reflective, "You know, I'm still attracted to him. But you know what, he even lost interest in me. He'd always say he was too tired, or maybe we should wait until tomorrow night. Then he'd want to move really close to me in bed and hold me and he'd be sound asleep in about one minute."

"Some of the guys I've been with should stick to cuddling anyway. I'm starting to like this guy more all the time."

"It was great before we got kids. We made love all the time. Over the past year, a lot of nights, Martin would doze off in his chair and I'd take the dog for a while last year after

I out for a run in the neighborhood just to work off some steam. I mean, a lot of the time it was nine o'clock and Martin's lying, there sawing logs."

"Liz, I think your problem is you've got too much energy. Read a book, that's what *I* used to do."

"Hey, I'm a woman, too. Not to sound trite, but I've got needs too, okay? If I've got to force the guy to make love to me every night, it doesn't do a lot for my sense of self-worth, either, know what I mean? I mean, what's the matter with me? I think I still look pretty damn good for having kids. *I'd* sleep with me." Now Liz was smiling too.

"I'd sleep with you, too," said Stephanie. And then they both laughed hysterically, getting looks from everyone.

"Look," said Liz, "this isn't about me getting enough sex. But take Todd, for example. Remember last year, the club was running the "buy six sessions, get six free" special on personal trainers? I was getting stale working out, so I wanted to do something a little different, and I signed up."

"Yes, I remember. I thought you signed up because Todd was going to be your personal trainer."

"I swear, not at all. In fact, when I signed up, Todd wasn't even working here. You couldn't pick your trainer anyway. The club assigned you one. Otherwise, everybody would've wanted to pick from only the three best ones, and the whole reason they did the promotion was to get work for the less popular trainers; you know, get them acquainted with some new customers."

"For now, I will believe you. Anyway, go on."

"So, I get a call from a guy—says he's Todd—he's just graduated from SMU with a degree in exercise physiology and he's going to be my trainer, so we set up an appointment for my first session. I get to the club a half-hour early and I'm warming up and stretching and this guy comes over by me on the mats and starts stretching himself. He's amazingly limber and he's in awesome shape."

"And of course, it's Todd."

"At first, I thought it could be him, but this guy was older, he certainly wasn't just out of college. But after we both stretched, neither of us talking, we ended up standing over by the sports desk where we'd agreed to meet and of course, it did turn out to be Todd."

"What's the point?"

"The two of us got to know each other pretty well. I mean, you're together a couple of times a week for an hour or more and you're sweating and working together and talking."

"You had sex with Todd."

"No! I didn't, even though I know half of the people that work up there thought we did."

"Okay, again, so what's the point?"

"Well, after about the tenth session, we knew each other pretty well. I had already told Todd I wasn't going to be taking any more personal training sessions because it was just too expensive, and I didn't really need a personal trainer, year-round anyway. And he started telling me how great I looked. He went back to that first morning when he had seen me warming up on the mats. He described in detail the thoughts that were going through his head, what he'd like to do with me, how he wanted to make love to me, what he thought would make me feel good. At the time, I was, first of all, embarrassed, and then I was so turned on I couldn't hardly do anything the rest of the day. I almost got in a wreck over on Post Oak, because I was daydreaming about what he would do to me if we were together."

"Oh, this is good." Stephanie was leaning forward now, speaking in soft tones. "So, what did he say he wanted to do to you?"

"Yeah, like I'm going to tell you that. I'll tell you one thing though—he said he'd love to spend a whole day with me just making love. At first, I was embarrassed even thinking about it, but you know, after I thought about it for a while, it made me mad. I can't get my husband to even do it with me, and here's this hot-looking, young guy that wants to sneak off with me for the whole day. I'm sorry, but that's just not the way it's supposed to be. We spent most of the last two so-called personal training sessions talking dirty to each other. I didn't care, for me the fantasy was worth it. In fact, after he was done telling me the stuff he wanted to do to me, I started telling him the stuff I was going to do to him."

"You are so bad. I had no idea you would talk dirty to a man like that."

"Well, I never had. I never cheated on Martin, either. After my final session, Todd and I were friends and we would chat from time to time, but we just kept it friendly. He even called me at home and asked me if I wanted to go out for lunch. Basically, I just told him that I thought that we had had some fun together, but I just couldn't spend any more time with him or I would give in to my desires, and I wasn't about to sleep with him when I was still married to Martin."

"But he called you at home."

"Well, he had called before, just to schedule workout times and stuff, so it wasn't like he had to go dig out my number. But this was a couple of weeks after we stopped our training sessions, and I could tell he was pretty disappointed because he thought we were going to get together. Trust me, I was disappointed, too. Anyway, a couple of months later, I told Martin that "getting by wasn't good enough any longer." Todd didn't have anything to do with us separating, but he did get me thinking about a lot of things."

"I know what you mean about thinking about things. Once I got thinking about not being married, it wasn't very long before I got divorced."

"Well, I've got to go. I've still got to get one of the kid's glasses fixed or I'll be crucified at dinner for being a terrible Mom."

"Liz, it was really good talking to you. I also think your racquetball game is improving. I know how much you hate to lose, and that makes it even more fun for me."

"It's not quite so bad losing on a closed court. Next time, we'll play tennis and you can get some public humiliation from me."

"Sounds like a date. Take care."

CHAPTER 30

IT WAS ONLY A TWENTY-MINUTE DRIVE BACK TO DEEP Lake Lodge. Larry was feeling pretty good about his day's work. He decided to take the long way back, driving down Highway H south for almost ten miles to Delta, and then coming back up to Highway 2 on the backroads. It was another gray and dreary December day, and the cold drizzle on the windshield was slowly turning to slush as it collected around the wipers. Inside the car, though, it was warm and dry. Country 101 from Superior playing in the background. Larry was almost finished up. The only problem had been Melvin Baker, but there was always one. Newspaper article had read "Elderly Man Dies in Fire." That had been the end of it.

Larry found himself looking back. He and Hilton Sinclair had been friends for a long time. Well, they weren't friends, but they had known each other and worked together off and on for a very long time. They had made some money together, and Hilton had bailed Larry out a few times when money got tight. Back in the early seventies, Hilton had run a startup exploration and production company. Oil had gone from about five dollars a barrel to thirty-five dollars, and every square inch of Texas and Louisiana was being leased up for oil drilling. Larry had started off as a landman with what used to be Gulf Oil before they were bought up by Chevron. It had taken him a couple of years to learn the ropes and know the right people before he had gone out on his own, kind of a "freelancer," he had told people. Hilton's company had focused a lot of their expertise around the Austin Chalk area, and Larry had gone to high school in Belleville of all places, basically right in the middle of The Chalk, as they called it. Larry had been scouting on his own and taking some of the prime tracts under lease in his own name when Hilton called him for the first time and wanted to have a meeting. They had started off at nine in the evening at one of the urban cowboy kind of bars and ended up closing down Allstar's, one of finer gentlemen's exotic entertainment establishments, also known as a strip joint.

Larry found himself smiling now as he reached Delta and turned north for the drive back. The Delta Lodge, Store and Restaurant had burned down about seven or eight years ago and now there wasn't even a building left standing, but there was still a sign that read, "Delta" and then underneath in real small letters: "Unincorporated."

That had been one helluva night. After they had been to the strip club for about fifteen minutes, Larry discovered that Hilton knew most of the girls, and Larry was asked at one point which one he liked the best. After some serious discussion, he and Hilton had agreed that the tall, leggy blond dancing over on one of the side stages was definitely one of the choicest women they had ever seen, although they were concerned that she might die at any moment from silicone poisoning. At the end of the dance, Hilton had gone over and talked to her and brought her back to the table. Before he knew it, Hilton had given her a thousand dollars and told her that her job was to keep Larry happy for the night. Hilton looked Larry straight in the eye and just explained that it was a business expense. And that was just his first meeting with Hilton. There was an oil boom down in Texas and money was flowing. About that same time, Larry was invited to Hilton's annual "fishing trip" over in Destin. Hilton would fly in eight or ten of his best business associates from the last year, and then eight or ten "hostesses" from the strip clubs in Houston. They would all go out on the Gulf fishing for the weekend on a chartered yacht. Needless to say, fishing wasn't the only recreational activity on the agenda. Years later, people would come up to Larry and ask him in quiet admiration what the "fishing trips" were like.

Through it all, Hilton just seemed to get richer and richer. While Larry made some good money, he was always just the hired man. Even though Hilton always paid him the going rate for his time and took care of him, he never offered Larry equity in any of the deals and he never asked Larry's advice on anything. He would just call him up, tell him what he needed and expect him to go do it. Sinclair was such a pretty boy, had everybody else do his dirty work for him. At first it was just getting leases almost anywhere he could in Austin Chalk. That had been pretty easy for Larry because he knew the area and many of the people. Once in a while, Hilton would ask Larry to put the lease in Hilton's name, not the company's name, and even though Larry knew it was trouble, he did it anyway. Things were moving so fast, in those days some of the investors didn't even care if you were holding a little back for yourself, if that's what it took to keep the money flowing in. There had been a few areas where they had made some pretty good oil discoveries and Hilton had really put the heat on him to pressure some reluctant landowners into signing up. Larry had grown up rough and tumble. After Vietnam, violence never meant much to him one way or another. It was just something people did when they wanted something that somebody else had, usually a woman or money, or in the case of Vietnam, some real estate. Larry had learned long ago that most of the time when you scare someone, or threaten to hurt them, they generally do what you want them to do.

Fifteen years ago, there had been a new discovery south of Bastrop. Hilton had somehow found out that one of the other independent landmen had already signed up five big landowners on his own. Hilton had asked Larry to "go over and talk to the guy about it." A couple of days later, the landman had signed over the leases to Hilton. Hilton was the type of man who would do anything to get something he wanted. Larry hadn't even had to show a gun to the guy. He just followed the guy and waited outside a bar by the guy's car. It was after midnight when the guy came out of the bar. Larry got him in a choke hold up against the car and he just told the guy he really needed to get those leases because he was concerned the guy or someone in his family might be in "an accident or something." He told the guy to think it over and left him his phone number. The next afternoon the guy called him up matter-of-factly and told him he had some leases he wasn't going to pursue and offered to sign them over. Hilton gave the guy ten thousand dollars in cash and gave Larry twenty-five thousand dollars for roughing the guy up. Then Hilton and his investors took more than two hundred thousand barrels off those leases over the next three years. Larry had done all the dirty work for them. And he got a pittance.

That was a long time ago. In those days, there were almost five thousand drilling rigs running in the US, and now there were only about six or seven hundred. Hilton's exploration company had gone bust a long time ago too. Hilton wasn't broke, but he had lost his big money. He had been divorced at least a couple of times too, so he had given away half of what he had left, a couple of times. Somehow Hilton had gotten into the trading business and seemed to be doing all right again. Hilton had been calling him, but Larry wasn't picking up. If Larry pulled this off, if he had all the leases in his name, he was going to have to deal with Hilton and with Martin, too. Technically, Martin was the one who had hired him. One thing at a time, thought Larry. Things were coming along nicely. One thing at a time.

CHAPTER 31

MARTIN HAD CALLED TAYLOR AND SET UP HIS DINNER IN Chicago. Officially, at the office, he was headed for the Chicago API Conference. It was pretty common for geologists and geophysicists to go to these conferences, so it hadn't attracted any attention when he said he was going to be gone a couple of days. Many of his co-workers, and Martin himself, had presented papers at these conferences. Martin had also been on work groups in the industry, trying to solve common problems like blowout prevention, protecting the integrity of surface water while drilling, and any number of subjects around advanced horizontal drilling and downhole production technology. Today it cost half of what it did just ten years ago to find and produce a barrel of oil in the United States, and most of the industry was pretty proud of that. These improvements also had enabled the US to significantly ramp up domestic oil and gas production. Fifteen years ago, everybody was worried the Arabs were going to freeze them to death. Now nobody in Washington or New York seemed to care about secure energy supplies anymore.

If their heater or air conditioner was running, and they had gasoline to put into their cars, who cared where it came from or what might happen five or ten years from now.

As usual, the plane to Chicago was late. They weren't circling ,either, they were still sitting on the ground in Houston because, of all things, a malfunctioning altimeter. They didn't keep spares at Hobby Airport, so someone was driving the part down from Intercontinental. Even on a good day the drive could easily take an hour. They didn't want to let everyone off the plane either, because if they pulled back up to the gate, they would lose their place in line in the landing queue in Chicago. So, there they sat, waiting for the part to show up. When they finally pulled up to the terminal in Chicago it was nearly 8:30 p.m. and the flight was originally scheduled to arrive at 6:00 p.m. Taylor answered on the first ring and basically said she was just worried that something had happened to him. She didn't know what airline he was flying so she couldn't check flight delays, and the weather had been perfect, so she couldn't see why he would be so late. After they talked for a few minutes, she started to relax, and he felt a lot better that she was worried about his welfare, not angry for being late. He still had to pick up his bags and get a taxi; it would be nearly ten o'clock before he would arrive. Dinner reservations had long since passed at the restaurant. It seemed very awkward, but after reviewing their options and joking about the scandal of it all, he finally agreed to come to her room and she would order room service for them. Not the kind of elegant dinner he had been looking forward to with her. But the thought of going to Taylor's room for dinner at ten in the evening was tantalizing.

Like most big cities, the old Midway airport was actually pretty close to downtown, but it seemed like there were a thousand stoplights getting to the lake shore. Coming in over the city at night he had always marveled at its size and order. A light orange hue, a grid that stretched off into infinity, and that long row of tall office buildings and condominiums along Lake Michigan. Chicago had become a pretty popular place, especially when you considered that the Indians had first called the place shi-kaa-kwa, meaning skunk, or smelly, after the garlic plants that used to line the Chicago River two hundred years ago. Even though he couldn't wait to see Taylor, he needed the time in the taxi to get his thoughts together. He kept running scenes through his head and became totally confused with what to say first. There was a time, when they were students back in Madison, that he thought he might marry Taylor. She was three years older than him. He would always study in the third floor "cages" in Memorial Library. They were actually research rooms surrounded by wire mesh, where students working on their doctorates could have a little privacy and lock up all of their stuff. One night in March, during mid-term exams, he had fallen asleep over his books and a woman had come in at midnight to gently awaken him and politely ask him to move to one of the first two floors which were open all night. At the time, he was taking nineteen credits and working twenty-four hours a week for a local engineering company. He was always tired. He hadn't actually seen her on that night. By the time he could wake up and get focused, she had gone, but her smell—her wonderful smell—still hung over the small little room. It wasn't perfume either, it was *her*. It was the outdoors, and leather, and the smell of a woman's hair. About a week later, in the same cage, at the same time, he had fallen asleep again. This time Taylor came over behind him and gently placed her hand on his shoulder to wake him up.

"Hey big guy," she had said quietly, "might be time to head home." She kept her hand on his shoulder as he stirred, and when he turned, her face was close to his, smiling quietly. He smiled back sleepily. "Two nights in a row. I think you need some sleep."

That smell again from last night. She worked at the library and was a student, too. He had seen her downstairs back in the card section, filing books or setting up microfiche or doing something over a typewriter. Apparently, one of her jobs was also to go through the library at closing time and make sure they got everybody out before locking up. On most Saturdays, Martin's routine was to get breakfast at McDonald's shortly before the library opened up, and then stay until six in the evening when it would shut down.

"Sorry," said Martin. "Pretty pathetic when I'm dozing off at 6:00 p.m."

Saturdays were always one of the heaviest student study days. A few years ago, they added a wealthy woman on the University Board of Regents. Her husband had passed away at a fairly young age after making a fortune in manufacturing plumbing supplies. After he died, she had gone off the deep end on religion. She had determined that since college kids weren't going to church, they needed to close the libraries at 6:00 p.m. on Saturdays. So many kids had bitched about the library closing, that The Cardinal had run a story on it back in those days. It was a big profile piece on this wealthy woman, making her out to be a clueless, wealthy old capitalist who was trying to control the masses. In this case, they had been mostly right.

The young woman standing over him—Martin still didn't know her name—almost always worked on Saturdays. He hadn't seen her on campus, so he didn't know if she was a student doing work study or was simply an employee at the library. He'd also seen her riding a British ten-speed down State Street from the Capitol, so she must either live off Langdon, or East Johnson or maybe Mifflin.

Martin packed up his stuff and headed outside. But instead of heading directly for his place, he hustled over to McDonald's, got two small coffees, and hustled back to the bike rack. He wasn't sure which one was her bike, or even if it was there, but when he got back, she was just getting it unlocked from the rack. Carefully he had handed her the coffee and thanked her for waking him the last two nights. Mid-terms were almost over. Turned out she was a second-year law student, the last thing he had imagined. They sat closely together on a small bench overlooking Lake Mendota to the north. That was a little over twenty years ago.

Now Martin was nearing the hotel. He did have real business to discuss. It wouldn't take long. If he didn't bring it up right away, he might not get another chance. If he started to discuss it and she thought he was crazy, it would ruin the entire evening, and he did not want to ruin the evening. He collected his things and paid the fare. He had booked a room across the street at the Swiss Hotel. From his work back at Amoco he had learned it had a much bigger fitness center, on the top floor of all things, overlooking the lake. It was awkward for him to skirt past the valet, and the doorman and the bellboys who all politely reached for his bags or asked for a room number as if he were checking in. Martin simply replied that he was "just stopping to see a friend." He was sure that was not exactly believable at ten thirty in the evening. Bird's eye maple paneling in the elevators—that might be new from the last time he had stayed here at The Fairmont. She was all the way at the end of the hall. The API rarely paid their speakers, but they got a lot of funding from the big oil companies and they flew you first class to the conference and got you a really nice room. As Martin tapped firmly on the door, he knew not what lay ahead, but he did know that if his plan were to work, he needed the full cooperation and the complete confidence of Taylor N. Thompson.

CHAPTER 32

IT WAS TUESDAY, AND LAST FRIDAY HILTON HAD SAID HE might call for lunch, so Anita had set her alarm a half hour early to give her plenty of time to get ready. There was nothing like an extra hot shower and a slow leg shaving to get her in the right frame of mind. She had already gotten one of the other secretaries to cover her for a long lunch today, just assuming he did call. She told the girl if she hadn't shaken her yeast infection, she was going to have to go see the doctor—a convenient fabrication. That way if he did call, she could easily take a couple of hours, or even the rest of the day. If he didn't call, Anita would just eat in the office and tell the woman that things seemed to be clearing up.

Somehow, if she knew in advance they might get together, she could go for days without hardly eating a thing. She wasn't getting any younger and she needed every advantage. Besides, at the Oil Baron's Ball, she had seen that Hilton's wife was putting on a few pounds—maybe more. That wouldn't do for Hilton, or any other man she had ever known. Most of them were smart enough to never say anything to a woman about her weight, but she had been at a few too many happy hours where the boys would joke about "wide-bodies." The men could be roly-poly little bastards themselves, and still bitch that their wife just didn't look like a twenty-one-year-old anymore.

She could never decide exactly how to dress around him. He only gave her genuine compliments when she was wearing something sexy or a skirt that was short by an extra inch or two. But dressing like a whore wasn't ever going to get Hilton to take her seriously, and besides, Anita thought, there were too many whores to compete with anyway. She picked a sheer cream-colored shift from the rack and hung it over the shower curtain bar. For some reason when they built these apartments, they never installed real exhaust fans in the bathroom, just one of those cheap charcoal filters that supposedly recycled the air. She needed to keep the door closed or she would wake up her daughter, still sleeping quietly in the other bedroom down the hall. Now, after her hot shower, the big mirror over the vanity was still heavily fogged over and she took one of the fresh towels from below the sink and wiped off the mirror. After blow-drying her hair, she passed on the hair spray. Hilton had told her long ago she didn't need to spray her hair for him, which was his way of saying he didn't like it. She never got any exercise, but if she just didn't eat, she looked damned good. She took the corset, hanging from the towel rack, and slipped it on, fastening it at the front, which pushed up her breasts nicely. She carefully removed the dress from the hanger and stepped into it, reaching behind her to zip up. Standing erect in front of the mirror she looked herself over. At first glance, she was very dressed up and looking formal enough for a very nice business lunch. While standing there, her thoughts turned to making love with Hilton, and then, surprisingly, with Martin, as well. It was possible that Hilton would not call her for lunch today as he said he would. Anita thought about it for a moment as she stood examining herself. If Hilton didn't call today, it was definitely going to be his loss.

CHAPTER 33

TEAMWORK WAS INTEGRAL IN AN OIL AND GAS EXPLORATION company. During the exploration phase, management would meet with accountants and geophysicists and geologists for hours to define groups of investments they could make. Big companies would compare exploration opportunities on a global basis, and it wasn't as simple as estimating how many barrels of oil were under the ground. Discussions would focus first on the oil, how much there was, how deep was it, where was it, was it light, heavy, sulphurous, acidic and so on. Next the discussion would turn to drilling. The first question was could they get a drilling rig to it, and if it was in the water, what type of drilling rig would they use? What had others used? Was a rig likely to be available, what would it cost, how long was it likely to take to drill? How rocky and gaseous, and salty and uneven was the subsurface? What were the environmental conditions like, both from a physical and regulatory basis, and how long would it take to get drilling rights and permits? What had been the record of others drilling anywhere in the area or in similar conditions around the world, and what were the contingency plans should difficulties arise?

The land department would report the status and end dates on all acreage the company owned around the area. In producing areas, the ownership was not just defined at ground level, but was likely to be defined in horizontal zones or completion zones where a company might own 50% of the mineral rights to 5,000 feet, 25% to 12,000 or 14,000 feet and still own 100% of the rights below. The landmen might explain that brokers and landowners and federal and state and county and Indian and school agencies might have an overriding royalty of one to twelve percent in each horizon. This meant that they would not share in the cost of drilling, but this would entitle them to get a piece of the production should oil or gas actually be found. A report would be made on who owned the surrounding acreage and how much the acreage cost. Title work would determine how long the owners had held it. An estimate would be made of what it would cost to get more acreage and who would likely be oil company partners. These partners would not only share in the revenues but also the cost of finding and producing the oil. Gone were the days of the 1800s where everyone drilled his own well on his own small patch of acreage. The land department, along with federal or state environmental agencies, would determine to what extent conditions would require combinations of acreage, a process called unitization, intended to enable efficient drilling, management and production of the oil and gas. This could result in the pooling of the interests of dozens, perhaps thousands of interests from generations of families, oil companies and regulatory agencies.

The oil or natural gas from a well would not flow out of the ground in a day and be sold. The production department would describe the number of years and flow rates of production. They would work with facilities to describe the

structure and the cost of production and they would determine the transportation facilities required to get the oil out
of the ground and transport it to market. These days, hard-
to-find new production would be located in harsh conditions
with arctic cold, or deep water or civil unrest and security
issues. In deep-water production areas, like the North Sea,
facilities would require billion-dollar production platforms
that could house a small city of three hundred men around-
the-clock. Much of the oil and gas would be mixed together
and contain water, or metal, or even the poisonous gas, hy-
drogen sulfide. Complex processing and purification units
might be needed at the site or in the area to remove impuri-
ties. Storage and treatment facilities might be needed to
recycle and even re-inject the offending materials. Pipelines
underwater or over mountains might be built to get the production either to a market, or to a final liquefaction and
loading facility for movement to market. Drilling one well
wouldn't do it, either. A ten or even twenty-year drilling
program might be defined. As the wells aged, they would
need to be refurbished, and injected with heat or pressure
or acids to sustain or renew declining production levels.

Planning people, accountants and economists would es-
tablish current and projected prices for an entire range of
products around the world for the next twenty years in order
to evaluate current and future production levels. Production
levels by product would be multiplied by these prices to
determine all of the future revenues that could reasonably
be expected from a potential field. Assumptions regarding
capital costs, and operating costs for material and labor
would be estimated over a corresponding time frame. Assumptions regarding currencies, discount rates and interest
rates would be applied in an attempt to determine the net
present value today of dozens, or in a huge company, hundreds of investment opportunities. Political consultants and
industry advisors would review current and likely political

scenarios in target countries. This would provide a frame-work for assessing a range of factors in lesser developed countries related to stability of the current government, health of the economy, strength of opposition parties, exis-tence of radical elements or terrorists in the region, and an entire range of additional factors. The risk profiles would be used at the front end of the process to define a number of regions as off-limits due to unacceptable corporate risk. Then the framework would be used again at the end of the evaluation process in an effort to set a value on an incredibly large and attractive pool of oil in a remote, unstable country in West Africa, for example. The framework would then compare the West Africa oil with a risk-adjusted value for a smaller reservoir of deep natural gas in the politically stable area of the North Sea, where the product would be easily marketable but technically very difficult and expensive to drill and produce.

All of this work and analysis would come together in a lengthy annual portfolio review process by the management team of the exploration company. There was tension in the internal company process—and competition, too. People had invested much of their last six months in preparation for the portfolio meetings and there would be winners and losers. Management tried to mitigate the problem by shuf-fling people across different teams so that everyone would be a winner. Hopefully, the losers would not be so obvious, but hurt feelings and egos were at stake. Paychecks weren't as important as pride and credibility. It was very simple. If your projects and your proposals got approved and got funded, you were likely to manage them, and you would form the "A" teams to lead the company's exploration and drilling activities over the next year. If management didn't "buy" your prospects, or the damn economists or accoun-tants poked a lot of holes in them, you'd be assigned to support the "A" teams over the next year. You'd basically be a grunt for the guys who got their stuff approved. You'd get your chance to develop new prospects next year.

There were three classes of people in this process. The Management Committee was at the top. Some of them were former engineers themselves who knew good work when they saw it. For this meeting, they were joined at Basin Oil, by the top three exploration directors who had a record of getting their deals done. A third group was at the bottom of the pecking order, made up mostly of technicians. They were either younger graduates, still learning the ropes, or older gentlemen, who had always focused on the technical aspects of the business. Maybe in their younger days these older guys had cut a deal or two, but mostly they were extremely strong technical people not very interested in management. In the middle of these two groups was a mixed group of people trying to make it to the top. Some of them were fairly recent college grads who wanted to do everything immediately and did not want to wait their turn for promotion. The balance were some very good experienced engineers who just couldn't seem to get traction with senior management. Even Martin knew it was this last group in which he found himself.

Martin had been quiet the first two days of the five-day meeting. He had presented several routine prospects with his various team members. Most of the plays were extensions on existing fields or enhancement programs on mature fields. The money wasn't all that big, and the decision making was pretty straightforward.

On the afternoon of the third day of the five-day meeting, he was leading the presentation on the Kazakhstan field, in the Former Soviet Union. He had spent half of his time in the last year working on this prospect. The Tengiz field. It was natural gas and there was plenty of it. Europe needed the gas, too, so there was a market. There were two major issues. The gas was in relatively complex formations more than two miles below the surface. Secondly, either a pipeline would have to get the gas to market, or a gas liquification plant would have to be built on the shore of the Caspian Sea. The pipeline would be costly and risky, but the effort would have international backing and the cost would be shared with a number of other large oil and gas companies who had already announced major investments in the region. The investment was significant, but if Basin Oil wanted to be a respected player in the industry, Martin felt they had to show that they could do projects like these. His team wanted this project badly. The chance to work on such a large, international project that had such complex challenges was an engineer's dream. The project would be a lot more interesting than recompleting some tired old wells in Louisiana or West Virginia. Such a project would also look good on everyone's resume, enabling them to command more money at Basin Oil, or some future job.

Martin had let one of the best analytical young reservoir engineers describe the size and location of the gas and there had been little discussion. The President, the Chief Financial Officer and three Exploration Directors had listened intently. The gas was there. Martin's boss was one of the three Directors, and he had been supportive of the effort over the last six months.

The conference room had been set up in a U shape with a large projector, large screen and various forms of technical computer hook-ups in place to access the data. The teams would come in and sit on both sides of the U, leaving the executive panel sitting in five big leather chairs at the back. They would act as a sort of tribunal during the presentations. Sometimes they were quiet until the end, asking a few questions and then quickly approving or rejecting a project. More often, they would get stuck on a thorny portion of a project and then test the work very hard before determining whether or not to move forward with it. Everyone had been on a break, and as they settled back in, Martin got up to discuss the pipeline aspects of the project. The room was very quiet. His credibility was on the line. His team was watching carefully, ready for him to bring this baby home.

"Okay," Martin started in, "we've seen that the gas is there, and the drilling is very doable. In the next twenty minutes I want to tell you what the market looks like and how we're going to get in this pipeline."

"First let's talk about the market." He quickly went through ten slides. The current sources and use of natural gas in Europe. The growth of the Green movement in Europe was generating a huge demand for clean-burning gas, instead of heavier, dirtier oil or coal. The outlook for the European economies was reasonably good. When you put them together, the market looked very favorable. Basin Oil would have no problem finding big, long-term buyers for the gas, even before they began the drilling. That was why so many of the other major players were going forward in other areas of the country. Once Martin had reviewed the market demand, he turned to the pipeline. The pipeline could go north through Ukraine, or south through Turkey. Martin began with a favorable discussion of the political climate of Turkey.

"I think your risk factor of Turkey is low." said the President. "Those bastards got all nervous and mushy just letting Western planes fly over their territory during the war with Iraq, saying they were afraid they would piss off the Muslim fundamentalists in their parliament or whatever they call it."

"It's not a parliament," Martin corrected, "it's a National Assembly in Turkey, pretty much the same as our House of Representatives."

"Whatever, I saw President Kozlov whining in the newspapers that the United States was putting him in a difficult position, and he wasn't going to tolerate our bombers flying over his airspace."

"That was just political rhetoric," said Martin. "He publicly says that to keep his people quiet, but you can bet at the same time he's making plans with the State Department for a whole new round of foreign aid and capital investment."

"I still think your political risk indicator is too low."

"Okay, well let's come back to that, and let me tell you about building the pipeline."

Martin's boss stayed quiet. From Martin's perspective, his boss would suck up to management on every single issue. To Martin, it was a question of integrity. You stood up for the people who worked for you and you did the right thing based on what the engineering and the facts told you. To Martin's boss, it was more a question of making sure you ended up on the same side as management.

About ten minutes into the pipeline discussion, the Chief Financial Officer asked a question about material costs. Since it was going to take two years to build the pipeline, why wasn't the cost of purchasing the pipe indexed to go up over the two-year period? It was a good question, but they had a good answer. The team had arranged to get a fixed-fee bid for the pipe that would rule out the risk of price increases during the construction period. It was an equally good answer, but the financial officer went on to ask a few questions about product pricing. One of the team members had gone pricing during the initial part of the session. Now Martin was flipping back to much earlier slides, explaining where they got those numbers, what the assumptions were and why. Finally, when he got back to the pipeline facility, his patience was wearing thin. After a few minutes, his boss joined in with the questioning.

"I can't believe you don't need redundant compressors along the pipeline," said his boss. His tone was caustic; his boss already knew the logic behind the compressor plan.

"Compressor technology has come a long way in just the last three years, basically eliminating the need for redundant compressors," said Martin.

"Well what do you do when one breaks down and you've got thirty big wells on-line?" asked his boss.

"Generally, you don't wait for the compressors to break down. I know in your position it is difficult to keep up with new technology," Martin's comment was squarely intended to belittle his boss, "but unlike years ago, today the compressors have dozens of microprocessors that monitor operation of the unit. Using satellite dishes, we transmit the compressor operating data back to the operations center continuously so that we can predict failures and service compressors before they fail."

"Yeah, I know about predictive maintenance, I'm just saying, what do you do if they fail?" he asked again. "I think you need back up compressors."

"What I'm telling you is we don't wait for them to fail and that's why we don't need back-up compressors. Nobody uses redundant compressors on pipelines like these anymore." Martin was getting steamed. There were forty compressors along the line and he knew exactly what they cost. If the political risk was assessed higher, and they had to add the capital cost of forty more compressors, the deal wasn't going to get approved. Plus, the Chief Financial Officer was expressing doubt over the pricing assumptions which the CFOs own damn people had helped prepare.

It was Martin's boss. "Well Jim and I were talking in the bathroom over break about whether we really want to sink this much money into Russia right now. If we're talking about adding even more to the cost, I don't know..." his voice trailed off.

"We're not sinking money into it, we're investing money in it—by the way, this isn't Russia, its Kazakhstan." Martin was losing it.

"Russia, whatever," continued his boss, "I think Jim and I were just wondering if we want to put this much money into it or not."

"In the future I am wondering if we could all discuss our concerns here together so that they can be addressed, and not try and settle this while you guys are taking a piss together."

"Now Martin, you need to just settle down and watch your language," said his boss.

"No, I don't need to settle down and I don't need you, of all people, telling me to watch my language. You know what our plans are for this project and you've already seen the pipeline schematics. You signed off on the compressor plan. If you guys have already decided this in the john, why am I up here wasting my time?"

"Martin," the President interrupted, "we haven't decided anything. We were just talking about how big of a bet this is for a company of our size. I'm not sure we, or our investors, are ready for it. Most of them own our stock because they know we are one of the most cost-efficient in getting oil out of the ground in North America and the Gulf, and this is a big step up."

"It's not any bigger than the step we took two years ago when we partnered on the Tamarron deal, and you guys were okay with that. If we're going to be respected in the industry we've got to show we can do these projects. This is a good project and you guys know it. The only difference I see is that you were pushing the Tamarron project,"—now he was staring squarely at his boss—"and I'm pushing this one. That's the way it always is, right? You guys play big dog and hold court over us here today like you're some kind of kings or something, and we peons sit around and wait for your holiness to bless us with your opinion."

"Now Martin, you're way out of line. I think that's enough. The guys at this table have all earned their place here." It was the President and he was suddenly red in the face.

"Oh bullshit. I'm a better engineer here than my boss and you know it."

"Let's not put your boss on trial here, okay? I'm just saying that we've all worked really hard to get where we are okay? It's nothing personal," said the President.

"You know what? It is personal. The only reason we did the Tamarron deal and don't seem to want to do this one, is Tom probably licked your ass until you said "yes" and I'm not going to do it. I've made more money for you and Basin Oil than you can believe. And it's not getting me anywhere, okay? Trust me, after a while it is personal and I'm not going to keep putting up with it."

"Martin, you've got a lot at stake here to be saying things like this. I know you're going through some tough times at home, but why don't we just move along and wrap up the presentation?" said the CFO.

Martin looked around the table at his team. Most of them sat in rapt attention listening to the discussion. A couple of them had slid down in their chairs and were drawing distractedly on the paper pads in front of them.

"You know, I don't think you need me to wrap up the discussions. I'm going to ask Lynn to come up here and take you through the final slides. I've got some thinking to do. If I'm not the right guy to help build this company, maybe it's time for me to stop pounding my head against the wall. I don't give a shit whether you do the project or not, but I'm not going to keep sitting here busting my ass for you guys and not get any respect for doing it. Now if you will excuse me gentlemen, I am through for the day."

Martin's boss looked over at the President shaking his head.

"I am sorry for that. I know Martin is under a lot of stress lately. Lynn, maybe if you could get up and complete the discussions with us we can move on.

To the group, it had seemed like an inevitable outburst from Martin, a really good guy who felt like he deserved a place at the top and wasn't getting it. It was no surprise that he had finally snapped and told management exactly how he felt. But people were shocked by his anger directed not only toward his boss but the President. He hadn't actually quit either, he just walked out and said he was going to think hard about things. From what his boss had said, it sounded like Martin was going to have to do some serious apologizing. They felt sorry for Martin and sorry that this had all turned out so badly for him.

Martin, meanwhile, did not have to pack his briefcase; it was ready to go behind his desk. Martin didn't have to check around the office, either; he had everything he need-ed. He stormed out of his office, slamming the door behind him and stomped past Anita down to the parking lot. In twenty minutes, Martin was poolside at the Houstonian.

Just for fun, earlier in the morning, he had even packed his swimsuit in his briefcase. Ordering a vodka rocks from the pool attendant, he reclined comfortably on the lounge chair, soaking up the mid-afternoon sun. On a scale from one to ten, he was giving himself a ten. It had really helped that Tom, his boss, had been the one to start picking the deal apart. That had made it all the more believable, natural, and frankly easier for Martin to seem to lose his cool. He knew his colleagues would be calling him, to try and coax him back. He had guessed that Tom would be indignant at first, probably looking for the chance to make him crawl back, but then would kindly ask him to return because Tom needed him.

Going over his plans, Martin had actually picked this day more than two weeks ago. Now with his eyes closed, replaying the series of exchanges, he tried to gauge the effectiveness of his little tirade. He might have pushed it a little too far, but he was pretty sure that if he really wanted to stay at Basin Oil, he could apologize, swallow his pride and keep his job. Even more importantly, if he suddenly announced that he was leaving, no one would be the least bit surprised. He sipped his drink purposefully, in the afternoon sun, and then set it down on the side table, walked over to the edge of the pool and dove in. He glided smoothly under the water, feeling it slide past him evenly and silently before emerging. He glided over to the far side of the pool and peered up toward the blue, cloudless sky. Perfect.

CHAPTER 34

TAYLOR HAD THOUGHT IT ODD THAT MARTIN HAD HIS GOLF bag with him—it was the middle of winter in Chicago. He could've been coming back from a vacation break and just connected in the airport. Maybe after the conference he was taking a few days in Arizona or Florida. After breakfast, they had lay on the big, overstuffed couch, dozing in each other's arms while the warm morning sun poured in the windows. Taylor awoke with a start, jumped off the couch and ran to get ready. She was speaking in twenty minutes and had not yet even checked in for the conference. In ten minutes, she had kissed Martin gently on the cheek and agreed to meet him again around seven. She would speak and politely attend the other sessions in the afternoon and then go to the closing day press conference.

Martin was instantly up and moving as soon as the door clicked shut. The API Conference turnout was so big for this conference that they had to move it down to McCormick Place, just a five-minute taxi ride away. From the conference bulletin, Martin knew there would be more than three hundred vendor booths and nearly five thousand attendees meandering among the exhibits. He had called Geovision ten days earlier since it was one of the older geophysical vendors that he had never done any business with. He got the name of one of the technicians who would be attending the conference. In a call to the man, he had identified himself as a research assistant in the geology department at the University of Texas. He indicated he needed to transfer some large digital files to old format, sixteen-millimeter digital tape. Would Geovision have a digital converter at the conference that he could try out? It was a bit of an odd request to go from modern format to an ancient format that had become obsolete nearly forty years ago. But yes, Geovision had a new conversion machine that could translate more than forty formats and ran at speeds ten times faster than their earlier model. And yes, it would be fine to bring the digital master disk and the tapes by at the conference and they could run them through.

Martin got dressed, grabbed his golf bag and took a cab to the Exhibit Hall. Walking directly to the restroom he entered the handicap stall and took the travel cover off his golf bag. Inside were the tape canisters and master disk which he had carefully covered in bubble wrap and stacked one on top of the other for the flight up. He also had one aluminum alloy transport carrier for digital plotting. There had been no other obvious way for him to transport the tapes and because of their digital nature they needed to be protected well for the trip. He carefully removed each of the canisters and placed them one by one in an oversized UT Longhorns duffel bag and then headed out into the Hall carrying his now empty golf bag in one hand and the duffel bag in the other. Finding one of the bigger, more active booths, he nonchalantly walked over to the back corner of the exhibit and quickly slid the golf bag under the fabric. Then he shouldered the duffel bag and headed for booth 228, Geovision. In less than fifteen minutes, the technical geek at Geovision had loaded the master disk and written out more than two gigabytes of data onto the seven sixteen-millimeter tapes. The guy was talking to another customer at the time too, so there wasn't a lot of discussion between the two of them. As each tape filled up, Martin would place it carefully in the bag and thread the next one, making sure to use a fine cotton cloth to keep the tape clean and his fingerprints off the casing. As soon as the transfer was complete, Martin took the last tape off the tape drive, grabbed the master disk and disappeared back into the crowd.

Not a lot of Martin's colleagues knew it, but today's writing devices such as this, engraved a small microcode signature on the outgoing digital which enabled you to determine the time, date and actual physical device that had completed the transfer. If anyone ever started asking questions, an expert would eventually trace the machine back to Geovision, and would even know that the transfer was made at this conference. If they were lucky, they would find the technician and he would even remember doing the transfer for some guy who was supposedly from the University of Texas. Martin had lost some sleep worrying about somebody tracing these tapes back to the big machine at Basin Oil. But now the tapes were untraceable. He would sleep more soundly thinking about anyone who tried to link some student at UT, with Geovision, and then with Martin. The Geovision guy never even got his name or card. He returned back to the big booth and again picked up his golf bag and headed to the restrooms at the opposite end of the Expo, keeping his head down, pretending to read a handout from one of the fluids companies. At the end of the hall he ducked into a new set of bathrooms and carefully wrapped the new tapes and canisters. Then he layered them in one on top of another and crumpled up the duffel bag into a plain brown bag and dropped it into the trash can on the way out. He then took a taxi back to his hotel and dropped off the golf bag with the valet and checked in. A quick call to Anita confirmed that he had no messages and things had remained quiet as usual back in Houston. He had missed Taylor's speech, but he proceeded over to the conference and registered, then went out of his way to generally stay in the lobbies and be seen. After grabbing a handful of vendor flyers, koozies, caps and a fairly nice shoulder bag giveaway, he watched patiently for the occasional associate from Houston, who Martin would saunter over toward and with whom he would exchange meaningless pleasantries. Word would be back to Houston tomorrow, that so and so had seen him at the conference; yeah, the weather had been nice but cold, and why didn't they have the damn thing in Phoenix or Scottsdale this time of year? It was important for Martin to be normal, to be seen and to be suffering through another ho-hum conference with the rest of them.

At five, he headed over to his hotel and changed into his running clothes and a wrinkled, maroon windbreaker. Martin took off for a run south down the lakeshore. He ran easily and slowly on his way down to the yacht basin, stopped a couple of times at stoplights to catch his breath and wait for a break in the traffic. He ran easily down along Lincoln Park down to the Observatory, a gentle north wind at his back nudging him along. When he turned to head back, the wind seemed to stand up to meet him. Biting into his cheeks and cutting into his eyes, the wind sent tears steadily running from the corners of his eyes that glanced back off the shoulders of the windbreaker before dropping to the pavement below. Clenching his bare hands tightly in the pockets of his windbreaker, he lowered his head and charged into the wind, knowing no one or nothing would stop him. Every quarter mile or so, a rogue wave would crash in over the bulkhead, sending a shower of icy mist over him. He felt his heart pumping strongly and surely. He could feel each surge of blood up the arteries in the side of his neck giving him warmth, strength and peace even as the wind rose up to meet him. Calmly, as he considered those he knew and those he loved, he found himself different. From this day on, decisions would be easier. He was angry and determined, and from now on he would not let anyone stand in his way.

Back in his room, he turned on the hot shower and sat down on the shower stall floor with his razor and shaving cream. He let the shower fall squarely on his back, intermittently closing his eyes and leaning over backwards as the water cascaded onto his face. He applied the shaving cream generously over his early-evening beard and then vigorously soaped the rest of the body, as the shaving lather did its job. His shave was close and smooth, then he took the bottle of body wash and poured it over himself before rinsing off and dressing for dinner. Exactly at seven he called Taylor's room and asked if she could pick him up for dinner. He explained that for appearance purposes he decided he better check into his hotel, and since she had a car, he had made reservations at Morton's for dinner. She was running a little late, but when she pulled in to pick him up, he was standing curbside by the valet, and for some reason he asked her to unlock the trunk so he could throw his clubs in the back. Morton's was really a man's place, with those big steaks and huge servings of Caesar salads with anchovies and sautéed mushrooms. Taylor was in her element in such a place. Although it was packed, he had requested a small booth for them, and with Frank singing "Come Fly with Me" in the background, they could talk for hours in complete privacy.

Taylor was relaxed. "So, are we going golfing tomorrow? You know I don't even have my shoes with me." She was showing the big smile, the one that he loved. Liz used to have that smile too, but she didn't show it much anymore. Taylor's speech had gone well, and the press conference even better. A lot had happened in the last twenty-four hours-for both of them.

"Yeah, there's a great course at a place called Princeville on Kauai. I bet there's a late flight too, which of course would mean that by tomorrow morning we should be teeing off." He found himself smiling easily and broadly back at her. They were so natural together. Everything just seemed to fit.

"Well, I have to be back by... Friday. I believe I've got a huge meeting on that day." She was still smiling. "That is, of course, not this Friday, but a week from this Friday." The thought of spending a week in Hawaii with Martin brought all kinds of very nice thoughts into her head, all while sitting at a steak house in Chicago.

After they had ordered, Martin turned suddenly serious. He started with a long discussion of how disappointed he was in his job. He was bitter—more bitter than Taylor could have imagined. He described in detail a series of situations at work where he had been left out of key meetings, where he had accomplished things for which others—namely his boss—had taken the credit. He had been passed over for promotion while they told him that it took time to develop. Finally, after nearly twenty years in the oil industry, they had promoted a guy two years behind him in the company as his boss. He was mad at the industry, too. For most of the last ten years they had been cutting costs, saying they needed to be more productive. Yet management seemed to be getting paid more and more every year. It was no secret that two years ago, when a major independent right in Houston had made three or four good discoveries, the President alone had made thirteen million dollars on his stock options. Most of the big oil companies had made more money in the last ten years than in any other period in history and they just kept downsizing. Now they were starting to call it "rightsizing" as if that was something different. He didn't share it with Taylor, but even as he talked, Martin thought about secretly cashing in the retirement account he shared with Liz.

Martin shared with Taylor details about his marriage. Martin thought to himself that Liz was just frustrated. For a long time Liz had been supportive, telling him how he was going to get his chance. About six or eight months ago though, she would grow sullen when the topic came up. She would say very little as he would replay the injustices of the week. About four months ago, she turned in a different direction and started to suggest the problem was him. She started to say that maybe in his heart that just getting by was good enough for him, and she made it clear that it wasn't good enough for her. She started to act different, too. Usually, if they hadn't made love for a few days, she would wake him up when she came to bed and tease him into it. At about the same time, she started just crawling into bed after him, and just going to sleep. One day Martin actually got the calendar out and determined it had been nearly a month since they had made love. Martin told Taylor that it was about this time that Liz started dressing up more when she left the house and wearing more make up. She took a new personal training class down at the club., Martin was actually jealous of how fit she was, telling himself he didn't have the time to work out, because of his job. And Martin had met her personal trainer, Todd—a good-looking young guy who was in perfect shape. Bad news. Some days she'd forget to remove the extra make up before he got home and to him she looked oddly out of place hanging around the kitchen with the kids, making dinner, hearing about their day and helping with homework.

On the night she told him she wanted a divorce, it was no surprise. Martin told Taylor that he thought Liz already had a lover. Martin had stopped by the house a few times in the afternoon to see if he could catch her. He had even taken friends to lunch over at the club to see who she might be seeing. He even thought about hiring a private detective before realizing that would be just as likely to make things worse. If she wanted him to know, she would; if she wanted to keep it a secret, it would be very hard for him to find out. Now that they were separated, she was dating a fair amount. Martin had seen her out twice, but his buddies would give him a full report every time they saw her. She had even been out sailing—and God knows what else—with Hilton Sinclair on his boat down at Clear Lake. Of all people, Tom, his boss, had been eating at Landry's Seafood House, right on the narrow cutout into Galveston Bay. Here comes Hilton in his big boat with Liz, Tom describing in detail how great Liz looked. She's standing at the wheel, piloting the sailboat out through the narrow cut, and Hilton's standing behind her with his arms around her, helping her steer. Tom couldn't wait to see Martin's face when he told him, telling him of course that, if their positions were reversed, he knew he would want to know.

Taylor had wanted to ask Martin a million questions as he talked and talked. Most of all, she wanted to know if he still loved Liz, but she was afraid of the answer. She couldn't interrupt him anyway, so she just listened carefully to every word. She knew Martin very well. He wasn't feeling sorry for himself and he would never make excuses. He wasn't beaten down, either. But he was angry—angry and determined—and she knew that meant trouble for whoever he might be facing. She had been far too ashamed, and frankly her ego was too big, to ever admit that she had given in to the big oil companies. They had blackmailed her. She felt dirty and disgusted with herself, even as she heard Martin talk. But by the end of the evening, Taylor had told Martin everything about her job and her life.

She and her staff had started off planning to just kill the refinery expansion in Superior. It was a bad idea. The area had some of the most pristine wilderness in all of North America. There wasn't a market for the products in the Midwest anyway, that couldn't be served just as easily from existing facilities somewhere else. Everything they were going to manufacture with the expansion, was going to Chicago and Cleveland and Minneapolis, anyway. The first two feasibility meetings with the DNR had gone very poorly for the oil companies. Jason had told Taylor from the beginning that he was adamantly opposed to the project and he got plenty of budget money from Taylor to put a DNR research team together that cut huge holes into the oil company plan. It had gotten personal. Jason even hired a couple of senior professors from the chemical engineering department at the University. Years ago, one of the professors had actually taught engineering to some of these oil company executives when they were students in Madison. The old professor ripped apart the design of the refinery expansion, suggesting that perhaps the executives should have paid a little more attention when they were back in his classroom. The sessions had made headlines that made it all the way back to the executive offices of the oil companies. Taylor assumed they would just pack up their stuff and go someplace like Louisiana or New Jersey, where it would be easier to expand their existing refineries. But a couple of days after the initial hearings, she got a phone call from the governor's office. It wasn't the governor, it was one of his campaign advisors, Ricky Amery, the campaign finance director, who said the state was concerned about the "messages" she had been sending to corporations wanting to invest in Wisconsin, something about giving them a break. Even when she talked to the governor later in the day, he was agitated with her. Governor Conlan said that these oil companies were important to the state. Maybe they should have a third feasibility meeting where the oil companies could regain some respect, suggested Conlan, even if Taylor still shut them down later. Reluctantly, she agreed and sent a junior team to meet with the companies at the third session, telling them to "just listen." After that meeting, the headlines had read, "Oil Companies See Improved Chances for Expansion." Jason had brought it over to her house and stuck it in her face the next morning when he came to pick her up.

She replayed for Martin, in detail, her dealings with Dick Jansen and Sheldon Mack, the oil company representatives—"snakes" she called them. She even told Martin that Mack had taunted her once, telling her that she had the "best tits of any bureaucrat he had ever met." Lastly, she told Martin about the meeting out at the governor's mansion. She told him how they blackmailed her, how they'd gotten pictures of her with the lieutenant governor. She told Martin how they threatened her with political ruin if she didn't approve the deal. There was no doubt the governor was crooked, taking some big money backdoor from Big Oil, assuming they hadn't dug up dirt on him, too. He could talk all he wanted about "industry being good for the state." Taylor wondered with Martin if they had given Conlan cash; maybe a condo down in Florida. Who would ever know?

Taylor reminded Martin how she had worked her way through school. She was smart, but her parents were poor. When Taylor and Martin had been dating back in college, Martin had been to the parents' place south of Iron River.

Taylor told Martin that even last year she had paid for their new roof and bought them a used car. All the years she had spent in Madison working in the cafeteria as an undergraduate and then at the library when she was in Law School; all those years she had dreamed of making a difference. She dreamed about standing up for something and being in a position where she could make a difference. She had given her life for this. Her life was her work. Any evening out had to be for some business purpose. With her schedule ,there was no time to get to really know somebody. Now that she was so well known in Madison, that was almost impossible anyway. She had had sex with the lieutenant governor only twice while they had been working on the Appleton Industrial Park, his hometown. For her it had almost been out of desperation, fear that she had forgotten what it was like to be with a man. Now she hated them all, hated the governor, the oil snakes, Amery, and it was her against them all. If indeed she was elected lieutenant governor, she saw it only as a stepping stone to governor. Suddenly, she stopped, realizing that she had been talking a long, long time to Martin. It was getting late. She smiled at Martin and then shrugged her shoulders.

"Well," said Martin as he lifted his wine glass, "we were a perfect fit for each other twenty years ago. Based on what you are saying, I think we are still a perfect fit for each other. Let me tell you a little story about that golf bag."

CHAPTER 35

ON MONDAY MORNING, TAYLOR WAS BACK IN MADISON, and he made a routine call to the DNR's controller. It had taken her no more than ten minutes on the net to find an article on computer disaster recovery and file storage. She now looked over a list of "Ten Commandments of Computer Storage." The controller was obviously nervous just talking to her. She never called accounting. Taylor indicated she had read an article over the weekend on disaster recovery of computer systems. While she personally didn't have very much time to worry about these things, the article had said that top-level executives periodically needed to ensure that the right steps were being taken. Taylor wondered what type of program the DNR had in place to address the issue and she proceeded to go down the "Ten Commandments," careful to sound only casually interested in any answer. "Were all files catalogued and indexed? Was all data backed up on off-site locations? Occasionally, she would ask a follow up question just to keep the controller engaged. Just before wrapping up, Taylor asked a couple of questions about the area of records management. Yes, the state meticulously maintained paper and electronic records. These days, what with all of the environmental work they did and the legal liability of much of this, records retention was a big deal. The state never destroyed old files. No, the DNR didn't actually run the Records Facility Management office, that was actually done at

the state level for all of the departments that needed Records Management and a storage facility for old files. Yes, the DNR kept two months of records onsite in their offices, but anything over six months old was managed by the Records Facility Management group. At that, Taylor said she felt better knowing the DNR sounded as if they had thought through the issues, and she said if she ever got asked a question, she could respond to it.

Still at her desk, she looked in her state government phone directory under Records Management and sure enough, they had offices right in the Capitol building. The Capitol was big, but it wasn't that big. Taylor had never recalled seeing them. Even in her days as a page intern, when she ran all over the Capitol, she hadn't seen any big file rooms. At the time, Taylor was studying political science as a sophomore and she had gotten a job as an intern with the state representative from Ashland.

She looked again at the phone number. It was an internal four-digit number from her office. Indicating that she and the controller had been chatting about this just the other day, Taylor was following up with a casual call to understand how Records Management worked. She was in the public eye a lot, and if someone ever asked her the question it was worth a few minutes of her time now to ensure she had a background.

The supervisor, a Mr. Gantry, was a real talker. It turned out that the RM offices were in the basement of the Capitol, of all places. Taylor didn't even know that the Capitol had a basement. Seems that all of the bulky paper files and microfiche, items that did not require air conditioning or a controlled climate, were stored in a huge warehouse down on South Beltway. They regularly picked up items from all of the state agencies in Madison and transported them to the warehouse for cataloguing and storage.

Digital media, was different though, the supervisor continued. It needed to be in a cool, dry place. Back in the sixties, they had started by storing electronic tapes and disks in the capitol basement, more for convenience than anything else. At the time, the state's computer department was still pretty small and it was located in the basement, too. The basement temperature hovered in the upper sixties year-round, saving them a fortune in climate control. In 1975, the computer department had grown so much they were ready to move to their new facilities. They took all of the critical records with them when they moved, but anything dated before 1970 they had left right there in the basement. That had avoided a lot of additional moving costs and wouldn't fill up their new facility with stuff that almost never got used. It didn't cost anything to guard the records either, since they already fell under the security of the capitol itself. Besides that, the stuff was so old, the guy joked, there wasn't much of a risk that a terrorist was going to target a bunch of fifty-year-old files.

There was a great filing system too, he volunteered. Taylor had actually used it a few times in her legal work at the DNR. The guy explained that anything with a "D" in the third position of the file reference was stored in the basement of the Capitol, and anything with a B was out on the South Beltway.

More recently, Taylor had gotten familiar with the state filing system while doing research on some of the big environmental cases at the DNR. At lunch time, she was meeting Jason in the dining room of the capitol. She left her of-

fice about fifteen minutes early and took the elevator down
to the ground level and then found the stairs down to the
basement. At the end of a dark, narrow hallway she passed
through two sets of swinging double doors and found Mr.
Gantry sitting at an old, gray, steel desk. A couple of silver-
haired clerical ladies were working on the computers behind
him. Taylor had stopped by just to say hello and thank him
for answering a few silly questions. He was pleased that she
had come and even took a minute to show her around, apologizing that there wasn't much to see, just row after row of
tape racks and storage containers. After a couple of minutes,
she politely thanked him one more time and wished him a
pleasant day. For Taylor, this was a reconnaissance mission.
There were no security cameras in the basement, or the
stairs. Not even one. There was really no security in the
basement at all.

The afternoon moved slowly. She was still laying low
from the Superior case and her head was spinning from her
time in Chicago with Martin. Jason told her at lunch she
looked tired and needed to take the afternoon off. She
smiled to herself. If Jason only knew why she had missed
some sleep for a couple of nights he would go crazy. Actually, he'd be very happy for her. More than once he had told
her point blank that there was a lot more to life than politics
and work. At 4:00 p.m. Taylor got her stuff together and told
her secretary she had to meet someone out of the office.
Rather than call a car, she took the elevator down to the
main floor of the rotunda and walked out the west doors
down State Street. She walked slowly, watching the college
kids coming back from classes. She remembered the long
bike rides she used to take along the lake on the way down
to Nielsen to play tennis. The wind would be blowing in
her hair as she raced along. The sound of the gravel would
crunch under those skinny tires in the early morning stillness, the lake waves lapping along the brushy shoreline be-

hind Elizabeth Waters dorm. Then on her way back, she would weave quickly through the people and the cars over to the library.

Martin. Martin. She didn't know where she was going with Martin, and she didn't know where he was going with her. She wanted to ask him, but she knew he probably didn't know anyway. She thought he still loved her. It was the way he listened to her when she talked, the way he moved when he was with her, especially by the way he held her head after they had made love. She paused to look through the window at the silver jewelry in one of the stores. She saw herself in the reflection. She was older now. Professional. Her hair seemed shorter than she had remembered it being, and then she realized she was comparing herself to when she was a young co-ed back in college, riding her bike with her long hair flying in the breeze.

Martin might marry her. He had almost married her once. It was she who had said they were too young. She had law school to finish. No money. He needed to go somewhere outside the state to get a job; it ended up being Texas. There was no way she could give up law school to follow him. He knew she was on a mission too. Didn't expect her to follow him, wasn't sure he wanted her to. She looked back at her image in the window, turning slightly in the late afternoon sun. The crow's feet around her eyes were pronounced, partly from squinting in the sun, mostly from the years of battling in her job. Too many weeks with too little sleep, the hours of late meetings where she was known to negotiate a settlement all the way until morning. Martin had told her when he had met Liz. He hadn't said he was attracted to her, just that he was playing tennis again and really enjoying it. He had a great partner named Elizabeth. She could tell by the tone of his voice that she was in trouble, that he was slipping away. But Taylor had a dream job and she loved living in Madison. Over the next six months, they talked less and less. When Martin came back home for the Fourth of July weekend, they had walked here along State Street arm-in-arm. Over an iced coffee down on Union Terrace, he had told her that Liz had grown very special to him. They had both cried. When they rose to leave, they had hugged for a long time. She could feel the tight muscles in his arching back. They walked slowly back up State Street hand-in-hand, and when they got to her street, they had simply dropped hands and she had walked off toward home in one direction while he walked off in another. It was better that way. She could never have said goodbye to him standing by the front door. She would have pulled him into the house. They would have tried to make things work. And he would have gone back to Houston torn between hanging on to what used to be and grabbing on to what could be.

She turned back down State Street and walked a half block before turning left on a side street and walking back to her house on East Washington. She took a long bath, and then sat on the couch watching the early evening news and drinking a Diet Coke and eating some chips. She was never home this early, and it was a treat just to hang out. She made herself a grilled ham and cheese sandwich. After the news, she called her mom and dad and talked for an hour. Things were the same. They were always great. After ten years they had finally stopped asking her about grandchildren. Dad had been out chopping firewood of all things, and Mom had spent the afternoon worrying that he was going to overdo it or lose his concentration and hurt himself. Then her dad told her mom that he'd been chopping wood for fifty years and he wasn't about to stop. At 7:00, she went upstairs and called Jason. He was over at his friend's house. They were making Chinese food and they had rented "Evita," planning to stay-in for the night. That was good. He was one of the only people in the entire Capitol who worked past seven or eight.

She changed back into her work clothes, grabbed her briefcase and headed downstairs. Opening the door in the hall closet, she dragged Martin's golf bag out into the foyer and opened it. Placing a dark, nylon shoulder bag on the floor, she carefully grabbed the first tape to place it in the nylon bag. She paused and looked at the label that Martin had applied and compared it to the label she had written down in her office. Exactly the same number sequence as she had seen on her desktop at work, even the "D" that the Records guy had talked about was in bold print. The old tapes should be in the capitol basement. She didn't think these canisters and tapes were all that sensitive, but she carefully stacked one on top of another until all seven were in the nylon bag. Hoisting the bag over her shoulder, she grabbed her briefcase and pulled the door closed behind her. The lock clicked decisively. She walked down the street to the pay phone on the corner and called the Records Management office. No answer. Everyone was gone for the day. In minutes, she had hailed a cab to take her back over to the east side of the Capitol building. If some-one had seen her leave in the afternoon, she could easily tell them she was coming back to drop something off at the of-fice. If they hadn't seen her leave, she told herself, it would be easier to explain coming in off East Washington Street. She flipped her picture identification card at the security guard as she walked in, he waved back at her, engaged in a conversation with one of the maintenance guys. Her steps echoed as she walked across the marble floor of the rotunda and took the elevator to her office. Her magnetic ID card clicked in the slot and when the little green security light flashed back at her, she pulled open the door to the offices and dragged the heavy nylon bag into her office and low-ered it gently behind her desk. She rolled up the sleeves on her blue cotton blouse. She took her reading glasses out of her purse, placing them down on the edge of her nose. She then sat down at her desk and turned on her desk light, set her briefcase on the chair and opened it and took three working files and spread them across the top of the desk. Opening her second drawer on the right side of the desk, she searched through staplers, paper clips, and post-its and found two visitor identification cards she kept in reserve for unexpected guests, and she slipped them in her pocket. She opened her brief case and grabbed the list of file labels that Martin had given her. She hoisted the nylon bag back over her shoulder and walked out of her office with pen and yellow highlighter in hand. It was 8:00 p.m., unlikely that she would even see anyone in the basement; and even if she did, it would be unlikely they would question who she was or what she was doing. With work on her desk and an armful of files, if she got questioned it would be pretty easy to explain that she was reviewing some files late in the day and wanted to pick up some things from Records Management. She took the stairs this time all the way to the basement— no need to be stuck on an elevator with someone making small talk at this hour. Back down the narrow hallway, she went to the Records Management office. She quickly slid the visitor badge through the magnetic slot, but the little red door lock light glowed back steadily at her. She didn't want to use her card, but she was prepared to. Sliding the visitor card again, this time more slowly, the light quickly turned green and she pulled the door open. So much for Capitol security. The guest badge got her in. As she expected, most of the lights were off, part of the energy conservation plan that one of the DNR task forces had put together back in the Carter administration. She walked over to the panel of light switches and flipped them all on. If someone was going to walk in on her she could hardly be poking around with a flashlight. She walked briskly down row after row of tape racks and file cabinets eyeing the series of labeling numbers on the end of the aisle. When she got to her sequence set, she turned into the aisle and found a series of tape canisters with numbers that matched Martin's. With relief, she saw that there were exactly seven canisters with the same number sequence, and the canisters were exactly the same in size and appearance as those Martin had given her in Chicago. Setting down her paper files, she slipped the nylon case off her shoulder and unzipped it. Using the cotton cloth that Martin had first used to avoid fingerprints, she removed the seven canisters from the shelf and placed them on the floor. Then, one by one, she moved each of the seven canisters from the nylon bag to the shelf. The whole process took less than a minute. A few minutes later, she was back in her office where she repacked her things and walked back out of the Capitol through her regular exit.

It was very unusual for her to drive this late in the evening. After she had changed back into jeans, a sweatshirt and a baseball cap, she took the canisters and packed them back into the golf bag Martin had given her. She carefully wrapped the bag and covered it with duct tape and slapped Martin's Creole apartment address on it. Then she threw the bag into the trunk of her car. She drove over to a UPS shipping place on the East Side and paid for the shipment in cash. One day delivery. A hundred eighty bucks. Martin would have the original Wisconsin tapes by 10 a.m. the next day. By nine she was back at her house, sitting in front of her television watching CNN. The fake tapes which showed huge oil reserves under the woods in northern Wisconsin were sitting in official Records Management storage in the capitol basement. Now the fun was about to begin.

CHAPTER 36

IT WAS TUESDAY. ONE THING ABOUT HILTON, IF HE SAID he was going to be there at noon, he would be there at noon. Sometimes he was a little earlier, but he was never late. It didn't do their relationship any good for her to be standing by herself in the lobby waiting for him to pick her up or him to be idling outside the building in his white Mercedes waiting for her to show up. Hilton was in a great mood and they headed for the hotel. She walked directly to the bar while he went to the front desk. She ordered drinks for both of them and sat patiently for him to return. He said she looked great. The oil market was up some. He had had a good morning. He looked great, too, as he came walking back from the registration desk. They grabbed their drinks and took an elevator up to the room.

Did she have any information on his little friend Martin? Anita had been doing some research on Martin the way Hilton had asked. She had definitely found some things that looked out of the ordinary. Looking at the history files, she indicated Martin had processed a very large file that had been on the system that looked especially odd because she hadn't checked it in, and it wasn't set up for archiving. In the same directory she had found a set of spreadsheet documents with a related set of names, and she had printed them off. They looked to her like the reservoir-sizing spreadsheets they used in the economic valuation and planning phase. She had also found a few geophysical summaries that described the structures of the formations, but she didn't understand them. Anita had it all in a big folder which she handed to Hilton and she suggested he take a look. He sat down in a stuffed chair in the corner of the room. His eyes widened as he reviewed the first page, widening even more with the second and the third. He was certainly no geologist, but it was clear this was an economic analysis of an oil field—a huge one! The spreadsheets showed that at forty dollars a barrel, the net present value of the field was almost fifty billion dollars. The drilling costs were high, especially costs for drilling mud, but production costs were low. Hilton guessed the oil was probably deep, maybe even under an existing field, and the pay sand must be very thick and the porosity excellent. A field like this was as large as the original finds in the Permian Basin back in the twenties; as big as anything in the Gulf of Mexico in the last twenty years. He turned frantically from page to page trying to determine the location, a clue on the geography, or an errant location or field reference. Finally, he saw some latitude and longitude references and Martin plugged those into his phone. The coordinates fell in north central Wisconsin. The files were referenced by Martin as related to a folder he had named the "Chequam.file," which sounded a bit like Eastern Europe or maybe one of the Russian fields Basin was exploring. But Anita had said the directory was secured and no one other than Martin was using it. It was possible that this was just the profile on a new field Martin was working on in Russia, but Hilton had a feeling he was on to something. A field this huge came along once in a lifetime and Hilton had to find out more. Anita said when she got back to the office she would do more digging and let him know if she found anything else. Still peering at the sheaf of pages, Hilton turned from page to page and back again while he sipped his drink. Anita finally suggested maybe he would want to look through the material in more detail later. They had better things to do. She laughed.

They had their own little routine. She would go in and use the bathroom while he pulled the drapes, got undressed and got into bed. Then she would come out of the bath and slide in next to him. Today was going to be a little bit differ-ent. If she was going to keep doing this, she was going to get what she wanted out of it. She unzipped the dress and slid it down over her hips and then stepped out of it and hung it on the hook behind the door. She was on fire. From her purse she took lipstick and rouge to freshen up. Then she leaned back on her heels just as she had done in the early hours this morning and stared at herself in the mirror. She ran her hands up her smooth nylon covered thighs, over her hips and up to her breasts. She slowly opened the bathroom door and stood in the dim yellow light; her hips thrown to one side as she leaned lustily against the side of the door. Hilton was in the bed not five feet away, staring at her from under the sheets.

"Oh baby," he said quietly, "you look fantastic. Come on over here."

She stood quietly for a few seconds, looking at Hilton lying in the bed. She smiled. She was supposed to walk over and crawl in next to him like she had done so many times before. She walked slowly over to the foot of the bed and pulled back the covers as if she was going to get in with him. But she kept pulling until the sheet, the blanket and the comforter, all of them were pulled back off Hilton, over his feet and onto the floor. She stood there for a moment surveying him as he lay completely exposed in the dim shadows.

Hilton raised up off the pillow and began to move towards her. He reached his arm out toward her, trying to grab her.

She pushed him back on the bed. "Not yet, Hilton. You've got some work to do." And she quickly jumped on the bed and straddled him. "Okay," she said. "You know what to do."

He looked up at her momentarily, her dark hair falling over her shoulders, her breasts jutting out over her corset. She felt a wave of heat rush over her. Two years together, and for once, Anita was first. After she was done with him, he rocked her wildly and in five minutes he had spent himself and collapsed back onto the mattress. Immediately, she moved off him and retreated to the bathroom to shower off. When she opened the door again, Hilton was sitting quietly in the chair in the corner. As they walked down the hallway to the parking lot, he trailed behind her, nervously jingling his keys in his hand. He opened the door for her and then stood patiently as she took her time getting in the car.

She started conversation that was casual, but businesslike on the drive back to the office. When they arrived at the office, she quickly got out of the car and leaned down back through the door. He could see down through the V in the front of her dress that now she wore no bra, and her breasts hung down to meet his gaze. She didn't smile, and had nothing to say. She was starting to conclude that she was going nowhere with Hilton. She just looked him straight in the eye.

"If you want to call me again, you can call me again," she said. "But if you call… there need to be some changes in our future. I have no idea where we're going." Then she sauntered into the office building. Hilton sat in the car, watching her walk from the car. When he found himself still staring, he quickly checked his rearview mirror and then pulled slowly away from the curb.

Later in the day, he had called. It was either call, or never see her again. He was unsure of himself now. He asked what she meant. She had been matter-of-fact. She was tired of being second. She was tired of putting everything into their relationship and not getting anything back. She said that she had been with other men before and she knew how to handle them. Hilton was already half-divorced. If Hilton didn't want to make any type of commitment, it was time for her to move on. She told him that he should think it over and let her know. Then, just like he had done a hundred times before, she abruptly hung up the phone.

CHAPTER 37

MARTIN SAT DOWN AT HIS DESK AND TYPED IN HIS password, staring patiently at the traffic again lined up on the Katy Freeway for the morning crawl into work. First, he signed on the computer as a Group User that they used for some of their projects. Then he attempted to get into his Chequam.file Directory. He had password-protected it, of course and received a message indicating that access was denied. He smiled when he received the message; his little security system was working. Logging off as a Group User, he signed on with his own user password and went into the Chequam Directory. Scrolling down the listing of files, his eyes focused on the column headed "last accessed" and found them all to be the same day. But it wasn't the last date he had last accessed the files—it was the same day he had lunch with Hilton. In fact, there was even a "time" heading which showed they had been accessed around 2:00 p.m. in the afternoon. Hilton hadn't wasted anytime. Anita had come back from lunch and scoured through Martin's files and took the bait. She got access to the fake Wisconsin oil files. Martin had thought Hilton would check him out after their lunch. Martin guessed Hilton might call Anita in the next few days after Martin's lunch with Hilton and ask her to snoop around. In fact, he must have called her immediately after lunch and told her he wanted to her to comb through Martin's files. "What was Martin up to?" He could envision Hilton asking Anita. Hilton was a lot hungrier than Martin gave him credit for, and a lot more aggressive. By now, Hilton would certainly have concluded that the leases were for oil, not timber or metals. Hilton wasn't stupid. Martin assumed that by now Larry had certainly found the old "Elephant Hunting in Michigan" article, that Martin had left for Larry among the maps. Larry would certainly conclude now that this was about oil. Well, Martin couldn't be absolutely sure Larry had found the Michigan article, but Larry would have had to open those maps where Martin had tucked the Michigan newspaper article. Certainly, Larry was able to put two and two together. Did it make any difference if Larry figured it out on his own? By now Hilton would have told Larry it looked like it was all about oil. Hilton would still be putting the details together, but Hilton would know Martin was doing something with an oil find, and a big one, at that.

Martin smiled to himself. He had planted those files for Anita to find. Hilton must have been pretty excited when he saw the reservoir-size projections from the files. Performing a tricky search command on his workstation, Martin could see that, in fact, Anita was the only one that had accessed the Chequam files. Martin guessed Anita had not only discovered the files but had undoubtedly printed off some copies for Hilton. Again, Hilton must have gone crazy when he had seen those numbers. Larry had the locations of all of the leases Martin supposedly wanted. But it was time for another dose of information for Hilton and Anita. God knows Hilton would have Anita scanning Martin's files everyday looking for more information. Martin took one of his back-up tapes from his briefcase and headed down to the map room that contained one of the local tape drives. He easily snapped the tape into place and then walked back to his office. This file was for Chequamegon and it had all of the latitude and longitude markers, all of the elevations and all of the underground horizons data. This kind of detail would be discovered by Anita and then Hilton would know all of the information about the big oil find, locations, depths and size. It would only take a few minutes for Hilton or Larry to confirm that the oil reserves lined up with the leases Martin said he needed for timber.

On the way back to his office from the plotting room, Martin stopped on the way for one of his special coffees; this morning it was Indonesian Bali Blend. He selected the tape drive as his source device, and began to download the huge file into his directory. Every few seconds the computer would give him an update of the time remaining to complete transfer and after eight minutes he had transferred the entire tape. Then he walked down the hall, coffee cup in hand, and removed the tape. Now it was 7:30 a.m. Anita never made it into the office before quarter after eight and by then he would be busy on one of his other projects.

Only a few employees had shown up in the Basin office by now. Martin didn't see Anita actually walk in the door, but about nine he was meeting with some of the guys in the map room and he saw her walk by with a handful of files. At lunch time, he checked the access on the big digital file that he had loaded earlier in the morning and saw that they had, indeed, been accessed by Anita at nine thirty. Shortly before four in the afternoon, Martin checked activity against the file again and found there had been no further access. Clearly Anita had found Martin's latest file and gotten what she needed that morning. He pulled the file up on his screen and issued a simple delete command. There would be no physical evidence that the huge file ever existed. Then he found the directory with the assortment of spreadsheets he had prepared and deleted those off the company computers, as well. Basin Oil only did full back-ups after each month's accounting close. Martin had been careful to place the files on the server only after this closing date. Daily backups were done, but they were only three days deep. In two more days, there would be no record of anything.

The days after Martin's blow up in the office had seemed a bit awkward for everyone. Martin had come back to the office and apologized, saying that the breakup of his marriage had really been getting to him. Publicly he had agreed to be "suspended" for a week while management considered whether to continue his employment. Privately, Basin's President had made arrangement to pay him while suspended, so it had been like a vacation. For management, he was too good a geologist to let go, yet it would send the wrong message to the troops if there had been no reprimand or suspension for his behavior.

People had been careful around him for a few days when he first got back. No one stopped coming by his office to visit, but everyone was cool toward him. Anita wanted to be his best friend and kept bugging him, after his "little tirade," as his boss had called it. But things were pretty much getting back to normal—or so it seemed. He emptied the trash bin on his desktop and did a "find" command on "Chequam" getting a "file not found response." He smiled quietly to himself. A day's work done. It was exactly 4:00 p.m. By now Taylor had placed the fake tapes in Wisconsin Records Management and Larry was in northern Wisconsin getting leases signed. Given the circumstances, Martin didn't feel bad about leaving a little early. Nobody was going to say anything to him. He mouthed the words "see you later" at Anita and walked out to his car.

CHAPTER **38**

IT WAS TIME FOR MARTIN TO LIGHT THE FIRE. WHEN THEY were finalizing their plan, Taylor had given Martin the name of one of the more aggressive young research analysts in the Department of Natural Resources. Taylor insisted Martin's first call go to him. Martin pulled over in the bus lane at the corner of Ashford and Memorial. He grabbed his new burner phone and called the central number at the DNR. Then he asked for Extension 2944, the number Taylor had given him for the smart, aggressive young DNR analyst. The guy picked up on the first ring.

"Yes, I am calling from the Department of Energy in Washington, D.C. and I was just transferred from the Capitol switchboard. Is this the research department for the Wisconsin Department of Natural Resources?"

"Yes. Well, I work in the research department. How can I help you?"

"The Civilian Conservation Corp ran a series of seismic tests in the 1930s across a number of the states. I'm with the

DOE and we are trying to determine how many states still have those tapes in storage. Could you research that for me?"

"What kind of seismic tapes?"

"Not really sure," said Martin, trying to sound every bit like a Washington clerk, "but it sounds like they are the kind that show if there is oil underground."

"So, what are you calling about?"

"Well," said Martin. "Just wondering if you have the tapes or not."

"Why? What does the DOE care?" said the research analyst.

"Apparently one of the states, I believe it was West Virginia, stumbled on to them in the basement of one of their state office buildings. They analyzed them. Now they think they might have some big oil fields in their state. Think they're the Beverly Hillbillies or something. I just need to know if you have the tapes, okay?"

"Okay, okay. Do you know what year the tapes were made?"

"Let's see, on my list here, it shows the Wisconsin tapes were probably made in 1931 or 1932. I have reference numbers on them too, you know, the federal file numbers, but some states don't use the fed numbers; they use their own."

"We use our own numbers here, but we can cross reference to alternate index numbers as well. What are they?"

Martin had the sequence numbers right in front of him. He slowly read off the labels for the seven canisters. Even as he read, he could hear the clacking of the computer keyboard on the other end of the phone. Almost as soon as he had finished reading off the numbers the guy replied.

"Got'em. Well I don't actually have them, but I see them referenced and catalogued here and I assume they are in storage somewhere. Looks like they are in the basement archives. What do you want me to do with them?"

"Nothing right now," said Martin. "Right now, we're just doing an inventory and once we get organized, the Department of Energy might want to bring them to Washington for analysis. We'd have our geophysicists look at them to see if there might be oil underground in Wisconsin. They're doing some study on energy supply but I'm sure it'll be months before they get around to doing anything."

"Do you want me to verify that they're in our possession and give you a call back?"

"Well for now I'm going to mark you off as "in possession" and we'll worry about that later. Half of the states I've called have thrown them out or lost them. Even if yours don't actually show up later, it's no big deal. It's not like Wisconsin is sitting on top of an Arab oil field or something. Course that's what West Virginia thought, too," Martin feigned a laugh. "Now they think the state lands have fifty billion dollars' worth of oil on them."

"Jesus," said the research analyst. "Okay, well give me a call back if you need something."

"Oh yes, I'm not sure I got your name or extension," said Martin smiling. The kid was so helpful. Martin listened patiently as the guy recited the spelling of his name and phone number. When he was done, Martin said okay, he had gotten it down, and repeated the last four digits of the extension again. He thanked the kid for being so helpful and said he'd call again if he needed something. The kid never even asked Martin his name or follow up phone number. It was all pretty easy.

Walking later to the door of his apartment, Martin found the golf bag package leaning against his apartment door. Martin unlocked the door, dragged the bag with the original Wisconsin tapes into his apartment and pulled a cold beer out of the refrigerator. He flipped on ESPN and called Taylor.

"Well," he said to Taylor, "I think things are shaping up. Hilton will probably get the digital print-outs today from Anita and I just called your boy and gave him the tape sequence numbers and some story about West Virginia thinking they got billions in oil underground."

"Okay, well the tapes have been laying there for a few days now and I haven't heard or seen anything yet." Taylor was relaxed.

"My guess is that after they think about it, somebody in research is going to be giving you a call, and then the fun will start. The kid was pretty good; I think things were clicking with him," said Martin.

"Okay we'll see what happens," said Taylor.

"I've been thinking about us," said Martin.

"What have you been thinking?"

"Good stuff, well maybe bad stuff," said Martin laughing. ESPN had an NBA highlight film running. "Sometimes the bad stuff is the good stuff."

"I've been thinking about you too. Definitely the bad stuff," said Taylor.

"All right, I don't think we should talk long. I'll talk to you later, okay?"

"Okay baby, love you."

"Love you."

The very next morning Taylor had been sitting in her office reading the transcripts on the Wisconsin Power nuclear case, over in Genoa. They wanted to expand the nuclear generator. Her secretary came in and said the head of research needed to see her urgently. Taylor had a relatively light day scheduled in the office, but she asked her secretary to schedule it for after lunch. She didn't want to do anything to show her hand. She was wondering how many of them from the research department would show up. When she got back from lunch it was just two of them, the bright kid she had given Martin's number to and the head of the DNR research group. She was definitely getting older, she thought to herself. The "kid" was probably twenty-eight. She walked up and exchanged greetings. She knew from her library days that research was long, tedious and thankless, but usually meant the difference between winning and losing in the courtroom. They rose up out of their chairs to follow her into the office. The kid bent over and picked up seven gray tape canisters off the floor that were lying at his feet.

"May I close your door, Ms. Thompson?" said the department head respectfully. He had to be nearing sixty. Taylor recognized the suit, a cheap, light brown polyester. She eyed the stitching around the lapel. She was pretty sure her father had exactly the same one. The right stem of his heavy black plastic eyeglasses had been bent or broken and he had done an excellent job of taping it with black shiny electrical tape, the kind she kept around in the kitchen drawer for minor emergencies. It was a great patch job, but Taylor had been at the department now ten years, and as far back as she could remember, she would occasionally be in a meeting with this guy and he had always sported these broken frames.

"Sure, feel free to close the door." As they settled down into the old leather chairs in her office, the kid placed the tapes down at his feet and she motioned for the two of them to sit. "So, are we going to watch movies here or what?" Taylor said jokingly looking at the stack of tape canisters. Neither of them showed much of a sense of humor. The old man started right in.

"Alan here, got a call yesterday from somebody in Washington. DOE, he thinks. Fairly routine call, a guy just checking to see if we had some records that had been turned over by the feds back in the thirties. As you can imagine, we get calls like this all the time. Usually they relate specifically to some piece of federal land, a lot of times for a federal road project, or FAA airport, or some other such federal project. This call was a little different and I want Alan to tell you about it."

"The entire call was probably only a minute long. A guy from DOE was just checking to see if we had some tapes. I did a quick look up and of course we had them. Well, I wasn't sure we had them, but I looked them up on Filex when I was talking to him and told him we had them catalogued."

"Okay, what's on the tapes?" said Taylor impatiently.

"Geological information. Underground seismic information from the 1930s," said the kid.

"Where in heaven's name did that come from?"

"I haven't been able to verify the source for sure, but the guy said that during the thirties a CCC work project made seismic tapes across a number of states."

"Why?"

"Probably just a public works project during the depression, who knows? But the guy said that the Department of Energy is planning to do a study on energy supplies and one of the areas they wanted to look at was domestic oil supplies, so he was wondering if we had our tapes."

"So, the tapes would show if we had oil underground?" said Taylor. "Gentlemen the last time I checked, I live in Wisconsin, not Texas where they actually do have oil." Taylor was smiling.

"I know what you mean, but he also said that one of the other states, West Virginia, looked at their tapes and they think they might have found a big oil discovery that they didn't know about. By the way, I did some quick research. Not all of the oil is in Texas and Oklahoma. The Rockefellers didn't make their money from oil in Texas or Oklahoma or Louisiana—they made it from oil in Pennsylvania and Ohio, and even New York state. Standard Oil was incorporated in New Jersey. And it's not just the East Coast, either. Illinois had four million barrels of oil production last year. Michigan, more than that."

It seemed they were getting Taylor's attention. "Who owns the tapes?" asked Taylor.

"Well," said the old man, "the law is not really clear on that. Officially, the Feds probably owns them, usually the agency that paid for the research. But when they shut down the CCC, they turned the tapes over to us. They're seventy years old, for goodness sake."

"Who called us?"

"Stupid me, I didn't even get the guy's name or phone number. I get a dozen routine inquiries a day and if I can answer the question over the phone, I don't even log the call. The guy was either from the DOE or the USGS, I'm not even sure which."

"And he wanted the tapes?" asked Taylor.

"Actually no. He said he was just doing pre-op work on a planning study and wasn't sure he'd need them."

"The tapes are probably just garbage anyway," said Taylor flatly. This was going exactly according to the plan that she and Martin had put together.

The department head spoke up, "Well, after we did some digging yesterday, we found the tapes in the basement of the capitol. Alan asked if he could take one down to engineering or geology over at the university and have somebody take a look at it."

Alan interrupted. He was excited. "The tape's in perfect condition. They've been sitting in the basement right here in the capitol at sixty-six degrees and they're not brittle or anything. And this is the good part. After the engineering guy got the tape working, it's some weird old format that nobody uses anymore. But he called one of the professors over in the geology department and they sent a post-doc over to look at the print outs. The guy wants more time, and I promised to say that everything was off the record, but he took one look at the plots that had been printed and said they showed very, very large deposits of oil on them."

"How large is very, very large?"

"The guy wouldn't say. And I only had one of the tapes with me anyway. That's not the best news either."

"Go on."

"The oil's under state land."

"Where?"

"It's only one tape, right? But the post-doc said some of the deepest deposits were under the Chequamegon State Forest. The state owns it if it's in the State Forest. The oil in Illinois and even Michigan is mostly under private land, so all the state gets is an excise tax, kind of like a sales tax, when the oil's sold. But as I said, if the oil's under state land, we own it—the state owns it—and we can do whatever we want with it."

Taylor remained calm, "Well, if it's in the middle of a state forest, I'm not sure we'd to do any oil drilling there." Now she leaned back slowly, folded her hands and rested her chin thoughtfully on her hands. She continued. "This could be huge. At the same time, I believe we should treat this very cautiously until we know more. I need to brief the governor. You guys keep a lid on this and I'll see if he's around today and I'll give you a call. And for God's sake, take good care of those tapes."

CHAPTER 39

ANITA HAD SENT THE COURIER OVER TO HILTON WITH the latest file she had lifted from Martin. Hilton looked over the file, some of the same maps, but this time with all of the detailed data. Sure enough, it was northern Wisconsin. And it wasn't timber, like Martin had suggested. Now Hilton was sure. It was oil. Huge oil. Martin had tried to throw Hilton and Larry off the track by talking about some crazy timber idea. Now Hilton just needed to put some major heat on Martin to get him to back out of the deal. That probably wouldn't be too hard if Hilton used the right kind of persuasion. Larry usually did this kind of work for Hilton, but he was in Wisconsin. Hilton hadn't heard from Larry in a few days either. Larry had left a message the other day and said his cellular phone didn't work once he got thirty miles from Superior. His cabin didn't have a phone, either.

These maps were fantastic. The oil was in large, deep reservoirs. Some of the fattest damn pay sand Hilton had ever seen. In Wisconsin. Who would have guessed? He put the seismic shots up against the spreadsheet; a billion barrels of oil. An elephant. Only one or two of these came along in the oil industry every decade or so. The last one had been in Irian Jaya, somewhere down in Indonesia. Usually people only found these after spending hundreds of millions looking for them in West Africa, or the Arctic, or some other godforsaken place. This was not exactly like the small stuff he had drilled up in the old Austin Chalk. As good as anything he had seen in the deep waters of the Gulf Coast, and this was on dry land; drilling would be inexpensive. In Wisconsin, of all places. Seemed like Martin had mentioned he was from Wisconsin. He must have been poking around on his own looking at geology studies, and somehow stumbled onto this stuff in Wisconsin.

If Hilton was going to put pressure on Martin, he needed to do it fast. When word of this leaked out, nobody would be leasing anything anymore. The major oil companies would swoop in on top of Martin and lock Hilton, and everyone else, out of the play. Hilton needed to get some cash, too. It was going to take money. Money and force. The carrot and the stick he used to tell his guys. If he just used force, Martin might just go to someone else, but if he used money *and* force, Martin would cave in and hand things over without being a problem. Once Martin got the picture he would come around. Hilton had seen it a million times. For ten or twenty thousand he could get someone to put a gun to Martin's head, but that would complicate things and add a couple more people to the equation. With Larry out, and with the size of this opportunity, Hilton couldn't trust it to someone else. He needed more than fifty thousand for this. Hilton thought maybe three hundred thousand would do it. He settled on a half million. He didn't have that kind of money lying around. Truth of the matter was that other than the equity in his house, he could scrape together maybe two hundred thousand. For the last two or three years he had been spending twice as much as he had made.

And he had been losing money on his secret trading with Gannon. Hilton had run his net worth down to almost nothing. Gannon owed him a few favors. Gannon needed to get him some money.

After spending half of his day dealing with Gannon, Hilton parked his Mercedes down in the common area designated for visitors and then walked across the pool area to Building K. Like most of the big apartment complexes built in Houston back in the seventies, Memorial Creole was huge and spread out. In Manhattan they build up, in Houston, with its cheap land, they build out. Sometimes the buildings were named after trees or flowers, but usually they were just letters shown plainly on signs by the side of each building. Memorial Creole was no exception. Pretty nice place, it was one of the nicer in the area. Word got out that a lot of well-to-do men were living at The Creole during or after a divorce. After that, it wasn't long before the women started moving in, too. From time to time, Hilton had ended up back here at their place with them, before, during and after his marriages. Nice guard house, too. Very secure. But in a late model Mercedes in Houston you could drive right through security. A nod or a casual wave to almost any of the security guards and the gate went up. The turnover was ridiculous at these security jobs, and no new security guard wanted to stop someone who might have been living in the place for five years. That could cause a complaint to the resident manager. This guard was a young one, too. Hilton hadn't even bothered to roll down the window as he went by.

Hilton took the shiny new key and slipped it into the lock. Without even jiggling it, the door opened. Anita had whined a little bit when he told her he needed an imprint of Martin's apartment key. But when he had asked nicely and told her he just needed to sneak in and look around to see if he could find out more on the Chequamegon maps, she finally agreed. She took the clay ball that Hilton had wrapped up carefully with a piece of saran wrap and headed down the hall toward Martin's office. Lots of times Martin would leave his keys hanging in a desk drawer or just lying out on his desk the entire day. She had encouraged the guys to ask Martin out to lunch to get him to loosen up a little. Then it was a simple matter to stop by his office with a stack of mail and make a quick imprint of the key. There were a couple of car keys and a few smaller keys on the chain, but only two that looked like they could be apartment keys. She made an imprint of one of the keys on the front of the clay pad and the second key on the back and handed it off to Hilton that afternoon. An hour later, Hilton had two nice, new, shiny keys. He was sure one of them would open Martin's apartment. He was right.

Hilton opened the door slowly and listened for a moment, calling Martin's name. He had called Anita on his car phone to confirm that Martin was still at work, but there could be a guest, a repairman, a cleaning person; who knows. When he got no answer, he entered and softly closed the door behind him, being sure to turn the deadbolt behind him. He set the briefcase up on the kitchen table and ducked down the hall to glance in the bathroom, two bedrooms and back to the living room. He got a feel for the layout. Nobody else was around. There wasn't a garage, but there was covered parking out the sliding door by the breakfast room. Hilton moved the briefcase over to the coffee table where it was out of line of sight from the breakfast area. Then he opened it. He took the handgun in his right hand and laid it gently on the table. He took a few moments with his left hand to straighten the neat stacks of money lining the briefcase. If Martin was smart, he was about to come into a lot of money. Hilton closed the case back up and sat it under the coffee table.

Gannon had been cooperative. Hilton had called him up and told him he was wiring over six hundred thousand dollars from Prolea. When Gannon asked what for, Hilton had explained that five hundred of it was for forged oil trading contracts that Gannon needed to prepare and fax over. Fake contracts to cover his ass with Prolea. The other hundred was for Gannon. Initially, Gannon had protested. Then Hilton said he wasn't sure he even needed the contracts, that he was coming into a lot of money, and just needed coverage for a week or so. Then Gannon had agreed. To an average person this would seem like a lot of money, but transfers of this size were standard in the oil trading business. Hilton simply had his secretary write up a wire transfer form, sign it and fax it. Within half an hour, the money was wired from Prolea to Gannon. Gannon had called his bank to tell them he would be coming in to make a large cash withdrawal. Hilton drove to the bank's parking garage and Gannon handed over the money. Hilton opened the suitcase and glanced at the money but didn't even count it. Gannon walked to his car with his hundred thousand. Then they both drove off in different directions.

Hilton took one more look around the apartment. He checked the closets, drawers and stacks of papers lying about. He had hoped to find more evidence of the Chequamegon field—maybe some additional reports or geological data in files—but there was nothing. The apartment was pretty sparse. Martin was still at that odd point in a divorce where you don't want your apartment to look too nice or too comfortable. Yet you want the basic stuff like a bed, your favorite clothes and some living room furniture and a television, so if you do have somebody over you don't look like you're camping out. Nice picture of Liz with the kids—what a great piece of ass. Why dumb shit Martin was walking out on that he had no idea. There were a few books. A stack of magazines on the coffee table.

Hilton mentally walked through how he wanted to do this. Best to get Martin under control first, then scare the hell out of him. Might as well show him the money right away. First few seconds are important. Need to get him under control, show him who's boss. Just as Hilton was getting things ordered in his head, he heard a car idle up very close to the door and park. Hilton jumped to his feet with the gun and got in position. Then he heard Martin turn the key and push open the door. Hilton put his back to the wall and held the .357 tightly in his right hand. With the silencer—actually a suppressor—the barrel was extra-long. As Martin stepped into the apartment, Hilton stepped up behind him, smashed him over the head with the gun, and pushed him with all of his strength up against the wall. He pushed the muzzle of the silencer up against Martin's neck and told Martin not to move a muscle. Foggy from the blow to the head, Martin stood frozen to the wall while Hilton quickly took handcuffs from his belt and snapped first one and then the other of Martin's hands behind his back.

"What the hell," said Martin. He was stunned from the blow to the head.

With the handcuffs firmly in place, Hilton grabbed the chain of the cuffs and rapidly spun Martin into the living room, where he tripped over the armchair and went sprawling to the floor. Hilton was over him, kicking him repeatedly in the back and legs while Martin tried to roll away from him, his hands still cuffed firmly behind his back. Hilton was strong from hours of lifting weights and working out at the Houstonian. Martin was helpless. Finally, Hilton stopped beating Martin around the head and let Martin lie there, panting and groaning. Martin rolled from side to side on the carpet. The entire exercise had taken less than two minutes. Tucking the gun in his belt, Hilton reached down and grabbed Martin under the arms and lifted him up onto one of the hardback chairs at either end of the couch. He eased him down onto the chair, pulling his arms behind the back of the chair, still firmly handcuffed together. Then Hilton reached under the coffee table and evenly lifted the briefcase off the floor and placed it directly in front of Martin on the table. He opened it slowly and carefully, watching Martin's eyes narrow as he realized the pile of cash before him.

"You've been a bad friend, Martin," Hilton started in. "You came to me for help and I said I would help you, but now you are not including me in all of your fun."

"What in the hell," said Martin. "Handcuffs?" Martin twisted around in the chair.

"Yeah, handcuffs. Actually won them in a poker game about twenty years ago. Only used them a few times," said Hilton.

"Hilton, what in God's..." As Martin began to speak, Hilton took the flat of his hand and slapped Martin as hard as he could across the face, nearly knocking Martin over sideways with the chair. If it had been a fist, Martin would be missing a few teeth.

"Shut up and listen, you piece of shit. I'm the one doing the talking now." Hilton hovered over him.

Martin closed his eyes and sat motionless. His entire body felt as if it were on fire.

Hilton pulled the gun from his conceal-carry holster on his belt and sat down on the edge of the couch. Martin had been around guns and looked it over. Probably a Colt, a big revolver with a silencer. One by one, Hilton began to remove each bullet from its chamber and set the bullets upright on the edge of the glass top coffee table. He continued to speak as he removed each bullet, examined it thoughtfully, and then placed it on the table.

"You're a good man, Martin. In some ways I actually like you. There's no doubt about that. But you haven't been treating me very nice." Hilton paused an especially long time looking at bullet number three before he set it on end. The chink of the metal on the glass was deafening in the silence.

Hilton continued. "I know all about the oil you've found up there in Wisconsin. I know all about that bullshit story you gave Larry before sending him up there. That bullshit about the diversification and timber and paper business. Very good. I liked that. How else to get a bunch of farmers to sign up to long term mineral leases on their land? Even Larry was a sucker for your story, and he's been around awhile. Of course, for ten grand Larry would believe almost anything."

By now Hilton had all six cartridges lined up in a row and he momentarily sat gazing at them. Then Hilton rose from the couch and walked past Martin into the kitchen. Martin grimaced as he went by, expecting a blow from behind, but Hilton just kept on walking to the sliding glass door and soon Martin heard the shades being drawn over the window. On the way back, Hilton opened the refrigerator. Martin heard the clinking of glass before seeing Hilton return and sit back down on the couch. The arrogant bastard had poured himself a drink.

"I'm going to make you an offer Martin, and you are going to take it."

"I don't want an…" Martin started to speak and Hilton hit him in the throat. Martin gasped for air.

"Just shut the fuck up," said Hilton, still holding the drink in his hand. "So… I'm a businessman, and businessmen understand that sometimes it takes convincing for a customer to come around. So here it is. I'm going to buy you out of your deal in Chequamegon. Everything. Your files. Your seismic tapes. Your spreadsheets. You will forget you ever heard of the place. All of them. I'm sure that by now

Larry has most of those leases signed, and I'm going to transfer those leases over to me. I'm going to pay you for this, too. More money that you've ever seen before. And I'm leaving the money right here for you. Five hundred thousand dollars in cash, tax free." Hilton walked over and grabbed the suitcase. He placed it on the recliner in the corner of the living room and opened it. Inside there were neat bundles of cash.

"Not a bad payback for the time you've put in, huh? Of course you were doing this while Basin Oil was paying you, right? But I'm not going to tell anyone about this. I'm not going to tell your employer. You can keep your job and you'll be half a million better off than you were a week ago. Tax free. Anita is the only one who knows that something is going on, but I can keep her quiet. By the way, you really need to talk to her about security at Basin Oil," he snickered. "From the sounds of it, people can carry just about anything they want out of there." Hilton laughed again at his own little joke and then paused to sip his drink.

Hilton sat back down on the sofa. "Now here's the good part. You know, Martin, I've learned a lot over the last twenty-five years. One of the things I've learned is that human life is very fragile. A blowout occurs drilling an oil well and a couple of guys die. Life goes on. A steam cracker explodes at a refinery and takes a few people with it. A week later, nobody even remembers their names. Life is very fragile. People get down, get depressed, and blow their own brains out in the back yard. It's sad, really." Martin watched silently as Hilton took his index finger and counted down the row of the six bullets lined up on the table, selecting number three and dropping it into the handgun. Then Hilton spun the cylinder once and then again, put the barrel to his own head and pulled the trigger. The sharp click of the firing pin was followed by a laugh from Hilton.

"You're fucking crazy," said Martin. He had seen Russian roulette in the movies, but never, never in person.

"You're not the first person to tell me that, Martin. Crazy, maybe, but my friend, life is fragile. Even for someone like you. Healthy, good looking, you're been depressed because your wife's thrown you out. You're having troubles at work. You're living alone." Hilton spun the chamber again and then again; he quickly placed the barrel up to Martin's forehead. Hilton pulled the trigger as Martin tried to twist away from the gun, gritting his teeth at the last instant before the hammer again slammed down on an empty chamber.

Hilton was standing directly in front of Martin, "A guy just decides it's not worth it anymore and kills himself in his apartment. Other than his mother, nobody really gives a shit... His ex-wife doesn't care, she gets the life insurance. So, you will take this money and get lost. I'm leaving this half million in cash and you go on your merry way. I get the oil. If you try and mess with me, then me or one of my associates comes back to visit you and you run the risk of looking like one of those sad suicide cases that you read about in the paper all the time. Or maybe next time somebody is waiting in the back of your car in the parking lot for you. Maybe they grab you as you're leaving the grocery store. Or maybe somebody knocks you over the head when you're going into work early in the morning before anyone else is around. Somebody brings you back here to your apartment and you die. Trust me, it will look like suicide."

"You're a fucking predator, you think..."

Hilton tapped the gun against the side of Martin's head. "I thought I told you to shut up." Martin groaned again. "You know you wouldn't be the first person to call me names."

Hilton settled back into his chair and sipped his drink while staring blankly at Martin. It must be twenty years ago since Larry had first told Hilton about the Russian roulette trick. You needed to make damn sure you got the dummy bullet into the chamber, but the best part of it was making someone believe you were not only crazy enough to kill them, you were crazy enough to kill yourself. Hilton had spent an hour in his office simply putting the gun to his head with the dummy bullet, spinning the cylinder and pulling the trigger, just to get comfortable doing it.

Hilton studied Martin, who was now sitting quietly. Larry had told Hilton that half of the guys would just breakdown at this point, blubbering like babies when you put the gun to their head and pulled the trigger. Martin was composed. His hair was certainly disheveled, and his clothes were torn. Hilton's muscles rippled underneath his designer dress shirt. Martin was a tougher son of a bitch than Hilton had calculated. It was a good thing Hilton had the element of surprise and a gun with him to handle this guy. Martin's face still showed the imprint of the hard slap across the face. The mark would be gone by morning. Hilton had tried to make sure he didn't bruise the face. It might not be a problem to have him going to work with a black eye, but it wouldn't make things any easier for Martin to explain either. Hilton finished his drink and looked Martin squarely in the eye. Expressionless, confident, Martin looked back at him, unblinking. The thought occurred to Hilton that Martin seemed too cool. Maybe Martin actually felt like he had nothing to lose. People were dangerous when they felt like they had nothing to lose.

Hilton continued. "Okay, so I am out of here. You get together all of your electronic files, all of your research. Get together everything you got on this Wisconsin deal and I will take it from here. It's just business Martin, think of it as just doing business."

Martin studied Hilton quietly before Hilton spoke again. "So now I'm going to quietly depart. I've thrown the keys to those handcuffs under your bed. It might take you awhile to get the keys and get those off, but you'll figure it out. Thanks for having me over for a drink, Martin. Sorry I've got to run. And Martin, if you mention a word of this to anyone, I will know. I know everybody. You tell anyone about this and we will come for you. Take the money and go away." Hilton picked up the briefcase packed with stacks of cash and dumped the cash onto the couch. He put the gun back in his holster and pulled his shirt over it. He also threw the scotch glass into the case. On the glass were the only fingerprints Hilton had left at the apartment. Hilton clicked shut each of the brass latches and turned the little combination lock to a new set of numbers. Patting Martin on the head as he walked by, he looked out the window, and then opened the door, holding a towel from the kitchen to avoid leaving any finger prints. He casually walked out, closing the door behind him. He walked left behind the K and J buildings and then took the tennis court path back to the visitor parking lot. He was taking the long way back to his car. There was no sense in someone seeing him both coming and going. Even though he had taken care to avoid parking directly under the streetlight in the parking lot, the white Mercedes stood out in the early evening darkness. Drawing the key from his slacks, he pointed it at the rearview mirror as he walked up, and the doors clicked dutifully open. There was a new guard now on the evening shift. Hilton looked away just as he passed the guard shack. It wasn't even Christmas, but the bushes around the shack were covered in white, Chinese twinkling lights. Very nice. Even though Hilton needed to turn right to get to the restaurant, just for purposes of deception he turned left onto Memorial without stopping and barreled off toward downtown.

The guards were supposed to record the visitor license plate number both on time of entry and departure. The night guard only got the first few numbers of Hilton's plate, but he looked down his long list of visitors for the day for the entry time. Nobody had logged the guy in so might as well blow him off. Other than Martin's bruised and aching body there was no evidence that Hilton had ever been to Martin's apartment at the Memorial Creole.

CHAPTER 40

HE WAS A LITTLE EARLY TO THE RESTAURANT, BUT HE TOOK a seat at the bar and ordered two glasses of champagne. His dinner date would be along any minute. They always liked it when he ordered them a glass of champagne. Made him seem kind of sophisticated, too. It had been a long afternoon, but a good one. The wire transfer had been routine. Gannon had done a good job showing up with the money and would be no problem. As long as Prolea didn't do some surprise audit, Hilton had until the end of the month to cover the dummy crude oil purchase contracts. It had been no problem getting into Martin's apartment. That had gone pretty well too. Martin had seemed under control when he left, pretty cool for such a little shit. Wasn't a little shit either, pretty big guy. Martin had just sat there. Probably just in shock, sitting there in shock that Hilton had even found out about the deal. Certainly, in shock that Hilton had somehow gotten into his house and put a gun to his head. Good thing Hilton got the jump on him. The gun thing had worked. Martin got the message. Martin also spent a lot of time staring at that five hundred thousand. That was a fair price. Hilton would be set for life if he pulled this deal off. Easily twenty or thirty million dollars just for brokering the deal. He wouldn't be able to get any rights to the oil under the state forest, but by now Larry would have signed up all of the private landowner leases around the area. Once Larry got going on something like this, he'd work seven days a week from eight in the morning until nine at night talking to the landowners, getting their confidence and getting them to sign up. One time Larry had told Hilton that Sunday was one of the best days to get people to sign. It was the only day that many people ever took time to think about their family or step away from their jobs and realize they were broke. If you worked in a few comments about "sharing it with the Lord," even the woman would be telling the husband to sign. Larry always did pretty well putting the women at ease. Once in a while he would get a stubborn man and it'd take five times longer to get a signature. But Larry would get the signatures one way or another. Hilton was confident of that.

Hilton finished his first glass of champagne in a series of quick gulps and directed the bartender over for a refill. Even better if it looks like he's waiting for his date to show up before he takes his first drink. He could've just had someone kill Martin, even forge the contracts, but this way was better. Killing Martin would bring investigators prying into Martin's private affairs, his work. Hilton needed to get those contracts down here in Houston and get them signed over from Martin. What could Martin do later? He'd have no proof that someone had forced him to sign things over. Even if he wanted to report it to someone, how would he explain where he had gotten half a million dollars in cash? Martin could hide the money somewhere, but sooner or later he would start using it and half a million in cash is a lot of money to leave lying around. No, Martin would be just fine.

He was onboard. Martin had just sat there looking at the money. It was a lot of money to a guy like Martin.

"Hi, sorry I'm late. Soccer scrimmage tonight was supposed to be for an hour, but it ran over and I had to wait." It was Liz. Martin's estranged wife. Liz.

"No problem. I just got here and ordered us a glass of champagne. Hope that's all right," said Hilton.

"Champagne, how nice. What's the special occasion?"

"Well two things really. For one thing, I had a very profitable day. More importantly, I'm spending dinner with a beautiful woman. To you." Hilton raised his glass, his fat gold Rolex peaking from beneath his sleeve.

She raised her glass in return. Hilton was looking very nice tonight. Great suit. Navy, double breasted, her favorite. She could tell he'd had a long but apparently rewarding day. "Here's to you, too," and she put the glass to her lips sipping the champagne. Placing her glass back on the bar, she noticed her lipstick marks on the glass. "So, what made it such a rewarding day?"

"Oh, nothing special, I guess. You know, I'm to the point where I mostly just manage people these days, but today one of my key guys was out, so I had to get my hands dirty." Hilton smiled to himself. "Yeah, I had to do a little ass kicking today. Kind of good to know you haven't lost your touch." Hilton looked again at Martin's wife, smiling back at him.

She smiled back at him and picked up her glass. "Here's to not losing your touch."

Hilton smiled and clinked his glass against hers. "To not losing your touch." He drank down the rest of his champagne, watching her lips through the bottom of her glass. He had arranged this date more than a week ago. Even though the French were in town, he told them he had dinner plans. A lot of times the French didn't even head out for dinner until nine. Now he smiled again at the irony of it all and waved the bartender over for another round. It was less than an hour ago that he was putting a gun to Martin's head. Now he reached out with his left hand and gently brushed Liz's hair back from her face and then ran his hand slowly down the side of her face and over the bare shoulders of her black spaghetti-strap dress. She could have pulled away from him or given him a knowing look, but instead she sat motionless and looked back into his eyes as he ran his hand over her shoulders and down her back.

The maître de led them to a booth in the corner that Hilton had picked out earlier. He slid in next to her and ran his hand up her thigh. This was all about power. Money and power. Beating the shit out of Martin and leaving him to grovel around on the floor in handcuffs had been one thing. Now, just an hour later, Hilton was sitting in a dark bar, feeling up Martin's wife.

CHAPTER 41

"SO, THERE IS OIL UNDERGROUND. A LOT OF IT?" ASKED Governor Conlan.

The governor had been out sailing on Lake Mendota with one of the insurance executives from Milwaukee. It just so happened that this insurance company had not only been one of the largest donors to the governor's last campaign, they also kept a large yacht at anchor down by the Edgewater Hotel. You could walk from the Capitol steps to the dock in five minutes. It wasn't even a very exclusive thing anymore to go out on it for an afternoon cruise or an evening dinner. State senators, representatives, the attorney general, almost everyone that worked in the Capitol referred to the boat by the name that had been cleverly painted in forest green script across the stern, "O'Fishal Business." It got a lot of use when the legislature was debating health care reform, or when the Wisconsin Insurance Commission was doing rate reviews, and of course, when an election was nearing. When her secretary had been told that the governor was out on "official business" for the rest of the day, Taylor called one of the governor's aides on his cellular phone, and about an hour later the boat was docking back at The Edgewater. They took an empty conference room at The Edgewater.

Conlan began, "So it's a huge oil find. And it's under state land?"

"We don't know that yet," said Taylor. "All we know is that some guy called from the Department of Energy in Washington and was looking for some old digital tapes that could show whether or not there is oil underground. It's crazy. Apparently, they are seismic tapes made back during the Great Depression. We really don't know for sure exactly where the oil is or how much."

Rick Amery was there. "But Dr. Reich here, just said that the tapes showed there was a lot of oil underground. Isn't that what you said Dr. Reich?" Reich was dean of the School of Geology at the University of Wisconsin. Texas and UPenn were the top-rated schools in the US, but Wisconsin was rated a respectable seventh.

"Well I only looked at one tape this morning, but yes, it definitely showed evidence of a major oil field underground."

"How big is it?" asked the governor.

"That's very hard to say governor. I've only looked at one tape, but it looked very promising."

"Promising," said the governor, "what's promising? Is there a million dollars of it, a hundred million, what?"

"It's impossible to tell…" said Dr. Reich.

"Yeah, yeah, yeah. Just give me a number?"

"Governor, the man is telling you he really isn't prepared to give out a number yet. Before word of this gets out, we need to perform due diligence." Taylor frowned at the man as the governor moved to the edge of his big wing-backed chair.

"Just be quiet for one minute, Taylor, and let the man talk. This is a great break for my re-election campaign and I'm not going to let six months of your bullshit 'due diligence' take it away from me. You need to lighten up. Ever since that refinery expansion deal you've been a pain in the ass and I'm getting sick of it." Taylor, flushed with rage, fought to hold her tongue. The governor looked back at the professor.

Conlan was direct, "You know I control funding to UW Madison, and your geology department, right?" He paused.

"The underlying structures are both very broad and very deep. The geophysical images, just the range that I looked at this morning, have hydrocarbon sands that are as large as any ever found in North America, with the possible exception of the North Slope."

"And the number is…."

"The field could easily be worth ten billion dollars, maybe more. And yes, almost all of what I looked at is under state-owned forest land." Taylor shook her head and stared at the ceiling as the governor whooped for joy.

"Ten billion! Ten billion dollars? Are you out of your mind?" said the governor.

"The find would be huge by North America standards and cause a short-term shakeup in oil prices. As you may know, governor, only every ten years or so is one of these giant oil fields discovered. They are called "elephants." One was found in Abu Dhabi in the Middle East about six years ago. The Sultanate is about the size of Rhode Island and over the last six years it has produced over one hundred billion dollars of oil from its reserves."

"Right," said the governor barely containing his enthusiasm, "and we were sitting right here on top of the damn tapes until we stumbled onto them, right?"

"Your voters may not find it especially flattering to hear you say that we 'stumbled onto them,' governor." It was Amery, and the governor shot him a dirty look.

"Right, right, I know. Jesus, Amery, I'm not going to tell anybody we stumbled into something. Let's see, we need to say we were undergoing a strategic review or something. Let me think about that. Ten billion dollars, maybe more. How soon can you look at the rest of the tapes?"

"We can look them over tomorrow and see if the other six are consistent with the first one. The tape is in very good condition but it's on a rare, obsolete format that takes us a few hours per tape to convert."

Taylor smiled to herself as she recalled Martin talking with such enthusiasm at the super-fast new digital translator he had used back in Chicago. These guys were the kiddy corps.

"So on Thursday at 1:00 p.m. I could hold a press conference," the governor said.

Taylor jumped in, "Jeez governor, give them until next week. What difference will a few days make? On something this big we have to have all of the facts."

"Taylor, again would you please just shut up. This is my baby now. If my memory serves me right, you are appointed by my administration, and you serve at the discretion of my administration."

"So, if I disagree with your approach, you're going to fire me?" Taylor asked intently.

"We're not saying we would fire you, we just need you to be a team player," said Amery, the governor's campaign finance lead.

"I won't stand in your way on this governor. I'm not sure I could even if I wanted to, but if someone asks me, I'm going to strongly remind everyone that I believe we should proceed with extreme caution until we know the size, the location and the characteristics of our discovery." Taylor was being stately, judicious, careful.

"Fine," said the governor, "if someone asks you, it's fine with me if you ask for caution. Tell them all you want about the need to take time on this. I just don't want you running your mouth at my press conference on Thursday."

"Fine." Taylor gritted her teeth.

"And between now and then I want a lid on this—not a word to anyone. If I found out somebody even talked to their mother about this I'm coming after them. Got it, everybody? Research, that includes you, too. Lock down your department if you have to." He saw everybody nod in agreement, except Taylor, who was staring out the window, seemingly bored.

"Get it Taylor?" He asked.

"Yeah got it. I only talk to my mother on Sunday nights anyway." Taylor was smug.

"Good," said the governor. "Meeting adjourned."

CHAPTER 42

AFTER HE HAD ROUGHED UP MARTIN, HILTON HAD GOTTEN increasingly nervous. He hadn't heard from Larry. He had always fancied he had some sort of sixth sense that would tell him when things were wrong. Larry wasn't returning his calls. He knew that something was just not right. First thing in the morning, Hilton had told the people in accounting that he wanted to look over the expense accounts for some of his direct reports and contractors. Accounting had brought in a huge stack of personnel and payroll files. Hilton had long had Larry on the vendor list as an approved independent contractor. Prolea was actually paying Larry's expenses. As soon as accounting left Hilton's office, he went straight for Larry's expense receipts. They had been processed only yesterday. He made notes of where in Wisconsin Larry was staying, where Larry was eating dinner. He also found a Hertz receipt. Larry had rented a gold Oldsmobile Aurora; a four-door. Larry would be easy to find. His work finished, Hilton left all of the files lay on his desk for two hours, while he did other business. Then he shuffled through the rest of them and called accounting to come and get them. He shared the thought with the accounting lady that he needed to keep everyone on their toes on expense reporting. Little did she know that his only purpose had been to track down Larry. On his cellular phone, Hilton had called his personal travel agent to make travel arrangements, a direct flight from Houston into Minneapolis. He asked that the bill be addressed to him personally. There was no sense in leaving a trail on this one.

Hilton had an easy flight and drove to Iron River, Wisconsin, and had gotten to Deep Lake Lodge that evening. Only two of the cabins were even rented. Hilton found it easy to find the gold four-door Aurora in the parking lot. It was Larry's rental car from Minneapolis. Hilton had stopped along the way and bought coffee, a bag of donuts, some microwave frozen entrees and the local newspaper. He wasn't going out. Best to not be visible to anybody in town unless he had to be. Hilton booked a cheap room down the road at the Northstar motel. The next morning, Hilton was up at 5:00 a.m. He made coffee in his room, had a quick snack and then drove over to Deep Lake Lodge and parked up the hill. Hilton watched patiently until 8:15 a.m. when he saw Larry drive out of the resort, stop dutifully at the four-way stop, and head west on Highway 2, probably to get some breakfast.

Once inside Larry's cabin, Hilton worked quickly but carefully, sifting through Larry's suitcases, a duffel bag, and a hardback Italian leather briefcase. After five minutes, he had found nothing of interest. He looked over toward a black, potbellied stove and then he saw a fat red accordion business file sitting on a hard-backed wooden chair by the kitchen table. He had missed it earlier. Careful to maintain the position and the order of the papers inside, Hilton spent half an hour reviewing document after document. He found the Michigan newspaper article about "Elephant Hunting in Michigan." He found Martin's business papers and checkbook that Martin had given to Larry. If all were going according to plan, Hilton would replace the materials and drift silently back out of the cabin and back to Houston. Larry would never know that Hilton had visited. But slowly, with rage building upon rage, Hilton found that Larry had, in fact, leased fifteen of the eighteen large private tracts within the borders of the state forest. But on the third page of the lease, the signatory block, where each of the old farmers had perhaps grudgingly made their mark, Hilton found that Larry had not signed these leases on behalf of the company that Martin had set up. He hadn't signed them in Prolea's company name either. Larry had signed these leases in his own name. They were made out to Walker Resources LLC. It was Larry Walker's own company. Hilton knew Larry could be dangerous, but he thought he could trust him. Hilton had often employed Larry when Larry was down on his luck. Now clearly, Larry had taken this chance to double-cross Hilton and make money for himself. Hilton could get these leases fixed—he had friends who could easily mimic the signatures of the parties. Hilton put all of the papers back into the big file and wrapped it up. As long as the landowners got their money, nobody would ever know the difference. That was not the problem. Larry was the problem. Hilton had already bought out Martin. It had cost him some money, but it had been easy. Now it looked like he had to deal with Larry. Permanently. He could threaten Larry all day long, but Larry wouldn't crack. And Larry was dangerous. Martin was a cupcake compared to Larry. Scaring the shit out of Martin and paying him off was easy enough. Hilton knew that he had to take care of this today, in a small, dark cabin in northern Wisconsin. He glanced over at the stove again, and then he saw a heavy, three-foot long, iron poker.

Still spitting snow in the dark hours of early evening, Larry Walker saw a nice crowd of cars at Deep Lake Lodge. Just for a moment, he considered pulling directly into the upper parking lot right by the bar to avoid the walk back up the hill. Then, because he wanted to get into a more comfortable pair of pants and because he had picked up a few things at the grocery store, he relented and drove down the narrow birch-lined drive to his cabin down by the lake. The groceries did not need to go into the refrigerator. In this cold they would be fine in the back seat. But he had planned on being back before dark, and now he wanted to get everything into the cabin before it got too late. He had stopped to see one of the three remaining landowners who had not yet signed. The guy had actually invited him in. It turned out the couple's daughter had just gotten accepted at St. Olaf's over in Northfield, and the whole family was quietly proud. The girl had even talked about being a Pastor someday. Yet, while the girl had qualified for substantial scholarships, it seemed the family was still caught short trying to find tuition at the exclusive Lutheran liberal arts college forty miles from Minneapolis. After more than an hour of low-key visiting and coffee drinking, the man had asked Larry to propose a deal where he got enough upfront cash each of the next two years to cover tuition. While the deal for Larry was easy to do, Larry had moved very slowly and deliberately to describe and then enter the terms into the standard agreement that the man would sign. While Larry knew that a single elderly eccentric like old Mel Baker would never sign, he had held out hope for this couple and his patience had been rewarded. They had signed, and they were happy. It had been a good day.

Going down the lane in his car, he could peer down the hill, noticing the roof of his cabin covered with a dusting of snow. In the moonlight he could still see the asbestos shingles in a wide, red circle around the stovepipe from the old pot-bellied stove he used for heat. The steps down to the cabin were made from reclaimed railroad ties. Larry stepped carefully on each of them because they were a little slippery. He carefully looked for traction on each step before putting his full weight forward and moving to the next step. Carrying his old, leather briefcase with the stickers in one hand and the bag of groceries in the other, he slid his key into the rickety old lock and pushed the door open. Making his way into the dark cabin, the smell of a damp, cold hearth reminded him of the need to restart the fire in the old wood stove which was waiting silently for him over in the corner. Leaving the door ajar, Larry stepped toward the kitchen table, bending at the knees slightly to ease the grocery bag onto the table. From behind the door, Larry heard the slightest movement and as he turned, he felt the crush of cold steel across the back of his neck. Immediately his legs collapsed under him and he fell backward, his briefcase falling to the floor, the groceries spilling back over him like so many little Christmas packages. Taking a blow that would have immediately killed most men, he laid on his back with eyes open, his spinal column severed. A large, dark mass loomed above him as he laid motionless in terror. His instincts were to pull himself up, to crane his neck around to address his attacker, but dumbly his body lay there in an odd, glowing warmth. In wispy, fleeting moments, he recalled awakening in the morning in the mountains in a cozy, down sleeping bag in the cold morning air. He could visualize the moisture from his breathing gathered in a silvery dewy meadow across the top of his tent. Drifting in weightlessness, out through the flap of the tent, he saw the clear snow-covered peaks of the Canadian Rockies and recognized himself on a backpacking trip he had taken to the Canadian Rockies when he was just nineteen. Suddenly, his eyes focused, and he surveyed the bare wooden trusses forming the rafters of his tiny cabin that had been his home for the last few days. In the faint light, he could see where steel plates had been used to join together two-by-fours in an even line across the roof of his kitchen. Then, fighting to focus his eyes, Larry saw towering above him the familiar face of Hilton Sinclair. Hilton's angry face was framed by those kitchen rafters. Larry saw Hilton raise up the black, roughly formed, iron poker that Larry had used to stoke the fire. As a tyrant now, with both hands clenching the weapon, with all his might, Hilton again brought down the heavy iron rod with full force across Larry's forehead. Then everything went dark. Hilton gathered up all of the files, all of the leases that Larry had signed, anything that looked like it related to business and carried it out to his car and headed back to Houston.

The owner of Deep Lake Lodge had three sons. They were great boys. Really super at helping run the rental cabins and the restaurant. It was Saturday and the boys were off school. The oldest one had loaded up the pickup with firewood and was restocking the cabins. Only two of the cabins even had occupants. He parked outside the cabin and got his first armload of wood. He dumped the wood on the porch and then knocked on the door. No answer. The Aurora was sitting nearby. Odd the renter wouldn't answer. He knocked again and then took out his master key and pushed open the door. Larry Walker was lying on the floor in a pool of frozen blood.

CHAPTER 43

It was Thursday morning in Taylor's apartment. She and Jason were having their morning coffee.

"So now we're not only in the refining business, we're in the oil drilling business." Jason could get pretty cynical.

"Before today I couldn't tell you a thing, Jason. Conlan would've crucified me," said Taylor. It had killed Taylor not to tell Jason about the oil discovery, but sometimes even Jason couldn't keep a secret. This had been so big, even she couldn't take any chances. Plus, Jason was smart, and the less he knew about it, the better the odds of this staying on track and keeping Jason off the warpath. Now she and Jason were headed to the press conference, and there was little to lose by telling him some of the details on the ride over.

"I couldn't stop this, okay. I couldn't sweep it under the rug because Records Management would have just gone around me. Once we told the governor about it, he went crazy. He was immediately talking about how this was going to save him in the election. He said he absolutely needed to go public with it before it either leaked or the feds came back asking for the tapes."

"So, what's he going to do at the press conference?" asked Jason.

"I have no idea. Probably make a fool out of himself," said Taylor.

"And has he asked you to play a role today?" Taylor could tell from the tone that Jason thought Taylor might actually be working with the governor on this for political gain, after all, she was more or less on the ticket for lieutenant governor. Little did Jason know.

"No role whatsoever. I'm up on the podium with him, but he's warned me to keep my mouth shut unless someone asks me a direct question."

"What question would you like to be asked?" said Jason cannily. "I've got a lot of real curious friends in the press, you know. If they knew you had something to say, they'd love to be the one asking the question, especially if it's at odds with "His Honor, Governor 'Con-Man.'""

"Funny, but don't use "Con-Man" in front of anyone," said Taylor hesitating. "Listen, I know I worry too much at times, but I just think this whole thing is moving too fast. I told the governor we should take our time, go through due diligence, and then see how we move forward. Basically, he told me that I wasn't going to steal this away from him and his re-election bid. Even threatened to fire me if I got out of line. Said I served at his "discretion," if you know what I mean."

Governor Conlan had taken a page out of Taylor's book and scheduled the press conference on the Capitol steps. It was a gray, overcast day, but the turnout was huge. Nobody knew what the topic was, they were just told it was a headline story. They asked the driver to leave them off in front of Rennebohm's and they walked the last half block to the east veranda of the capitol building. The staff had erected a small wooden riser over the steps and put a half dozen chairs on the platform. As they neared the area, Taylor found it was much worse than she could have imagined. Dick Jansen from Empire Oil and Sheldon Mack from Arbor were there. Obviously, they were continuing to cater to Conlan on the Superior refinery project. He had invited them to the event today, obviously telling them why, to be present at the press conference. This just kept getting better. Taylor had told Martin it might take two or three weeks to get this far. The governor had taken the bait and gotten way out of control and brought in these guys in the last forty-eight hours.

"Your buddies are here." She had never tired of Jason's dry, razor-sharp humor.

"Oh, this is going to be interesting," said Taylor.

"Look," said Jason. "Jansen's already up on the risers. It must be that your esteemed company on the platform will be the people from big oil. Maybe you can get a job with Empire Oil when this is all over."

"Out of control. Conlan is totally out of control this time," said Taylor. "You know I bet you twenty bucks that Conlan's already cut his oil buddies in on the deal."

"So, do you want me to plant some questions or not?" Jason had a way of getting to the point. She was about to go up on stage.

"You bet. The only question I need is "Taylor, are you convinced this is all real?" said Taylor.

"No problemo, amigo," and he melted off into the maze of reporters, government press staff, cameras, tripods and microphone booms.

The governor started in: "People of Wisconsin, ladies and gentlemen, esteemed colleagues and guests, thank you for coming today. I believe today marks the start of a new era of development, growth and opportunity for the people of Wisconsin, their children and their children's children. Today we embark on a new journey to ensure the vitality, the security and the education for the people of this great state. When I took office, I pledged to myself and to my Party that I would become an architect of greatness for all that is right in Wisconsin, and today I stand before you ready to take a next step along that path."

This was so bad, Taylor was ready to throw up. The film was running though, and even the reporters stood with bended ear. A number of the reporters held a microphone in one hand and a cellular phone to their ear, ready to relay any big news directly to the news center, for processing long before the press conference would conclude. All eight chairs were lined up in the same row behind the governor. The three oil company executives were sitting together, and Taylor was sitting right next to Sheldon Mack. The stark, plywood-plank flooring stared back at Taylor and she made a series of little circle indentations in the soft wood with the bottom of her black pumps as the governor droned on.

"Some time ago, we started a strategic review to look at ways for government to partner with industry to create value in our state. We wanted to break down current paradigms and consider possibilities that our predecessors had never dreamed of before. I am proud to tell you that today that we believe we have met with some great success. We have discovered that in Wisconsin; yes, here in the state of Wisconsin, our research and analysis, confirmed by the university, has found that we have in excess of twenty billion dollars of oil underneath the state lands and neighboring private lands of the Chequamegon State Forest in northern Wisconsin. This find will represent one of the largest single oil discoveries in the history of the United States. With this oil money, we will provide improved resources for the education of our children, the care of our sick and aged, and the training of our less skilled poor. Effective immediately, I will ask the legislature to begin to construct a tax savings plan that will recognize the immense revenue contribution of this discovery and return many of the tax dollars projected for the next few years, back to Wisconsin workers."

The noise was deafening. Reporters shouted into their phones. A dozen reporters in the front row jumped up and darted to the front of the podium, jamming microphones into the air, begging for the governor to take questions. The governor was on a roll and enjoying it. Letting things go out of control for a few minutes, the governor then made a motion for the people to quiet down, promising to take questions afterward.

"This day also marks the beginning of a new partnership; a partnership based on trust and a common vision for the future. For too long, in too many past administrations, we have failed to join forces with strategic business partners in a positive way to build the future. My administration is out to change all of that. At this time, I would like to ask Mr. Richard Jansen of Empire Oil and Mr. Sheldon Mack of Arbor Energy to please rise and be recognized."

There was a smattering of applause from Conlan's staffers. The press sat with curious silence.

"These men on the stage with me are senior representatives from some of America's largest oil companies. I, in close consultation with my leadership team, have asked these men to help us over next few days to evaluate the data and develop drilling plans. I would like to express our thanks to Mr. Richard Jansen and Mr. Sheldon Mack."

Taylor saw Jason in the crowd and smiled. Conlan must have invited these "tar-balls," as Jason called them, immediately after Conlan learned about the discovery. The part about the "close consultation with senior state officials," was just cracking her up. Nobody was in on Conlan's scheme. In fact, both the lieutenant governor and the attorney general had called her yesterday, to ask her what the big press conference was about. She had left them clueless, telling them she was totally unaware of what the governor was up to this time. Now Conlan was digging his own grave.

"Over the last few days, these men have worked closely with me to sign a joint venture agreement, whereby Wisconsin will team with these two companies to drill and produce the oil from this huge new field. Starting on Monday, we will make key digital and seismic data associated with this discovery available to these companies so that we can expedite the drilling process. These men meet the highest tests of integrity and we are fortunate to have them as partners."

When Martin told Taylor at the API Conference in Chicago about his plan, she liked it immediately. Martin had made the fake oil tapes. They would arrange to have the tapes "discovered" in the state's archives. And Conlan would "find out about it" and go crazy. In the meantime, Martin was going to get rich playing the oil market. He had incredible inside information. Taylor had immediately known back in Chicago that she could nail the governor over something like this. She had flashbacks to that dark night back in the wood paneled library at the governor's mansion, with these same three bastards, Conlan and Mack and Jansen. It had occurred to her that the governor would get together with these snakes behind closed doors on the refinery deal. She had no idea that he would be brazen enough to independently bring them in on this deal without bids or competition or any sense of proper protocol. The effect was essentially to legitimize them as valid players from the start. Like Conlan, the oil companies thought their companies would make billions. Taylor told herself Conlan was certainly getting a million dollars or more under the table on this deal. And the governor was probably getting an unlimited oil company campaign pledge for the rest of the campaign.

The governor announced that he would take questions. Jason was standing next to a tall, thin, handsome male. Taylor recognized him as one of Jason's friends from the Milwaukee Journal. Taylor nodded at Jason, and then watched as his friend moved to the front of the pack of reporters vying to ask a question. The first several questions were related to the size of the field and how big the tax cut could be. The governor took his time answering each one of these, savoring the attention as he let slip the few actual facts that they had. When one reporter asked how these oil fields compared to some of the other great finds in the world, the governor was eager to respond. He said that this discovery compared favorably with Oman, a "country the size of Rhode Island that had produced more than one hundred billion dollars' worth of oil over the last six years." Taylor smiled politely. Conlan had messed up a few facts, but he was still putting the hundred-billion-dollar number out there. It would be headlines tomorrow. Finally, Jason's friend had his chance.

"Governor, obviously there are environmental implications to all of this. We haven't heard from Taylor Thompson today. My question, Taylor is, do you think this is all real? Are you onboard?"

There was no way to defer the question the way it had been asked. The question couldn't be answered by the governor either because it had been directed squarely at Taylor. Frozen for a moment, the governor motioned for Taylor to come to the podium. She slowly rose from her chair and moved graciously and deliberately across the stage to take her place behind the barrage of cameras and microphones. In heels, she was noticeably taller than the governor as they stood side by side. Even more, her composure and presence compared favorably with the seedy governor.

"You've asked a very good question sir. Obviously, there are significant environmental implications to this matter, and I assure you we will deal with them in a diligent and comprehensive manner. However, there is a larger issue: I think it is too early to say very much at all about this so-called gigantic discovery. I am always very supportive of the governor, but I believe we should move forward with caution. And we should only move forward once we have done our homework. Frankly, while the news appears good, I am concerned that if the governor experiences unforeseen difficulties in this entire process, or if the data is wrong, then we will have to hold him accountable. So, I, for one, am recommending a much more slow and deliberate approach to this entire development."

At that point, the governor reached with his left hand in front of Taylor and moved the microphone back in his direction. He strained forward to recapture the spotlight and to get control of the situation. The news was still there, and his child-like exuberance still bubbled over, but the enthusiasm in the audience gave way to skepticism and the press conference rapidly came to a close. There were a few more questions, but the press conference was over.

As she found Jason in the crowd, she asked, "Time for a drink?"

"It's practically the middle of the day," joked Jason. "What if my boss finds out?"

"I won't tell her," said Taylor. They headed to Eno Vino on the top of the Marriott. Amazing views over the Capitol and the three lakes that surround Madison.

"I don't know if you know what's going on here or not," said Jason. "If you can't tell me, I don't want to know."

Taylor paused. "Jason, even I don't know if you could've kept this oil discovery a secret. Conlan threatened to fire anybody who leaked it. I couldn't tell you about the oil."

"It's not the oil discovery I'm talking about; it's something else," said Jason. "Either you're just being petty with the governor and you're mad at him for stealing your oil reserves discovery, or you sense something bad about this whole deal. Whatever it is, you put a really big target on his head with your comments. If this thing blows up a month from now, they're going to be playing your comments over and over again until the guy just crawls into a hole."

"That's where rats go, right? Into holes?" Taylor laughed. She had set the trap and Conlan had walked right into it.

"Girl, you've got some attitude today." Jason was joking, but he wasn't cracking through her toughness the way he usually did. "All I know is, I think the Governor is going to give his little DNR girl a serious lecture about raining on his parade."

"You know what Jason, I'm sick of that old crook. I'm really sick of those snakes he's always crawling around with and I'm sick of playing his little games. Just so you know, he threatened me with political ruin on that refinery deal and I gave in. This time we'll see who's facing political ruin."

"So that's what happened on the refinery expansion, he threatened you?" asked Jason.

"He threatened me. They all threatened me. Said I needed to be more reasonable and accommodating or else."

"Or else... what?"

"They had pictures of me. Bad pictures of me and the lieutenant governor when we were working the Appleton review."

"Oh, shit. You and Clark Everson slept together? Oh, shit. You should have told me."

"I'm sorry. I wanted to tell you, but what would I have said? I'm sorry I did it. Clark wasn't even my type; we were only together twice. Somehow the oil company guys got photos of us." Taylor took a sip of her drink.

"Oh, shit," said Jason, letting out a low whistle. "They had photos."

"Hell ya. They showed me a couple. But it's okay now. Clark even confessed to his wife, said Taylor. "And by the way, I apologized to Clark."

"So, Everson's wife knows?" asked Jason.

"Yeah, but that's what Conlan and the oil guys were using to shut me down," said Taylor. "That's over. This time I'm taking Conlan down, and you know what? He doesn't even know it. The guy's digging his own grave and he's taking his oil buddies with him. Right now, I just can't tell you any more than that."

"I'm sorry, Taylor. I never should have doubted you. I didn't know what was going on with the refinery stuff." Jason was emotional. "I even thought you were on the inside with the governor on this one. If there is anything you need me to do, just tell me. I'll do anything to bring him down."

"I might need your help, but right now I just need you to keep quiet about all of this. It's business as usual, okay?" Again, Liz smiled.

Finished with their drinks, together they walked out the door and walked back toward the capitol. Briefcase in her right hand, she reached her left arm around Jason's waist as they walked. He uneasily slid an arm around her waist as they walked on in silence. Other than an old high five, or that New Year's Party at his place three years ago, it was one of the only times they had ever even physically touched, much less walked arm-in-arm. They were a great team. Taylor wanted this as much for Jason as she did herself. She understood he would never have any sexual interest in her and that was just fine. He was just a great friend to have on her side of a fight. He deserved a better shot at the top, whether he wanted it or not, and she was going to get it for him.

"You know," Taylor said, "this has been really wonderful talking with you and sharing a quiet moment." She stopped to bid him goodbye. "Thanks for being my biggest fan, Jason. Thanks for being my bestest friend. I love you."

Jason began to speak but couldn't find the words. He felt the same kind of love for her that she had for him. No woman had ever told him she loved him. She loved him, she loved him as he was. His eyes welled in tears and he looked away. He looked back at her again, tears streaming unashamedly down his face. She stood on tiptoe and kissed him lightly on the cheek, and then turned lightly and walked down Mifflin Street toward her apartment.

CHAPTER 44

AFTER HE HAD FOUND THE KEY AND GOTTEN THE CUFFS off, Martin had gone into the bathroom and examined himself in the mirror. His head hurt. He had several big red welts around his ribs which were already turning an angry dark blue. His lower back ached when he stood up straight —probably a bruised kidney—but other than that, he was in amazingly good shape. That game of Russian roulette had really freaked him out at the time. Looking back at it now he couldn't believe how crazy Hilton could be. It wasn't the smooth, confident Hilton with whom he had gone to lunch. This Hilton was desperate. Once Martin had convinced himself that he was in one piece, he scoured the apartment to see if anything else had been touched. There was no evidence that anything had been moved about, but the place still felt dirty. He had no idea how Hilton had gotten in; probably had learned to pick locks somewhere along his illustrious career. Martin checked the locks anyway. From the time he had started this, he had known that Hilton, or one of Hilton's thugs, would come for him, but he hadn't known where or when. He thought a logical place would be the parking lot before work. Martin had been on the outlook for trouble. He even thought Hilton might call him and simply arrange a meeting. This place, an apartment complex with the security and all the apartments one on top of another had always felt pretty safe to Martin. Martin wanted to take a shower, but the thought of Hilton, or someone else coming in was overriding. The television was still on, but he shut it off, listening for the smallest movement of the lock or the lightest scratch on the window. An occasional thud of a neighbor's door made him jolt. After an hour, he gathered up the money, putting it into his briefcase, and selected some of his favorite clothes, and packed them neatly in a carry-on bag. He peered at his car through the small window over the shower. He saw nothing out of the ordinary. Moving to the kitchen, he peered again from left to right and back again. Nothing. Readying his keys, he quickly opened the door and locked it behind him. He moved swiftly to the car and opened the door and quickly threw his bag and his briefcase into the passenger seat. He hopped into the driver's seat and slammed and locked the doors. Then he fumbled to get the key into the ignition while scanning the area around the car in all directions. The car started, and he backed away from his apartment and out onto Memorial Drive.

He checked his rearview mirror repeatedly. After about a mile, he stopped alongside the road at the big bend in the road out by Woodway, but no one seemed to be following. When the light turned red, he made a U-turn back down Memorial and drove down Post Oak Lane. He checked himself into the Ritz Carlton using an assumed name and paid for three days in cash, explaining sheepishly that he was visiting from Dallas and hadn't expected to stay overnight. Arriving in his room, he suddenly felt very tired and very relaxed. It was Wednesday. Taylor had told Martin that Conlan's big press conference was coming up tomorrow, on Thursday. Conlan and the big oil guys had taken the bait. Oh, sure thought Martin, Hilton thought he had it all under control. Hilton knew nothing about the tapes from the capitol that had been "discovered." Hilton was working off the same data as the "discovered tapes" but Hilton didn't know that together Martin and Taylor were out to get Hilton and Governor Conlan. In his hotel room, Martin stared at himself in the mirror. A few bruises; he'd get over it. He took two Tylenol and drifted off to a tormented sleep. Tomorrow was going to be a big day.

CHAPTER 45

BIG PRICE MOVES IN OIL WERE NOT IN THE LEAST BIT unusual. A big refinery fire could raise gasoline prices in minutes. A huge new crude discovery, especially one that was easy to produce, could move crude oil prices dramatically—especially in the country of discovery. In 1973, the Arab Oil Embargo raised crude prices from three dollars a barrel to twelve, almost overnight. In 1980, prices doubled almost overnight when Iraq invaded Kuwait. Oil prices were just known to be volatile and prices moved fast on big news. That's why oil traders could make so much money—or lose so much—in a comparatively short period of time.

Martin was going to bet that the discovery of a giant new oil field in the heart of the Midwest would drive down crude prices—dramatically. He was at the first stockbroker's office at 8:00 a.m. Word was going to get out about the big Wisconsin oil discovery as soon as the press conference started. Taylor had set the hook with the governor and his buddies, and now she said they were going crazy.

Martin was racing against the clock. When he got to the first stockbroker's office, he had been a little nervous. He didn't want to seem too anxious or cause too big of a stir. He had done enough research to know that, assuming the brokerage house or bank was actually complying with the law, cash transfers of more than $10,000 had to be reported to both the Federal Reserve and the IRS. He had chosen seven brokerage houses around the Galleria to spread around the transactions. It was pretty well known that these offices around the Galleria were frequented by wealthy clients from Mexico, Venezuela, and Colombia. Even some Russians with oil money dealt with a lot of these banks. The banks wanted the business, and the fees, and they were more than willing to handle large amounts of cash in a confidential manner. There were rules about reporting large cash transactions, but in a complex international bank it was easy to hide money simply by moving it around from one country branch to another. Most of the law enforcement was focused on chasing down drug money, not oil money. Martin had heard stories about guys being stopped at the airport with millions of dollars in cash in their luggage. When he had opened his accounts, Martin had chosen a mix of banks and brokerage companies that were both US and foreign-owned. He guessed that doing so would make it a bit more difficult to track or consolidate his activity. Two of the offices were owned now by the Germans and one was owned by the Dutch. The transactions weren't going to be huge. Martin had taken care to break the money into lots of $70,000 each and had made several copies of the withdrawal slip from his profit-sharing account transaction. At each institution, it showed how he had pulled money out of his pension account. Once he had been shown to a broker's desk, he would explain that he was moving money to a new self-managed account and wanted to deposit $70,000 of the $87,000 into an investment account at each institution. He'd show the receipt he had gotten for the $87,000 cash withdrawal. At each office, once the account was set up ,he would place five thousand dollars into a big blue-chip stock ETF and leave the balance in a money market trading account, explaining that he wasn't ready to make other stock selections at this time. The offices all had online Internet access, too and Martin signed up for online banking. Just to make sure, he had gone out and visited each website to make sure they were fully functioning sites. When he filled out each of the account deposit applications, he made sure that he completed the form that would enable him to trade electronically. Because he was opening his account with cash, the funds were available almost immediately. In fact, in the second office, a cute girl from customer service walked him over to the trading customer service center and helped him while he logged on for the first time and saw his $70,000 balance staring back at him from the other side of the computer screen. At each subsequent office, he asked to do the same thing and all but one of the remaining offices were able to get him online even before he left the office.

Some were a bit faster and some a bit slower, but it more or less took a half hour at each place. It was noon when he left the last office. He had a little less than $10,000 left in his briefcase and a trunk full of bank and stockbroker brochures and pamphlets on bank services. One of the places had vacation giveaways and he had picked up a nice new ice chest.

Hilton had surprised Martin by bringing $500,000. Perhaps Martin had underestimated Hilton's wealth. Anybody that could come up with half a million in cash in a day had some serious assets. When he first made his plan, long before Hilton had attacked him, Martin thought there would be at least one meeting—and probably two—where Hilton would pressure or threaten him. Martin had planned to hold out for $300,000, but under pressure he had determined that $250,000 would be more than enough. It surprised him even more how Hilton had just brought all of the cash over to the apartment and left it there. Martin had thought that there would be some negotiation and then Hilton would take a day or two to get some money together. Either way, it had gone fairly closely to the plan that Martin had laid out. Just faster. It still made him shudder when he thought about Hilton jumping him in his own apartment and putting a gun to his head. He just never appreciated how ruthless Hilton could be.

Martin drove back to his hotel room at the Ritz, changed into jeans. and plugged in his computer. He was starving, so he ordered room service. He went to the first investment office web site, found his account, and signed in with no problem. Using some simple calculations, he went to the "investment purchase" section and clicked on the commodity futures and options box. Martin picked an option contract that would reserve the right for him to sell one thousand barrels of oil at a set price any time before the end of next month. Oil traders at big companies used these options all the time to guard against price swings in the market. Even farmers used such options or futures contracts with corn or wheat to lock in a good price. Speculators used them all the time when they expected a big change in market conditions. Options were relatively inexpensive, but they were just a contract giving him the option to sell. If prices generally stayed the same through next month, an option to sell at today's price was worthless. But if prices went down, the option could be worth a substantial sum.

For $352, Martin could lock in an option to sell one thousand barrels at the current price. The cost of this "put" option at the current price averaged out to about thirty-five cents a barrel. With the $60,000-$70,000 cash balance in each bank's account, he could buy an option to sell about 185,000 barrels of oil. The option was simply a bet. If the price dropped a dollar a barrel, he could make a hundred and eighty-five thousand dollars back on each of his seven accounts. If the price stayed the same or went up, his option was worth nothing. His bet would expire, and he would lose all of his money. He clicked "OK" and saw the transaction begin to process. In a few seconds, the transaction was confirmed. It restated his account balances to show the investment in the blue-chip stock, the 185 oil options contracts at a thousand barrels each, and a few thousand in cash left over in his money market cash account. The New York Stock Exchange and the NASDAQ close trading in late afternoon, but you could trade oil and most other commodities around the clock these days. He quickly repeated this process at all seven bank and trading offices. When he was done, he had "put" options on almost 1.3 million barrels of oil. It was Thursday afternoon. The Governor Conlan press conference was about to begin. Martin was ready for everything. When the news broke, Martin would make a fortune if the price of oil dropped on news of the big oil discovery in Wisconsin.

CHAPTER 46

MARTIN SAT BACK AND MARVELED AT MODERN NEWS sources. He was flipping between CNN and Bloomberg on the television, and he had Reuters and Google News open on his laptop. A Reuters reporter had been the first one to break the news when he stepped out of the early part of the Conlan press conference and made a phone call. It was only six minutes after the Wisconsin governor had announced a major new oil discovery. The report was running as a news-flash banner at the bottom of the Reuters website. Bloomberg and DowJones and other companies employ dozens of people whose sole job is to sit all day and follow news releases from all of the major networks and decide which stories get routed to their network. In another ten minutes, all of the major newswires had the story online. The Bloomberg digital business feed that ran on the desks of nearly every trading house in the world ran the story with the banner, "Kuwait-like Deep Oil Field Discovered in Wisconsin." It was 1:30 p.m. in Houston. The commodity traders were back from lunch and working at their desks.

The price of a barrel of oil immediately dropped one dollar on the news. The oil industry executives present at the governor's press conference gave the story added credibility. The price continued to fall and was down another two dollars over the next hour. The governor himself had made the announcement after what sounded like a careful study by the university. Several commentators said this field sounded bigger than anything in North Dakota—maybe as big as the old Permian Basin down in Texas. On one of the cable channels, one of the analysts interviewed had been in college in Michigan and recalled the date in history when the big Saginaw field was discovered in that state for the first time. There had been oil in Michigan when no one expected it. Maybe it wasn't so surprising that a giant field could lie deep under the northern forests of Wisconsin. Oil dropped almost two dollars more per barrel. There was a slight rally when one of the analysts reminded the markets that it would take years to fully develop and produce this oil. Prices came back up a dollar or so, but rapidly dropped off again. Heading into late afternoon, the price was still four dollars a barrel lower than it had started the day.

Martin spent the entire afternoon watching the prices fall on his computer screen while replays of the press conference itself had now covered every major network. The financial networks played their expert interviews over and over again. An occasional clip would even show Taylor on the stage with the governor, encouraging everyone to ask for further analysis to be completed so that they could move forward with "all of the facts." She was good. Damn good. She looked great, too. He desperately wanted to call her but could leave no trail between the two of them. He didn't really have anything to tell her anyway; he just wanted to hear her voice and find out what she was thinking.

Martin watched and waited. He knew the New York Mercantile Exchange didn't close until 7:00 p.m. eastern time on weekdays. It was open much later than the stock markets. At 4:00 p.m. he sold out his first account when oil had fallen four dollars and forty cents below the strike price on his first set of option contracts. He kept his calculator and a yellow legal pad in front of him and jotted down the trade confirmation number. He sold out the next two positions at nearly five dollars per barrel below his option price. When the drop got to $5.30, he sold it all. He sat back to tally up his records. His back was drenched in sweat. He had exercised all of the options. In total he had sold his 1.3 million barrels at a profit of $5.08 per barrel. On paper, he had made $6.6 million.

Oddly enough, it was Hilton who had told Martin over lunch that a good trader could make just as much money when the oil price was going down, as they could make when it was going up. Hilton was the one who had explained how to take big oil futures positions when the oil price was going to move. Hilton was bragging about his own exploits at the time. Martin had been listening carefully. Martin went over to the mini-fridge and looked over the contents. There was ice in his ice bucket—typical Ritz-Carlton service. He filled a glass with ice and poured over a Tito's. Six million dollars. A month ago, he and Liz had his $87,000 401k and some equity in their house. Now he was worth six million. Liz. That image from dinner lingered before his eyes. Their last dinner together. Had she been right about him? Did he have the "killer instinct?"

He had the $6.6 million spread across the seven accounts. It was an hour before the commodities market closed. Martin held his breath and logged in to the first account, only he was getting an option to buy this time at the current market price. The price was five bucks lower per barrel than it had been a few hours ago, and the only two people on the planet that knew it was fake were Martin and Taylor. When it was discovered that the giant new oil field was fake, prices should shoot back to where they were before the big market move. Somebody would be digging through the details. Somebody would discover it was fake. When that happened, prices were going back up.

He spent almost six million dollars on "call" options to buy at this low price. Martin reflected on this. On the first round he had only a half million to place his bet, but on this round he had six million dollars to invest. Again, he had the orders spread across each of the seven accounts. He completed his last transaction just as the market closed. He was exhausted from the pressure-packed day. He was relieved. He pulled a chair over to the window and looked out over downtown Houston from his hotel window, cradling a second Tito's in his lap. He smiled. Finally, he called the front desk for an early wakeup call and then fell into bed for a fitful night of sleep.

CHAPTER 47

THE UNIVERSITY HAD CREATED TWO COPIES OF THE ORIGINAL digital tapes and sent one to Mack's company and one to Jensen's. Conlan was putting the heat on them to review the data and rapidly determine the first four drill sites. The next day the polls had shown Conlan's popularity had risen almost seventeen points in one day. Conlan was already planning a second press conference to announce commencement of drilling activities. In fact, the governor had given his staff a picture of the Oval Office of the White House and he asked them to recreate, as much as possible, the exact same look and feel. First, they had hauled in a different desk and chair. Then they had spent the last three days cleaning and painting his office, taking down the Wisconsin flag and replacing it with the US flag, carrying out old files and finally putting in the gallery section for the press.

Taylor was sitting in her office when the governor walked in alone and unannounced. He closed the door behind him.

"Enjoyed your little show over at the press conference," offered the governor as he strolled slowly over to her window and looked down West Washington Street.

"I didn't mean to cause a problem governor," said Taylor. "You said it was fine as long as I only responded to questions when asked."

"Don't give me than innocent act. I know that your boy Jason had his little boyfriend ask you that damn question and I know you arranged it."

"Governor, you're way out of bounds here."

"Don't lecture me, you little bitch. This time I'm giving the lecture and you're listening." The governor turned to stare out the window again. "You know Taylor, I was serious about working you in as my lieutenant governor if you played ball with me on the Superior refinery deal. God knows you couldn't be any worse than Clark, although apparently you have a much more...intimate appreciation for his capabilities than I do."

Taylor found herself bristling at the reference, but the governor continued.

"Thought you'd make a good running mate. Experience and re-invention, man and woman, the party that puts environment first, all of that crap. God knows at the time I needed a boost in the polls. You blew it, Taylor. I gave you a chance. I asked you to bend a little and play ball with the system and you screw me. Actually, you didn't screw me; it might even be better if you did. That wouldn't be half bad." The governor turned from the window snickering at his own little joke and looking over at Taylor with amusement. He continued, "First, I've got to threaten you in order to get you to smooth over the refinery thing with our oil friends. Then in front of my own people you tell me that you are the one who "owns" the oil discovery like you are the one who's the damn governor. Finally, you make me look like a dumb shit at that press conference by telling everyone we need to exercise caution and that if it were you, you would have "all of the facts" before coming before the people blah, blah, blah." He was worked up. Taylor sat silently. "It's not all about you, all the time Taylor, okay? I'm the governor, dammit! And I don't need you anymore Taylor, you're through. Now I've got the oil discovery. I'm going to win easily. Oh, you can stay here in your little office as long as you like and be a pain in the ass on the environmental stuff, but I've talked to our friends in the party and we can't trust you anymore, Taylor. You're not one of us anymore, and you've proven to be unreliable. When we really need you to come through for us, we can't have you taking some holier-than-thou stance when we're trying to get something done for one of our friends."

Now he turned and walked slowly toward the door as she sat patiently waiting for him to finish. When he reached the door, he opened it and began to step out, turning one last time. "Oh, and you're not coming to the press conference this afternoon—in fact, you're not coming to anything I'm doing anymore. It's a shame darling, but you're finished."

The new "oval office" was packed as the governor walked into the room, cameras flashing, film running. The atmosphere was electric. First, the governor made another enthusiastic speech about the strategic effort he had sanctioned to explore all options to "build a better tomorrow," implying that this had all been his doing from the beginning. Jason and Taylor, just one floor below, watched it all on the tiny black-and-white television Jason kept in his office. Then the governor went on in his best presidential manner to explain the "demanding process" that the state is making the oil companies go through to come up with the four drilling sites. Then he asked representatives from each company to come forward and make their recommendations. Both guys did a nice, brief job talking about forming a partnership with Wisconsin, identified four "likely drilling sites," committing to nothing, and then it was over. The reporters stayed to ask questions, which were very straightforward, and the press seemed satisfied with a great headline story for both tonight's and tomorrow morning's news, "Drilling Soon in Northern Wisconsin." In closing, the governor put up a huge chart that showed the huge potential size of the field. The chart projected that the state's revenues from the royalties on the next twenty years of production were likely to reach seventy billion dollars. This amount said the governor, "could even perhaps reach as high as a hundred billion dollars," depending upon future oil prices. Taylor watched the proceedings in cold calculation and quietly whispered under her breath, "Okay Conlan, I'll give you a day, maybe two…"

CHAPTER 48

A<small>IR</small> F<small>RANCE</small> <small>HAD A LATE FLIGHT FROM</small> N<small>EW</small> Y<small>ORK TO</small> Houston that left at 7:30 p.m. Gerard and his three young analysts all sat together completing some of their work and finalizing their options. They sipped Latour champagne and joked about the stupid Americans. Gerard had tried to reach Hilton directly on the ride to the airport in New York, but Hilton had been out of the office. Finally, Gerard had called from the plane and reached Hilton at home. Gerard told Hilton that he was flying to Houston to conduct a special meeting. Hilton needed to be at Gerard's meeting, and he needed to bring his vice-presidents of crude and product trading to the meeting. The meeting would start promptly at eight the next morning. There was nothing more to be said.

"Perhaps you can refresh our memories from the last meeting," said Gerard peering over his glasses toward his lead analyst.

"Last time, we sat at approximately ten million barrels of fuels inventory, primarily gasoline at one dollar and seventy-six cents per gallon." The young Frenchman clicked off the statistics like a machine as Gerard sat at one end of the table and Hilton sat at the other.

"And the expectation of management here in Houston was what?" said Gerard.

"The agreement was that we would hold our position and management here was firmly convinced that prices were going to improve," the young analyst snapped back dutifully.

"And after the last two days, since the Wisconsin oil discovery have prices improved?" asked Gerard.

Rather than simply be sent to the firing squad, Hilton was slowly being tortured here by Gerard. Gerard, who hadn't known a damn thing about the oil trading a few years ago when he came to Houston, was now giving Hilton a lesson for the benefit of everyone to see, including his own trading staff.

"Can we cut the crap here Gerard?" Hilton asked. "You know exactly what prices did yesterday. West Texas Intermediate oil dropped five bucks a barrel on the MERC."

Gerard never looked at him and continued on, nodding for the analyst to continue.

"Prices have not improved as management here in Houston had assured us they would. In fact, as Mr. Sinclair has mentioned, since we were here at our last meeting, crude oil has dropped a total of five dollars and ten cents a barrel and New York Harbor Gasoline is down eleven point three cents a gallon."

Now Gerard turned decidedly towards one of the other analysts. "What is our current position on trading activities here in our Houston operations."

"Why are we singling out Houston here?" asked Hilton. "I bet our Singapore and Paris operations are under water, too. Or did they know that a billion barrels of oil were going to be discovered in Wisconsin?"

"We will deal with Singapore and Paris in Singapore and Paris. We will also deal with Houston in Houston. Do I make myself clear?"

"I'm just saying…" Hilton began to talk but Gerard expertly cut him off.

"I will need your full attention now to the business at hand. Do I make myself clear Mr. Sinclair?" This was not good. He was referring to Hilton again as Mr. Sinclair. Not a good sign.

"Yes, you make yourself clear," said Hilton. Gerard was giving him no option.

"Now what is our current trading position here in Houston?" Gerard asked again.

"We have lost nearly thirty-seven million dollars since our last meeting. Crude volumes are up thirty-two thousand barrels from our last meeting and products volumes are down three thousand barrels. Since the market opened yesterday morning, we have lost 34.6 million US dollars." The air conditioning was still coming on late in the morning. The analyst quickly rattled off a few more statistics as the group sat quietly in the still air of the conference room. Hilton was perspiring and looked down the table at his traders. The head of crude was leaning back away from the table with legs crossed. His custom-made ostrich cowboy boots looked almost vulgar next to the expertly tailored young Frenchman sitting next to him.

Gerard looked down the table, measuring each person and each item on the table until he stopped at Hilton. The room was in total silence as Gerard spoke. "Hilton, I believe that last time, you suggested that prices were 'firming,' as you described it."

Hilton looked back at Gerard. "They were, Gerard. Supplies were starting to get tight. Any one of our traders here can tell you that."

"Yes, and yet prices have in fact gone down dramatically over the last two days."

"Jesus, Gerard, nobody saw this coming. This is the Iraqi invasion, the oil embargo all over again. You can't blame me for some jokers up in Wisconsin finding out they're sitting on a bowl full of oil." For just a second Hilton got a glimpse of Martin sitting tied in the chair in his apartment. Oddly, he pictured himself at the helm of his yacht, reviewing the latest production reports from the leases he owned on the private land surrounding Chequamegon. Hilton had nothing to lose here. He was going down and he wasn't about to go down easy. The meeting attendees looked from Hilton to Gerard and back to Hilton. Gerard began to speak. "I am not blaming you, but I am holding you accountable."

"And what's that supposed to mean Gerard?" asked Hilton.

"That means that the next time you lose thirty million dollars at a company you might want to give your management a call and let them know the actions you are taking to manage the situation." Gerard was in control.

"And just for the record, Gerard, what actions were we supposed to take when oil was dropping through the floor? If you and the boys here had some great ideas maybe you should've called me up and told me about them."

"Just for the record, Mr. Sinclair, I did try to call you yesterday and your secretary informed me that you were out of the office." Gerard reached for a cigarette.

"I had a business meeting, but I was on the phone with my guys here several times. You can check with them. There was just nothing we could do. Prices are going to come back; the market is overreacting to this news and prices are going to bounce back over the next week." Hilton was on edge.

"We tried to understand when you were completely out of favor in the market six weeks ago. We were patient even though your position had actually worsened when we were here a month ago. But this time Hilton, you have gone over the line." Gerard had made up his mind.

Hilton stared back at Gerard. "I can recover from this, Gerard. Prices are going to come back. We can buy strongly when the market opens this morning and book the gain when prices recover over the next few days."

"I am sorry, Mr. Sinclair, but this time we will not be relying on you to recover anything. In simple fact, we will not be relying on you, period. You are free to collect your things now. Effective immediately we are terminating your responsibilities at Petrolea Energy."

"Based on what?" asked Hilton.

"Based on the fact that you have lost us another thirty million dollars. Based on the fact that you have lost the confidence of management. Based on the fact that you aren't qualified to be the president of a large international oil trading firm. Need I go on?" Gerard actually smiled.

"I've taught you everything you know." Hilton replied angrily.

"Based on your record here, one can only hope that I prove to be a very poor student," Gerard said haughtily, his staff joining with him in laughing at Hilton. "Hopefully, your condition will not prove contagious." Again, a laugh around the table.

"I'm sick of this company. I'm sick of these little shits you keep dragging in here to look over my shoulder and I'm sick of you running down here like a nursemaid every time some friggin' frog in Paris yanks your chain." Hilton's voice was elevated now.

Gerard spoke, "I suggest you be civil, Hilton. We will pay off your employment contract according to our original agreement, but that is at our discretion after we have reviewed all of your files. Now Hilton, if you please, remove yourself."

"I give a shit about my contract. I'm the president of this company and I don't have to listen to you or your little jerkoffs here suggest that there was some brilliant action I should have been taking yesterday when prices were falling." Deep inside, Hilton was kicking himself for not seeing this coming. He had no idea how the Wisconsin authorities had found out about the oil just hours after Hilton had. Had he thought about it, he could have predicted a big fall in prices when the news broke. He still had those leases on private land that would be worth millions.

"With all due respect Hilton, you are not doing yourself any favors here. Much of your employment contract incentives are based on goodwill, which is quickly eroding. I will not tolerate you referring to my staff in such terms." Gerard blew out a puff of smoke.

Hilton slammed his leather portfolio shut and stood up, his chair wheeling back against the wood paneling of the conference room with a thud. Hilton knew that with those leases in his hands he was going to be a very rich man from that oil in Wisconsin.

"I'll tell you what I'm not tolerating. I'm not tolerating a bunch of smart-ass French boys in here telling me how smart they are. If you're so smart, go ahead, you run the damn company and I can't wait to join one of your competitors and beat your brains out in the marketplace."

Gerard was completely calm. "It's really quite simple, Hilton. You have failed. I will be taking things on from here as you have suggested and if you can now pack up your things, I will ask one of the men here to call security to escort you out of the building."

"I don't need an escort. I will pack my things and you will be hearing from my lawyer," said Hilton.

"Very well then, wishing you all the best." Gerard gazed out the window.

"Oh, go to hell," said Hilton. With that, his days of employment as the president of Prolea abruptly came to an end.

There was a small armload of stuff to take with him. It was bad luck in the trading business to take all of your old things with you to a new job. The security guard did finally show up. Hilton dumped out his wastebasket and swept his desk items, a walnut inlaid clock and his favorite golf trophies into the basket and handed it to the guard. Then he opened his right bottom desk drawer and removed a stack of personal financial papers, tax files and his own oil trading account activity with Gannon and stuffed it into his briefcase. He had maybe a week before the $600,000 wire transfer to Gannon would show up. By then he would have more money than he knew what to do with. He could explain to Gerard that this had apparently been an oversight on his part and would gladly repay the money.

Once Gerard got the cash back from Hilton, Hilton reckoned Gerard would be happy to keep it quiet for two reasons. First of all, no trading house wanted to publicly admit that they had discovered fraudulent in-house activity. Sometimes it took years to get over that stigma with trading partners. More importantly, if Prolea in Paris found out that Hilton had been able to easily wire transfer $600,000 into his personal account, it would not reflect very well on the oversight and control that Gerard was supposed to be providing for the North American operations.

It was barely 9:00 a.m. and the last thing Hilton wanted to do was go home. He drove down to the Houstonian, bought himself a morning paper and went into the Men's Grill for breakfast. On the bottom of page one was a big story about the Wisconsin oil discovery. There was a large picture of the Wisconsin governor, surrounded by American flags and a long story about the size and depth of the field with a lot of quotes from a professor in the geology department up at their university in Madison. Hilton carefully read the article and smiled. The state was going to get rich off this oil, but so was Hilton. It was just a matter of time.

After lunch, Hilton headed down the Southwest Freeway and exited Chimney Rock, headed north as far as Richmond, and then turned left. Driving slowly along the boulevard, his eyes swept from left to right, eyeing massage parlors, strip clubs and modeling studios. When he got to Gessner, he made a U-turn and drove slowly back toward the freeway and finally pulled into one of the massage parlors, telling himself he needed to clear his mind. He opened his briefcase and grabbed a handful of cash from his wallet. Then he slipped off the big gold Rolex and tossed the watch and his phone into the briefcase and locked it in the trunk.

CHAPTER 49

JANSEN AND MACK KNEW THEY HAD THE WISCONSIN STATE public lands sewn up, but there was private land over the oil fields as well. They had wanted to send their men to Iron River, Wisconsin immediately after the governor had first called them to get the private land leased. In an hour after talking to Conlan, Jansen had a private jet in the air with four of their best landmen, three company attorneys and $200,000 in cash. But the governor made them wait until after his press conference. Jansen and Mack had decided that Mack and Arbor Energy got the nine landowners on the east side, and Jansen and Empire Oil got the nine on the west. They weren't battling each other. They just wanted to keep other oil companies out.

As soon as the press conference wrapped, the acquisition teams started rolling to their respective private landowners. But as they got to each homestead, they had the same conversation over and over again. Yes, they'd love to lease their land if there was oil under it. No, they hadn't leased their oil rights to anyone. They had clear title to their properties, too, except for the timber lease they had signed just last week with a nice fella from Texas named Larry Walker. Larry had come around the house and took his time, several of the people had gotten to know him, and everybody had signed up with him. Going to develop high grade timber on the properties. It was going to take some time, all right. Even Larry had said you didn't grow a sixty-foot oak or a four-teen-inch walnut overnight. Didn't know if that would in-terfere with the oil drilling, but the owners said, if it was all the same, they'd just as soon still let Larry's company get on with planting the trees, too.

The oil guys looked over Larry's contract. It was a Pro-ducer's 88, a standard oil and gas and minerals contract. It had held up on appeal for fifty years in Texas and Oklahoma courts. Occasionally, a landowner down in Texas would claim he'd been delirious or under medication, when he'd signed an oil lease down in Texas after he found out what he was sitting on. Once in a while someone would sue for fraud or misrepresentation on the lease document or say that they'd signed it only under duress from their spouse, anything to try and get the lease contract nullified. But the Producer's 88 had stood up in appeal after appeal and judge after judge now for the last sixty years. It was bulletproof. At the top of each contract, in bold letters, it clearly stated: "Lease of interest in timber rights and various other mineral rights as may be defined herein." But once you got past the title, the text was straight off the Producer's 88 and there was no mention of timber, planting, pulp or anything that even sounded like paper. In fact, if you looked real closely below the header you could see fine gray line where the header had been pasted over the standard oil lease. Larry had given them all of the time they needed to read the lease. Larry had even suggested they have their attorney look it over—not that any of them had an attorney. The only attorney this side of Solon Springs was some quack with an office behind the Spur station in Iron River and he charged forty dollars an hour just to get the family business settled when one of the older relatives would pass on. The younger land men had never seen anything like this before, but the veterans smelled it right away. Somebody had gotten advance notice of this oil discovery to this Larry Walker fellow, or whoever Larry worked for. With this advance notice, whoever it was had gotten this area sealed up even before the governor knew what was going on. Oh sure, the oil companies were going to get all of the state forest land for oil drilling, but some private individual was getting all of the private land from these eighteen farmers.

Over the weekend, Dick Jansen and Sheldon Mack arranged a meeting. They accused each other of secretly hiring this man named Larry Walker. They demanded answers from each other. And more than anything they wanted to find Larry Walker. Larry would know the story. A couple of the older land men even remembered Larry from his Austin Chalk and Permian Basin days, but they had lost track of him. Larry had always been kind of a loner, a tough cookie, and not the kind of guy you wanted to claim as your friend. He was dangerous, too. One of the land men had recalled a night when Larry had been in a bar over in Pasadena, Texas, over by the Ship Channel. Larry got up to use the restroom, and when he returned, a muscular young man had taken his barstool. When he came back, Larry had asked the man politely to return his barstool, and the man had told Larry in no uncertain terms to go to hell. Larry had broken a beer bottle over the bar and then used it to rip half of the man's face off with the jagged edges. Larry never said a word. When they carried the poor bastard out on a stretcher, Larry just sat back on the same bar stool and continued to quietly sip straight vodka the rest of the night. Nobody said a word to him for four hours, and at closing time, he dropped a hundred-dollar bill on the bar and walked out.

Hilton squinted as he emerged from the shadows of the massage parlor. He walked briskly to his car, grabbed his briefcase out of the trunk, hopped in, and locked the doors. He opened his case and returned what was left of his cash to his wallet. He clicked the big Rolex back around his wrist. Time to check in with Martin.

CHAPTER 50

Taylor had asked Jason to arrange her press conference for the top of Bascom Hill. Abraham Lincoln sat stoically in his chair behind her as she began her speech.

"Ladies and gentlemen thank you for coming today on such short notice and thank you for giving me a small opportunity to share a few of my thoughts with you about the future of Wisconsin."

It really hadn't been short notice by press standards, but all of the cameras would eventually pan the crowd that was engulfing her as she spoke. Just the idea that so many people would attend her press conference on what seemed to be short notice added immeasurably to her credibility.

"Over the last three years, I have worked hard to maintain the integrity and dignity of the office which I hold. As you know, I have worked tirelessly for you, the people of our state, to conduct our affairs with surety, fairness and a fact-based framework that enables us to make the right decisions for *all* of the people, not *some* of the people." Even Jason was hearing this for the first time.

"In the last week, as our governor has become aware of what may be potential oil reserves of benefit to our people, and he has embarked on a non-stop campaign that is, I believe, reckless, irresponsible and in the end, self-promotional for the governor himself. I have asked the governor to exercise due diligence, and he has declined. I have asked to let the people of our state be a partner in this, not a spectator, as the huge oil companies move in to take our natural resources and harm our environment. Unfortunately, the governor has told me that he—and the party—have lost confidence in me and cannot attempt to respond to my simplest request for fairness and equity. In fact, I believe strong forces within the oil industry are pushing the governor's programs forward, including this ill-conceived quest for oil riches. Despite my repeated attempts for justice, for prudence and for due diligence, the governor has pushed relentlessly forward with his half-baked ideas and ill-informed programs."

Taylor continued, "Nobody is perfect. Everybody makes mistakes. It is easy to make a bad decision. Over a year ago," Jason was shaking his head, "no, no, no" as Taylor continued, "I had a brief affair with a married man. A good man. It was Clark Everson, our lieutenant governor, and I am deeply sorry for that. I have apologized to Clark and his family. It was a mistake. But for me, it is time to move on."

Jason's eyes were wide with disbelief. For the press, this was too good to be true. First, the oil story was the biggest in a decade, and now a public battle was shaping up at the highest levels of Wisconsin state government. Taylor was easily one of the most popular and familiar faces in state politics. A fight between Taylor and the governor over this oil thing was too much to ask for.

"I have asked myself why the governor is moving ahead at breakneck speed. He has been unwilling to respond when I have directly asked him the question. I believe the reasons are twofold. First, as a man who has been in politics a long time, he now finds his own political future to be waning and he is desperate to revitalize it before the elections by bringing forward this sensational but unproven claim of oil wealth. Second, his close personal and professional relationship over the last few years with the big oil companies has compromised his integrity. He now relies on these people as a primary source of financial campaign support and he must be under tremendous pressure from these companies to proceed with this program at this alarming rate."

She had stayed up late rehearsing her speech. First, she had written it out in long hand. Then she typed it into her home computer and printed it out. She knew what she wanted to say; it was just a matter of putting it in concise terms, with enough color and easily quotable phrases to obtain maximum public impact.

"As your steward and your servant," Taylor continued, "it is my job is to protect the interests of the people from reckless and selfish acts that benefit a few at the expense of the many. I have enjoyed and I have been proud of our many fine accomplishments in the Department of Natural Resources during my tenure here. Regrettably, over the last week or so, I have found my hands tied by the governor, by others in the party and by others in the industry. I ask the people of this great state to call upon the governor and those around him to act with diligence and to proceed judiciously with this oil program. As for me, it is with regret but with finality that effective immediately, I am tendering my resignation as Director of the Department of Natural Resources."

CHAPTER 51

THE BIGGEST OIL COMPANIES WERE HUGE. IT WAS HARD for an average person to understand the sheer magnitude. One recent project, off the coast of Newfoundland in Canada, was going to cost more than ten billion dollars. In terms of assets and technical capability, only the automotive industry came close. As big as they were, they preferred joint ventures. The bigger the field and the greater the investment, the greater the desire to form a joint venture to spread their risks and spread their costs of oil development. Research laboratories at such companies had historically been rated the best in the world when compared with any other industry or any of the great universities. Over the years, the scientists from major oil companies had filed thousands of patents, from fuel additives to diamond drilling bits. The petrochemical arms of these companies had invented the nylon and Lycra compounds that paved the way for a revolution in everything from tires to women's bras. Leading science and engineering graduates fought to join the ranks of these companies where they could continue to work in the finest labs with rich research budgets—at much better pay than they could expect as a college professor. But cost cutting over the years had taken its toll. First, they just stopped hiring new graduates. Then they began offering "early retirement" to the most senior researchers, and anyone else who was willing to "take the package." They stopped buying new equipment. When an old piece of equipment that was expensive to maintain stopped working, they just let it sit there and ran fewer tests and fewer models and accepted smaller projects that could add immediate value to the business. After several years the Exploration Research Departments were no different than any others. They had a small number of very powerful computers. They had a skeleton staff of personnel, who, by working very smartly and planning their work well during the year, could perform the analysis and run the models needed for new exploration.

When the nine tapes arrived on the Empire Oil company plane from Madison, it took them more than four hours just to unscramble the format. Newer equipment from companies like Geovision could process and store data like this a hundred times faster, but those machines were expensive. Only a handful of oil companies—and both big oilfield service companies—had the latest Geovision platform.

The old magnetic tape format was a complex but effective format that was widely used fifty years ago but never used today. The tapes were large, and data was packed in double density. When they ran their fastest computer against the tapes, it chugged along for more than two hours. By the time they had started the third tape, it had completely filled up all available storage on the computer. Word went up the line from the engineers and the geophysicists to management that this was going to take some time. Business management had convened to consider the economics and run their numbers. A large array of technical computing infrastructure would be needed to analyze all of this data that had suddenly appeared on Empire's doorstep. Not only was all of this data from Wisconsin showing up, many other oil companies had found out that this had all originated from old CCC seismic tapes. Empire and Arbor and the other oil companies were scrambling to contact other states to see if they had tapes like these for their states. Its exploration research potentially worth tens of billions of dollars. Which state would be the next Wisconsin? The mountains of data coming in would be almost unfathomable to the skinny, tired out little work forces that had survived fifteen years of cost cutting. And the stripped-down computers, decimated by years of budget cuts, were no match for the mass of data and analysis to be performed. It was now known throughout the industry as the Chequamegon field. When word was announced at Empire Oil that they had gotten a concession for half of the state's oil, a cheer went up in the exploration department. This was virgin territory; essentially unexplored terrain. The fact that the discovery had been made after a routine inquiry into the state's archives made it all the more intriguing.

Pradeep had worked at Empire Oil for nearly thirty years. He was quiet, meticulous, organized, and obsessive. Over the years, his wife had grown accustomed to his work habits. Frequently, she would call him at eight or even ten o'clock at night when she hadn't heard from him. She would worry that he had been in some terrible accident or mugged and beaten senseless in the parking lot. But time after time, she would find him completely immersed in his work, often even unaware that it was long past dinnertime, endlessly apologizing that he had failed to call. Ultimately, she realized that Pradeep just loved his work. She had seen his behavior at home, too. When their old television had broken a few years back, Pradeep had spent an entire weekend taking the television apart and then testing every single component until he found a bad relay switch, which he then re-built from scratch using his soldering iron out in the shop in his garage. After ignoring the family over that entire week-end, he came to bed late on Sunday night, simply observing that it had certainly taken longer than he had expected to fix the old TV.

Everyone had been called in on Saturday. At 9:00 a.m. they were still waiting on the decoded tapes until they were finally distributed at 9:30 a.m. When Pradeep first looked at the digital interpretations from the CCC he was impressed with the quality and clarity of the data. The oil was deep, about a mile below the surface, and yet it showed up beauti-fully on his seventeen-inch Unix workstation. He had heard the tapes had been stored in metal canisters in the base-ment of the Capitol. Heat is what ruined tapes like these. If you kept them cool and dry, they would last forever. The blasts used to do the soundings, back in the 30s by the CCC, had been large too, especially for onshore formations. He could see the impressions the sound waves had made as they coursed through the layers of sediment and limestone. The charges had been spaced far apart, meaning the deto-nated caches had to be larger. Such an approach was often used undersea, where the environmental impact and cost of each detonation was much higher. Better to have fewer large detonations than lots of small ones. On land, the economics and the environment were different. Lots of small blasts were preferred on land. Odd that the CCC hadn't used a lot of small blasts to send out shockwaves. In fact, Pradeep knew that some shallow oil seismic waves in the old days were generated by repeatedly dropping huge, heavy blocks of weight from giant trucks that would drive over the land-scape. The impact would create the sound waves needed to profile the oil reservoir, somewhat like a giant ultrasound. Pradeep's guess was that the CCC had plenty of explosives which had compensated for what had to be the primitive equipment that was the norm back in the 30s. So, they chose to do fewer bigger blasts. Still, these images were very, very good. It was going to be easy to find the key formations to drill.

They had given him the first half of Tape Number 3 to analyze. Navigating the data was somewhat like riding in an underground digital submarine. First, he quickly jumped vertically down to the layers of oil sand. In some areas, the pay sand was more than eighty feet thick. Amazing. Kuwait and Saudi had pay sand like this. Some areas in the Gulf of Mexico and Alaska, but Wisconsin? Empire Oil had drilled onshore wells when the sand was less than fifteen feet thick. The porosity was excellent, too. He had a vague recollection from his college studies that the Midwest generally had poor porosity, especially in the farming areas of southern Wisconsin, Minnesota, Iowa and Northern Illinois. He also recalled a heavy sedimentary belt that ran across the Great Lake basin from Winnipeg on the west to Erie on the east. That might explain the excellent porosity. Large, even granularity, little evidence of gypsum, the oil was likely to be light. One perforation in the well casing in the middle of each formation and the oil would flow from hundreds of yards in every direction. With modern production techniques and some chemical enhancements, it could flow from more than a mile away. Easy to find and easy to produce.

Pradeep had been told he had only twenty-four hours to complete his initial analysis. They were going to reconvene on Sunday morning. Time was critical, and in the morning, there would be a large caucus where each of the explorationists would profile the top sites in their segment. Then the group would rank in order the top three formations recommended for drilling. Pradeep wanted to find the top prospect for drilling.

He spent several hours combing slowly over his entire set of data, cataloging each of the reservoirs, calculating their gross size and key characteristics. Even though the biggest formations were easy to find, there were a number of outlying smaller formations that he documented, as well. This was no time to be careless. In the afternoon, he began to analyze the five largest formations in painstaking detail. He loaded each of the reservoirs into a 3-D software program that enabled him to more accurately calculate reservoir size. He sliced off the "tops," or the highest portions of each of the big formations to determine the curvature and thickness of the "ceiling" of each reservoir. Ideally, the drill casing would enter the formation in an area where it would not splinter or fragment the rock formation that had trapped the oil, ensuring that the oil—and gas, if there was any—would remain in place and not escape into neighboring formations. It took him several hours to examine each of the highest points in each of the three largest reservoirs and find the best "top" to drill, or best path into the reservoir. At each stage, he recorded copious notes and observations in an electronic exploration log that he always used, and he captured hundreds of digital frames that documented each step of his analysis. By eight in the evening most of his colleagues had looked over the tapes, found their top drill sites, and summarized their findings for the Sunday morning meeting. It was Saturday night, and they wanted to get out of the office and not ruin the entire weekend.

Pradeep had completed his second round of analysis, but then he went back over each step he had taken a third time, making a tiny adjustment or correction here or there, and adding to his exploration notes. By midnight, he was confident that his analysis of the reservoirs was accurate. It was getting late. Now he needed to do a drilling profile for each of the three target sites. He started at the top of the first reservoir. His calculations indicated the zone was 5,456 feet below sea level. He meticulously scanned upward through layer after layer of the ground documenting the type of sediment, estimating the density and possible acidity, and determining the depth and estimated time of drilling through each horizon. Thirty years ago, when he was still in college, he had worked a couple of summers on drilling rigs in West Texas. He knew that eventually a well logger would be comparing the notes he made here, this evening, to the actual results as the well was drilled. This was called taking well cores from drilling and logging the results. The kind of documentation he was providing now would prove incredibly valuable and reassuring to the drilling crew during the many days it would take to drill this well. Some of the horizons were very consistent and hundreds of feet thick so the work went relatively fast. By three a.m. he was nearing the surface level and the layers of sediments and rock were narrow and highly differentiated. Surface casing would have to be driven into the ground more than two hundred feet to get below the water table and make sure the drilling mud and drilling fluids did not leak out into the surrounding ecosystem. Pradeep took his time cataloging each of the detailed layers of soil.

Then, using some of his spectrographic equipment, he went back to the pay sand. The ratio of sand to shale was an astounding 67%. Pradeep found it extremely odd. Swinging to another area of pay sand, he ran the test again and got 66%. The only way to get a reading this high, is when the oil is under an ocean, or under the Gulf of Mexico. Dying crustaceans, and sedimentary sand, over millions of years, are the only thing that can produce this high a ratio of sand to shale. The highest he had seen onshore was 38%, and that was in southern Louisiana which had once been under an ancient, saltwater sea. It was possible perhaps, that some very large geological event could have created such an unusual fingerprint several thousand years ago. However, it was totally uncharacteristic to maintain such a perfectly even and precise level across a broad expanse of geography.

Well-defined formations would run for several hundred yards on his profile and then end abruptly at this line of aberration. He took more than twenty minutes to document this odd piece of geology before continuing. Finally, he went back to the well bore and continued the path upwards, documenting each of the final layers as he had before.

At 3:30 a.m., Pradeep began his surface work. He set the longitude/latitude coordinates carefully and then analyzed the topography above ground. In his second year with Empire Oil, he had been sitting at his desk one afternoon when one of the senior vice presidents had come storming into the work area looking for Pradeep's boss. It turned out that his boss had sited a well without checking the topography. When the drilling company headed out to set the well, the coordinates put the well right in the middle of an old cemetery in West Texas. Unable to drill, the rig sat there for three days, at a day rate of thirty thousand a day, while the whole department worked to find an alternate site for the drilling rig. Eight years later, at the guy's retirement luncheon, they were still giving the guy grief; even presented him with a tombstone commemorating his years of service with the company. Pradeep didn't need to be reminded to check the topography for the drilling rig. What was on the surface? He scanned the surface level of the seismic maps.

It was hilly—very hilly. Probably not too steep to drill on, but Pradeep had never realized that northern Wisconsin had such elevations. Some of the hills rose more than thirty-two hundred feet. Pradeep continued his detailed note taking. There might be significant delays while they built a road to the drilling site and leveled it for drilling. For one of his highly rated drill sites, he wondered, is there already a road close to the site? He pulled up the USGS surface maps from Empire's own digital library. He plugged in the coordinates. The screen popped up in front of him, showing roads and surface elevations. The area was flat as a board. This was a completely different set of data that did not come from the Wisconsin tapes—it was data that Empire owned. This data and these maps showed houses, schools, roads and cemeteries—basically, all of the ownership of private land in the county and any houses or other improvements on the property. He used maps like these all of the time. He double checked the coordinates. The CCC seismic showed very hilly land surface, again, over thirty-two hundred feet of elevation. But on the left side of his screen was the topographic map which showed the area was almost flat. He plugged in his exact drill site coordinates for his preferred well site and pulled it up on his Topo screen. It showed his drill site to be perfectly in the middle of a seven-hundred-acre lake. It was named Canthook Lake. He searched the internet using "highest elevation in Wisconsin," and got back Timms Hill, elevation 1,951 feet. Then "lowest elevation in Wisconsin," Lake Michigan, 581 feet. That meant the highest possible elevation in Wisconsin would be about 1400 feet.

Thinking that perhaps his topographical coordinates could be wrong, he went back to the original digital map, found the top of the reservoir where he planned to position the well, and checked the east-west coordinates. They were exactly as he had recorded them. How could the coordinates be correct on the underground digital map? The topographical map from the CCC data showed mountains, and the USGS data from Empire showed a seven-hundred-acre lake. He slowly rose from his chair in the early morning hours and went to the bathroom. It had been noon when he had eaten the cheese sandwich he had brought from home. 4:30 in the morning. He stopped by the vendomatic and bought a container of dried soup, added some water, and stood idly as it rotated in the microwave. Something was terribly wrong. In thirty years, he had never seen such a thing. He removed the steaming soup, picked up a plastic

spoon, and headed back to his desk. He checked the coordinates on the well bore and then slowly moved the cursor
up, layer by layer, horizon by horizon. When he got to two
hundred feet, he stopped and stared blankly at the screen.
Dragging his cursor, he highlighted a rectangle on the map
and then clicked on the microscope button to enlarge it the
maximum 500%. Tracing along the razor thin line he saw
sediment after sediment cut off unnaturally by this strange
horizon. For some reason, someone had digitally pasted the
two maps together here, two hundred feet below the surface. The quality of the digital map was so good—*too* good.
The odd layer of sediment with the high sand/shale ratio,
and then the thin razor line running evenly beneath the surface. Then it came to him. Someone had doctored the CCC
maps. Or they were fakes. Oh, they were real digital maps
all right, and they showed oil that was really there, but they
had been taken from some other oil field somewhere in the
world. It would be almost impossible to tell where. Whoever
had done this was an excellent geophysicist—maybe a geologist. Pradeep went back over the line where the two maps
had been pasted together and noted that the seam had been
digitally scrambled using a randomizer to mask the seam.
Very nice work. The entire industry had assumed that these
old tapes had just been innocently lying in the basement of
the Capitol for fifty or sixty years. Certainly, none of his colleagues had suspected anything. They had all left quietly
while the evening was still young. Now Pradeep was going
to have some fun at the 6:30 a.m. so-called consensus meeting. He captured several digital slices from each of his files
and routed them to a high-resolution color printer. Then he
took the color pages and stood over the copy machine while
it warmed up. He was going to need some overheads to explain himself. Empire Oil and Arbor Energy had just made a
huge, public commitment to explore and develop a mammoth oil field in northern Wisconsin, and now there was no
oil. Pradeep slid blank transparencies in over the paper

drawer and then pushed the copy button. In a moment, he had ten color overhead slides that told his story.

Sunday morning. He had slept three hours in his office. It wasn't the first time. He was fourth on the list of explorationists to talk. As the meeting began, he quietly asked if he could go first, but the exploration department general manager courteously replied that he wanted to stick to the original agenda. Pradeep sat quietly enjoying himself while the first three geophysicists made total fools of themselves. Each of them outlined and described the size of their three biggest reservoirs and quickly targeted the preferred drilling sites. Everything was very business-like and to the point. Finally, it was Pradeep's turn.

"Ladies and gentlemen," he began. (Last year they had finally hired their first female in the department). "Unfortunately, I believe there is no oil on the section of maps that I was asked to analyze. Or if there is oil, these maps do not reflect that."

Pradeep was acting funny. So, there was no oil on his section, fine, that happens all of the time when you divide up a prospect. Still, he was just standing up by the projector smiling. The guy looked like crap. He must have pulled another one of his all-nighters. Hadn't even shaved. A good geophysicist though—you had to give him that.

"Now, despite what my three colleagues have just told you, I believe there is no oil on the section of Wisconsin land that they have analyzed, either. While it may be statistically possible that there is some oil, it would certainly be nothing like the oil pictured in the presentations they have just shown you." The room grew quiet. Where was this headed? Pradeep put his first slide on the projector.

"Here is a very nice reservoir that I looked at yesterday. My estimates show that, by itself, it holds more than one hundred million barrels of oil. There are two other slightly smaller reservoirs on the section of the tape that I was asked to analyze. The problem is that the tapes are fakes. They are frauds."

"Where is this heading, Pradeep?" the department manager's voice was quivering as he spoke. Maybe from anger, probably from fear.

"Let me show you what I found," Pradeep said quickly. "After finding the best point to enter the reservoir I set my coordinates and moved up through the elevations to the surface. Next, I ran two standard checks on the target drill site. I ran the topo check and I found the site to be extremely hilly—elevations to seventeen hundred feet." He popped the slide up on the overhead. Everyone could see the hilly sections of over the drill site.

"Next, I checked the USGS surface map, but I found this." Some squinted at the screen; all of them leaned forward in their chairs to see the well site and coordinates squarely in the middle of a lake. "The land surface is flat. Actually, it's a lake."

"Ladies and gentlemen, it's impossible for a lake of this size to be sitting over an area with this thirty-two hundred feet of change in topography. In fact, the maximum possible topographic change in Wisconsin is about 1500 feet." He flipped up the slide, with Wisconsin's highest and lowest elevations. Then he quickly flipped back to the previous slide, and then returned to the lake slide.

"After retracing my steps, I rechecked all of my coordinates and found them to be correct. As you may recall, I tend to be a bit anal at times..." He drew a small laugh from the crowd. As I retraced the digital map lines, I found this." He put up an overhead slide which showed the area two hundred feet below the surface. "Unless someone is playing a very bad trick on only me, I am quite sure that all of our digital maps look like this. If you magnify this section at five hundred percent, it will look like this," and he placed the next slide on the overhead. "Ladies and gentlemen, two separate digital maps from goodness-knows-where have been digitally pieced together to make these tapes from Wisconsin. Additionally, my guess is that the oil reservoirs we are looking at are from an undersea formation some-where. The sand-to-shale ratio is about 67%. Clearly, a mix we find undersea, but not on land formations. What we have is rubbish. These maps are all frauds."

Everyone sat in complete shock and silence. This little man whom they had given so much grief to over the years had made an irrefutable case.

"Okay," said the manager, flushed in the face, "fifteen minutes. I'm giving everyone fifteen minutes to go check their sections. Check what Pradeep said, and come back here immediately. I don't want anyone breathing a word of this. If I see anyone either making a call or answering their phone in the next fifteen minutes, I will personally fire you on the spot. Get out of here." The room jumped to its feet and people pushed out through the door. When the meeting reconvened fifteen minutes later, the Executive Vice President of Global Exploration was sitting just to the right of the exploration department manager. Dick Jansen was standing just inside the door.

"I assume that everyone confirmed Pradeep's findings?" No one spoke, but they all slowly nodded their heads up and down. "Pradeep, maybe I can ask you to take Mr. Jansen here, really all of us, through the little presentation you did for us earlier."

CHAPTER 52

EMPIRE OIL EXECUTIVES WERE SCATTERED ALL OVER THE world, but Jansen had immediately called an emergency video conference with the executive committee. It was Sunday afternoon. The Empire President was in London where it was already 4:00 p.m. Jansen laid out the facts. With very little debate, they concluded they had to go public immediately with the findings, no matter the consequences. If word of this got out to the market before they announced it, they would have enough lawsuits filed against them to fill a library. There was some debate over how to involve the state of Wisconsin. At the end of the day, they agreed it was best to make a joint announcement with the governor. In fact, it would be best if they actually had Wisconsin make the announcement on their own.

Jansen had everyone he knew in Madison looking for the damn governor, and nobody knew where he was. Late Sunday afternoon. Nobody at work had seen him, but they thought he could have stopped at the country club to work out on the treadmill. His assistants weren't with him, and he did not have either of his cellular phones on. Jansen was frantic. He had to go public with this. Finally, he got the governor on the line. The damn fool had stopped by the driving range to drive some balls and then had a few drinks in the bar. He was enjoying his best standings in the polls since he had taken office.

"Jerry, this is Jansen. We've got a problem." There was an unusual sense of urgency in Jansen's voice.

"What's the problem?" the governor asked lightly.

"We spent all Saturday analyzing the tapes we got from you. This morning we had a big meeting. They're fakes, Jerry. All nine of them. They've been doctored."

"That's impossible. We had our guys at the university look those tapes over and they confirmed themselves, the same size oil fields as your guys did."

"Oh, the tapes show there's oil all right, and plenty of it. But I've had a dozen of my guys study them, and they've been digitally altered. The data is from another oil field somewhere in the world. It's been made to look like it's located in Wisconsin."

"That's impossible, I don't understand," the governor was dumbstruck. "I can send the tapes back to the geology department down at the university and have them look at them again."

"Jerry, listen to me. The tapes are frauds. It took one of my best guys to make the discovery that they are fake, but we've confirmed it. We've got to go public with this and we don't have a lot of time." Jansen was direct.

"No, no, for God's sake, we can't go public with this until we know more." Conlan sounded frantic.

"Jerry, listen to me. We need to make a joint announcement. I've got a draft of a joint press release we need to release, and we need to release it now. It's Sunday night. The markets are going to open early Monday and we have to disclose this now. If you want, I will fly up and we can do a press conference first thing Monday morning." Jansen was pushing.

"I can't. I can't go to the people and tell them this was a mistake. It will ruin me. I'll be the laughingstock for years to come." Conlan's Sunday was suddenly not going so well.

"How do you think *I* feel?" said Jansen. "Empire's going to hang me for this. Our only chance is to back out of it with grace and dignity, and stress the fact that fraudulent activities have occurred that led us to act the way we did."

"You are out of your mind, Jansen," said the governor. "I gave you a copy of the tapes before anyone else had even seen them. I set this up for you guys. Now you're coming back to me and you want me to take the fall on this. You are out of your damn mind."

"Jerry, I don't want to talk about stuff like this over the phone. We both know how, ah, let's say, "beneficial" our relationship has been for you over the last three years. I don't think you'd like it if all of a sudden people started asking questions about how that pitiful little investment company you set up supposedly bought that condominium we got for you in Aspen. That would be embarrassing for you now, wouldn't it Jerry?" Jansen paused.

"It's not going to work Jansen. If you want to expose me, fine, expose me, and I'll take you and all of Empire Oil and Arbor Energy down with me. I'll plea bargain my way out of it and you bastards won't be able to set foot in the Midwest for the next twenty years. I ain't going to go do some press conference and tell everybody this was my fault. You go do your press conference if you want, and I'll have my comments later in the day. That's the best I can do for you." The governor had called his bluff.

"You're going to regret this, Jerry," said Jansen.

"We both regret it now, don't we Jansen?" and the governor slammed down the phone.

CHAPTER 53

THE EMPIRE OIL ANNOUNCEMENT HAD BEEN DRAFTED and reviewed a dozen times by everybody in management. They would release it at 8:30 a.m. New York oil trading opened at 9:00 a.m. Martin was still at the Ritz. He had called in to work and told them he was ill. He had worked out and then showered back up in his room. He turned the TV on at seven. Everything was quiet. Martin knew it could be a day, or two or even three days, but once Empire and Arbor got their hands on the tapes, one of their experienced geologists or geophysicists would discover the tapes weren't real. He flipped from CNBC, to Bloomberg, to Fox Business and back again. He ordered breakfast. It was a little after 8:00 a.m. An announcement was made that Empire Oil was holding a press conference at 8:30 a.m. Martin had all of his investment account positions in place expecting a big rise in the price of oil.

It could have come from one of the technicians tuning the video conference equipment, or a security man standing outside the meeting area. A secretary could have done it after revisions to a memo, or a hotel clerk could have seen it coming off the fax in London, or Los Angeles or Singapore. One of the young analysts who worked in public relations might still have a friend from college who joined Reuters or Dow Jones, or the New York Times. A geologist could have told his wife. A telephone operator could have overheard a call. Everyone wants a scoop. It didn't really make any difference. At 8:15 a.m., a manager came running into Jansen's office with the news that there was a rumor that the oil find in Wisconsin was a fraud. Martin saw it scroll along the bottom of the screen, "Questions asked about giant Wisconsin oil discovery."

Fifteen minutes later, Empire Oil released their statement while simultaneously Jansen held a two-minute press conference where he read the exact same statement. He stated the billion-barrel oil field in Wisconsin was a "mistake, possibly a hoax."

Acting on the rumor, just fifteen minutes earlier, traders in London were buying as many contracts as they could write. The oil price was going to go back up. On a typical day, the New York Mercantile Exchange, or NYMEX, alone trades more than twenty times the amount of oil actually used in any one day. On a day like this, they might trade two hundred or even four hundred times an average day's actual physical global consumption.

Martin was watching TV and hovering over his laptop. The price skipped along every minute or two, taking jumps up of ten or fifteen cents. It would be Jansen's last official act as an executive at Empire. The price was now up a dollar and not slowing down. It took fifteen minutes for the price to come up three bucks a barrel. Martin started to pull the trigger on some of his positions. He sold all fifteen million barrels. In the last three days, he had turned the $500,000 dollars from Hilton into $45,000,00. He flopped on to the bed and stared at the ceiling. His plan had worked perfectly. There was still more work to be done, though he couldn't help but smile as he thought about his plan, his work with Taylor, and the absolutely stunning outcomes.

CHAPTER 54

HILTON HAD BEEN OUT OF THE OFFICE. COULDN'T EVEN turn on his phone when he was in Wisconsin because he didn't want to be tracked later if he somehow became a suspect. He was thinking back on his dealings with Larry. Hilton wasn't used to killing. He had known Larry a long time and Larry had done him a lot of favors. But Larry had double-crossed him. Larry was dangerous, too. One false move and Larry could have overpowered him in seconds. After Vietnam, Larry could kill a man without giving it a second thought. Hilton himself was good with his fists or a gun. In the early days, long before he was a white-collar executive, he had spent a lot of time himself in the oil fields. And he had been in more than one fight in a bar where he more than held his own. The only way he could have possibly ended up with this oil was to kill Larry and take the signed leases and forge them over into his own name. As long as the landowners got their money, they didn't care who paid them. Larry didn't have any family, or if he did, he never mentioned them. Didn't have any friends, either. Nobody knew what Larry had been doing on this except Hilton and dumbshit Martin. Hilton recalled that he even had several old powers of attorney he had signed with Larry on other deals. He could probably use one of those to legally get the leases in his name. One of his lawyers would fix them up for him. Martin should be out of the deal. He had taken his half-million and that was the last Hilton had heard from him. If there was a problem, maybe Martin wanted another little "Russian roulette" demonstration.

After finishing Larry with a final blow to the head, Hilton had looked around the cabin. Larry ran a pretty tight ship. Hilton gave some thought to hiding the body, disposing of the murder weapon, and even burning the place down. Then he realized there was nothing in the world that linked him to Larry in this place, at this time. Nobody had seen Hilton. No one knew he was here. At the same time, Hilton had no idea that the entire oil discovery had been melting away. Hilton went through Larry's pockets and wallet but found nothing of any value and nothing that linked Larry to Hilton. In the end, Hilton had quietly picked up the red accordion file that contained the signed leases, and all of the stuff that Martin had prepared, and he stuck it all into Larry's briefcase. Hilton grabbed Larry's gun and cell phone and put them in the briefcase too. Hilton took a wet washcloth from the old chipped sink and wiped down the door knobs, the suitcase handles, anything that Hilton thought he might have come in contact with. When he had everything in the briefcase, Hilton looked around one more time and then walked silently back to his car and drove out of Deep Lake Lodge.

CHAPTER 55

IT WAS SUPPOSED TO BE A ROUTINE MEETING. THEY HAD a staff meeting like this every two weeks, where each of the section heads would give an update on activities and plans for the next two weeks. Then Martin's boss would give an overall summary update and cover any remaining administrative items. It never lasted more than an hour. Anita hated these meetings because they always started right at 8:00 a.m. and she had to stop by Shipley's and pick up donuts. It was also her job to make sure there was plenty of coffee in the conference room. Martin chose his spot carefully in the big conference room. He was one of the first to give his standard section briefing. As usual, he had been in the office before anyone and he already had packed the few essential and personal items he cared about in the trunk of his car. He also had taken the extra, remaining tape canisters from West Virginia and hauled those out to his car for disposal. Everything—every single thing he had ever done with Chequamegon—was erased from his computer. He had even combed Anita's files and cleaned out a few items that she had stolen from him and given to Hilton.

Each of the section heads went through their report, and then Martin's boss began his overall briefing. Martin listened carefully, waiting for an opening. Finally, his boss announced that they had finalized the capital budget for the coming year. It was to be 20% lower than last year due to overall sluggishness in the oil market.

Martin started in. "Do you mean to say that we are actually going to have a smaller exploration budget next year than we did this year?" Eyebrows raised around the table at Martin's sudden reaction.

"Yes, that's what I said. 20% less than last year," his boss driving the point home. He wasn't going to take anymore crap from Martin. He had already talked to the President about the need to "do something" about Martin.

"Did our Kazakhstan project make the cut?" asked Martin.

"We won't be announcing the final projects until next week," his boss dryly responded. "We just set our overall spending level this week and now we'll be going back through the projects to see which ones get final approval."

"You know right now whether or not Kazakhstan made the cut, don't you?" said Martin sarcastically.

"We will discuss it next week, Martin," his boss said emphatically. "That is not the purpose of this meeting."

"Are we doing the Kazakhstan deal or not? I'm not leaving the meeting until I know. Now did you approve it or not?"

His boss looked around the room carefully. They all knew that if the budget was cut 20%, the chances of them doing a project as large and as risky as Kazakhstan were almost zero. Martin sat glowering at everyone from the other end of the table. It was time for a showdown, and Martin's boss seemed to be holding all of the cards.

"Well, Martin, since I need to treat you differently from everybody else in the room, I will tell you. No, your project did not make the cut. We're not doing it next year; we might not even do it the following year. It's too big and it's too risky and I don't think we should spend any more time screwing around with it. Does that answer your question, Martin, or do I have to further explain it to you?"

"No, you don't have to explain a damn thing to me or anyone else in the room, do you? Everybody else in the business is expanding, raising their budgets with the increase in crude prices since last year. We just sit here fat, dumb and happy while you guys at the top just collect your big bonuses." Martin looked grim.

"Please don't start in, Martin. It's eight o'clock in the morning, for Christ's sake. We really don't have time for this," his boss said firmly.

"Oh, I'm not going to waste everybody's time. Because you know what? I'm finished. I'm finished working on projects that never go anywhere. I'm sick of working at a company that's got no future," said Martin.

"Martin, that's enough," his boss tried to intercede.

"And most of all I'm tired of kissing your incompetent ass with the hope of getting a 7% raise next year instead of 5%," Martin interjected.

"Martin I've had it with you. You're a talented geologist, but you need to go pack up your stuff. You're fired." His boss slammed shut the folder in front of him.

"No, no, I'm not fired. I quit. I'm out of here. Now if you will excuse me, I wish all of the rest of you nothing but the best." And at that, Martin rose from his chair and headed to the door.

"This is it, Martin. This time you will not be welcome if you come crawling back."

Martin paused momentarily and looked his boss squarely in the eye, "In your dreams. I'm finally out of here, this time for good." There was a long pause as they all watched the big door slam shut behind Martin. Then Martin's boss looked down his list of handwritten notes and paused for a moment.

"Okay," he said, "now that we have that out of the way, I only have a couple more things I want to go over."

Back at his hotel room again, Martin lay sprawled across the bed watching television. It was Taylor, and she was absolutely outstanding. He loved her. Missed her. Professional, sharp, witty, attractive. Their time in Chicago had been awesome. Word of the oil bust was out, and thanks to Jason, the TV crew in Madison had "caught her" coming out of Magnolia Café with a breakfast coffee and a bagel.

"Given that the oil is apparently just not there, Miss Thompson, do you have any regrets now over your resignation on this matter?"

"Absolutely not. I never look back. I believe that principles are still important in the business of government. When the governor went forward with plans to proceed with this action before we had done all of our homework, I had to resign."

"Can you describe your relationship with the governor as it stands today?"

"I told the governor in no uncertain terms that if I were running the show, I would have done things completely different, but he didn't want to listen to me. He told me I wasn't a team player. He told me since I wasn't doing what he wanted, and what the party wanted, that I was finished politically. He threatened to ruin me over my affair with the lieutenant governor. I thought we needed to put integrity above politics on this, but frankly I think the governor saw this as his ticket to re-election."

Martin smiled broadly in his hotel room. He could see where this was headed.

"Taylor, there was a report this afternoon in a Milwaukee Journal poll that shows the governor's popularity is crashing. Is he still a viable candidate after this?"

Jason said he wouldn't need to coach anyone to ask that question. The question was pretty obvious.

"Oh, that's not for me to decide, that's up to the voters," said Taylor smiling broadly. "I will suggest however, that once he's out of office, the governor may have more time to go dove hunting down in Mexico with his oil executive buddies."

"Can you see a scenario where he doesn't seek re-election?" asked one of the reporters.

"That would be only speculation on my part, and I never speculate," she said. "I would wonder though, if given the way this entire episode was handled, if the governor still has the confidence of the people of Wisconsin. At this point, can he effectively lead?"

Masterful. Here it comes, thought Martin. He was up sitting on the edge of the bed watching the "impromptu" interview.

"Taylor, we have to know. All of the people are going to be asking the same question. Are you now a candidate for governor of the state of Wisconsin?"

"I'm very honored that you would even ask me that question. I haven't really thought about it. I guess if the people and the party came forward and asked me to represent them I would do it. As governor, I believe I could serve with the dignity, with the honor and with the sense of purpose that the people of Wisconsin should expect. It is far too early to carry on a discussion such as this and I hope I have been responsive to your questions today. Now I'm going to go home and eat my breakfast. Thank you very much."

A small crowd had gathered around the TV camera and the reporter. As the interview concluded, a funny thing happened—there was applause. She was still on camera, but she had stepped back from the microphone. There was a mixture of journalists, neighbors, and students, at the conclusion of the interview. She had bowed her head ever so subtlety, and spontaneous applause came from the small crowd. She stood smiling just for a moment and then gave a little wave and walked off towards her apartment.

Martin picked up his burner phone and called her on her private cell number. She was walking back to her house alone and she answered on the first ring. Only two people had this number—Jason and Martin.

"Just wanted to talk directly with the next governor of the state of Wisconsin."

Taylor was having some real fun now. Exhilarated from the press conference, especially the unexpected applause at the end. "I think you're jumping to some pretty big conclusions Mister," said Taylor, joking with Martin.

"Let's see, would that make me the First Gentleman of the state of Wisconsin, or the Mr. First Lady?" Martin was so happy for her.

"Do you believe this?" asked Taylor. "I think the governor exceeded all expectations in his degree of stupidity on this. The buzz on this is unbelievable. Jason said we got a call from CNN and *60 Minutes* this morning."

"Are you going to do it?" asked Martin.

"60 Minutes? No idea."

"No, no, I mean are you going to run for governor?" asked Martin.

"This is the chance of a lifetime Martin," said Taylor growing suddenly serious, "I've got to do it."

"There was never a doubt in my mind. I just had to hear you say it." Martin was silent.

"You were great in all of this Martin. You're just great, period. I, I love you."

"God, I love you too, Babe. Listen, I just want to make sure we know where we're going on this whole thing." Now Martin sounded suddenly serious.

"Wow, you like getting to the point, don't you?" said Taylor. "Where do you think we're going?"

"I don't know what to think. I thought I knew and then with everything happening I've sort of lost my way," said Martin.

"We don't need to rush anything, Martin. You know I'm going to be busy for a week just watching this thing take shape. What do you think about seeing where you end up with Liz on this whole thing?" Taylor paused.

There was a long silence on the other end of the phone. Martin felt the tears form in the corners of his eyes. Martin wasn't going to lose Taylor this time. He wasn't going to walk away. He loved Taylor. She was awesome. Exciting. Beautiful. Taylor had always loved him. But he loved Liz, too; at least, he thought he did. He did all this for Liz. He had been angry at Liz over the separation. Angry at Liz for telling him he didn't have the killer instinct, wasn't making enough money. He had already shown he could outwork and outsmart everyone. He wanted to tell Taylor that he would come for her. He wanted to say he wanted to be with her.

"Umm, okay how about we talk in a week, probably need to limit our phone calls for a bit," said Martin.

"A week sounds good. Surprise me. Love you." said Taylor.

"Love you, too. Bye."

Martin lay on the bed for a few minutes, staring at the ceiling and wiping the tears from his eyes. It was nearly 2:00 p.m. in the afternoon. He was now a very wealthy man. But he still had a bit of business to do.

CHAPTER 56

MARTIN HAD CALLED LIZ AND TOLD HER IT WAS IMPORTANT; told her it was something about the house and he needed to see her. She had suggested Saturday. When he told her he was off work today, and then pressed her again and explained that it was urgent, she finally said if it didn't take too long, he could come by around 3:00 p.m. Promptly at 3:00 p.m., he pulled into the familiar drive and parked in his usual spot in front of the right garage door. He got his brief case and a big leather portfolio out of the car and walked across the stepping stones to the back door. He had laid these stones with Liz almost twenty years ago. They had driven up to Marble Falls one weekend and bought ten flat stones and thrown them on a blanket in the trunk of the car. The drive back had been crazy that night. The stones were heavy and weighed down the car. Every time they hit a bump on the road, sparks had flown as their old car had hit bottom and they laughed like kids all the way back to Houston. It was good to be home.

The back door was locked, and Liz was in the kitchen. She had probably heard him drive up, but he knocked anyway. He watched as she pretended to see him and then he followed her as she came over and unlocked and opened the door. She stood there momentarily, just looking at him and then smiled.

"Hi." She finally spoke.

"Hi." Martin stood in place.

"Come on in, I'm starting dinner." She turned as quickly as she had appeared, and he trailed her back into the kitchen. It was the first time they had been alone in the house since she had asked him to move out. She went back to washing fresh vegetables over the kitchen sink and he eased down on one of the old gray bar stools at the breakfast counter. They had always talked about getting nicer bar stools, but these were just so comfortable. Not having seen them for a while, Martin noted just how beat up they looked.

"How have you been?" asked Martin.

"Fine. I've been doing fine." She began to scrape the skin off the carrots with a small knife. "And you. How have you been?"

"Busy. A little busier than usual, but you know—busy."

This wasn't going at all as he had planned. He wanted to just tell her everything. He didn't want to make a fool out of himself. He still had Hilton to contend with too, so maybe it was a little early to even be over here talking to her. She was being cool; not that he expected anything any different.

"Listen Liz, I need to talk to you, okay?" He wanted to ask her to stop and look at him, but he had no right.

"You said it was urgent, right? About the house, right?" She was still working on those carrots.

"Well, we do need to talk about the house, but we need to talk about something else first." He stopped talking, she stopped scraping carrots and looked over at him. She dropped her knife and dried her hands on the dishtowel lying on the kitchen counter. Then she walked around the end of the breakfast counter and settled onto the end barstool, slinging one leg over the arm as she often did when talking on the phone. "So, what do we need to talk about?"

"Well we've been separated now for a while. And I've been doing a lot of thinking about what you said when you asked me to move out." Martin paused.

"Like what?"

She wasn't going to make this easy for him. "Like everything," Martin said.

"And?"

"And we need to talk about some stuff." He might as well just blurt it out. This was getting them nowhere.

Liz was one to take charge. "Martin don't take this personally, but you said we needed to talk urgently about the house, and we don't seem to be getting anywhere." She was smiling.

"Okay, I need to ask you a few questions and you have to answer them. Okay?"

"What kind of questions?" asked Liz.

"Just say you'll answer them okay?"

"Okay, okay, I'll answer the questions."

Martin hesitated; he looked around the kitchen. She was heating up the water in a pot on the cooktop. "Okay, here's the first question. Do you love me?"

"Martin," she protested.

"Just answer the question. I need to know the answer."

She hesitated for a long time. She had spent sleepless nights asking herself the same question. Where to begin?

"You know Martin, I've decided that's a very complex question. I know that I used to love you with all of my heart. I used to love our nights together, the way we talked, and the way you held my hand when we walked—even in the grocery store. I loved you like the crazy young woman that I was back then. I loved you when we brought our babies home from the hospital and you stayed home from work to take care of me because you didn't want my mother doing it. And I loved you when you bought that swing set with a million pieces and put it up in the backyard and made handprints of the kids around the concrete you poured around the bottom."

Liz paused to find Martin listening quietly. He still looked great. He looked tired, too. Didn't look like he had slept in a week. Still looked good, though. Years ago, she referred to him as her Marlboro Man. He had never smoked, but at a back-to-school mom's coffee a few years back, in front of everyone, one of the new mothers was trying to figure out who went with who. The new mom wanted to determine if she had met Liz's husband. Liz had been describing him and then one of her friends had jumped in and blurted out, "You know, he's the one that looks like the Marlboro Man." Then the woman had known immediately who Liz's husband was and they had all laughed like teenagers over it.

Liz continued, "Look Martin, maybe I've changed, maybe you have. I don't think it makes a difference anyway. But that part of our life seems to be gone; or, if it's still there, I just can't see it anymore."

"Tell me again why you wanted me to move out. I know I've changed over the years. Is that why you asked me to move out?" asked Martin.

"Actually, that's not the main reason I asked you to move out. Somewhere, deep down, I think you're still that same person; it's just that other things have buried the real you and turned you into someone else. For the last couple of years, the Martin I've known has given up. He's mad at his job but he doesn't have the guts to do something about it. He's frustrated that he doesn't get the respect and acknowledgment of others, but he's not willing to go after it. He's working as hard as he ever worked, but he's lost his edge and it's eating him up inside. The last two or three years it seems you've just given up and decided that you will just "get by" these next twenty years. The real reason I asked you to move out Martin, is that 'getting by' isn't good enough any longer. I wasn't being selfish either, Martin. To be honest, I had always thought I'd be living a better life, and that includes having some more money in the bank. Getting by isn't good enough for me, and it isn't good enough for you, either."

"You know Liz, there's some truth to what you are saying. I can see that now," said Martin. "I was afraid to venture out, to go out on my own. But we had a house payment, kids to feed, I was doing okay in my job. I had job security."

Liz listened quietly, sympathetically to Martin, "I don't know about security. I think sometimes people have to take risks. Go for it. You know they say, 'Nothing ventured, nothing gained.'" She continued to look quietly at him.

Martin nodded his head, "Yes, yes, at this point I know that better than a lot of people do. I really do think I'm a different man than I was six months ago."

"I don't know Martin. It's hard for somebody to change. I know over the last two or three years, you just didn't seem..." Martin interrupted Liz.

"So, do you still love me?" Martin asked again.

"Of course, I still love you. Maybe I love you in a different way than I did ten or twenty years ago." She had changed over the years, too. She missed him. She wanted to talk to him like they used to talk. She wanted him to hold her, to take care of her. She had options; she knew that. Some of the guys she had met she found very interesting. And some had been very successful. If she had to, she could do just fine on her own. She would have to work full time on her fundraising jobs, but she could get by. She wanted a man—a man who was strong, to take care of her. Was that Martin? It didn't have to be old Martin. It could be somebody new.

"What about the other guys you've been seeing?" Martin could help himself.

"First of all, it's none of your business, and second of all, what about them?" said Liz.

"The guys at work tell me whenever they see you out with someone. Obviously, I know about Hilton, too. For Christ sake Liz, Hilton's a married man. Why are you going out with someone like him?"

"So, a bunch of us went out sailing on Hilton's boat, big deal." Liz was stretching the truth a little bit. "And he's married, but they're getting separated too. Sound familiar?"

There was supposedly going to be a group of them going out to sail; Hilton had told her it was going to be a group. Then it was just Hilton and her. Martin would never know the difference. She continued. "You know what? I like Hilton. He's got a great job. He's fun to be around…"

Martin interrupted, "I don't suppose the fact that he's rich and has a giant sailboat even enters into the equation."

"You know Martin, as long as you brought it up, yes, it does enter into the equation. I'm just not getting any younger, Martin, and I don't want to be selling my furniture to raise money to put the kids through college. I don't want to be living off social security when I'm seventy, either. If I can't have you, if I'm going to be marrying someone else, then they might as well have money. Believe it or not Martin, I've found some guys still find me pretty attractive for an old woman, and some of them, like Hilton, have got money—a lot of money." She looked him straight in the eye and smiled. She was just so alive, so honest. She just enjoyed life. She wanted more than he had given her.

Martin looked at her carefully.

"What about you, Martin?" asked Liz. "You're a good-looking guy, you been out on any "hot" dates?"

Taylor flashed before his eyes. The dance at the restaurant when he was deer hunting. Chicago.

"Well," said Martin, "I bumped into an old friend from college, but we didn't exactly go on a date."

She looked back at him with a puzzled expression. Finally, she spoke, "Maybe we switch topics. The kids are going to be home pretty soon. You said you needed to talk to me urgently about the house."

Again, there was a long pause, and Martin slid off the bar stool and went over by his briefcase to the big oversized leather portfolio. He carried the portfolio over to the breakfast bar and sat it on edge, carefully pulling the long narrow zipper around three sides of the case and then opening it flatly on the counter in front of her.

"Yes, the house. You know how attached I've become to this place, but I've been thinking a lot about what you've said, and I think we should bulldoze this place. For the value of the lot it's sitting on, it's not worth fixing up and it's sure not worth adding on to."

"And what do we live in once we bulldoze this house?" Momentarily, she had forgotten they were separated.

"I need to talk it over with you, but I'm thinking something like this." Martin pulled back the light waxy paper covering a sheaf of oversized pages and there was a front elevation view of an extremely large house. It was a French Colonial—her favorite. Huge round fieldstones, clapboard siding and cedar shingles on the roof. It was not only her favorite style; it was an architect's design of her favorite home plan. For years, she had kept the plan in a stack of magazines by her bedside. Somehow Martin had got his hands on it and had some plans drawn up.

"How, how did you get this? Where did you get this?" she stammered. This was the last thing she had expected.

"It was easy. It's Home Beautiful right? You've only had it lying on your nightstand for the last five years. I just had Terry get the basic plans from the magazine and then I had him do some working drawings to get it sitting the right way on our lot. I had him make a few changes, too. I had him add a sitting room off the master and a three-car garage. This is just a first draft; I didn't want to go any further on it without you."

"Martin why are you doing this?" Liz was stunned.

"Doing what?"

"Showing me these plans. I know what something like this costs. We could never afford anything like this." Liz was confused. What kind of game was he playing? Why did he go to all of the expense to hire an architect and tease her with this? It all seemed like a dream to her.

"Well, I think we can afford something like this if we want it," said Martin.

"And just how do you propose we pay for it?" asked Liz.

"I've got the money, Liz. Right now, we need to keep it quiet, but trust me, I've got the money." Martin was speaking in quiet tones.

"If you don't mind me asking, where did you get it? Did you rob a bank or something?" She laughed. "Martin I just don't understand." Could what he was saying be true? They had saved years just for vacations and cars and now he was showing her plans to a million-dollar house she had always dreamed about.

Martin smiled comfortably. "Well, as a matter of fact, something did happen at work, too. I quit my job, but that's another story."

"You quit your job?" Liz was incredulous.

He continued on, "The truth is I've made some very, very good investments that have really paid off. For right now, though, in case anyone asks, I plan to just tell them that I inherited some money. If anyone asks, I'd prefer you tell them the same thing."

"Who's going to ask me that?" asked Liz.

"Well, nobody right now—except our architect friend, of course. Terry already wanted to know if we had won the lottery or something."

They had met through church. Last year, Liz and Sandy had been on the Sunday School Christmas Program Committee together. Terry specialized in designing big custom houses out in Memorial. For a moment, Liz could just imagine the discussions Terry and Sandy were having in their kitchen, too.

"What did you tell him?" asked Liz.

"Told him an old maid great aunt had died. Told him we had been saving up anyway for years, and this is something I really wanted to do." Martin said confidently. "You know I am an only child."

"What did he say?" asked Liz.

"Nothing. Actually, he said, "good for you." I think it's pretty common, Liz. You just assume that everybody you know is making a lot more money than I am, and in fact, a lot of parents are helping their kids build these big houses in Memorial. A lot of these couples, like this, moving into these houses, are getting big money from their parents, even if it's not an inheritance. I don't think Terry gave it a second thought."

"So how much will we have to borrow?" asked Liz carefully. Maybe this is where the fantasy came to an end.

"We can pay cash for it if we want to. I've got the money—and more. I just think it might be prudent, and actually better, tax-wise, not to pay for it all in cash."

Liz leaned back on her barstool. She looked at the plans lying on the counter. She couldn't comprehend this in a few minutes, or even in a few hours. This changed everything, and yet it changed nothing. She couldn't help from looking at Martin in a completely different light. But she didn't want to go back to where she was with him; she wanted to live, and she wasn't sure Martin was being altogether honest with her. There were just too many unanswered questions.

"So, what do you think," Martin asked. "Do you like the plans or not?"

"Yes, yes of course, what's not to like? Martin, this is all just taking me so much by surprise." She heard the creaking brakes of the bus out in the cul-de-sac and the roar of the big diesel engine as it took back off down the street. "Listen Martin, I don't know what this means. You've got to give me some time, and now the kids are coming in on the late bus, so we can't talk anymore today."

"Yeah, yeah of course. I know this is a surprise. It's not just the house Liz, I'm different too. I listened to what you said. I did what I had to do. Is it okay if I just leave the plans for you now to look over and we can talk about it later?"

Liz hesitated. "Well, yes, I guess. I just don't want you to read anything into this. I haven't decided anything about you or about us though, okay? I'm just looking at plans. It doesn't cost anything to dream, does it?"

Martin paused again a long time before responding. "This isn't a dream Liz. You take some time to think things over. I've got to go now anyway. Thanks for agreeing to meet."

Oddly, he reached out to shake hands and she reached out to touch him, for the first time since they had been apart. Then he quickly walked back to his briefcase by the backdoor, picked it up, and walked out without looking back. She peered out at him through the side window by the laundry room as he met the kids in the driveway. He dropped his bag and got down on his knees, giving each of them a big smile and a hug. His older daughter stood back behind her little sister waiting, and then gave him a high five before falling into his arms. Liz had never been more confused in her life.

CHAPTER 57

HILTON HAD GOTTEN IN LATE FROM WISCONSIN AND WAS up early. He was dressed in casual clothes, driving over to the Houstonian. No more dealing with the fucking French people over at Prolea. He was out, and ready to start on those leases in Wisconsin. Needed to come up with a package to talk to investors. Need to lay low after the Larry Walker thing. Time for a nice workout, then maybe a lunch, poolside. Wonder if Liz will be there today?

Hilton was daydreaming on the drive down Memorial. They're finally widening Memorial Drive, he thought to himself, as he sat in morning traffic. Listening to Bloomberg on satellite radio, he suddenly heard a clip from an earlier Empire Oil press conference. He cranked up the volume. "And so, the Wisconsin oil is simply not there. It was a mistake. Possibly a hoax. The state of Wisconsin is conducting a press conference later today. There will be an investigation." What the hell? What had he just heard? He tuned to another news channel to try and get another report on this. Somehow the Wisconsin oil was not there? Hilton felt a sickening knot tighten in his stomach.

What happened? How had the state and Empire and Arbor "discovered" this oil? Hilton had the damn data. He had studied the seismic data himself. Did they somehow get the same maps he had stolen from Martin? Were Martin's maps in error? They certainly showed huge oil deposits. Martin had even calculated the size of the reserves on his spreadsheets—the ones Anita had stolen from Martin and given to Hilton. The oil *had* to be there. Hilton had just killed a man in northern Wisconsin to take over the leases to a bunch of Wisconsin land that might be worthless. He had paid Martin a half a million dollars to back out of the deal and keep his mouth shut. But again, Hilton had proof that the oil was there. Somehow the tapes in Madison had gotten mixed up. Or it could be a computer glitch. It didn't make any difference to Hilton. Bloomberg radio played more clips from the oil executives. Hilton was just pulling into the Houstonian. Another oil industry man was being inter-viewed. "The maps are useless. Mistakes were made." Hilton's leases were worthless. Had to get his half million dollars back from Martin and return it to Prolea before they found it missing. Hilton could go to prison for embezzle-ment. Martin was also a liability. Martin was the only link between Hilton and a dead man lying in a cabin in northern Wisconsin. Hilton could make Martin go away. Permanently. They could hang you once for killing a man, but they couldn't hang you twice for killing two. Hilton felt his grip tighten on the wheel as he flashed back to swinging the iron rod forward to crush Larry's spinal column. Larry was simply expendable. Then he thought about how he had roughed up Martin. Martin was expendable, too.

Back at Prolea there was a package delivery for Hilton Sinclair, the President of Prolea. The good-looking delivery guy who was making the delivery had the package on a trol-

ley. He leaned over the desk calmly as the receptionist
signed for it. After he took back the clipboard, he indicated
the delivery was pretty heavy and asked her if it made sense
for him to just wheel it on back to Mr. Sinclair's office. "I
think it's golf clubs," he said. "I can unwrap it if you want."
She smiled to herself. Little did the guy know, Mr. Sinclair
was officially unemployed. She wasn't going to miss Hilton,
either; he had always acted so arrogantly around the office.
There was some question in her mind whether the package
was for Hilton or the "position" of President at Prolea. The
bottom line was that she didn't want the thing just sitting
out in her reception area all afternoon. It could be hours before the idiots in the mailroom got around to carting it off.
The delivery guy was all business; kind of cute in that uni-
form. She directed the man down the hall to Hilton's former
office and he walked briskly down the hall. In a few minutes, Martin, posing as the delivery guy, had unpacked the
original Wisconsin canisters, and put them in a drawer in
Hilton's old desk. Then he gathered up the wrappings—and
the golf bag—and hustled out to a waiting elevator and into
the parking lot.

CHAPTER 58

IT WAS NEARING LUNCHTIME AND HILTON CALLED ANITA. "I want to see you," he said coldly.

"Wow, aren't we Mr. Happy today?" Anita chided him, but he did not seem amused.

"Is Martin around?" asked Hilton.

"News flash: Martin resigned," said Anita.

"What? When?" Hilton asked.

"There was a big meeting and Martin got all pissed off and walked out," said Anita. "Not a big surprise, really. He had a big altercation a couple of weeks ago during annual planning. I think he has told a lot of people he's had it with Basin Oil."

Hilton thought this over carefully. Not really a surprise. Martin told Hilton he was thinking about making a change. "Meet me at the hotel at the regular time." He wasn't asking her—he was telling her.

"Aren't you picking me up?" she asked.

"I'll leave a key for you at the front desk. I'm running a little late today. Just meet me over there." Click.

He hung up so quickly that she literally looked into the phone receiver as if to see if he was still there. Then she slammed the phone back into the cradle and said, "I really missed you too, you bastard."

Hilton got to the hotel before Anita. First, oil prices had stayed down when he had been at Prolea and he was on the ropes with his oil trading. Then he hands five hundred thousand dollars to Martin, to get rid of him. For nothing. There was no oil. One of his oldest friends double-crosses him, over what turns out to be a bogus oil field. Jesus, how bad can it get? Now he has gotten his ass fired, and on top of it, Anita is whining to him about when he's going to get "serious." Yes, it was time for him to take matters into his own hands. He dropped his gun down on the dresser top and went into the bathroom. Anita would show up any minute.

She had called her lunchtime replacement down in Legal and told her she was going out for lunch after all. If the lady could be sure to come up right at 11:45 a.m. it would be great. Anita had on an old dresses, but a favorite. Alone, she walked out into the parking lot and drove off in her old clunky car. The car was starting good now that she had gotten it fixed. She really wasn't in the mood to see Hilton. When he asked her to meet him in the room, it was pretty clear what he was after. She had driven over to the hotel a few times before by herself when he had asked her, as a favor, to meet him. This time he hadn't really asked her; he told her to be there. Still, she couldn't just say "No" to Hilton and risk losing him—or could she? She picked up the key at the front desk and took the elevator up to the third floor. She slipped the key into the lock and withdrew it quickly, but the lock didn't open. Just as she was reinserting it a second time, she heard the lock click and Hilton threw open the door and motioned her in.

He was wearing only a towel. His clothes were on the chair. Her dress was a black one with seven large, white buttons down the front of it. He stood in front of her and began to unbutton her dress, first the top button, then the second.

"So how are you doing? Are you glad to see me?" Anita asked.

"Shhh." Hilton was moving very slowly, moving to the third button and then the fourth.

"How was your trip?" Asked Anita.

"Quiet," said Hilton. It was as if he were talking to a dog. He unbuttoned the last buttons and pulled her dress off, throwing it onto the chair. He reached and quickly unsnapped her bra.

"Hilton, I want to talk; at least a little bit." This was how you treated a prostitute, not your girlfriend.

"I said 'quiet,'" Hilton barked, and he pulled the bra down roughly over her arms and threw it on top of her crumpled dress lying on the chair.

"Damn it, Hilton, stop. I want to talk first!" Now she was getting angry.

Suddenly, he grabbed her roughly and threw her face down onto the bed, forcing himself upon her. He was angry. She was naked and helpless. She tried to move her head from side to side in the deep pillow to get air, but each time she moved, Hilton clamped her neck all the harder and forced her head deeper into the pillow. She tried to scream, but her lungs were nearly empty, and her desperate shriek was barely audible through the pillow. She reached back with her hands flailing at Hilton while she fought for each breath, but he pulled her arms behind her back and forced the last bit of air out of her lungs. Finally, after ten minutes of rough treatment, he flopped down on the bed and she could get her breath. After a few minutes, he rose up off the bed and went into the bathroom.

She lay still, for a moment not realizing that she was free. Then she forced herself to move, and seeing her dress on the chair, she found the energy to quickly move toward it and put it on. She glanced at the dresser and stared at the gun. She looked for her shoes as she hurried to close a few buttons on the dress. Still barefoot but with her shoes in one hand and her purse in the other, she turned for the door. Suddenly, inches from the door latch, Hilton grabbed her by the collar of the dress and dragged her back into the center of the room.

"I didn't say I was finished with you," Hilton said bluntly. In his right hand was the gun. Anita shuddered at the sight of it. Hilton, seeing her reaction, smiled, and held it in her face before slipping it inside the top of her unbuttoned dress. "You told me one time you like to play rough, right?" Still holding her by the collar of her dress, Anita felt chills run up her back as he ran the cold steel of the gun barrel over and around each of her breasts.

"Hilton. No. You hurt me." He had turned into a madman. Clearly satisfied with the result, he finally swung her again by the collar and she went sprawling onto the bed, her shoes and handbag flying across the room.

"Now stay there until I get dressed," said Hilton. And he walked back into the bathroom still naked. In a moment he came walking back out, now fully dressed. He went over and sat down on the chair and began to lace up his shoes.

"You stay here for an hour after I leave. Settle down a bit. If you want, you can call your office and tell them you need to go home because you're feeling sick or something. I'll call you the next time I need you."

"There won't be a next time," said Anita quietly under her breath.

"What did you say?" he raised his voice even though he had heard her perfectly.

"I said there won't be a next time." She cowered under the covers expecting him to strike her.

Hilton glowered at her. "Oh, there will be a next time if I say there will be. And a next time and a next time. Nobody messes around with Hilton Sinclair. Not the French. Not Larry. Not your dumbshit boyfriend Martin, either. Nobody. If you don't understand that then maybe I need to give you another lesson before I leave here today."

He tied his shoes, and stood up, placing the gun under his belt in back. "Now you stay here for a while and get yourself cleaned up. You look like shit. I'm going to pay your little friend Martin a visit. He owes me some money. Oh, and don't get any ideas about calling the cops on me. If anyone tells me that you've even mentioned me, or Martin, or Wisconsin in the same breath, you won't live long enough to regret it." He slammed the door and was gone.

CHAPTER 59

AFTER SPEAKING WITH LIZ, MARTIN HAD HEADED BACK
to his apartment at the Memorial Creole. Anita called him
on his regular cell phone as he drove through the gate.

"What did you do to Hilton?" Anita sounded upset.

"I didn't do anything to Hilton," said Martin. "What are
you talking about?"

"I just saw Hilton at the hotel. He is acting crazy. He
beat me. He threatened me. He has a gun," Anita wasn't
crying but her voice cracked when she said the word "gun."
"He said you owe him some money."

"Jesus, he has a gun?" Martin felt a chill go down his
spine.

"Yeah, and he said he was going to pay you a visit." Anita
was worried. "What did you do to him?"

"If you just knew…" Martin paused. He couldn't tell
Anita anything. "I did talk to him about some business
ideas," said Martin. Anita had no idea that Hilton had

roughed up Martin, "stolen" the oil leases and dropped five hundred thousand dollars in Martin's apartment.

"Martin, I shouldn't have done this, but I gave Hilton some of your files. Is that why he is all crazy? Hilton knew you were up to something. I went into your work files. He asked me to do some digging on you and I gave him your "Checq Files." I made some printouts for him," Anita confessed.

"Oh Christ Anita, you never should have done that. Those were secret files. You gave those to Hilton?" Martin remained calm. He knew damn well Anita had given Hilton the files. He had set it all up and it worked out perfectly. Hilton got played. Hilton believed that he had forced Martin to give up the oil discovery. Hilton thought the leases were worth hundreds of millions of dollars. Even for five hundred thousand dollars, Hilton thought he was getting a bargain. Martin couldn't help but smile, even as he shut off the car and sat talking to Anita.

"Answer me, Martin. Is that what this is about? That stuff I gave to Hilton?" Anita sounded concerned.

"I don't know Anita, but you must never, ever tell anyone you did that. You could go to prison. Hilton might do something really bad to you if you told anyone about this. That was super confidential information and it's probably what has Hilton waving a gun around." Martin sounded concerned about Anita.

Anita paused. There was a silence. "He just left here three minutes ago. Like I said, he said he was going to pay you a visit. I'm afraid. I'm afraid for you, Martin. Hilton is in a rage. I know what he is capable of."

"All right. Thank you for warning me, Anita. You mean the world to me. And don't ever tell anyone you gave those files to Hilton. Nobody will ever know. And don't tell anyone that there's a connection between you and me and

Hilton. It could be bad for all of us." Martin was still very calm. None of this was a surprise to Martin. He knew Hilton would come for him. He knew Hilton had a gun. Probably that same gun that Hilton had used for the Russian roulette demonstration.

"I won't say a word, Martin." Anita had settled down.

"Okay. Good. Listen Anita, I've got to go. Thanks for the call." Martin hung up.

Martin changed quickly into jeans and work boots and a T-shirt. He hadn't been working out much, but he had been slowly getting back into shape after he moved out. He still had the build of a linebacker. He took one of his softball bats and leaned it against the couch. Then he ducked out the backdoor. He started his car and moved it out of his assigned parking space, far down on the end of the apartment complex. Returning to his front door, he stood on his tip toes, reached up and unscrewed the light bulb over the porch by his front door. Then he did the same to two of his adjacent neighbors. If his plan was going to work, when nighttime arrived, he was going to need the cover of darkness. He came back into the apartment and walked around to check all of the window and door locks. Martin was pretty sure that when Hilton came for him, it would be through the front door again. The last time, Hilton had apparently picked the front lock because there were no signs of forced entry. Martin hadn't even bothered to change the locks after their last encounter. It seemed futile. Martin hadn't been here for a few days anyway—he had been camped out at the hotel. Martin had always knew at some point Hilton would come back for him, especially when the fake oil was discovered. Definitely for Hilton to get his five hundred thousand back. Maybe to kill him. Martin had spent time earlier in the day, visiting the seven banks where he had set up accounts and Martin withdrew seventy-five thousand from each of them in cash. He had the five hundred grand hidden in his closet. He retrieved the locked suitcase with the money and poured the cash into 3 big shopping bags. Martin couldn't be positive that Hilton himself would show up. Hilton might send one of his goons. Might even be Larry, if Larry was back from Wisconsin. There was no real way to know if or when Hilton would show up. Martin kept telling himself to relax. Focus. When Martin had reflected on it, he felt like he now knew Hilton. He knew Hilton had a huge ego. He knew Hilton thought Martin was weak. Hilton would probably enjoy coming over and threatening Martin again. Hilton really was probably on his way to the apartment right now.

Martin was pretty sure that Hilton still didn't know what had happened. Hilton might have looked back over the papers and files that Anita had given to Hilton, but they really told him nothing. Hilton knew the stuff he had gotten from Martin showed oil. Where was the oil? Not in Wisconsin. By now Hilton would certainly have heard there was no oil. The damn governor had said there was no oil. But Hilton would have no idea how Martin and Wisconsin and Empire Oil and Arbor Energy had all "found" these oil reserves at the same time. How could they have all gotten it wrong? Basin Oil and Arbor were established oil companies. Could it have been coincidence that Wisconsin and Martin had somehow found this old data at the same time?

Thoughts rushed through Martin's head. Martin's heart was pumping wildly. Martin wondered what the conversation was like between Hilton and Larry when they found out there was no oil. It couldn't have been pleasant. Martin wasn't afraid of Hilton any longer. Martin wasn't afraid of anything anymore. Liz had made Martin this way. Liz had shaken him up. Telling him he wasn't driven enough, wasn't hungry enough. Hilton wasn't catching Martin by surprise this time. It would actually be tempting for Martin to just give Hilton his money back and be done with him. Nobody knew it, but Martin had over forty million dollars in the bank. He had the five hundred grand ready to hand over. But in fact, Hilton was a predator. He would keep coming for Martin. Or maybe he just wanted the money. Yet, Hilton might somehow find out Martin had made a fortune. Hilton might finally figure out that Martin had tricked him, planted the false documents where Anita could find them. A banker might inadvertently tell Hilton about one of his trading customers named Martin who had "hit it big." Hard to keep a secret around Hilton. There were a lot of risks. Martin's thoughts flashed back to his boss at Basin Oil leaning into Martin's office to tell Martin in hushed tones how so-and-so had seen Hilton with Liz on the sailboat. Martin gripped the softball bat even tighter. He was done with taking crap from people like Hilton. Guns didn't bother Martin either. He had grown up with guns. Hunted with guns since he was twelve years old. Hilton couldn't just shoot Martin. How would he get his money back? Even if Martin lost everything now, he was okay with that. He thought of where he had come from. He had more than toughened up. It was now Martin who had the killer instinct.

Martin had turned off all of the lights. He needed to be quiet. Hilton had no idea what Martin knew, and would think the apartment was empty. Martin leaned back in the stuffed chair in the corner of the living room and held the big aluminum softball bat in his hands, turning it over and over again, waiting for Hilton. After what seemed like hours, Martin heard footsteps. Gravel crunching near his front door. Martin quietly got to his feet and stood behind the door with his softball bat. He saw the lock turn slowly on the front door. Hilton cracked open the door and carefully took a half step over the threshold, the gun held firmly in his right hand. Martin swung down the bat with full strength on Hilton's arm and the gun went flying. Hilton groaned and stumbled forward into the living room. As Martin reached back for a second swing, Hilton regained his balance and charged headlong into Martin. But Martin was already in midswing and brought the bat down across Hilton's back with a dull thud. Hilton yelled in agony but hung on to Martin and dragged Martin to the floor. Hilton landed on top of Martin and pounded on Martin's face with his fists. Suddenly Hilton stopped his onslaught and lunged in the direction of the gun. Martin dove on top of Hilton just as he reached the handgun. Martin landed on Hilton's back and heard the air rush out of Hilton's lungs. Hilton still clung to the gun. Martin put his hands over Hilton's hands and they fought for the gun. "You piece of shit," said Martin. "I'm twice the man you'll ever be."

"Where's my damn money?" Hilton and Martin were both completely out of breath. Both clutching the gun. Martin still lying on top of Hilton on the floor.

"Guess what, piece of shit! I'm giving you your money back. It's in those bags by the wall." Hilton turned his head slightly and saw the grocery bags. "It's all there," said Martin. "You can have your stinking money. I don't know what happened to the oil," Martin lied, "but I don't want to have anything to do with you or your sidekick Larry Walker."

"Well that was stupid, showing me the money." Hilton half croaked, "Anyway you won't have to worry about Larry." They were both out of breath, still grappling for control of the gun.

"What's up with Larry?" said Martin.

"Bastard double-crossed me," said Hilton. "Let's just say he isn't ever going to do that again. To anybody."

"You killed Larry?"

"He had it coming," Hilton snarled. "Actually, you got it coming, too, but I'm willing to overlook that. I just want the money. Let me up or I will kill you."

Martin felt the anger. Hilton was never going to stop. Hilton really was a predator. Ruthless. Can't trust him.

"You think it's smart threatening me right now, you scumbag?" said Martin. Martin got his hand on the barrel of the gun and vainly tried to rip it from Hilton's grip.

"Yeah, that's not going to work." Hilton hung on doggedly. "I'm used to dealing with pussies like you." Hilton violently rolled sideways, trying to get Martin off his back. "You ain't got the balls to deal with men like me. I'm just better than you."

"Your bullshit doesn't work with me, Hilton," said Martin. They continued their battle for the gun. "I'm better than you. I'm stronger than you. Smarter than you. And I'm tougher than you." Martin knew when he first made his plan, when he first met Hilton, that it might come to this. Hilton was a murderer. If he let Hilton go, Hilton would kill him. Or he would hire somebody to kill Martin. Hilton had no conscience.

Hilton tried to shake free again. They both were tiring. "Just so you know, I'm not stopping until I kill your ass. I don't know how you did it, but it wasn't just Larry. You double-crossed me, too. For a while, I was starting to like you." Hilton was still fiercely gripping the gun. "At least we got the same taste in women."

Martin felt a cold, steely rage well up within him. He thought of Liz and Hilton together. Smashing Hilton's head into the floor with his elbow, Martin grabbed the long silencer of the gun with both hands. Hilton rose to all fours and they were both now on their knees fighting for the gun. Hilton pulled the trigger and a bullet tore into the sofa. With both hands, Martin now had control of the barrel and he suddenly twisted it unexpectedly into Hilton's chest. Hilton's finger was still on the trigger and the gun went off. Hilton's body went limp. They were still kneeling face to face. Hilton's head dropped oddly to one side. His eyes rolled back. Martin pulled the gun from Hilton's hands and Hilton toppled to the floor. Shot through the heart. Martin lay on the floor staring at the ceiling. Gasping for breath. His heart still pounding. The gun felt cold in his hands. His breathing slowly returned to normal.

Martin rose slowly to his feet and retrieved a bottle of tequila from the cabinet over the refrigerator. He put ice in a glass and filled it to the brim with straight tequila. Standing in the kitchen, he downed the tequila and stared at Hilton. He filled the glass again and walked over to Hilton's motionless body. He pushed on it with his foot. Hilton was gone. "Hilton," said Martin coldly to the lifeless form, "if you'll wait here for a minute, I'll bring your car up to the door." Martin retrieved Hilton's car keys and wallet from Hilton's slacks. Then Martin went back to his closet and rummaged through his deer hunting gear until he found his wool gloves and an old baseball cap. He wasn't leaving prints on anything. He put on the gloves, picked up the gun and spent a good five minutes wiping away fingerprints. He even poured some tequila over the gun thinking it might wash away any DNA. He kept the gloves on, pulled the cap low over his face and eased out the back door. He walked into the dark parking lot and clicked the remote key and heard the beep from Hilton's car. He walked through the shadows over to the car and got behind the wheel. He pulled the car around to the parking area by the back of his apartment. He was glad he had unscrewed the light bulbs earlier. He rolled down the driver's side window and shut off the engine. Martin sat quietly for several minutes. It was another humid evening in Houston. Quiet. He could hear the cars driving down Memorial Drive. With the silencer, nobody had heard the gun. Martin cracked open the driver's side door and reached up to click off the dome light. Then from inside the car he threw open the passenger door and slowly walked back into his apartment. Hilton was a big guy. Hard to move. Martin removed Hilton's belt and looped it around Hilton's chest and under his arms to get a handle on Hilton. Then he rolled the body up in a blanket. He half-carried and half-dragged Hilton out to the car and pushed him headfirst into the passenger seat. He walked back into the apartment. There was blood all over the small rug where Hilton had fallen. Martin rolled up the rug and carried it out and tossed it in the trunk of the car. He returned and carried the three shopping bags of money out to the trunk and closed the lid. He moved quickly and silently back to the apartment and looked around for any of Hilton's things. He grabbed the tequila bottle, locked the apartment, and then walked slowly back out to the darkened car. He slid into the driver's seat and drove off. As he was driving, Martin took a hit off the bottle of tequila and poured the remainder of the bottle over Hilton's body. He stopped on a dead-end street that sided Buffalo Bayou. He smashed Hilton's phone on the pavement. Then he dumped the rug, the blanket, the tequila bottle, the wallet and Hilton's phone into the dark water.

CHAPTER 60

WHEN THE CALL CAME INTO THE HOUSTON POLICE Department, it wasn't domestic violence or robbery. Turned out it wasn't on the Southeast side either. The car was found in a damn parking lot in some big office building off Post Oak. The caller had simply said, "The man who killed Larry Walker in Wisconsin is in a car in the parking garage at 460 Richmond Avenue. White Mercedes." It was such an odd call in such a nice neighborhood. A patrol car was there in less than five minutes. The keys were in the ignition and a guy in the front passenger seat appeared to be passed out and wreaked of tequila. Turned out the guy was dead. A quick check showed he owned the car. He had been in some kind of fight or something, had a fractured right forearm. Took one in the chest. Three grocery bags full of cash in the trunk. Did the killers not even look in the trunk? His wallet was gone. Robbery? When they counted the money down at the station, it was just under a half-million. Then dispatch radioed back. In fact, a man named Larry Walker had been found dead somewhere up in Wisconsin a few days ago. They were contacting the Wisconsin police. Homicide division showed up. Like a lot of Houstonians, it turned out the guy had a gun stashed in the front seat console and any cop could tell just by smelling the barrel, that the gun had very definitely been fired recently. Was it the murder weapon? Who leaves the murder weapon at the scene? It turned out the guy was from Houston; name was Hilton Sinclair. They locked down the crime scene.

After two days, things became pretty obvious to the police. Hilton had killed Larry Walker. Hilton's DNA matched prints found on the murder weapon, an old iron fireplace poker in some Wisconsin cabin. They performed ballistics on the handgun. Sure enough, it had recently been fired. Wisconsin detectives had previously noticed that Melvin Baker had signed one of these oil leases and then suffered an accidental death. Seemed odd. After some digging it was determined that the slug found in Mel Baker's body came from the gun in Hilton's car. They couldn't determine if it was Larry or Hilton who killed Melvin. Couldn't tell if the gun was the Hilton murder weapon because the bullet had gone straight through and exited. It didn't really matter.

Turned out Hilton had stolen six hundred thousand dollars from Prolea using a guy named Gannon who had an office near the Montrose neighborhood. Gannon admitted accepting a fraudulent wire request. Gannon had passed the cash on to Hilton. Gannon had honored the wire request that Hilton had signed for as president of Prolea. But Gannon swore he didn't know what the money was for. Hilton had told Gannon that he was going to settle his account within the week. Initially, Gannon "forgot" to tell the detectives that he kept a hundred thousand for himself, but when the cops started snooping around in Gannon's bank and business records, he suddenly remembered. He handed his hundred thousand over to the authorities. The cops discovered that Larry and Hilton had worked a few times together over the years—mostly oil- type jobs in Texas. Clearly, they were working together on the big Wisconsin oil discovery. They were signing up a bunch of leases from old farmers and landowners up around Iron River. They found Hilton's plane ticket to Minneapolis which was dated the day before Larry was murdered. Turned out that in Hilton's old office at Prolea, Hilton had left several aluminum canisters hidden in his desk. After some research, and some calls to detectives in Wisconsin, it was determined that these canisters were apparently old seismic data from Wisconsin. These were just like the canisters and tapes that were found in Wisconsin. These were the originals. Hilton must have planted the fakes. They never could determine who actually killed Hilton. Maybe Hilton had screwed someone on that Wisconsin oil deal. Maybe one of Larry Walker's buddies took care of Hilton. Larry had run with a tough crowd. Maybe the big oil companies had hired somebody to knock off Hilton. Perhaps they thought Hilton was behind the big fake oil discovery. The cops had interviewed Dick Jansen. They interviewed Sheldon Mack a number of times. They interviewed Governor Conlan and the lieutenant governor and the head of the DNR in Wisconsin. Everyone characterized the entire ordeal, the fake oil, the murders, as tragic. But nobody had any answers.

The police continued their due diligence. Hilton was clearly a bad guy. He clearly killed Larry Walker. Hilton had the gun that killed Mel Baker. They had recovered the Prolea money. Six-hundred thousand dollars that Hilton had stolen from Prolea. Houston had five thousand cops. They did some digging. Frankly, nobody in the police department really cared who knocked off Hilton. Nobody in Houston really cared about a fake oil discovery in Wisconsin. Or the murder of Larry Walker in Wisconsin. After a week they really weren't finding any new information. They kept the case open another week. After a few meetings downtown to review findings and discuss options, the case was closed.

EPILOGUE

BY NOW, THE SO-CALLED "WISCONSIN OIL DISCOVERY" was old news. No "elephant" oil fields. Hilton's death had made headlines in the Chronicle, for sure. But the case had been wrapped up. Hilton wasn't the first guy to doctor some oil reserves data. He had embezzled six hundred thousand dollars from Prolea. Apparently, Hilton killed two men up in Wisconsin: Larry Walker, one of his longtime business associates, and an old farmer named Melvin Baker. It wasn't a big mystery why somebody wanted Hilton dead. Hilton had lots of enemies. In Wisconsin, Governor Conlan was still running in the primary. Other than looking stupid, it didn't appear that Conlan had done anything wrong. He had owned his Aspen condo for two years. Even though the oil companies had set him up with it, nobody knew about it or even asked about it. Jansen and Mack, the oil company representatives, were obviously as surprised as anyone by the "fake" oil discovery. Jansen had been offered "early retirement" over the deal. With Taylor gone, the Superior Refinery expansion was rapidly approved by the state, but that wasn't illegal. The bad news for Conlan was simple: Taylor Thompson had barely started her campaign, and Taylor was already the easy favorite to be the state's next governor.

Martin had not wasted any time. He rented a small office on the fifty-sixth floor of Williams Tower. It had breathtaking views of downtown. Martin had set up a company and named it Venture Oil Limited. He put ten thousand dollars in start-up money into Venture. He re-opened his retirement account and re-deposited the exact same eighty-seven thousand dollars into the account. Martin apologized to the banker; told him it was probably better to "just leave things the way they were," given the separation that Martin and Liz were going through. Martin was going out on his own as an independent oil explorationist. Martin knew a ton of people in the business and he had a reputation as a top-notch geologist. His office was already packed with new maps and old maps, a white board and all of his personal and office stuff from Basin. As a present for himself, Martin had bought a fancy new desk chair. Up in his office, it was six in the evening. The sunset's golden rays were reflecting off the office towers downtown. Martin was packing up his briefcase. He was done for the day.

Martin got to Cody's ten minutes early for his seven o'clock reservation. The hostess informed him that his guest had already arrived. She had already been seated. Goodness knows Martin had spent enough nights at Cody's to know the exact table that he had reserved for tonight. Nevertheless, he let the hostess ceremoniously lead him to their table, through the bar, through the dining room, and out to the terrace overlooking downtown. As he walked up to the table, she pushed back her chair and practically jumped into his arms.

"Oh Martin," said Taylor. "I am so glad to see you."

"Best table in the house," said Martin, smiling broadly. "Hope you like this place."

It had been Taylor's idea to pay him a visit. The Wisconsin oil thing was over. Her campaign had barely begun. She was perfectly positioned for governor. She knew Martin had made a ton of money; no idea how much. She wasn't exactly sure how he had made the money. "Oil trading," was all that Martin had said. She said it was time for them to celebrate. She looked amazing; better than ever. And rested. Black cocktail dress with spaghetti straps. She looked over Martin. Nice-looking designer jeans. White linen shirt. His arms well-defined, as he rested his elbows on the table, and leaned toward her. The wine steward arrived.

"Excuse me, the waitress informed me you wished to order wine?" The steward asked.

"Yes," said Martin. "I believe you have Petrus, correct?"

"Very, very good sir. Yes, sir. We have the 2002," said the wine steward.

"That would be fine," said Martin.

"I will bring it immediately, sir," said the wine steward.

"Well, we're not really in a hurry," responded Martin. "Not with her."

"Yes, sir." The steward said as he backed away from the table.

"You know," said Taylor, "I'm just a small-town girl from Iron River, Wisconsin, but if I'm not mistaken, that stuff's fifteen hundred dollars a bottle."

"Yeah, I know. Actually the 2002 is going to be more than that," said Martin, smiling. "But you will be glad to know, that other than buying myself a three-hundred-dollar office chair, I've hardly spent a nickel. I rented a small office. I'm living in an apartment with my life packed into three suitcases. I'm still driving my eight-year old 325 Beemer." The wine was poured.

She lifted the glass, "Okay, Big Spender, here's to a new beginning."

They clinked glasses. "To new beginnings," he said.

She gently placed her glass on the table and turned her head slightly, the slightest smile on her face. "So, Martin, where do we go from here?"

"You remember, I told you that I loved you, right?" said Martin. It was not so much a question as a statement.

"I think I told you the same thing." She smiled. Then seriously, she almost whispered to him, "Martin, I really do love you. I've missed you, for so, so long. For twenty years, I guess."

Martin nodded silently, looking into her eyes, "You think we made a mistake back then?"

"You know what I think?" asked Taylor. "I think we all just do what we've got to do. At the time, nothing would've kept me from finishing law school. Nothing would have stopped you from getting a good job and using your geology degree. Then you just came back into my life like a dream."

"Here's to dreams, you amazing woman," said Martin. "Here's to us."

"Here's to dreams, my love," said Taylor. Then once again they clinked glasses as the golden rays of sunset slowly settled over the winding bayous of the Magnolia City.

The End